DRY BLOOD SPRINGS

A Battle of Hope Versus Darkness Set in the West

A Novel Written By

BRYON K SAXTON

Acknowledgements

Julie Williamson for her Editing; Sean Newton for his Original Cover;
Eric Brandley for Cover Editing;
Chase Saxton for Marketing and Public Relations.

Special thanks to the late Marley, who served as inspiration for Ranger.
Thank you family and friends for your support
in battling darkness with hope.

CHAPTER 1

The life of Abe Vigil looked as if it had been drained from his body. Vigil's face, all white and drawn, wore a look of frozen fright. His usually-deep set eyes now as wide as saucers, but nonetheless just the same, Vigil lay dead in the dirt in the comfort of the tall cheat grass.

Generally not much scared Vigil. At 6 feet tall and 240 pounds, Vigil could take care of his self, and, for the most part, had. Yet here he lay in his goin'-fishing clothes near the banks of the Dry Springs River – ironically, a river that is the lifeblood of the little Western town about a mile away bearing the name: Dry Springs.

The weatherworn wooden sign reading: *Dry Springs, population 113* marked the town border. The sign, posted well before the Murphies or Berries had their babies, but well after the death of widow Sally Johnson some months ago, left the town count tally on the sign relatively close.

With the rapidly setting sun, despite his failing eyesight, Gibby Jones looked over Vigil's old worn out frame, before removing his sweat-stained tan cowboy hat from his head and stroking the gray stubble on the end of his chin that always seem to remain the same length. Being a sworn sheriff's deputy of Dry Springs, Gibby realized it was his responsibility to pack up Vigil's motionless body in a respectful manner in taking him back to town.

Using an old, dirty, gray cotton blanket rolled up in the bed of his rickety buckboard, Gibby proceeded to wrap up Vigil mummy-style.

"Hard to figure," Gibby muttered under his breath, further examining the corpse while shifting it around. No bullet holes, knife wounds or torn clothing, Gibby thought odd.

"What do you think?" Gibby said, directing his question at Ranger.

Ranger, being a dog, did not reply. But the dog did cast a glance toward his owner as if he understood exactly what he was saying before briefly wagging his tail. The golden-colored Australian shepherd/border collie mix had become Gibby's best friend since Gibby's wife, Bev, died of the whooping cough two years prior.

Ranger, continuing to give his master a quizzical look – the kind where a dog will cock its head from side-to-side and raise its ears – had become good company for the cantankerous Gibby Jones.

Gibby then ambled back to his wagon to grab the rope needed to tie the now wrapped body off. Gibby was hoping wrapping the blanket tightly around Vigil's body would prevent it from taking a beating on the mile trip back to town over one of the roughest roads known to man.

Besides, his gentle touch would earn him a compliment and a slap on the back from town doctor Ben Howard, actually a veterinarian, who also served as town mayor due to the small size of Dry Springs.

Moving Abe's body around, wrapping it and lifting it into the buckboard, that creaked under the new weight, caused the middle-aged Gibby to break out in a small sweat, putting dark sweat puddles on his shirt beneath his arms and on his chest. After all, Dry Springs, located on the edge of the Utah Territory, was a mountainous desert town, with high heat during the day and cool winds at night.

Ranger, without given a command, took his position next to Gibby on the squeaky bench seat of the wagon before Gibby gave the "giddup" order to his faithful horse Stu to begin pulling the wagon over the rocky terrain back toward town.

Gibby was grateful for the smell of him and his dog, a combination scent providing them both much-needed relief from the decaying smell of Vigil's already decomposing body that was now their cargo.

"Poor Abe," Gibby said, flashing Ranger a forlorn look.

With Vigil being unmarried, having lost his wife some years ago when she ran off with another rancher, Gibby was relieved part of his duties as a lawman wouldn't include him having to chase down a widow or children to break the news of the death.

As Stu began pulling the wagon slowly through the brush and back out onto what the townspeople referred to as Break Road, Gibby, from habit, balanced his double-barrel shotgun a crossed his knees, cracking it open, in making certain he had placed shells into it, before standing the gun upright on it stock just off to his side. He never knew when a wild turkey would cross his path. Besides, Gibby was a cautious man, particularly where the night sky had begun to envelop him and his dog.

Seeing the dark creep up on them, Gibby also trimmed his oil lamp, hanging it off the side on a wagon hook, in hopes the light from the lantern would help him avoid the deeper ruts that over time had been worn into the hard-packed dirt road. The night sky, full of stars and a full moon, would also be of help in keeping Gibby and Ranger to the road.

CHAPTER 2

Gibby's annoying habit of whistling, which could be heard over the moans of the old wagon clomping along, was causing Ranger's ears to raise and lower to the piercing sounds of the pitchy tones.

But the dutiful Gibby was feeling better about himself having accomplished his task.

The sheriff's deputy had been asked to scour the riverbank for a body based on a tip from a passer-by, never thinking he would find his friend Vigil, who he suspected succumbed to a rattlesnake bite where there were no serious wounds that he could see when wrapping up the body.

Besides, there was always at least one town member per day who was claiming they had encountered or spotted a rattlesnake in their day-to-day activities.

"Bit puzzling," Gibby shared with Ranger about the death as the wagon continued to creak its way toward the torchlights burning off in the distance. The welcoming torches were those that regularly burned on the Dry Spring's Main Street this time of night.

The pair hadn't traveled much further, when Gibby in staring down Break Road, laid out straight as an arrow, spotted what appeared to be a shadow of a man standing in their path a couple of hundred yards up ahead.

The figure, hid in the dark, their form only silhouetted by the rising moon, appeared to be dressed somewhat formal, Gibby thought, like one of those "fancy Dan" East Coast characters he had seen in mail order catalogs.

The man appeared to be wearing a long, hooded dark cape, a white long sleeve shirt, a dark vest and black flat dress shoes that reflected the shine of the moon.

Whether it was coincidence or a preamble of things to come, the wind had also began to stir, swirling hard enough to send sprays of dirt and dry leaves tumbling across the road in front of Gibby's wagon. The breeze was also strong enough to tear from the few trees dotting the desert road what few leaves remained on them this early fall night.

And then as fast as the wind had begun swirling, it stopped. Like nature had slammed a door shut. And a second look ahead by Gibby down the road revealed the figure was now gone. "What the ..." he muttered, scratching the front of his head covered by his sweat-stained hat.

But just as Gibby finished muttering to Ranger about his annoyance over the situation, the wind picked up again, with the figure having now repositioned itself directly in the path of the wagon less than 50 yards ahead.

The return of the figure and the unnatural wind that followed sent a shudder down Gibby's spine. Even Ranger, now staring straight ahead, was out of sorts with the unwelcome stranger.

Gibby began fidgeting with the deputy badge pinned to the chest of the long-sleeved wool shirt he wore. The long-time resident of Dry Springs had taken an oath to protect and serve the people of the town he loved, at least until another full-time deputy could be hired or coerced into taking the job, a job that paid so little. Gibby was wishing now his duties had not taken Ranger and him out on this little adventure.

Enough, Gibby thought, bringing Stu and the wagon to an abrupt halt, before standing on the bench seat deck of the buckboard, and yelling "Who goes there?"

But Gibby's yell, which echoed off the rocky terrain surrounding them, brought no reply.

"I've got a gun," Gibby said, in holding his shotgun aloft, hoping it would frighten the stranger away. But again there was no response, other than the stranger having now moved within 30 yards of the pair.

"I'm a deputy sheriff. I represent the law," Gibby added, becoming more agitated with their uninvited, and mysterious, guest.

The tense tenor in Gibby's voice put Ranger into full barking mode.

"Now look what you have gone and done – upset my dog," Gibby yelled at the figure. But before Gibby's words could reach the stranger, the figure was once again gone.

Out of sight, and more importantly, no longer in their path, Gibby figured it was time for Stu to make double-time toward town.

Gibby quickly took his seat, before popping the reins hard and giving a forceful "giddup" to his horse. The wagon lurched forward, causing Vigil's body resting in the buckboard to roll some, before coming to a thudding stop against a side of the wagon.

Despite Stu's speed, and the road ruts, Gibby and Ranger sat on the wagon bench like two boulders, barely shifting, hurrying back to civilization.

The torchlights of Dry Springs Main Street were beginning to grow as the pair moved closer toward town.

But no sooner had the thought crossed Gibby's mind that the remainder of his trip back to town might be uneventful, the wind picked up to a screaming howl, smacking together the limbs on the trees, raising over the road a dust cloud the size of a small mountain the pair would have to pass through.

CHAPTER 3

Cutting through the blowing dust storm temporarily blinded Gibby, as he squeezed the reins tight in keeping the wagon moving and on the road.

But Gibby and Ranger hadn't moved fast enough, both being knocked off the wagon bench, as if they had been kicked up-side the head by one of Howard's stubborn mules.

The impact caused Ranger to fly and yelp, and Gibby to gasp in pain, with the jolt landing the unsuspecting pair into some nearby rocks and brush.

Disoriented from the fall, Gibby stood as quickly as a man his age could, looking for what had knocked him and his faithful companion from their perch. But before being able to piece together the mystery, a punch came from out of the dark and buried deep in his soft midsection, knocking what little wind he had left in his lungs.

Then a hand, with a pasty white hue and fingernails as long as eagle talons, scraped him along the right side of his face, the marks instantly drawing blood.

Gibby was under attack from something that stood like a man, but fought like a beast. To even the odds, the deputy knew he would need to make his way to his loaded shotgun likely still resting in the wagon, which had come to a stop some 20 feet up the road due to ol' Stu's laziness.

But in his scramble to the wagon, the attacker managed to leap after him, in knocking him down, before securing a tight a hold on his right foot by digging his talons deep into Gibby's thick leather boot. If he was going to free himself from the hold and reach his gun, Gibby figured he was going to have to wiggle his right foot free from his boot and go about bare-footin it.

It was then Ranger rejoined the fight, burying his teeth deep into the attacker's hand, holding the bite long enough for the attacker to loosen the viselike grip he had on Gibby's boot.

For a moment Gibby was free, stumbling across the road in the dark toward his gun he could now see still resting on the bench seat of the wagon, its barrel shimmering under the stars.

The attacker annoyed by the pair's persistence, now had Ranger in his clutches, flinging the dog 20-feet into the air as if he were half a bale of hay and into the road side brush. Ranger let out a whimper upon hitting the ground with a thud and slide.

But the dog's pestering of the attacker had bought Gibby the time needed to grip his gun, and swing it around in getting a clear shot at the monster.

"Take that," Gibby yelled, his heart nearly leaping from out of his chest as he fired the gun. It had been some time since Gibby had shot at anything outside of his next meal.

The discharge of the gun was loud, with the jolt of the blast causing the shotgun to kick back against Gibby's torso. It was like his old hunting days were coming back to him. And for an instant Gibby was thinking the fight was over.

But once the ringing of the shotgun blast died, the attacker stood ready to resume the fight, having no wounds, but now wearing a menacing expression on his face as dark as death.

Before Gibby could get off another shot, the creature slapped the gun away from the deputy, sending it flying like a stick.

Out matched once again, Gibby found shelter underneath the wagon, pulling from his waist-band leather sheath his dull 8-inch knife. The same knife he used to gut fish and clean the dirt out from underneath his fingernails.

With the knife in his right hand, the now winded Gibby lay on his stomach beneath the under-carriage of the wagon, sticking the knife into the hand of the attacker every time he would bring his hand within reach. It was like a wild game, with Gibby cheering himself each time he successfully found the creature's hand with his knife.

Ranger again joined the fight by positioning himself beneath the wagon next to Gibby, snapping at the hands of the attacker each time they would pass.

On occasion, Ranger would also catch a piece of the attacker's fingers, hand or arm between his teeth, allowing Gibby to get in an extra deep thrust with his small knife into whatever it was they were fighting.

But there was something different with this enemy. The knife wounds and bite wounds Gibby and Ranger were inflicting tore at the attacker's flesh, but never drew blood.

Tiring of the game, the attacker, who had gotten down on his knees in an attempt to get cleaner swipes at his victims, now stood, lifting with him the wagon Gibby and Ranger were finding refuge under, and tipping it onto its side.

The attacker's demonstration of strength left Ranger and Gibby exposed to the nighttime sky. It also snapped the reins and harness holding Stu in place, allowing the old horse to make a getaway during the clamor.

Gibby angrily jumped to his feet, wildly swinging his knife at arm's length at their attacker, while Ranger bit at the monster's feet and legs. But their cloaked foe was refusing to retreat.

Sharp razor-like pain dug into Gibby's face each time the stranger was able to reach him and rake his talons across his flesh. But the cowboy, out of fright or pride, remained silent while the blood from his wounds mixed with his sweat.

To prevent his foe from doing further damage, Gibby began swinging his knife faster, hoping his desperate approach would land the lucky blow needed. But his old arms were beginning to tire.

In the meantime Ranger continued snapping at the caped figure's heels, until Gibby realized the dog's attacks were to no avail, and his friend should save himself.

"Scatter," Gibby yelled forcefully at Ranger, who upon command took cover in the brush, while the deputy slowly and clumsily backed his way around the wagon now lying on its side. There, on the other side of the wagon, near where Vigil's body had tumbled out of the buckboard and into a heap, lay the oil lantern at Gibby's feet, the same lantern the resourceful deputy had fill and trimmed for the ride back home.

As a desperate measure, Gibby quickly bent down, using his right hand to snatch up the lantern surprisingly still holding a flame, while switching his knife to his left hand in order to keep his attacker at bay.

Gibby's thoughts were that he might be able to strike the attacker with the lantern, considering his options at this point were limited where he had backed as far as he was going to be able, with the back of his legs now resting up against Vigil's wrapped corpse.

"Gibby Jones isn't it?" the fiendish foe whispered to him.

The attacker knowing his name caught Gibby off guard just long enough for him to take advantage of the old deputy, lunging at him, and wrapping his strong hands around his throat, squeezing his airway shut like it were a reed, before using his razor-sharp nails to inflict the fatal stab wounds to his neck.

Gibby could feel the life draining out of him, likely very similar to the way ol' Abe Vigil died.

Buckling to his knees and sucking for air, Gibby out of reflex or concern for his friends, smashed the lighted lantern onto the cotton blanket in which Vigil's body was wrapped.

"Sorry, Abe," Gibby gurgled, as the blanket his dead friend was wearing burst into flame. Gibby hoped the fire would serve as a warning to Dry Springs it had a monster on its hands.

The fire, which burned intensely for a short period, also provided Gibby a place to finally find refuge, as the hot, unpredictable flames kept his attacker at bay, giving him the peace needed in saying good-bye to Mother Earth.

Gibby gave one last look around before his last breath wheezed from him. Everything on Break Road was dark except Vigil's burning corpse.

Chapter 4

Sheriff Deputy Jason Ajacks was proud of the tin star he wore on his brown leather vest. But at the moment the young man's eyes were full of his girl, Prudy Richards, whom he hoped someday to marry.

Ajacks, a tough-talking young cowboy, was smitten.

The town's most eligible bachelor and bachelorette were walking hand in hand along the Dry Springs Main Street, with Ajacks occasionally breaking the connection to perform the menial task of rattling the doors of the Main Street businesses in ensuring they locked.

But it wasn't like the door-rattling task was necessary. Dry Springs hadn't had a crime in over a year. The last being some child stealing a pie off a bakery cart during a town celebration. The boy ate the evidence preventing him from being prosecuted.

Yes, life in Dry Springs was rather slow for its three lawman.

Ajacks had lived in Dry Springs for only a few years. The town was to be a temporary rest stop on his way to California, where he had a hankering to put down permanent stakes. That was until he laid eyes on Prudy. "Prudy the beauty," he called her from the beginning.

Prudy had initially been brought to the town by an aunt, who had since married and moved away. Prudy, in addition to being beautiful, with auburn hair, a slender figure and doll-like features, was equally intelligent, having landed the job as schoolteacher for the 15 school-aged children who lived in or around the town.

During their stroll down the boardwalk, the two lovers were giggling and talking a lot about nothing when Prudy spotted a fireball off in the distance, followed by a steady stream of smoke.

"What's that old-timer up to?" Ajacks said, always a wee-bit impatient with fellow Deputy Gibby Jones.

Ajacks had given Gibby the order to go and retrieve a body someone had spotted out near the riverbank. Ajacks was actually given the order to perform the task by Sheriff Harry Wiley prior to the sheriff leaving town. But Ajacks, despite his youth, outranked Gibby when it came to delegating deputy duties.

Besides, Ajacks wanted to spend all the time he could gazing into Prudy's eyes, versus Gibby who had no one to spend time with outside his flea-bitten dog.

But now there were flames and smoke reaching skyward near where Gibby Jones would have been traveling.

Seeing the fire and smoke initially alarmed the young deputy, but standing next to his girl, he wanted to make certain he remained composed.

Gibby's instructions were simple, bring the body back to town so Howard, makeshift town doctor, could examine it in determining the cause of death prior to preparing the body for burial.

"Maybe Gibby's fishing a spell and needs the fire for some warming," Prudy surmised.

But her words nearly went unnoticed.

Prudy being a schoolteacher possessed great book sense.

Ajacks, on the other hand, considered himself to be smarter than he was, having a lot yet to learn, being only 24 years of age. The problem was, the only man Ajacks answered to was Sheriff Wily, who, being an ambitious lawman, was regularly out of town chasing down bad men in other parts of the territory in making a little extra money.

"I'd better go round up a few riders to see what that old coot is up to out there," Ajacks said in a put-out tone, out of habit rubbing his pearl-handled six-shooter. He had special ordered the gun from the Sears & Roebuck catalog and displayed it every chance he got.

"I would ask you to walk me back home," Prudy said to Ajacks, "but it appears you have more important duties to attend to."

"You sure? "Ajacks asked, not wanting to be dealing with an upset girl the following day. "It would only take me but a minute to walk you to your cottage," he reassured her.

Of course, the petite Prudy would never come right out and demand she be walked home. Such a forward, open attitude would run contrary to the lessons she often delivered to her students at school.

"I can handle myself," said Prudy, who lived in a small home near Means' saloon and close to the hardware store, the area of town that enjoyed the largest amount of foot traffic.

"You be careful now," she told Ajacks in a flirty tone before planting a wet kiss on his cheek. Prudy was never afraid to show her affection in public.

Wearing a fresh smudge of red lipstick on his cheek and stars in his eyes, Ajacks went about assembling a makeshift posse to ride out with him to where the fire appeared to still be burning less than a mile from town.

Chapter 5

The makeshift posse Ajacks assembled was a mix of characters.

There was Ray Wolcutt, a middle-aged former lawman with a sparse crop of gray hair under his hat and a thick gray mustache. The years had not been kind to Wolcutt.

But having Wolcutt along, eager to ride to Gibby's rescue, gave Ajacks a sense of relief, where Sheriff Wily was out of town.

Also on the ride were brothers Stan and Ike Peterson, who happen to be at the General Store picking up a few supplies when Ajacks's urgent call for riders went out.

The Petersons appeared to be close in age, Ike appearing slightly younger, while Stan was a little more refine, having sense enough to wear a kerchief over the bottom half of his face for what would be a cool ride.

The two brothers had recently settled in Dry Springs to care for the estate of their father and mother, Darwin and Mabel Peterson, who had met with untimely deaths.

The Peterson spread, the largest in the territory, was located just north of town.

And then there was James Edward Furst III, a.k.a. Jef, the be-speckled, novice cowboy who had more smarts and mouth than guts.

Jef, a newspaperman, had volunteered to tag along with the posse after overhearing just outside his office Ajacks extend an invitation to the Peterson brothers of needing help.

Jef figured the ride would give him column fodder for his next edition. So, using his wife Lola's horse he had ridden to town earlier that day, Jef joined the posse, armed only with his sharp wit and tongue.

Adventure was nothing new for the faithful Mormon, who had trekked his way to Dry Springs with what was then his young Hispanic female friend, now his wife, to care for her family and a small 4-acre plot of ground they farmed.

Ajacks didn't much mind Jef was a Mormon. What annoyed the deputy was Jef's overzealous desire to want to be a newspaperman in such a small town, where many living there just wanted to be left alone. But when challenged about his choice of career, Jef was always spouting the nation's Founding Fathers' interest in protecting a free press when framing the U.S. Constitution.

Ajacks was hoping their adventure would not be splashed across the front page of the Dry Springs News over the next couple of days. But desperate for riders, Ajacks agreed to let Jef tag along.

The ride down Break Road toward where the smoke rose into the night sky was now lit only by the moon and two torches Ajacks took the liberty of procuring from the General Store, all in the name of the law.

"Put it on Wily's tab," Ajacks told Jasper, the store clerk.

"Bit brisk," Jef whined as the riders galloped down the road through a cool fall breeze. But no one in the posse offered Jef a response, the other four riders letting their horses' breath, which could be seen curling in the breeze, do the talking for them.

Wolcutt, riding hard, said little, and just spit. Ajacks was equally quiet, but more due to nervousness. The Peterson brothers were a bit more talkative.

The brothers openly groused about what chores they would each be rendering at their late father and mother's ranch upon their return. Because of the heat of the day, despite it being fall, the Peterson brothers mentioned they preferred working at night.

The posse had not traveled far when they came across ole' Stu, Gibby's horse. Stu was quickly clomping his way in the opposite direction the posse was heading. The strange behavior of the old pulling horse put a fright into Jef, while it seemed to amuse the Petersons.

"Maybe we are in for an adventure after all," Stan Peterson said, his dull eyes lighting up under the shadow of the bill of his hat, it tightly pulled down on his head.

"I've never seen that old horse move so fast," said a bewildered Ajacks. "If I didn't know better I would think that horse had seen a ghost." But Ajacks's nervous chuckle that followed died in what wind there was.

Jef remained silent, brushing his brown moppish hair from his eyes before straightening the gray, flat cap resting on his head.

After witnessing Stu's fiery determination to keep moving the other direction, the men were now even less talkative in making their way down Break Road toward the lingering smoke.

Chapter 6

Although the much-used road beating a path from Dry Springs to the best fishing hole in the area was five-riders wide, the impromptu posse, out of fear or habit, rode closer to the center of the road, with Ajacks holding a torch, leading the way.

Wolcutt, with the other torch in hand, rode to the side of the young deputy. The Peterson brothers followed, riding side by side, with Jef bringing up the rear.

The group had only traveled another 200 yards after spotting Stu when they began to smell the odor of burning flesh.

"That smells worse than bad buttermilk," Jef said of the offending smell.

"That's the smell of death," Wolcutt said coldly. "I've smelled that smell before. Its death and it's come to visit. Let's hope it doesn't stay long."

Hearing Wolcutt's words made Ajacks nervous, causing his fingers to dance over his pearl-handled pistol. The Peterson brothers said nothing in exchanging glances. Jef, who seldom sweat as a result of hardly ever working outside in the sun for too long of a period of time, could now feel beads of cold sweat sticking to his shirt collar, his heart skipping an occasional beat.

The only thing that drove the Mormon cowboy to volunteer for the posse was the first-hand opportunity the experience would provide him in writing a story for the town newspaper, which he owned.

Yes, a slice of greed rode with Jef, who in looking around the group, had come to realize he was the only family man in the posse. That, along with the fact that he was unarmed, gave him all the rationale he needed to be bringing up the rear of the group.

Jef's hope was his real cowardice wouldn't surface. But just the same, it was moments like these, although he hadn't had too many of them like this, that he relied heavily on his Mormon upbringing to see him through.

The group traveled a little farther in silence, the only sound being their horses' hoofs digging into the hard ground, when they caught a whiff of burning wood. The smell served as a welcome substitute for the smell of burning flesh the group had been inhaling and exhaling for some time.

Gibby's tipped-over wagon in the center of the road was still smoldering as the group slowly approached the scene. Scattered small pockets of fire were still burning on the wagon, but for the most part, the wagon had already seen the worst of it, blackened where flames had licked it.

Ajacks brought his horse to a stop, immediately jumping from it with his pistol in one hand, and a torch in the other. The kid had guts, but sometimes no sense.

Wolcutt gave Ajacks an odd look before joining the young deputy on the ground. But Wolcott moved cautiously, unconvinced whoever was responsible for what they were witnessing had not yet left the area.

Moseying around the scene, Wolcott caught first glimpse of Gibby's half-burned body lying next to the wagon. His head and torso were badly charred, while his legs looked as if they had nearly gone untouched by the flames.

The Peterson brothers, Ike and Stan, remained on their horses but also had drawn their pistols.

"I get the sense eyes are on me," Ike Peterson told his brother. "And I don't like it."

Jef remained on his horse, his head spinning like a string toy, his heart beating like a drum, his brain trying to take a mental picture of a scene he would have to recreate on paper. But Jef didn't want to get too close to where Ajacks and Wolcutt were now standing out of fear it might make him sick to his stomach. And to be sick to the stomach was something he certainly didn't want to do in front of the other men.

"Looks like it might have been wolves," Ike Peterson said, inching his horse closer to where Gibby's body lay.

But Wolcutt, now inspecting the ground, was skeptical of Ike's surmise.

"I don't see any wolf tracks," Wolcutt said, bringing his torch closer to the ground for a better look. "Those look like dog tracks to me, likely Ranger's."

"Got to be wolves," Stan Peterson said. "Wolves got Gibby. Probably got the man you sent Gibby out here to recover, Ajacks."

"Wolves would have certainly sent that old pull-horse a flying," he added speaking of Stu.

Ajacks made his way around to the side of the wagon to get a better look at Gibby's body. There his fellow deputy laid, his fishing knife clutched in his left hand.

And then there was the second charred corpse in which Gibby partially laid on top of.

"What the ...," Ajacks stammered, the second corpse burned to a point of being unrecognizable under the light of the moon and their torches.

"Ya figure that was the body he came to recover?" Wolcutt asked Ajacks, whose face wore an expression of shock and guilt.

"I reckon," Ajacks said, still taking everything in, wondering where Sheriff Wily was when they needed him.

Next to the wagon was a smashed oil lamp, which both Ajacks and Wolcutt figured was the cause of the fire.

A further inspection of the area also revealed Gibby's shotgun not far from the burned-out wagon.

Wolcutt popped open the gun and found one unspent shell.

"Based on the lack of blood at the scene, this Gibby fellow must have missed his target," Stan Peterson said.

"It is mighty strange Gibby would have altogether missed. He was getting older and certainly couldn't shoot the eye out of a target, but at close range he should have hit something," Wolcutt said, holding Gibby's shotgun in his hand.

"Is that your law experience talking?" Stan Peterson asked Wolcutt.

"More than 20 years' worth," Wolcutt stated matter-of-factly through his thick gray mustache.

"I don't know, maybe Gibby panicked, shot early and missed, leaving whatever it was to get him," Ike Peterson added.

"Maybe," Wolcutt said in continuing to survey the area in search of a clue as to what really had happened.

"For the time being, the cause of death is roadside bandits. At least until we can get this figured out," Ajacks interjected.

"But nothing is missing. It can't be bandits," Jef said, before realizing what he had just blurted out. "Gibby had nothing of value but his dog."

"At this point it doesn't matter. Regardless of how these men died, we're going to have to take both bodies back to town where we'll have Howard identify them and determine their cause of death," Ajacks said.

"Ajacks is right. We are going to have to pack these bodies back to town," Wolcutt said. "We leave them out here, wolves are certain to get them," he said, staring in the direction of the Peterson brothers. The stare was Wolcutt's way of telling the brothers not to question him - ever.

But the pair of brothers took no notice.

"I'm telling you, Wolcutt, wolves already got 'em," Stan Peterson persisted.

"The scene here doesn't indicate that," Wolcutt said, spitting on the ground as if to signify that would be the last word on it.

"I can ride with Gibby over my horse, but somebody else is going to have to pack the other body," Ajacks said, exhibiting a sample of the bravado Sheriff Wily must had seen in Ajacks when he hired him as his deputy several months ago.

"I'll take the other," Wolcutt said.

"I appreciate you two men stepping up like that," Jef said, relieved he wasn't going to have to pack one of the smelly, burnt carcasses home.

No sooner had Ajacks and Wolcutt gotten the bodies tied over the front side of their horses than the group heard rustling in the brush near the road.

Stan Peterson for the first time was off his horse with his pistol in hand.

"I told you earlier, something is watching us," Ike Peterson said, joining his brother, who was beginning to move slowly toward the roadside where the desert brush began.

"I tell ya, it's wolves, Wolcutt," Stan Peterson whispered.

"Wolves don't tip wagons up onto their sides," Wolcutt said. "Besides, Gibby's got his knife in hand. If it were wolves, there would be more blood spattered about," he said.

But the noise coming from the brush did concern Wolcutt, just not enough to force the former lawman to get back down off his horse.

"Take your torch over there, Ajacks. These boys might be onto something," said Jef, who still had yet to show any desire in getting down off of his horse. Instead, he took his glasses off his face and wiped them vigorously on his shirt before placing them back on the edge of his nose.

Ajacks sighed, in getting off his horse and making his way toward the brothers. He was hoping they wouldn't find anything in the brush. He had already seen enough death for one night. And to think, Sheriff Wiley was missing it all, he thought.

"Just keep your torch close," Stan Peterson scolded Ajacks, while Ike and he methodically crept from bush to bush, searching for whatever it was the pair sensed was tracking their every move.

Chapter 7

"I just seen a set of eyes," Stan Peterson cried out, quickly pointing his pistol in the direction of the sighting.

"Where?" Ike asked, freezing where he stood, in aiming his pistol at the same spot Stan stood pointing to with his weapon.

Wolcutt, still up in his saddles hoping for a quick departure, had also drawn his pistol. Jef remained close, looking on with curiosity, pushing his glasses up on his nose to get a better look.

"You ready?" Stan asked Ike, as he slowly peeled back the brush.

"Shoot it, Stan. Hurry, before it gets us," Ike screamed frantically.

Just as Stan rolled the hammer back on his six-shooter, Jef leaped from his horse and, out of instinct, grabbed Stan's arm, forcing it downward, causing his shot to fall just short of the intended target.

The bullet bounced harmlessly off the desert floor.

"What are you doing?" Stan said, pushing Jef away and staring him down.

"It's Ranger," said an excited Jef. "That's Gibby's dog."

But Ranger wasn't up for company, the fur on the nape of his neck raised like a row of wheat, as he snapped and growled at the men as if they were the enemy. Baring his teeth, the normally friendly dog appeared rabid.

"He's rabid, Jef. He's a rabid dog. Back away from him. It was a wolf, I tell ya, they've done bit him, and he is done for," Stan Peterson said, preparing to take another shot at Ranger.

But Jef, out of his love for animals was having none of it, standing in such a way in creating a barrier between the dog and the end of Stan Peterson's gun. "He's just frightened," Jef said, for the first time that night letting his feelings known. Now he was no longer just covering a story.

"He has got to be put down before he bites someone," Stan Peterson said, again raising his pistol in an attempt to take aim at Ranger, who still remained back from the road among the bushes, growling and snarling.

"No, wait," Jef said. "Ajacks, tell him to give me a minute."

"You got one minute," Ajacks warned holding up his index finger. "We need to be going."

Jef ran to his saddlebag, pulling out of it one of two dry biscuits left over from a lunch Lola had packed for him earlier that day.

"Get away from him with your guns," Jef said, gesturing with his arms for the Petersons to back away from the dog. "I'll coax him out."

"Ranger, I realize you have already had enough for one night, but if you don't come with me now, you might not make it back to town," Jef said, waving the biscuit he held out at arm's length in the direction of the snarling dog.

Ranger's growls weakened, before the blood and dirt spotted dog reluctantly came forward out of the bushes and in the direction of the biscuit Jef was holding outward.

"Hurry it up," Stan Peterson said quickly becoming annoyed with the time it was taking Jef to lure the dog out.

Before Jef could respond to Stan Peterson's complaint, there was a tail wag by Ranger as he moved closer to the biscuit, sniffing it, before one flash of his long tongue and a quick gulp by the dog made the biscuit disappear.

"You're lucky that wasn't your finger," Stan Peterson said.

"Better yet, your arm," Ike added with a laugh.

Ranger, now standing a few feet from Jef, was settling down but still unwilling to take his eyes off the group or come within petting range of his new friend.

"He needs another biscuit," Jef said, racing back to his saddlebag.

"Come on, hurry it up," said Ajacks, growing weary of the wait. "Whatever got them, I don't want it to get us," he said, motioning his head in the direction of the two bodies slumped over his and Wolcutt's horses.

Ranger gobbled down the second biscuit as fast as the first, allowing Jef to get close enough to pat the dog's head. "That a boy," Jef said, who made a smooth transition from petting Ranger, to getting his arms around the smelly dog in lifting him up onto Lola's horse.

Jef was the only rider in the group who didn't own his own horse. But he didn't mind. He lived fairly close to town and often would walk to work.

"When that dog chews your arm off up to your elbow and you get rabies, I'll be the first to tell your wife I warned you the dog was rabid," Stan Peterson said.

"Let's get out of here. You two ladies can discuss the dog on the ride back to town," said an impatient Wolcott before spitting to the ground.

The Peterson brothers followed Wolcutt, leaving Jef, who was having difficulty riding his horse and holding onto his new canine friend at the same time.

There was little said between the men during their ride back to town.

CHAPTER 8

Jef sprung up in bed as if it were Christmas morning, awakening to a fresh smell of oatmeal and smelly dog. The smelly dog was Ranger, who lay on the floor at the foot of the four-poster bed Lola and Jef shared. The smell of oatmeal was coming from the cabin kitchen. Lola was already up in getting 5-year-old James Jr. ready for school.

Jef was still wearing the clothes he had worn the night before. Clothes, that now, along with their bedding, bore the scent of a smoldering wagon and the odor of dog.

However, the smells did provide Jef with the reassurance that what he had experienced the night before was no nightmare.

The sun was just beginning to rise on a new day in Dry Springs, and Jef had work to do as he reached for his glasses on the nightstand where he out of habit tried to always leave them.

Jef's brain was already turning. He had a newspaper to publish, for the first time, having a real story to share.

Gibby's and the unidentified stranger's deaths were the first unnatural deaths in Dry Springs since Lola and he had lived there.

That was news. And Jef felt obligated to print it in his struggling newspaper, published bi-weekly, or as dollars would allow. What he made off the newspaper, being publisher, editor, reporter and carrier, wasn't enough to fill a sock. To make ends meet, Lola and he farmed the 4 acres of land they inherited from Lola's mother, Maria Sanchez.

The young couple originally came to Dry Springs seven years ago to care for Mrs. Sanchez due to her failing health. But after two years Maria was overcome with sickness, and upon her death the property she owned ended up becoming Lola's inheritance. Lola's only brother, Martino, headed off to California rather than work the land, leaving Lola and Jef the small farm.

To make ends meet, Lola and Jef also did odd jobs for others in town with much larger tracts of land to care for.

Lola also baked and sewed some, in helping put food on the table for her family, Jef, James Jr., and their 3 year-old son Bobby.

But Jef's real interest was in the publishing business, and what few coins he made off of his hobby was just enough to keep his old iron Columbian printing press with its Algerian typeset operating.

Jef was lucky if he was able to sell with each printing about 30 newspapers at 3 cents each.

Generally the Dry Springs newspaper consisted of articles on birthdays and move-ins, which in Dry Springs were not many.

Miss Peggy Higginson's recipes were also always a big hit. But his biggest single selling edition was one he published a few short months ago focusing on Mayor Howard's hire of Sheriff Harry Wily and whether a sleepy little town the size of Dry Springs needed a sheriff of Wily's caliber.

That edition sold about 60 papers. The mayor bought extra copies to mail to family in Texas. He even bought three copies for himself because he loved seeing his name in print. "Lookie there," Howard said the day the story ran. Jef could still picture the mayor with his thumb tucked inside his gold-colored vest, waving that particular edition around as if it were a flag.

Wily, on the other hand, was annoyed by the attention he received from the article. "Don't be doing that again," Jef recalled Wily telling him. As if the lawman himself was wanted by the law, or was trying to ditch a beautiful woman he had left behind in his rough wake.

But the mystery surrounding the deaths of Gibby and the other victim was a real story begging to be shared. A story Jef had taken a role in firsthand, providing him with his golden opportunity to prove to the rest of the town the value of the press while exercising his vanity.

Should he exercise some literary license with this particular piece, he might even gain the attention of the folks living in Twin Bridges, a town of about 80 people less than 40 miles east of Dry Springs.

No doubt the death of a sheriff's deputy in such a small town would be big news. Heck, the papers up Denver and Salt Lake City way might even be interested in such a story, Jef thought to himself.

But before the story could be told, he would have to visit with Squeak, his quiet, somewhat awkward friend whose duties in the town included prepping bodies for burial.

Squeak, who got his nickname when he was a kid because he was always squeaking when he spoke, inherited the job of taking care of the dead being he was the most gifted carpenter in town, and had no family that might object to him performing such work. Besides, Squeak never seemed shaken by the work that included corpse makeovers, building the coffin and engraving the tombstone.

If Squeak had his way, he would even deliver the body to the gravesite if not for Pastor Parsons not wanting to relinquish those duties.

Although the day was early, Jef was hoping Squeak, who Jef shared build-ing space with, would already have the second body recovered identified.

But before James Edward Furst could splash his face with water from the basin sitting on the nightstand next to his bed and bolt from the bedroom with his head floating with so many details, he would have to share some of what he knew with Lola in order to get past her.

After all, the cabin was small, with only one way in and one way out, and that was by way of the front door.

Chapter 9

Without Lola saying a word, Jef could hear her voice in his head: "James Edward Furst, a husband and father first, a newspaperman a distant third."

But before Jef could approach his wife, Lola, in her thick Spanish accent, was already posing questions. The first being: "What is Gibby's dog doing in our bedroom?"

Ranger, knowing she was talking about him, gave Jef a stare.

For a moment, Jef hesitated, hoping the question would evaporate in thin air while Lola busily helped James Jr. prepare for school.

James Jr. had many of the same physical characteristics as his father. They shared the same smile, brown moppish hair and lean build. But James Jr.'s personality and interests favored his tough mother. The boy was always eager to work the farm, where Jef showed little interest in such menial chores.

To avoid having to share with Lola the whole account of the night before, Jef was pretending to ignore her.

But Lola, desiring to know all things, asked again, this time in a louder tone with more emphasis on her accent.

Lola's accent over the years had softened some, unless she was angry, then it surfaced like well water.

Jef realized he was going to have to tell Lola about Gibby's death, but was uncertain how he was going to break the news.

"Ranger is going to be staying with us," Jef began slowly, burying the lead.

But before he could say more, James Jr. and his brother Bobby let out a whoop and a hooray. Ranger was by far the most popular dog in town.

"Why is that?" Lola sternly asked her husband, making certain he didn't forget who was really in charge.

"Dismiss the children," Jef reluctantly responded, hoping his talk with Lola wouldn't take a direction that would delay him much further.

The two boys immediately left the kitchen and went outside, taking with them Ranger, who seemed to be already warming up to the family.

"Is Gibby sick? Because I can't imagine him giving up Ranger's company unless he was really sick," Lola said. Lola had always had a soft spot for Gibby, who was quick with a wave and a wink, which always flattered Lola.

"Gibby's dead," Jef said, plopping down in one of the kitchen chairs. "He was killed by someone or something late last night. A posse run I made with Ajacks, Wolcutt and the Peterson boys was in response to Gibby's wagon being set on fire. Gibby was in the process of retrieving another body when he was attacked," Jef said, quickly blurting out facts in hope of reducing the sting of his story.

"Before you ask, Lola, I have to go see Squeak to determine who the other victim was," Jef said.

"Two murders," Lola said in disbelief. "Dry Springs hasn't had a single murder over all the years I've lived here," she said, plopping down in a chair next to her husband and grabbing his hand to ward off some of the shock.

"Two bodies," Jef confirmed. "I'm not certain the deaths are related. But I suspect they may be," he said, scooting closer to his wife to console her. Something he didn't have in mind until seeing how she was taking the news. Generally Lola was as tough as iron.

"Where did this occur?" Lola asked.

"About half a mile out on break road, maybe a little farther," Jef replied, while running the fingers on his free left hand up and down his black suspenders.

"Could it have been wolves?" Lola asked, trying to rationalize the cause.

"I don't think it was wolves. Although that is what the Peterson brothers suspect," Jef said.

"So, what's your next move?" Lola asked.

"Outside of caring for Ranger, who we found last night hiding in the brush near where the bodies of Gibby and the other man lay," Jef replied, "I have got to warn the other town members."

And Lola knew exactly what that meant.

"Before you go stirring your ink, get me the old washbasin in the barn so I can give this dog a scrubbing," said Lola, who was a bit of a neat-freak. "He can't stink if he is going to be inside with us."

"Lola, really, I've got a newspaper to get out if anyone is ever going to respect me as a newspaperman," Jef said.

"Think that's wise, putting out a story about the deaths before you talk to others?" Lola asked. "Hadn't you better talk to Sheriff Wily before you do such a thing?"

"Wily is out of town, left yesterday. Besides, a newspaperman should never have to wait on his sources," Jef said.

Now Lola had gone and done it. She had hit Jef's hot button.

"If you knew anything about the paper business, you would know news waits for no one," Jef said, pushing his wire-rim glasses up on the bridge of his nose. "Besides, with this particular incident, I am only going to write what I know," he said.

If only she could get Jef to be so headstrong when it came to shooting a gun or planting a row of seed, Lola thought. Skills that would be useful in helping her care for their property -- skills their two boys would likely want to see out of their father, she thought.

From childhood, Jef had a love for writing. A passion Lola was aware he had developed while growing up in New York. There, his father, a businessman, would often bring home a newspaper tucked under his arm.

Jef and his father would take turns passing the paper back and forth, each reading what they wanted, and then talking about it. It was then Jef first shared with his father that one day he was going to be a newspaperman.

Lola recognized Jef was sincere and intelligent and had set a lofty goal. But his newspaper dreams in a small town she had grown to love didn't seem to fit.

Of course, neither did their marriage, a Catholic/Mormon mix in which their religious differences were still being worked out as they arose.

But now that the town had an actual murder her husband would be writing about, Lola was concerned Jef's ambitious nature was about to run head on with how Sheriff Wily preferred to run the town.

"It's because Wily can't read he takes such offense to the newspaper," Lola recalled Jef saying on more than one occasion.

"Lola, I have to go. I'll catch up on the work around here later," Jef said, grabbing an apple off the table and his flat, gray cap hanging on the hook by the door.

Lola feared the West someday was going to eat her husband up. But he was a confident man, always talking about God being on his side. She was pretty sure it was part of that Mormon faith he practiced, which included daily prayer and scripture reading.

"Before you go, I need that washtub," Lola reminded Jef by nodding at Ranger, having taken a somewhat relaxed position on their porch.

"Can't it wait?" Jef said with a child-like tone.

Lola shook her head in silence, sending a marching, muttering husband off to the barn some distance away to fetch the tub they used to wet down their smaller livestock in the heat of the summer.

While Lola waited for her husband to return, she took in the smells of the fall and sounds of the chirping birds. But Lola hadn't ventured far into her thoughts when her trip was interrupted by the thud of an iron wash tub smacking the hard ground.

"There," Jef exclaimed, returning from the barn with the basin and dropping it outside of the cabin, a distance from where Lola was standing in the cabin door.

"See you small ones later," Jef told his children before jumping aboard Lola's horse.

"Tell them you love them," Lola said, getting in one last dig at her impatient husband.

But Jef was already off, and before she could realize it, cutting through the cloud of dust behind him was his new friend Ranger.

"Ranger," Lola called, trying to bring the dog back. But the free-spirited dog and Jef were well down the road. The dog-washing would have to wait.

The thought Jef had a new friend brought a smile to Lola's face. Until it dawned on her once again that while Jef worked his toggle joint and lever printing press in town, she and her young son Bobby would be stuck once again doing the morning chores.

Chapter 10

When the door to the print office opened, the cow bell hanging over it clanged as it always did. It clanged again when the door closed.

Squeak was just putting the first nails in the second coffin when Jef and Ranger arrived. Looking at Squeak, you couldn't tell he had been hard at work. He never broke a sweat.

Jef always marveled at Squeak's craftsmanship and how easy building and shaping things came to him. Little did Jef know – because Squeak said so little – that he equally marveled at Jef's gift of being able to strike up a conversation with anyone at the drop of a hat.

The admiration the two men had for one another served as their bond. That, and because the pair shared a building, Squeak's woodshop up front, Jef's printing press in back.

It saved both men, a little light in the pocket, operating cost.

"So, who's the second body? Were you able to identify it through all that charred flesh?" Jef asked, keeping his distance from Squeak's workbench where the body of the unidentified victim still lay out.

"Abe Vigil," Squeak replied gesturing toward the grisly corpse, staying true to his nature of being a man of few words. "His gold filling cap, a dead giveaway," he added with a snort.

"Not funny," Jef responded. "So what killed him?"

"Surprisingly, it wasn't fire," Squeak replied, concentrating more on the coffin he was building for Vigil than on Jef's questioning.

"The Peterson brothers suspected wolves got them both," Jef said.

"I don't think it was wolves," Squeak said, "or their flesh would have been torn. Gibby's flesh was sliced. Like his attacker was carrying a straight-edged razor."

Sliced? What a story that would make, Jef thought to himself, his wheels made out of words already spinning in his head in anticipation of creating his story.

"Abe Vigil, that's a shame," Jef said, refocusing on the other victim, but still from a distance. Jef had only but a few brief encounters with Vigil, most of the talk centering on fishing. It was just small talk for Jef, who had no real interest in fishing.

"Abe was drained of blood. Like a horse trough with a hole in the bottom," Squeak said, before realizing he had probably shared too much information with his reporter friend. But Jef and he had become close, having to share the same shabby building. Two mild-mannered men brought to Dry Springs out of their love for women.

Jef moved to Dry Springs out of dedication to Lola, while Squeak was there at the insistence of his mother, who had since passed. Sadly, hers was the first coffin he ever built in Dry Springs.

Squeak, being shy, and not having an adventurous bone in his body, decided to remain in Dry Springs rather than start somewhere new.

The two men together made one perfect cowboy: Jef provided the mental know-how and ambition to make things work, and Squeak was gifted with two strong hands and the willingness to get them dirty if he needed to.

"I see you got a new friend," Squeak said, nodding at Ranger, who was quickly becoming attached to Jef.

"Somebody had to care for Gibby's dog," Jef said, patting Ranger on the head. "The Petersons were going to shoot him, claiming he was rabid."

"Yea, Deputy Ajacks told me all about it. That is so unlike you, Jef, to actually take part in a ride," Squeak said.

Ajacks and Wolcutt, upon arriving back to town the previous night with the two bodies, had showed up at Squeak's small living quarters. Because the town had no funeral home, the duties of prepping the dead for burial were delegated to Squeak, who never seemed bothered by the work.

Squeak, who could sell only so much hand-crafted furniture in a small town, figured he could always use the extra money he received for building coffins and etching inscriptions into tombstones.

But the lingering smell of the bodies amid the smell of the fresh chipped wood of the furniture pieces squeezed into the little office was a smell Jef was having a difficult time getting accustom to. Of course, Dry Springs didn't have an overabundance of burials. Prior to the death of Gibby and Vigil, the last funeral service they had was a service for Darwin and Mabel Peterson, whose bodies were found in the west desert.

Stan and Ike Peterson had said they were hoping to solve that mystery.

"I'm intrigued by the amount of blood Vigil lost," Jef added. "What an odd way to die," he said. But Squeak was absorbed in getting his work done and had already said about as much as he was going to.

"Come on, Ranger, let this man be. We've got a newspaper to publish," Jef said, walking through a black curtain the two men had hung, the only thing separating Squeak's wood shop and Jef's print office in the Main Street building.

CHAPTER 11

Ajacks and Wolcutt returning to the scene of the smoldering wagon were in search of any clues to as who may have killed Gibby and Vigil.

With Sheriff Wily out of town, young Ajacks had taken charge of the investigation, turning to Wolcutt for some investigative insight.

In the light of the day, Wolcutt had found only two different sets of footprints circling the upturned wagon. That ruled out Gibby being done in by wolves.

The only other tracks Wolcutt and Ajacks found at the scene were paw prints they both suspected belonged to Ranger.

Even more concerning to the two men was there was very little blood at the scene, despite Gibby having fired his shotgun.

"Gibby's eyesight was failing, but how could he have missed someone, or something, that would have been right on top of him?" Ajacks asked Wolcutt.

"In all my years of law work, I've never come across such a scene," Wolcott replied.

Despite being middle-aged, Wolcutt still cut a muscular shadow. He feared little, but this particular murder scene had the former lawman stumped.

Wolcutt in rubbing his chin, paused, before spitting.

"Beast or bandit?" Ajacks asked his new partner.

"Not certain, maybe a mix of both," Wolcutt said, before determining the pair might want to start making their way back to town where the townsfolks would likely have questions galore, particularly one irritating gnat that went by the name of James Edward Furst.

"For the time being, I suggest we tell everyone the investigation continues, and to bolt their doors at night until we make an arrest," Ajacks said.

Wolcutt nodded, this time without spitting.

Little did the two men know Jef had already determined how news of the murders was going to be shared in having had gleaned enough information from talking to Squeak, and from his own posse experience, to tell his own story – in print.

Chapter 12

The Dry Springs News headline read: "MYSTERY SURROUNDS THE DEATHS OF TWO DRY SPRINGS TOWNIES."

Below that was the byline of James Edward Furst III.

Ajacks read the headline a third time before wadding the one-sheet newspaper into a ball and throwing it to the creaky wooden floor in the sheriff's office.

Ajacks was annoyed Jef had taken advantage of the trust he had placed in him by allowing him be a part of the posse to retrieve Gibby and Vigil's bodies. It now appeared Jef had volunteered only to advance his newspaper dream. The more Ajacks thought about it, the angrier he became at the bespeckled Jef, who often portrayed a sense of innocence.

But Ajacks wasn't buying it.

Jef was quirky, like his Mormon faith, but the ambitious newspaperman had to be watched or he was going to send the town into a full-scale panic, Ajacks thought.

When Sheriff Wily made his return, Ajacks was certain he would have words for Jef. But to keep the peace for the time being, now was not the time to confront Jef.

Today, the town was coming together to bury Gibby and what was left of Vigil. There would be time later for Ajacks to confront Jef privately about his insulting newspaper article.

Chapter 13

Pastor Ronald Parsons was presiding over the funeral services held jointly for Gibby and Vigil. Squeak purposely nailing their coffins shut prior to the service to prevent anyone from lifting the coffin lids and fainting right there on the spot.

Pastor Parsons, whom everyone just called "Parsons" for short, was a determined soul, who over the years had bounced from job to job to put food on his family's table. For many years Parsons served as a hired hand of sorts, building fences, plowing fields, and on occasion caring for someone's livestock.

It wasn't but only a few years ago Parsons had found God, in transforming himself into Dry Springs' conscience.

It helped Parsons could read and was an eloquent speaker. He hardly ever said the word "uh" when stringing together the sentences in his sermons. His preaching always seemed to come across to others as kind and compassionate. His hazel eyes were warm, and his hands actually quite large, likely from all those years performing odd jobs.

And his smile was contagious.

Parsons was married, having three older children. His wife, Shirley, a pleasant woman, over the years had developed a knack for baking. The pastor would often call on her baking to break the ice in asking people out to church.

"Here is some pie. Hope to see you out to church Sunday," Shirley would say, direct as a train. Parsons was a little less plainspoken and worked to be someone's friend before becoming their pastor.

Now Parsons stood before a small crowd gathered in the sturdy church. Despite Gibby having few friends because of his cantankerous nature, and Vigil not having any family, the chapel pews were nearly full.

Gibby, who stepped forward in filling the much-needed deputy position, making the sacrifice of foregoing his checker-playing days at the hardware store, was to be laid to rest in the city cemetery next to his wife, Bev. Gibby had doted on Bev during her years of sickness leading up to her death.

Vigil's resting place in the cemetery was amongst what the townsfolk referred to as "loner's row." Those buried there had no family.

Jef and Lola and their two children sat in a pew near the front of the chapel. The Furst family was seated in such a way, making it difficult for Ajacks to make eye contact with Jef in sending him a nasty glare.

Prudy sat next to Ajacks, keeping her strong, young mustang calm by occasionally patting his knee and whispering in his ear that everything was going to be fine.

"I swear," Prudy said, lovingly reassuring her impatient boyfriend.

Ajacks conceded there would be a more appropriate time to talk to Jef about the article that Ajacks had attempted to read, despite him being such a poor reader.

The combined funeral services for Gibby and Vigil were short and sad. Parsons spoke of how the two men contributed mightily to the fabric that made up Dry Springs, and how the men would find their peace in the next life, likely next to some fishing hole.

Jef was impressed at the way Parsons handled the service and the manner in which he elevated both Gibby and Vigil to near-sainthood.

The crowd in the church then quietly and respectfully filed out of the chapel when the services were complete. The group, dressed in their Sunday best, made their way down Dry Springs' packed dirt roads and onto the nearby cemetery.

Only murmurings and whisperings could be heard amongst shuffling feet.

The Furst family walked near the front of the group. Gibby's dog, Ranger, appearing to have his head bowed, walking stride-for-stride with them.

Behind the Furst family was Parsons, Shirley and the couple's children.

Following the Parson's family was Squeak, whose best dress consisted of a clean white shirt that was a little short in the sleeves and clean pair of black trousers that hit the tall, thin man of Scandinavian descent at mid-ankle. Squeak was no show pony.

Others in the procession included Mayor Howard; Miss Peggy Higginson, a world traveler who brought loud color to the otherwise gray town; Otis Thumper, a bear of a man who served as the town's blacksmith; Wolcutt and Ike Peterson. The younger Peterson brother appeared lonely without the company of older brother, Stan, who Ike explained was away on business.

In addition, there were other townspeople who walked in the procession, with Ajacks and Prudy, walking arm-in-arm like lovers do, bringing up the rear.

But on this day, Ajacks was walking a little heavier as a result of guilt he was packing, having been the one who had given Gibby the order to go check on the body by the river - the corpse that ended up being Abe Vigil.

Ajacks couldn't help but think that task was to be his, and would have been, had he not outranked his senior deputy.

But Ajacks sent Gibby instead, and Gibby, being the kind of man he was, took the assignment without grumbling.

Now Ajacks was alive and well and the top lawman in Dry Springs until Sheriff Wily returned, while Gibby was enclosed in a pinewood box, taking his last wagon ride to his final resting place.

Before a tear could form and roll from his eye, Ajacks stopped reflecting on Gibby, and began to selfishly worry about what might lay ahead of him.

There were no clear answers as to who, or what, killed Gibby and Vigil, he thought. But based on time and location, he was certain the deaths were related. Those same sentiments were shared by many of the townsfolk, who were demanding answers from the young deputy.

To keep the town calm, Ajacks and Wolcutt had been floating the rumor that they suspected bandits passing through Dry Springs had killed the two men.

The hope was the story would suffice until Sheriff Wily returned to town to sort everything out. The townsfolk had always placed a great deal of confidence in Wily during his short stint as their sheriff.

But if Ajacks was going to be able to make the bandit story believable, he was going to have to convince Jef to keep his ink in his quill until they had all the facts.

When Ajacks approached Wolcutt in the cemetery following the burial service, he told Wolcutt of the article Jef had published and how it already had some town members buzzing.

"I swear, Jef would kick a hornet's nest with his bare feet," Ajacks told Wolcutt.

Wolcutt shared similar frustrations with Jef's newspaper article, pulling from his coat pocket a folded-up clipping of the same story.

"Where does Jef's loyalty lie?" a frustrated Wolcutt asked Ajacks, before spitting to the ground.

"I don't know. This afternoon we'll pay him a personal visit and find out," Ajacks said with a smirk.

CHAPTER 14

"Bandits?" Jef said with a snort, his tone questioning Wolcutt and Ajacks's story. Wolcutt, sitting at the Furst's kitchen table, sat in a way that allowed his brown duster to hang open just wide enough so Jef could see Wolcutt was now wearing Gibby's charred deputy tin star.

"I don't think so," Jef said, refusing to buy the explanation the two lawmen were pitching. He was thinking Ajacks and Wolcutt's strategy was to try and get him to take a different direction with his newspaper articles in the future.

But Jef, who stood nearly 6 feet tall, had some fight in him, and he figured this was his one opportunity to etch his name across the stars.

"With all due respect," Jef said, pushing his glasses that had a tendency to slide, further up onto the bridge of his nose, "Gibby and Abe were both found to have money in their trousers, according to Squeak."

"And Wolcutt, you yourself found Gibby's gun at the scene. Bandits would have taken it," Jef said, who for two days had been processing all the information he had gathered to this point by himself.

"We're saying it's bandits until we know otherwise. We suggest if you do any more writing on the matter that you share with folks the same information. I'd hate to have to throw a newspaper man in jail," Ajacks warned Jef.

Ajacks and Wolcutt had ridden out to the Furst home, about a half mile outside Dry Springs, with the purpose of curtailing Jef's willingness to publicly share information surrounding the deaths of Gibby and Vigil.

The pair now sat straight across the kitchen table from Jef in an interrogating fashion, while Lola popped in and out pretending to be doing chores to cover her eavesdropping.

"It wasn't wolves," Jef said. "It wasn't bandits dressed like wolves. I believe Gibby set fire to his wagon as a last resort, like firing off a warning shot for the rest of us," Jef said. "We are dealing with something much more than just some passers-by bandits," he stressed.

"We may be," Ajacks fired back. "But it isn't like we are just sitting on our hands. As you can plainly see, I have deputized Wolcutt to help in this matter, and other measures will be taken should the residents of this town be put in any further danger. But you publicly taking us to the woodshed is not helping matters," Ajacks said, raising his voice, forgetting for a moment whose house he was in.

"I thought you said you suspected the deaths were the work of bandits passing through town," Jef replied. "Why should there be any future threat?"

Ajacks glanced over at Wolcutt, whose facial expressions were as cold as stone.

"That would be none of your business," Wolcutt told Jef.

Wolcutt's abrupt response delighted Ajacks but did not sit well with Jef.

Lola, regardless of the busy work she had been mustering up, couldn't help but overhear the men's conversation. To prevent the men's discussion from getting further heated, she darted back into the kitchen to ask any of them whether they wanted a nice cold drink of water, or better yet, some freshly squeezed lemonade.

But her effort failed when both Wolcutt and Ajacks declined her offer.

Lola didn't care. Acting like she had work to do in the kitchen, she stayed close, hoping her presence would supply her husband with the nerve needed to defend his story, even though she too did not approve of the article.

Ranger also remained close, resting at Jef's feet.

Over the past two days Ranger had become Jef's shadow. It helped that Jef was always throwing the dog table scraps from what the Furst children left on their plates following breakfast and dinner.

"I'm sure you men understand the importance of a free press keeping the town members informed of what you are doing to try to apprehend Gibby and Vigil's killer or killers," Jef said.

"Free press," Wolcutt said, blowing up his cheeks and then puffing air through his thick gray mustache almost hard enough for him to blow the hair off his face. "Where is your allegiance?" he scolded.

"It's to everyone who lives in this community," Jef replied.

"Jef, it sounds to me that you and I have the same job. Wouldn't it be best if we were to work together on this," Ajacks asked.

Wolcutt slightly nodded in an agreement with what Ajacks had to say, and was in the process of clearing his throat to spit on the Furst kitchen floor, when Lola re-entered the room and cast the tough, weathered cowboy a warning glare.

Wolcutt swallowed hard instead and after a brief moment of silence, again started in on Jef. "If you interfere in any way with this investigation, it will be our sworn duty to take you into custody," he said, slowly standing.

Ajacks stood with Wolcutt in attempt to make it look like it was his idea to stand.

Jef again slid his glasses back onto the bridge of his nose, before getting up from the table along with the two cowboys.

"We'll be keeping an eye on you," Wolcutt told Jef as he grabbed his black hat off the worn hat hook that hung on the wall next to the kitchen door.

"I will also be keeping an eye on you two," Jef said, trying to prevent his lower lip from quivering from the adrenaline now rushing through his body.

After the pair had shown themselves out of the Furst home, Lola breathed such a heavy sigh of relief Jef feared the two lawmen heard it.

She wasn't alone. Her sigh was matched by the sigh Jef heard coming from under the kitchen table. Apparently, Ranger too was relieved to have that meeting behind them.

But while Jef and Lola were sensing some relief, young Ajacks remained burdened by the course of events, wearing Gibby's death like a harness.

"Wolcutt, you ever feel like you made a mistake and will never be able to undo the wrong you committed on another fella?" Ajacks asked his new found partner as the pair began to ride back toward town.

"My experience tells me that God forgives lawmen for such mistakes, as long as that is all it was, a mistake, and not an act of cowardice," Wolcutt said.

"I just wanted to be with my girl," Ajacks said, knowing that was something Wolcutt, being separated from his wife, could understand. "I keep thinking whatever Gibby encountered, I may have been able to fend off," Ajacks said.

"Let it go," said Wolcutt, his long, distinguished career as a lawman speaking. His words helped ease Ajacks's conscience some.

"Thanks," Ajacks said as the two men rode hard toward the setting sun.

Wolcutt, generally reluctant to share his emotions with anyone, just spit and thought to himself he was grateful the two of them didn't have much further to ride because he had already shared more personal feelings with Ajacks than he wanted to.

Chapter 15

The night fell on Dry Springs. The streets were quiet. Only buzzing insects and a few lowing livestock could be heard. All of the businesses along Main Street were dark, with the exception of Means' Saloon.

The funeral services early that day had nearly everyone in town emotionally spent. Immediately following the service there was some foot traffic in town, but no social stops or gatherings. Everyone's heads were down, quick to nod at those who passed, in moving along to their homes. The ordinarily gray town was nearly in total mourning.

However, there was one lonely figure sitting on an empty wooden keg in the narrow alley between the saloon and Thumper's blacksmith shop, which had closed earlier in the evening. Thumper was a man who only put in the hours he needed to, and not a minute more.

The alley, where both businesses dumped their garbage until it could be taken away and buried, was serving as a temporary rest stop for Homer White.

White ducked into the alley to sulk after having lost nearly $8 in a friendly scratch poker game in the saloon.

White was no lush, but on occasion did frequent the saloon with his part-time work duties at the hardware store shrinking due to the coming change in weather.

The only one White had to care for was his wife, June. His son, Bert, had moved to Denver, while his daughter, Julia, married a man chasing the California gold rush.

White was sitting in the alley contemplating whether he should return to the saloon, using an I.O.U to return to the poker game.

But before White could muster the ambition needed to rise from the barrel he had been resting on, the alley suddenly became dark, giving him the impression something or someone was closing in on him.

A sudden burst of cold wind then tossed around some of the loose garbage lying at White's feet. It was a fast breeze, slapping him in the face like a cold splash of river water.

After the wind died down, White's attention came to focus on a 6-foot tall figure entering the alley off Main Street. The silhouette of the figure cut off what little light was shining down into the alley from the mix of Main Street kerosene lanterns and burning torches.

The alley was only about 5 feet wide and 25 feet deep, so it wasn't long before the slow-moving figure, taking elegant strides, had closed most of the distance between the two of them.

The approaching man, dressed in what appeared to exceed Sunday best, said nothing. White thought he knew everyone in town, but he had not seen this fella before. He would have remembered the unordinary look on the face of the stranger.

White thought he would break the ice between the two of them by striking up a conversation.

"Howdy, friend," White said.

But the stranger offered no reply, steadily moving closer, now crowding the space between them.

White was now growing uneasy with his newfound company.

"I was just about ready to duck back into the saloon for a friendly game of cards. Care to join me?" White asked growing increasingly weary of the intruder dressed in a high-neck, collared black cape. White thought certainly unfashionable dress for these parts.

But due to the darkness of the alley, White was having a difficult time making out all of the man's facial features. Based on what he could see, the approaching man's face appeared cold and lifeless.

It was a threatening look, causing White to nervously stand and rest his right hand on his six-shooter still in its holster.

"I already lost my money. I don't know...," but before White could utter another word, the stranger had cut off his ability to talk or scream by quickly reaching out with his right hand and wrapping it tightly around White's throat.

White tried to draw his gun up from out of its holster, but before he could level his weapon at the stranger, the stranger, using his left arm, grabbed White's right arm, forcing it downward, along with the gun. The stranger then squeezed White's gun hand with enough force to get White to drop his weapon.

Losing air, White instinctively raised his left arm in an effort to grab the collar of the cape his attacker was wearing. His hold on the collar was tight, similar to how a child would latch onto their mother's apron so as not to lose track of her.

Had it not been for the noise White was making in searching for air, he may have been able to hear the material on the intruder's cape collar give way just enough to cause a slight tear in the fabric.

"Just not your night," the stranger whispered in White's ear before sinking his razor-blade sharp fingernails into his neck, delivering the fatal blow.

With his left hand still wrapped around White's neck, the stranger lifted his victim 6 inches off the ground and walked him the rest of the way to the back of the dark alley.

The struggle between White and his attacker had gone still, with the exception of White's dangling feet, twitching for a second or two, before going limp in announcing his final surrender.

The stranger then slowly craned his head around the side of White's face, inflicting his victim with a bite on the neck. A bite the stranger held long enough to change the skin tone of White's suntanned face from peach to ash white. After a grimace, the stranger than released his grasp on White's neck, allowing his body to fall to the ground like a feather-stuffed doll.

The stranger was confident White would be telling no tales or be firing off any warning shot.

The stranger had just begun to gloat at taking his latest prey when his thoughts were interrupted by a loud male voice.

"Who is there?" a voice called from the Main Street side of the alley.

In a whirl of dust and wind, the attacker had quickly transformed from a man into a dark-winged bat, before taking flight out of the alley.

The dust the whirling wind had kicked up was just settling when saloon owner Russ Means, torch in hand, began to race toward where White's blood-drained corpse lay.

It wasn't until Means drew closer with his torch that he recognized the mass laying amongst the alley garbage as longtime friend and bar patron, Homer White.

It was bringing the torch even closer to the body that Means was able to see the stab wounds and the purplish-yellow strangulation marks on White's neck.

"Go get Deputy Ajacks, and bring me my gun, boy," Means yelled back down the alley toward Main Street, where his 13-year-old son, Todd, was standing.

"And keep your eyes peeled," Means warned Todd.

"Yes, Pa," the boy replied, eager to help his father.

Being down a dark alley where a murder had just occurred spooked Means and he wanted to be armed in case White's attacker should return.

Besides, Means had ulterior motives for wanting to move quickly. He didn't want Homer's murder, which he suspected was linked to the deaths of Gibby and Vigil, to frighten off any of his bar patrons.

Standing over White's body, it was all Means could do to keep from trembling in the chilly night air. "Where is that boy with my gun?" Means muttered under his breath.

CHAPTER 16

Despite Jef and Lola's bedroom being on the back side of their cabin home, the rapping on the front door woke Jef, who had been sleeping uneasily the last two nights.

Lola, lying next to him, also stirred at the noise. In a house so small, every sound carried, Jef thought.

"Who could that be at this hour?" Lola asked sleepily.

"I don't know," Jef said, grabbing his glasses off the nightstand and placing them onto his nose.

Ranger, who slept at the foot of the bed, had begun to growl, putting the Furst couple on notice that something was out of sorts. It was a muffled voice coming from the other side of the door and a knock on it that followed that irritated Ranger to the point of him eventually delivering a loud warning bark.

Ranger's ears pitched up, then down. The same movement the dog's ears made when last traveling with Gibby along Break Road prior to them encountering their attacker.

"Shush," Jef told Ranger, generally posted within arm's length of Jef since he took the dog in.

Again, there was the noise, rap-rap-rap, with Lola responding by reaching over to her side of the bed, in bringing back with her a Colt '45 pistol she always tucked away in her nightstand, despite Jef opposing the idea.

Jef figured providing protection when one slept is what prayers were all about. But Lola was much more temporal, despite her deep Catholic upbringing.

"What are you doing with that?" Jef asked in a whisper so as not to wake their children.

But in all likelihood Ranger's loud barking had already done that. The two boys slept in a separate room less than 15 feet from the door of Jef and Lola's bedroom.

"I heard there are bandits in the area. One of us needs to arm our self," said Lola, who had a streak of courage Jef envied.

Again, there was the persistent rap-rap-rap.

"Go see who it is," Lola said, encouraging her husband to take the lead. Besides, Lola was a much better shot, making it easier for her to cover for Jef than the other way around. She always feared Jef covering for her might get her shot in the process.

But despite their contrast in style, Jef and Lola worked as a team since first meeting years ago.

Jef always showed Lola and her Catholic heritage a great deal of respect, while Lola loved the confidence Jef's Mormon faith gave him.

Sliding his pants over his long johns, Jef began making his way from their bedroom to their front door, passing through the kitchen in order to arm himself with his wife's deadly rolling pin.

He knew when she threatened him with it, he was scared.

Lola, wearing a white petticoat, closely followed, her gun drawn and cocked. Lola was a crack shot, every so often taking target practice behind their home while everyone was away.

There was only so much beauty you could hide beneath a straw hat, and so Lola, never wanting to be taken advantage of in the tough West, continued to perfect her shooting, something her father, Amor Sanchez, introduced her to as a child by having her shoot at lizards scrambling across the rocks.

Jef was confident enough that he never saw his wife's strength as a threat to his manhood. As a matter of fact, he found his pretty wife's tough exterior quite alluring, as it kept other men in Dry Springs from making unwanted advances toward her.

Jef had now nudged himself up against the front door of their home. "Who is it?" he asked through the door.

"Squeak," a recognizable voice replied.

"Squeak?" Jef asked, puzzled, before starting to lift the wooden plank securing the door.

But before Jef could finish the task in allowing the door to swing open, Lola grabbed her husband's arm. "Wait a minute. How do you know that it is Squeak standing on the other side of the door?" Lola asked.

"Squeak, is that you?" Jef calmly asked to reassure his wife.

"It is," the voice replied through the door.

"There you have it, Lola," Jef said, setting the wooden rolling pin he was carrying on the kitchen table so as not to look silly in front of his friend.

Ranger had posted himself directly behind Jef and just in front of Lola, who kept her gun drawn.

Jef cast Lola a look as if to say: "Please, Lola, put the gun down."

But glare or no glare, Lola was having none of it.

"I am not putting my gun down until I see that it is Squeak," she said defiantly.

"Squeak, don't take offense, Lola is armed and she is not putting her gun away until she sees it is you," Jef said apologetically through the door. "She has become a little tense over this whole murder thing."

"I understand," Squeak said, always a man of few words.

Jef cracked open the door just enough for his rail-thin friend to squeeze his way through.

Seeing it was Squeak, Lola lowered her pistol.

"Hickory, Squeak, what are you doing knocking on our door at this time of night," said an impatient Lola.

"Another murder," Squeak blurted out before Jef and Lola could even offer him a chair or drink. "You have to come quickly, Jef."

"Lola, I'm going to need your gun, with it still being dark out and all," said Jef, who was often borrowing from his wife such necessities needed in living in the West.

Squeak grinned so as not to laugh. If this was marriage, Squeak figured, he could wait.

"Be careful," Lola insisted, kissing Jef on the cheek.

Squeak smiled. On second thought, maybe marriage wasn't so bad, he thought.

"I'll leave Ranger with you," Jef said. "Make sure you latch the door behind us," he told Lola.

Squeak envied the relationship Jef and Lola had. Having someone care for you, that would be something worth having, he thought, as Jef and he darted out the door in heading to town.

CHAPTER 17

Under the light of the lone lantern and the few candles Squeak had lit, Homer White's body, laid out on Squeak's wood work bench, was quite visible. White's flesh appearing almost transparent from the loss of blood.

The scene was enough to make Jef a little light in the stomach as soon as he walked through their office door, the cowbell above ringing out with an irritating clank.

On their short ride to town, Squeak told the story of how some men at the saloon had brought White's body in. He also explained to Jef how they would have only a short time before Deputies Ajacks and Wolcutt would be arriving to examine the corpse.

Their work would all be done in the dark of the night so as not to raise any further the concerns of the townsfolk.

"The deaths must be related," Squeak said, bobbing his head in the direction of where White's corpse rest.

Jef was having a difficult time with this, while Squeak seemed unfazed by death or having to handle dead things, or for that matter dead people.

Squeak grabbed one of the candles he had lit, taking it with him as he repositioned himself on the other side of the work bench in casting even more light over the body.

"You see anything." Squeak asked in calling out to an initially reluctant Jef who appeared that he really didn't want to be there.

Jef was generally not one to grow nauseous. But this was pushing his limits, as he nervously moved closer to where Squeak was standing, grabbing his flat gray cap off the top of his head and wringing it as if it were dirty laundry.

The cap, a gift from his father, was something Jef constantly wore day and night from his days of living in upstate New York.

Lola had begged him to ditch the hat for something resembling more of a Western fashion, like the Stetson cowboy hat in the general store she particularly fancied. But Jef insisted on keeping and wearing the hat he wore while making his trek across the plains with his fellow Mormons.

Jef, proud of the hat that set him apart from the other townies, had inched his way closer to Squeak, and more importantly closer to White's lifeless body.

"Well, look there," Jef said pointing to White's neck. "Give me a little more light."

Squeak responded by holding the candle for Jef so he could further examine the markings on White's neck.

"Almost like a dog bite, huh?" Squeak asked.

To avoid getting sick from the smell of the body, Jef tried to compose himself.

But upon closer inspection, as if by accident, the word "Vampire" fell from Jef's lips.

"What did you say?" said a startled Squeak.

But Jef remained silent, pushing his glasses back up onto the bridge of his nose, hoping Squeak hadn't heard him.

To regain his composure, Jef began slowly circling the work bench White's body rested on, looking for any additional clues. He walked slowly in avoiding falling over any of the partially completed pieces of furniture Squeak had strewn along the walls of his shop.

"The bruising on the neck indicates he was strangled," Jef said pointing at the body. "But obviously, looking at the body, there was some major blood loss," he added, trying to piece things together out loud.

"The marks on the neck are like puncture wounds," Jef said. "Did you happen to notice whether the other two bodies had puncture wounds to the neck?" Jef asked Squeak.

"No. Those bodies were badly burned, Vigil's body totally charred, Gibby's body burned from the waist up, as if he were trying to leap into the fire to get away from whatever it was chasing him," Squeak said.

"There are also two stab wounds," Jef said, giving his summation standing as far away from the body as he could.

"But it is those smaller marks a little lower on the neck that concern me," Jef said. "Like you said, teeth marks, or something," he told Squeak, before pausing to collect his thoughts.

"Yes, bite marks," Squeak confirmed, who had now moved to get eyeball-to-neck with the deceased Homer White.

"You frighten me," Jef told Squeak, referring to his friend's willingness to get so close to the body.

Jef for a second time circled the body in making certain they hadn't missed anything. Of course, in the poorly lit office, it was difficult to distinguish between what was real and what was shadow.

It was then that Jef made a new discovery. A small piece of torn black fabric clenched in White's left hand.

"What's that?" Jef asked Squeak, pointing to the fabric.

"Don't know," a surprised Squeak replied.

"Well, walk over there and take a closer look," Jef asked Squeak, still pointing at White's hand in a semi-clasped position due to the rigor mortis starting to set in.

Squeak, getting so close to White's hand that he could almost lick it, confirmed Jef's suspicion. "It's a small piece of fabric," he said.

"No, it's our first real clue. Bring it to me," Jef asked before giving his request a second thought. "No, wait," he said raising his arm to stop Squeak from proceeding. "Better yet, give me the piece of fabric after Ajacks and Wolcutt have examined the body. I'm certain they'll never even notice it."

"You think that little piece of cloth holds any clue as to who the killer might be?" Squeak asked.

"I don't know," Jef said, "but knowing Wolcutt and Ajacks the way I do, they are going to overlook such a detail in their examination of the body."

Squeak shook his head. "I don't know, Jef."

"It will be our little secret," Jef said, trying to comfort his suddenly nervous friend.

"I don't fear Ajacks," Squeak said. "But sooner or later Sheriff Wily is going to return and want answers, and I don't want to cross him by keeping secrets from him."

"By the time Willy gets back to town, you and I will have this solved," Jef said confidently. "One thing is for certain, these murders are not the work of bandits. By looking at the marks on White's neck, whatever grabbed him was strong and apparently thirsty."

Squeak nodded. "You'd better get before the others arrive," he warned Jef.

Realizing the Dry Springs murders had all occurred at night and while individuals were alone, Jef sheepishly asked Squeak to join him for a portion of his ride back home. The morning sun in Dry Springs had yet to peek over its eastern mountains, and Jef was not willing to take any chances.

"You don't fear Sheriff Wily, but you fear the dark," Squeak said with a giggle.

"You know what is even stranger, Squeak, is that you play with dead things, yet you fear Sheriff Wily," Jef responded with a quick retort.

"I'll grab my hat," Squeak said, realizing he had again been bested by Jef, a verbal assassin. Before leaving, the craftsman flashed a slight smile, prior to blowing out the candles and trimming the lantern in the office.

Chapter 18

Squeak, taking every shortcut possible in accompanying Jef back home, returned to town in time to see Mayor Howard, Wolcutt and Ajacks marching their way down the Main Street boardwalk toward his shop.

In the dark of the early morning, the trio looked like serious lawmen. Mayor Howard and Wolcutt looked fresh, like they had been up awhile, while Ajacks appeared to have just rolled out of bed, his hair askew with a rooster tail, and bed lines still creased into his face.

Reaching the shop door at about the same time, the men exchanged no words, with the exception of Squeak giving them a "good morning" greeting.

The cowbell clanged as the men walked into the office, the sound of the bell annoying Wolcutt, who let out a huff.

"Well, there he is," Squeak said, gesturing toward White's body, looking even paler than before, laid out on the work bench.

"It looks as if he was drained of blood," Squeak offered automatically, forgetting who he was talking to.

Wolcutt glared back. "Let us do the thinking around here," he said in a voice sounding a lot like a shovel turning dirt.

Squeak moved around the small office, trimming up the lantern to give the men more light to work with. He also lit a few of the candles he had lit earlier for Jef, knowing it would offer some additional light, as well as help clear some of the smell in the office of decomposing flesh.

"Odd," Wolcutt said. "What does this to a man?"

"The deaths do appear to be related," Ajacks chimed in, as he, like Jef before him, slowly circled the work bench positioned in the center of the small shop.

Mayor Howard merely nodded, as if it were too early in the morning for a body inspection.

"Looks like he may have been strangled," Wolcutt said, gesturing toward the deep bruise marks on White's neck.

"There are puncture wounds there as well, maybe strangulation first, and then a drawing of his blood," Mayor Howard finally spoke.

"Cause of death?" Wolcutt asked aloud.

"Bandits," Ajacks immediately responded, flashing Mayor Howard and Wolcutt a quirky smile, giving the appearance that the men were playing roles in some sort of secondhand stage show.

With Ajacks's comment everyone laughed but Squeak.

"Bandits?" Squeak asked, interrupting the men's inspection of the body.

"Bandits," Ajacks firmly replied.

"But nothing was taken," Squeak said, hoping for more of an explanation.

"Did White have anything in his pockets when they brought his body in?" Ajacks asked Squeak.

"No, but Means indicated White had lost all of his money in a card game before he stepped out into the alley," Squeak said.

"No matter. We can change the cause of death later if we figure it was something else. But for the time being it was bandits," Wolcutt said. "Right mayor?"

"I concur," Mayor Howard quickly replied as if he had breakfast waiting for him somewhere.

"Get his body in the box, and contact Parsons for a service," Wolcutt demanded of Squeak.

As the three men were leaving the office, Squeak couldn't help but over-hear them discuss having a town meeting and implementing some type of dusk-to-dawn curfew for the town.

Ajacks also shared with Wolcutt the possibility of deputizing another man until Wily returned.

One thing Squeak had learned from Jef was how to go unnoticed in eavesdropping on conversations.

As the men cleared the office door, Squeak couldn't help but grin in noticing the tiny piece of fabric still resting in White's clenched fist.

Jef was right again, Squeak thought. What a story his newspaper friend would have to tell. And when he did, Squeak could already envision the angry expressions on the faces of some of the town leaders.

CHAPTER 19

It was still morning dark when Jef returned home. He appreciated Squeak accompanying him for most of the ride. He had become a little unnerved that whoever was responsible for Gibby's death obviously wasn't finished.

Equally disconcerting was the attacker had the bravado to enter town to do his killing in spite of other men being close by, Jef thought.

Yet, the crazy murder, and White's body being drained of blood, so unnatural, selfishly would make for another incredible headline, Jef thought.

Often, while in town, Jef would bump into White. White was always cordial. And now he was gone.

And even though Jef was more known for being a wordsmith, he could do the math, and that was three murders in three days and for the first time he was beginning to fear for the safety of his wife and children. Dry Springs was a place where everyone knew everybody, and murder took place in the other cities. That is why people in Dry Springs were willing to go without some of life's niceties, in exchange for quiet and being kept out of harm's way.

Jef was also quickly losing confidence in Ajacks and Wolcutt to solve the mystery. Ajacks seemed to be a nice guy, someone with ambition, who eventually wanted to shake off the dust of Dry Springs and move on to something better, or at least somewhere bigger.

But he wasn't going anywhere without Prudy.

Wolcutt, well, he had law experience, but his closed-minded approach to doing things gave Jef cause to wonder.

One thing was for certain, if Wolcutt ever did come face to face with the killer, he'd likely have the courage to spit in the killer's eye.

With Jef's family still sleeping, only Ranger stirring, he figured there was no better time than the present to recharge his spiritual battery before returning to town when it was light.

The lid on the small wooden chest tucked beneath Lola's side of the bed where Jef kept his well-worn Book of Mormon was a bit dusty.

It had been sometime since he last cracked open the book of scriptures that held for Jef such extreme sentimental value.

Carefully sliding the chest out from underneath the bed, he was able to avoid waking his wife. He then popped open the chest, reaching inside it to grab his book that always seemed warm to the touch.

Just holding the book his father James Furst II had given him prior to him parting ways with the family in Laramie, Wyo., made him feel better. It made him feel not forgotten. His mother and father had worried Jef would forego his daily prayers and scripture study as a result of his decision to bound off with a female of another faith.

But Jef, for the most part, had stayed true to his word of remaining a Mormon even in the darkest hour.

Finding a corner in the house where he could light a candle and place it by his side, Jef opened the book. There, always the first thing he saw before reading scriptures was his dad's somewhat faded message scrawled on the inside cover: "Keep this book close, keep God even closer in remaining safe," it read.

Reading the message for what must have been the hundredth time still nearly brought tears to Jef's eyes as he pushed his glasses back up onto the bridge of his nose before beginning to read.

In that time when he was reading, his family and he were safe again. But Jef knew there would come a time he may have to confront the evil hanging over the town, and as his scriptures advised, he would need to put on the whole armor of God in order to be protected.

Just as Jef was finishing up, he heard Lola stir. He would now have to retell the story behind White's death. And after hearing it, Lola would say she was OK, Jef thought, but she would be churning inside.

Chapter 20

"THIRD MURDER IN THREE DAYS, SHERIFF DEPUTIES CONSIDER CURFEW

Like a carnival barker, Jef stood on the corner successfully selling his latest edition. Although it was still early, many out and about desired to pay to read what he had written. That, despite the town rumor mill already having informed many of them that Homer White had been found murdered in the alley between Mean's Saloon and Thumper's blacksmith shop.

Putting it in print somehow made everything official, he thought.

Standing next to Jef as he yelled to passers-by that he had newspapers for sale, was Ranger, his faithful and attentive companion.

But while Jef was visible to passers-by from all sides, he was blinded by the fact that Deputy Ajacks was quickly approaching having heard the familiar voice of James Edward Furst III and his cry of "Paper here." Ajacks didn't have to walk much farther before reaching Jef, standing on the corner in his long-sleeved white shirt and his gray flat cap.

There, tucked beneath Jef's right arm, was a short stack of freshly inked newspapers.

Ranger sat nearby as if he were expecting to receive a portion of the sales.

Ajacks wanted to swear at the pair, but the words hung heavy on his tongue much like that nasty-tasting wad of mix Wolcutt chewed on. So, rather than cuss, Ajacks quickened his pace in the direction of the corner the newspaperman often laid claim to in selling his newspapers.

Before Ajacks could even reach the corner, he could recognize enough of the large lettering printed on the newspaper to know Jef had written an article dealing with the latest murder.

"Third murder in three days," Ajacks said. "What is this?" the deputy demanded, grabbing the single newspaper Jef was holding aloft in his left arm.

"It's today's edition," Jef replied. "That will be 3 cents," he said, referring to the newspaper Ajacks had snatched from his hand.

"I am warning you, Furst," Ajacks said, shaking the newspaper.

But while Ajacks boiled over with frustration, Jef continued to work, barking out, "Papers here."

Growing increasingly weary with Jef's attitude, Ajacks took a more confrontational tone with Jef, attempting to move closer to him. But Ranger prevented Ajacks from getting any closer by repositioning himself between the two men.

"The truth needs to be told," Jef said, defending his work. "Because according to Wolcutt and you, those bandits who took the lives of Gibby and Abe are apparently still making their way through town," he said smartly.

"Have you no respect for White's widow?" Ajacks asked, trying to prick Jef's conscience.

"I have more respect for White's widow than apparently Wolcutt and you have for the truth," Jef said, raising his voice.

"Now, if you're not going to buy that newspaper, give it back to me and leave me be. I'm open for business," Jef said, turning away to yell to passers-by, "Papers here."

"We'll continue our conversation later," Ajacks warned, stomping off toward his horse tied to the hitching post out front of the sheriff's office. Ajacks frequently left his horse in front of the sheriff's office to give the townsfolk the impression he was at the office working late.

"The nerve of that guy," Jef said to Ranger, pushing his glasses back up onto the bridge of his nose.

Ranger appeared to listen, pitching his ears upward and then down again.

The cloud of steam Ajacks had created at the corner was just beginning to lift when Jef and Ranger heard the wheels of an approaching wagon.

It was Ike Peterson, making an early run to the general store, when he brought his two-horse team to a halt at the corner Jef and Ranger were occupying.

"Well, I'll be, if it isn't a boy and his dog," Ike Peterson said jokingly.

"How are you this morning?" Jef replied.

"My lazy brother Stan has got me chasing for supplies again," Ike said, generally wearing an ornery look on his face. "More importantly, what brings you two out so early?" the dusty cowboy asked.

"Our third murder in three days," Jef said excitedly. "You can read all about it," he said, holding a newspaper out to Ike.

"Well, maybe I will take you up on that offer," Ike said, jumping off the bench seat of his wagon to buy the paper. But before the worn cowboy could get close enough to Jef to make the transaction, Ranger went into an annoyed rage, snapping at Ike, forcing Jef to grab the dog by the nape of the neck to prevent him from biting his customer.

"I spared your life. Maybe I shouldn't have," Ike scolded Ranger, quickly grabbing a newspaper and climbing back up onto the wagon seat.

"That will be 3 cents," Jef told Ike.

"Here's a nickel, keep it," Ike said, tossing the coin down to Jef from the wagon. "With it, maybe you can buy that dog some manners."

"You know, dogs are known for their memory," Jef said in defending Ranger.

"Dogs got no smarts," Ike said. "They're dogs. They're not smart like a horse. Of course, you wouldn't know that, you ain't got a horse. Or at least a horse of your own," Ike said, openly frustrated by the way he had been treated by Ranger.

"I'm sorry about Ranger," Jef said, apologizing for the dog's reaction. "He generally is a good-spirited dog."

"Don't worry about it. Next time I'll just shoot him," Ike said. "Just kiddin'," he added.

"Thanks just the same for your patronage," Jef said.

"What does that word mean, patronage?" Ike asked before pulling away.

"It means being a customer," Jef said.

"Well, see, that's your problem Jef. You'd have more friends if people were able to understand what you were saying. That's what's wrong with you educated types," Ike said, getting in one last jab before snapping the reins on his two-horse team and moving on to the general store.

But Jef brushed off Ike's irritability. He was having a very successful day selling newspapers.

CHAPTER 21

Ajacks had made his way over to Wolcutt's place before the two of them paid a visit to Mayor Howard.

Ajacks, still hotter than a smoking gun after his conversation with Jef, wanted to get with Mayor Howard and Wolcutt before going over to have a talk with Squeak. Ajacks suspected Squeak was leaking information to Jef for his stories.

When the cowbell clanked and the three men walked into Squeak's dilapidated office, the craftsman already knew he was in for a tongue-lashing based on the look of the men's faces.

"What we discuss with you as to matters of the law will no longer be shared with James Edward Furst III," Ajacks warned Squeak.

The normally quiet Squeak stayed in character, saying nothing. It was his hope they would say what they had come to say and leave what had become an overcrowded office.

White's body had been placed in a coffin, the coffin eerily resting on Squeak's work bench awaiting delivery to the church.

"Strangulation was the cause of death," Mayor Howard told Squeak. "It was not puncture wounds to the neck, or bite marks, as Jef's article claims."

"I'd agree," Wolcutt said, staring at Squeak.

"But there were marks on the neck," Squeak said, defending Jef's story.

"Son, let us do our work," Mayor Howard said.

Jef was right. These three men couldn't spot a rose in a briar patch, Squeak thought to himself.

"Being a longtime lawman, you've seen your share of death. What was it that you think killed White?" Ajacks asked Wolcutt, drawing him into the conversation in hopes his answer would reassure Squeak.

Wolcutt spit his jerky-seed mix, plus another ingredient unknown to man, having it splatter like mud on Squeak's dusty hardwood floor.

"I think we ought to put in place a curfew and close off our streets at night until we find the person or persons responsible for this," Wolcutt said. "And we need to do it without Jef making our every move public," he added, eyeballing Squeak.

To avoid eye contact with Wolcutt, Squeak acted like he had something to wipe off in his cluttered work space, an office that seemed even smaller with White's coffin, him in it, sitting atop the work bench.

It was obvious Jef was not the most popular person in town. He appeared to be making enemies by the minute, Squeak thought.

"Let's just get White buried," Mayor Howard told Squeak.

Squeak nodded, as if to say that he would honor their request. Because after all, if White's widow didn't have the funds to pay for her husband's coffin, then it would be the Mayor or Ajacks who would have to reimburse Squeak from the town fund for the work he had done. And Squeak could use the money.

"What is it we tell the widow should she want to know who killed her husband?" Ajacks asked Wolcutt and Howard.

"Tell her we are going to find his killer," Wolcutt said sternly.

"And that is information we had better not see in Jef's next story, or we'll be finding us a new coffin-maker," Ajacks warned, turning the conversation back on Squeak.

To reinforce Ajacks' message, Wolcutt glared at Squeak for a second time, before spitting on his wood shop floor. The three men then exited the office, the clanging cowbell signaling their departure.

Thanks, Wolcutt, Squeak thought, as he looked at the spit splatters the deputy had left in his wake. It wasn't that his shop already didn't stink enough from the decaying bodies that had been brought there of late.

As promised, prior to placing White's body in the coffin, Squeak had wrestled from White's death grip the piece of fabric Jef believed held some clue as to who the killer might be.

If Jef and he were going to avoid being found on the wrong side of the law, Squeak was certain the two were going to have to go about their business a little more quietly.

CHAPTER 22

"It's silk, you silly," Miss Higginson told Jef.

"It's as soft as bunny ears. That's the way you can tell it is that real imported silk and not the Denver knock-off stuff you see sold in these parts," Miss Higginson said. "Oh yes, this has an old European feel to it."

To make certain, Miss Higginson had rushed to her large mahogany armoire to compare the fabric with some clothes she had purchased while traveling abroad.

"I thought so," Jef said, re-examining the piece of fabric Squeak had pulled from Homer White's hand.

Prior to attending White's funeral services in town, Jef had decided to stop at Miss Higginson's place to get an expert opinion on the material while his wife took the children for ice cream. Lola was hoping doing the day-in, day-out normal routine with the children would keep her mind off the murders, while at the same time prevent the children from being frightened.

"How do you suppose Dry Springs would come by having such fine material like this here?" Jef asked, holding the 1-inch-by 1-inch red lined, black piece of fabric out in front of her.

Miss Higginson stroked her heavily powdered chin, her lipstick as red as blood and nearly as thick. Although a younger woman, likely in her late 20s, Miss Higginson powdered well beyond what she needed to, Jef thought.

"A traveler, I would assume. Maybe it comes by way of someone who has spent some time back East. On the East Coast fine linens are shipped in and are as common there as hitching posts in Dry Springs," she said with a giggle, bringing her hand up to her face to be polite.

"Where did you come across such a fine piece of fabric?" Miss Higginson asked, she just as snoopy as Jef.

Jef and Miss Higginson also shared other interests, each having a love for literature.

Miss Higginson had originally come to Dry Springs by way of a sister who needed her help in making a go of it in the West. But like many others in Dry Springs who were alone, Miss Higginson was left behind when her sister, Bethany, married and moved on to San Francisco.

It was Miss Higginson's dream to one day be able to sell her little house and move to San Francisco to also be by the ocean's edge.

"I shouldn't let Lola know about that fine piece of fabric you're holding," Miss Higginson said with a teasing giggle that jiggled her body. "Knowing you, you're probably going to surprise her with a dress made up of it," she said. "Lola would look just stunning in black."

"Well, let's hope not," Jef replied with a gulp. Jef feared if he soon didn't solve the mystery behind the murders, Lola may soon be wearing black – widow black.

"Miss Higginson, we probably should keep our conversation today between ourselves," he said, shoving the fabric deep into the pocket of his trousers.

Jef and Lola kept no secrets from one another. But Jef didn't want to alarm his wife that he possessed such an item until he was sure how White had come by it. Jef suspected White had ripped it off the shirt, coat or maybe even the cape of his attacker.

But even with the clue, Jef was no further ahead in knowing who the killer might be.

Jef had never seen anyone in Dry Springs wearing such attire. Which concerned him, because it could mean the attacker was in costume when approaching his victims, making the attacker difficult to identify.

CHAPTER 23

Keeping what he knew from Lola would be difficult, Jef thought, as he blankly stared at Miss Higginson from across her parlor. Lola and he were like beans and rice, each complementing the other.

"Beans or rice" were two of the first words the couple shared in their odd courtship.

"Beans or rice?" the beautiful senorita asked him prior to Jef plopping down at the wood table for lunch in Fort Laramie.

"Can I have both? I'm hungry," Jef told her, not yet catching the beauty of the server.

"For both, there is an extra charge," she replied in a heavy Spanish accent.

Upon hearing that, Jef's jaw dropped and his stomach growled. Extra charge, he thought. He barely had enough to cover the cost of the daily special listed on the propped up blackboard where all those entering the chuck wagon cantina could see it.

"I have 10 cents," Jef said disappointedly to the server. "Better just give me the beans. The way my father is working me, I'm going to need the protein," he told the dark-haired Latina.

And it was then that he actually took notice of her. Despite her dirty apron and the flour smudges on her face, she glowed under the drab blanket covering that kept the noonday sun from beating down on the customers looking for a short respite from the tough west.

"You are a funny man in a funny cowboy hat," the server told him, referring to the flat gray cap Jef was wearing.

"I'm a pioneer making a …," Jef said, before noticing the server was already on her way to the next table, having no time for idle chit-chat.

Upon her short return from the kitchen, the server put before Jef a heaping plate full of beans and rice. There was even a flour tortilla lying over the top of the food piled high on his plate. The tort hiding the amount of food she had shared with him.

Jef was about to tell the young woman he had no way to pay for the meal when she shushed him and motioned for him to eat it. And when he went to offer her a hearty thank you, she shushed him again.

Jef, realizing that bringing attention to his new server friend might get her in trouble with those overseeing the cantina, remained silent. But the pretty lady and her generosity had left an imprint on his mind and heart.

Jef recalled the server looking at him and mouthing the words, "It will be our little secret," before flitting away like a hummingbird to serve another hungry patron.

But even while hurriedly spooning his food into his mouth as if it would be his last meal, Jef couldn't take his eyes off the server. The way the young woman moved in delivering and picking up plates was like watching one of those fancy dancers in a New York Broadway play. The grace and energy of the server seemed to be catching nearly every eye in the place as she kept pace with the hungry mobs filing into the Wyoming fort.

The fort was merely a temporary resting point for Jef and his family – father, mother, younger brother and sister – who were all headed farther west to live amongst the Rocky Mountains.

The trek for Jef was a result of his father converting to the Mormon faith while in New York and his desire to relocate with other church members wherever LDS Church Prophet Brigham Young would lead them.

The family was currently camping in a temporary Mormon settlement near the fort, awaiting other pioneers making the same trek west.

Initially, the stop near the fort was to last a week, possibly two. But when it lingered due to bad weather incoming trekkers were encountering, the stay became long enough that Jef seized the opportunity to work in the fort kitchen to make a few dollars. But more importantly, Jef had decided the work would give him the opportunity to make small talk with the server whose name he later discovered was Lola.

It wasn't just Lola's beauty that caught his eye. Jef adored her ability to put unruly, unclean men in their place when they became fresh with her. The kind of edge he could see he was going to have to develop if he was to survive out West.

"Jef," Miss Higginson said, bringing him out of his thoughts. "It appears you went away from me for a moment there," she said with a giggle.

"Are you thinking of Europe and those fancy clothes designers? I can tell you, it's not everything they make it out to be," Miss Higginson said.

That was easy for Miss Higginson to say, her home serving as a shrine to all the places she had visited before settling in Dry Springs.

But he had to hand it to Miss Higginson, after all the places she had been, she had been able to adapt to Dry Springs, no one's destination, but nevertheless a place that a killer was trying to make home – a finely dressed killer at that.

"I'd better get back to my family," Jef told Miss Higginson. "I left them on Main Street eating ice cream."

"Sounds chilly," Miss Higginson said, trying to bring a smile to Jef's face, which had turned stone-cold serious during his visit with her.

Upon leaving Miss Higginson's home off Main Street, it dawned on Jef he was eventually going to have to share what he knew with his wife if he was to keep his family safe.

"No more secrets," Jef recollected Lola telling him after their first meeting.

Now, just how and when he was going to tell his wife all he knew, he had yet to decide. But it would certainly have to be in a private. And it would have to be prior to anything appearing in print, or his printing office would become his home.

In going over in his mind what information he had to this point, he knew that all the attacks had occurred at night, and those attacked were alone. It also appeared as if the attacker was draining his victims of blood. That odd practice, combined with the European-made fabric White had torn from his attacker's wardrobe, whispered to Jef the possibility they might be dealing with someone who is, or believes he is, a vampire.

There was also that little matter about what appeared to be bite marks to the neck of victim Homer White.

Could a vampire be responsible for the deaths? What would a vampire be doing in Dry Springs? There wasn't an overabundance of wealth here, and there was no gold, silver or oil Jef was aware of.

Seeing his family come out of the ice cream parlor with smiles on their faces quickly brought him back to the present.

"Looks good," Jef said, calling to his family and Ranger to get their attention.

His vampire theory would have to wait.

CHAPTER 24

The walk from the church to the cemetery was a short one. The procession moved slowly, with Parsons leading the way.

The pastor had delivered another stirring eulogy, this one in behalf of Homer White, whom the town was now burying.

Despite the earliness of the hour, those gathering at the church for White's service likely couldn't help miss the neatly hand-lettered signs posted along Main Street: Town Hall Meeting Tonight 7 P.M. at the Courthouse.

The lettering on the signs appeared as if it belonged to Prudy Richards, near fiancée to young deputy Ajacks, Jef thought as his family and he passed two of the signs while on their way to the church.

Jef figured the next move Ajacks and Wolcutt would be making was to impose a dusk-to-dawn curfew on Dry Springs. A curfew might not be such a bad idea, Jef thought. The feeling in the town was one of fright and suspicion, each town member inching ever so closely to wanting to point a finger of blame at the other.

From the clues he had put together, Jef suspected the killer might be a vampire. But he wasn't about to share that with just anybody. He would have to talk to someone he trusted. And right now, outside of Lola, that list was short. One person he did believe he could confide in was Pastor Parsons, the same man currently leading the procession he was part of.

"Poor Homer," Jef said aloud, his mind actually fixed on the upcoming town meeting.

"What do you mean, poor Homer? What about his widow, Linda?" Lola said in a whisper, grabbing Jef's arm to make certain he heard.

"All I know is these funerals are becoming all too frequent," Jef said.

No sooner had Jef shared his sentiment with his wife than Wolcutt passed the couple, walking briskly through the crowd.

"I guess these funerals give you something to write about," Wolcutt said with a sneer in passing the pair. Wolcutt was making the motion to spit to the ground in the couple's vicinity, when Lola threw Wolcutt an icy stare.

"You'd better not," warned Lola, who was growing increasingly impatient with the way Wolcutt and Ajacks were treating her husband.

Jef was glad to have Lola on his side.

Chapter 25

The palms of Ajacks's hands were quickly filling with nervous sweat.

It was obvious speaking in public posed a challenge for Ajacks, who was normally cool, without a hair out of place. The lawman generally relied on either his badge or good looks to get by in a pinch.

But neither of those two things would be useful this night.

Seeing his darling Prudy seated in the front row of the courthouse gave him a short boost of confidence. But that was soon lost as he watched the rest of the crowd file in.

The town members were gathering in the sturdy Dry Springs courthouse to hear what "the law" had to say about the recent killings.

Ajacks was hoping to convince the crowd a night curfew was needed for their own safety. Taking people off the streets, he hoped, would force the attacker to go elsewhere. Of course, that was if the killer himself wasn't a longtime townie who had been keeping one heck of a secret all these years. At this point, the young deputy was willing to try anything to change the course they were on.

Besides, he feared for the safety of his loved ones, or in this case, loved one, that one being Prudy Richards, who at the moment was flashing a flirting smile his direction.

The flirtatious winks and nods from the beauty made Ajacks grin, but only for a moment, and not near long enough for anyone else to see.

With Sheriff Wily being away, Ajacks was concerned how town members would react to his request to stay off the streets after dusk. With winter approaching, dusk would be coming a little earlier each night.

"Folks, can I have your attention," Ajacks said, rising from his chair on the stand and stepping to the elevated platform where generally town Judge Art Handy handed out sentences once a month, or on occasion when needed.

"Please, folks," Ajacks said, trying to quell the murmur of the crowd that had grown to fill the courthouse and put people standing up against the back wall of the room.

Wolcutt sat in a chair on the elevated platform, just off to Ajacks's left. His face still like a bed of rock, except for his chin and jaw, which were noticeably bouncing as he worked over a fresh piece of jerky. Wolcutt's teeth were a permanent yellowish-gray from always having something rolling around in his mouth. It was a bad habit. But Wolcutt, who married once for about a decade, never to marry again, had no one in his life to tell him any different.

And no one ever dared.

But there would be no spitting in the courthouse. The courthouse was a building the former lawman treated with more respect than Parsons's little church, a building he had not seen the interior of for some time outside the recent funerals held there.

Sitting next to Wolcutt was the round-faced Mayor Howard.

"Thank you, thank you," Ajacks told the crowd as, one by one, they began to find their seats and face his direction.

Nearly everyone in town was now looking Ajacks's way, with the exception of saloon owner Russell Means and his 13-year-old son Todd. They were still at the saloon, hurriedly straightening chairs and wiping tables in an effort to make the meeting at the courthouse.

Russell Means was concerned a dusk-to-dawn curfew might be talked about at the meeting, and he wanted to be there to let the law know forcing him to close his saloon early would hurt his business.

At night was when the saloon was at its busiest, and Means was already trying to squeeze every second out of the day to make money.

To save a dollar, his son Todd worked at the family business stocking shelves and sweeping floors.

"You best go, boy. Save me a seat," Means said, dismissing Todd to the meeting that was half a block from the saloon. One last wipe-down of the bar and bar stools, and Means would be blowing out the lanterns and making his way to the meeting.

Chapter 26

Ajacks began the courthouse meeting by telling the crowd Wolcutt, a man who needed no introduction, had been deputized.

There was also a moment of silence out of respect for victims Abe Vigil, Gibby Jones and Homer White. Ajacks concluded the moment of silence by expressing his deepest sympathies for the families.

Prudy had helped organize Ajacks's speech.

But now was the meat of the meeting.

"While we investigate the cause behind these recent murders, I'm proposing we put in place a town curfew to keep people safe," Ajacks firmly announced. "Or at least until Sheriff Wily returns, and other decisions can be made," he added.

Someone in the crowd yelled out: "How long is Wily expecting to be gone?"

"Wily is due back any day now," Ajacks replied from the pulpit. "But between now and then I just don't want to take any chances."

"What are Wolcutt and you doing to catch this killer?" another voice yelled.

"We have examined the victims' bodies and visited those areas where the crimes have occurred to collect clues and evidence," Ajacks said.

Wolcutt, sitting behind Ajacks, could be seen nodding, as if to say, good answer.

"Do we still expect it to be bandits?" a woman's voice from the crowd asked.

"Yes, ma'am, we do," Ajacks said. "But at this point, Wolcutt and I have not ruled out anything or anyone."

Ajacks's words caused some in the crowd to stir, each likely questioning who the murderer might be, and might they be sitting next to them.

"I know a curfew is not going to be popular with all of you," Ajacks conceded, his words causing some in the crowd to groan. "But I'm trying to keep everyone safe, and this is the best way I know how."

CHAPTER 27

While Ajacks was at the courthouse exerting his new authority, Russell Means was scurrying to reach the courthouse. He had questions for the deputy.

But in his haste, he had failed to realize the sun had set on Dry Springs.

The wood boardwalk beneath Means' 200-pound frame creaked as he walked at a brisk pace toward the courthouse, well within sight. He imagined he could almost hear Ajacks's young, trembling voice trying to convince the crowd he had everything under control.

Then, as if the weather had flipped, there was a stiff, unnatural breeze, causing the horses tied to the courthouse hitching post to excitedly prance, and pound their hoofs in the dirt.

Even ol' Stu, Gibby's horse, held in the sheriff's unclaimed property corral next to the courthouse, danced around like a newborn colt under the rush of the eerie wind.

After the breeze had died, as fast as it had come, a shadowy figure appeared between Means and the courthouse. Realizing he was no longer alone sent a chill down Means' spine.

Means was hoping his tired eyes were playing tricks on him.

"Todd, is that you?" Means called to the figure, hoping his son had already made his way to the courthouse and was holding him a seat. When there was no reply from the figure, Means felt a little foolish and began to proceed to the courthouse at even a more brisk pace.

"Geez, what I am doing?" Means asked aloud. "I'm now scared of shadows?" he questioned, his nervousness causing him to talk to himself.

The courthouse was now within a stone's throw.

Then without warning, the figure quickly sprang before him in the dark, moving as if it had wings.

"You got greedy," the figure whispered to Means. And before the unarmed Means could react, his eyes were cloaked in total darkness, as if a hood had been thrown over his head.

"Hey," Means said, with a muffled cry, before feeling what felt like two needle-like puncture wounds to the side of his neck. The punctures went deep, as if they were inflicted by a barber's straight-blade razor.

Means swung his arms widely, thrashing about like a drowning swimmer about to go under for the last time.

"Good-bye, Mr. Means. No more overcharging for watered-down drinks," he heard the voice say before all went black.

Before Means' body could fall to the boardwalk like a sack of potatoes, about 100 yards away Ajacks was wrapping up his speech, having convincingly won over the majority of the town members that a curfew by dusk was a good thing.

"It might actually save someone's live," Ajacks told the group.

Outside a few protests from some business owners, the town agreed to give Ajacks's plan a go.

However, Ajacks was surprised having never heard from Russell Means, who he was well aware strongly opposed implementing a curfew. He did see Todd Means at the meeting sitting next to an empty space on one of the courthouse benches.

Prudy Richards had never been more proud of her man and the leadership he was showing in wake of the recent murders and in the absence of Sheriff Wily.

The couple left the courthouse, walking the opposite direction of where Means' body lay on the Main Street boardwalk. Ajacks walked with one arm interlocked with his girl, the other hanging closely at his side near his pearl-handled gun. Had the couple walked the other direction, they would have stumbled over Means' corpse just a spell away from the courthouse steps.

It would be only a matter of time as the crowd filed out of the courthouse that someone would discover Means, Dry Springs's fourth murder victim.

Chapter 28

Wrapping his cape around Means' head in applying his deadly bite had only extended the tear in his cape.

Holding the cape up, he could see the small rip, which first began when Homer White clasped onto his collar like a child would clasp onto their mother's hand.

"Do you sew?" the male voice asked, holding his prized cape in his hands.

"You know I don't sew," said a second male voice sharing the same room. "There has got to be some sort of seamstress in this one-dog town that could fix that."

"No," the other voice immediately responded. "That will raise too many questions. I'll take care of it after we leave this town," the first voice said.

"Now that you brought it up, how much longer do we stay here in Dry Springs?" the second male voice asked.

"Until our business is complete, and our business won't be complete until he pays for the mistake he made in crossing me," the first voice stressed. "Meanwhile, I need to provide him with reminders of who is actually in charge."

"And the others?" the second voice asked.

"When I leave this town I want to leave my mark," the first voice said with a bit of a laugh.

"Oh, by the way," the first voice added, "make sure you're careful out there. From what I understand, there is a dusk-to-dawn curfew in town. You just can't go anywhere anymore," he said mockingly.

"Blow out the lamp, you've had your fill for the night," the second voice said before leaving the room.

And then the eloquently adorned room where the two men had shared their conversation went dark.

CHAPTER 29

News about the death of Means spread through the town like a cold. Jef was shocked over how close the attack occurred to the courthouse where town members gathered. Equally frustrating for the newspaperman was that as far as he could tell the entire town was in attendance at the courthouse meeting, with the exception of Sheriff Wily.

In going over a checklist in his mind, he couldn't recall a single face that was noticeably missing. Maybe Ajacks and Wolcutt had it partially right. Maybe it was a bandit who decided to remain in the area because of the easy pickin's. But like the other victims before him, Means still had a few coins in his pocket, according to Squeak.

And no bandit would dress in the torn linen Jef had discovered.

"Go wash up, children," Lola said, her routine order to James Jr. and Bobby prior to them eating. Lola's voice brought Jef back to the dinner table.

No sooner had the two children exited the room to visit the iron hand-pump well just outside the back door of their home than Jef turned the tap loose on what had been running through his mind.

"Squeak told me Means had bite wounds on his neck," Jef told Lola, as if he were writing a lead for one of his newspaper articles.

Before Lola could respond, Jef had more to say: "Homer White had a bite to his neck."

"What are you saying, James?" Lola squeezed into the conversation.

"And then there is this," Jef said, pulling from his trouser pocket the piece of shiny black fabric with red-colored lining he had earlier shared with Miss Higginson.

"Where did you get this?" Lola asked, examining the fabric. Before Jef could answer, James Jr. and Bobby had returned to the kitchen table.

To conceal the piece of fabric like it was a dirty picture, Lola quickly shoved it into the pocket of the apron she was wearing.

"Not a word until later," Lola said in a hushed tone to her husband.

"Momma is scolding Daddy," Bobby said with a giggle, having overheard his mother.

"It's probably because Daddy didn't wash his hands," James Jr. said, peering over at his father.

"Go wash your hands, James," Lola told her husband, trying to convince her children that hand-washing was exactly what they had been talking about.

A few hours later, after the children were put to bed, Lola brought out the shiny piece of black fabric that seemed to hold her in a spell.

"Where did you get this?" Lola asked, reigniting their earlier conversation.

"Squeak pulled it from White's clenched fist and gave it to me. Don't worry, Lola, Squeak did it after Ajacks and Wolcutt had examined White's body. They didn't notice it," Jef said, answering the questions he anticipated from his wife.

"You haven't shown this to anybody, right?" Lola asked.

"I shared it with Miss Higginson to find out if she had an idea where such a fine piece of fabric might come from," Jef said. "She guessed it came from some sort of European dress, maybe off of a cape or coat."

"I can't believe it," Lola said. "I thought you and me were about no secrets. Remember, beans and rice," she said, an ember growing in her brown doe-like eyes.

"I want you to take this piece of fabric and turn it over to Ajacks as soon as possible. You tell him the truth. You explain to him Squeak noticed it and took it from White's hand and didn't know what to do with it. Do you understand me? And then I want no more talk of those murders in this house," Lola said, wadding up her right fist and pounding it into the palm of her left hand.

"Nor do I want to see any of this conversation in print and shared with the whole town," Lola demanded, her Spanish accent coming through loud and clear.

But Jef, normally agreeable to his wife's every whim this time stood his ground, much to her surprise.

"I can't do that," Jef said stubbornly. "We are not the only ones in danger. We have a whole town to think of, and the more they know, the safer they'll be," Jef said.

"That's the newspaperman in you talking, not the James Edward Furst III that I know," Lola said.

"I'm going to share with you, Lola, what I shared with Ajacks. I, like you, have everything at stake. And if we are going to remain in Dry Springs, the faster we find the culprit responsible for these murders, the better off this whole town is going to be," Jef said.

"I don't want you to be the lead on this thing. It may lead the killer back to us," Lola said, the fear in her eyes growing. "I want my children to be safe and not marked by your idle dreams," she said.

"As do I," Jef fired back, hurt by what his wife just said.

"Keep your voice down, James, or you will wake the children," Lola said. "They do not need to be a part of this."

"I shared with you to keep us safe, them safe," Jef said, motioning to the boys' bedroom. "They mean everything to me."

Trying to compose herself, Lola stared into Jef's eyes. "Tell me what you are thinking," she said, taking a breath.

"I'm thinking we are dealing with someone who thinks they are a vampire, or someone who wants the town to think they are a vampire to further frighten us," Jef replied, almost relieved to have shared his assumption with someone.

"Sounds crazy, I know," Jef said. "But based on what information and evidence I've been able to gather, it's what I keep coming back to."

It seemed like an eternity of silence passed, the only sound in the house being Ranger's panting as he lay at the foot of their bed where the couple had resumed their conversation.

"A vampire?" Lola asked incredulously.

"Yes," Jef responded, nodding his head as if that would confirm it.

"I don't know if it is one of those old Transylvania full-fledged vampires they often talk about around campfires, but nonetheless, Dry Springs has got some sort of blood-sucking criminal on their hands," Jef said.

"You know you put that in the newspaper, Jef, they are going to run us out of town," Lola said. "And despite your beneath-the-surface wishes to move to the Salt Lake Valley to be closer to your mom and dad, this is my home," she added.

Lola was right. There were times Jef thought the family would be better off in the Salt Lake Valley where other members of his family and faith resided.

Initially, his mother and father broke ties with him for marrying outside the religion, The Church of Jesus Christ of Latter-day Saints. But over the years, particularly with the births of their two children, his father and mother were softening some to the fact he had married Lola.

Besides, it wasn't like Jef wasn't living his faith, holding to his practices. Albeit at times he did feel isolated because there were no other Mormons in Dry Springs to share in worship services with.

But Jef remained confident that day would come.

"A vampire?" Lola again asked in astonishment.

"Well, like I said, or someone who thinks they may be a vampire," Jef added.

"Who?" Lola asked.

"I don't have any idea. But I have a plan," Jef said, tapping the side of his head.

Lola gave him a worried look. "I hope your plan doesn't interfere with what Ajacks and Wolcutt are trying to accomplish. Please, Jef, tell me it doesn't," she said pleading, as if the family's stay in Dry Springs depended on it.

"I make no promises that I can't keep," Jef said.

Lola sighed, shaking her head as if that might convince Jef otherwise.

"Remember, you told me to keep no more secrets from you," Jef said. "Which means from now on it is going to be a steady diet of beans and rice even if it means spoon feeding you nothing but the truth," he said with a look that screamed believe in me.

Lola almost cracked a smile but feared doing so. She did not want to let Jef know he had won this round. The stubborn Latina couldn't let that happen.

CHAPTER 30

It may have been Thursday, but Jef, with Ranger trailing close behind, was hustling his way to the church. Even though it was daylight, the foot traffic in town was sparse because of the earliness of the hour.

Jef had just completed the sale of another stack of newspapers, this edition with a front page headline reading: FOURTH MURDER IN 5 DAYS, CURFEW INSTITUTED.

As usual of late, the newspapers sold quickly. It seemed the townspeople couldn't get enough bad news.

And now he had his work behind him, Ranger and he were heading to the church. The pair moved at a brisk pace, despite Ranger periodically stopping here and there for a few seconds to sniff something out in the dirt. The dog would paw at the spot before catching back up to Jef, who was taking some lengthy strides along the wide-open Main Street boardwalk.

Four murders in five days had cast a gloom over the town and everyone living in it. People were now suspiciously eyeing everyone else, while Jef was becoming more confident he had it all figured out.

Each killing had occurred at night, allowing the townsfolk to freely move about during the daylight without so much as to having to look over their shoulder.

And the only one over his shoulder on this day, Jef thought, was Ranger, as the pair passed the sheriff's office.

Across the street from the sheriff's office was the courthouse, and next to it the corral where unclaimed livestock were held for up to 10 days in giving the original owners the time needed to claim them.

At this time the only animal in the corral was ol' Stu. Everyone in town knew Gibby lived alone and had no other family, his wife having died years ago. So it would be only a matter of days before someone could, and would, lay claim to the old pull horse.

Jef and Ranger had gone out of their way to cross the street to visit Stu.

"Here, here's a nice apple for you," Jef said, stopping long enough at the weather-beaten corral to give Stu an apple he had been packing for breakfast. Jef then patted Stu on the side of the neck in reassuring the old work horse he still had value.

Jef had a soft spot for animals, and Stu was comfortable around Jef, maybe because he was already caring for Ranger.

Lola and Jef had already talked about it and decided they would put in a claim on Stu when the horse became available. The old docile horse would make a great first horse for James Jr. and Bobby, Jef thought.

Working their way to the church, Jef and Ranger also passed several posted signs reading: *Dawn to Dusk Curfew By Order of the Law.* Ajacks, or more likely Prudy, had been busy as all the words on the signs were spelled correctly.

One day Prudy was going to make Ajacks a nice wife and settle that cowboy down, Jef thought, as Ranger and he continued on their way.

CHAPTER 31

The heavy wooden doors of the church, which Dry Springs town members years ago sacrificed their time and talents to build, were swung wide open in saying "Welcome."

And everyone was.

Parsons and his wife, Shirley, both had a kind heart and recognized the importance of being the caretakers of Dry Springs's only chapel.

Jef, although not of Parsons' fold, had business with the pastor this day.

"You stay here," Jef said, giving Ranger the command to stay on the small two-step porch out front of the church entry way. Leaving Ranger outside was Jef's way of showing his respect to the house of worship.

Before stepping inside, Jef even snatched the gray flat cap off his head, allowing his thick floppy brown hair to tumble into his eyes.

From the back of the church, Jef could see Parsons and his wife working furiously at the front of the chapel. They were dusting and sweeping underneath the pews in preparation for Means' funeral.

The neatly aligned rows of the 10 mahogany benches – the handiwork of Squeak – were pleasing to look at but uncomfortable to sit on. Jef figured Parsons liked it that way so no one slept during his sermons.

Oftentimes Jef would join Lola and the kids at the church for Sunday service. The stained-glass window on the south side of the chapel depicting a brown wooden cross on a green hill always gave Jef a sense of hope.

When the sun would shine through the window, it would cast colorful reflections onto the chapel's interior walls and those sitting in the pews.

On the north side of the building was a stained-glass window depicting an outline of the Holy Family – Mary, Joseph and the baby Jesus. That window when the sun would shine late in the day would bounce equally colorful reflective patterns off the chapel's otherwise colorless walls.

The north side stained-glass window reminded Jef of the importance of family, something his Mormon faith promoted.

The stain glass windows were also the sacrifice, work and talents of those who had come before both Jef and Parsons.

"Nice article," Parsons said, bringing Jef out of his thought. "I know your words meant a lot to the widow Means and Russell's son, Todd."

In his latest edition, Jef, in addition to sharing further details surrounding Means' death, had written a tribute to the saloon owner, whom Jef considered to be one of the town's best business minds.

It was sad Means' lifeless body was discovered by Todd, who nearly stumbled over his father's corpse in retracing his own steps from the courthouse back to the saloon that night.

But Todd Means was a tough kid with a good head on his shoulders. And mature beyond his years.

"You did a real good job," Shirley said, echoing her husband's praise without so much as missing a dust ball beneath the pews.

"So what brings you out?" Parsons asked Jef. "Means' funeral services aren't for a few hours. I'm sure there will be a seat."

"I was hoping we could talk," Jef replied. "In private," he added, so Shirley could hear.

Shirley just raised an eyebrow and continued on feverishly dusting.

"Well, I've got my office we can go into," Parsons said. "While you're at it maybe you could confess to me a sin or two so I'm not thinking you're perfect," Parsons said jokingly, always taking a jab at Jef because he was a Mormon.

"Someday we Mormons are going to fill this territory, and, Parsons, you'll be the minority," Jef replied, sending a friendly counterpunch.

Despite their religious differences, Jef respected Parsons and the job he was doing as Dry Springs's moral compass.

The flecks of gray in Parsons often furrowed eyebrows, and touches of gray at his temples, gave the impression that Parsons was wise beyond his years.

Chapter 32

Parsons's chapel office was small, appearing even smaller due to the large wooden desk nearly filling the room.

The desk had obviously been assembled in the office, based on the narrow width of the door. That made the desk, compliments of Squeak, impossible to rearrange without taking out a wall.

"You know Squeak," Parsons said gesturing at the desk looking more like the side of a house.

Jef smiled.

The office was dark and windowless. Parsons struck a match to light a candle he had placed on the desk before them.

"I'm sorry," Parsons said, apologizing for the tight, dimly lit quarters. "Windows are expensive."

"I understand," Jef said, his little house having only one window in it.

What Jef didn't understand was why Parsons's office chairs had to be so hard, unless it was done on purpose so no one got too comfortable with him when confessing their sins.

"So, what brings you here this morning?" asked Parsons, who, instead of wearing his traditional cleric collar, was wearing a long-sleeved cotton button-down shirt. The same shirt he generally wore when not conducting Sunday service.

The shadow of fresh whiskers across the bottom half of Parson's face revealed he had yet to groom for today's services.

Unlike when he shared with Lola his suspicion behind the town's murderous attacks, Jef would pace himself with Parsons, like a trotter-horse, to avoid his thoughts falling out of his mouth like poison.

"You believe in evil?" Jef quizzed Parsons.

"Where there is good, there is evil," Parsons said, "opposition in all things."

Jef now felt like he was heading the right direction with his questioning. "Do you believe in the undead?" Jef ask, his voice picking up with excitement.

"Where are you going with this?" Parsons asked, repositioning himself in his chair.

"Vampires," Jef said. "Do you believe in vampires, Parsons? Because I think we have one living here."

And then Jef had realized he had done it again, like an anvil the words fell from his mouth.

Parsons sat silent for a few seconds, trying to determine if Jef was serious.

"James Edward Furst, those are awfully bold claims you're making," said Parsons, who, being a little older, was always willing to look at things with a mix of faith and logic.

"I assume you mean the murders? You believe a vampire is responsible for the killings?" Parsons said, staring into Jef's eyes.

"I'm leaning that way," Jef said, stroking his boyish bald chin with his hand. "The attacks have all been at night. At least two of the victims had bite marks on their necks," Jef said, trying to assure Parsons he wasn't crazy.

Jef didn't want to sound like a kook. No one would read the column of a crazy newspaperman.

"Squeak put you up to this?" Parsons asked, having difficulty believing the large leaps in assumption his respected newspaper friend was making.

"You have other ideas of who might be responsible for the murders?" Jef asked Parsons, looking him straight in the eye.

"I obviously haven't given it as much thought as you have," Parsons admitted. "But regardless of who the perpetrator is, I believe I will be stayed by God's hand."

"As do I," Jef nodded. "But maybe it's time you consider sharing your faith with others, Parsons, by providing your flock with some protection-maybe in the way of some wooden crosses, for the believers and non-believers alike."

"Using Squeak's handiwork, I think you could make such a plan work," Jef added without blinking.

Parsons blew out a long breath before responding. "I see you have really given this some thought," he said. "Does that mean you would be willing to wear one of my crosses?"

"I have my own faith," Jef said, figuring he was immune from needing a cross, whereas, part of his Mormon doctrine allowed him a degree of priest-hood protection. It was his father James Edward Furst II, who through his righteous living, was able to bestow that sacred authority onto him.

"I'm merely thinking of others," Jef said in coming back to Parsons's original question.

"Such action might set off a town-wide panic," Parsons said. "And, if in fact our attacker is a vampire, the crosses may only get non-believers killed. It takes real faith in a higher being full of grace and light if the cross is going to fend off the attack of something or someone as evil as what you are describing."

"Besides, do you have any idea what type of response I would get if I told my congregation the town is under attack by a vampire?" Parsons added, staring back at Jef.

"Jef, I've already bounced from job to job during my stay in Dry Springs. I don't want to lose all credibility and be bounced from town," Parsons said.

Jef then reached into his trouser pocket and pulled out the piece of shiny fabric he had shared earlier with Lola and Miss Higginson. "What do you make of this?" Jef said, handing the piece of fabric to the pastor.

"What is it?" Parsons asked.

"I found Homer White clutching onto it as if it were the Holy Bible itself," Jef said. "I believe he tore it off the cape or coat of his attacker."

"What were Miss Higginson's thoughts?" Parsons asked, developing an interest in what Jef was now sharing with him.

"She said it was likely a European or East Coast piece of fabric and, based on its red lining, may have come from a cape or a cloak of some kind," Jef said.

"And with this tiny piece of fabric I am to put my ministry on the line?" Parsons asked. "I can tell you if I were to do that the next one that would be murdered would be me. Shirley would kill me."

Jef's face dropped with disappointment.

"Look, I want to help," Parsons said. "But within reason."

"Well, you can start by telling your congregation there is a very dangerous individual out there on the loose who is striking in the nighttime hours. I would also recommend you and your family keep your faith and your crosses close," Jef said sternly.

"You're serious," Parsons said, handing the piece of fabric back over to his friend.

Jef nodded sharply before standing to leave.

"I'm going to be putting together a plan. I am hoping you will be a part of it," Jef said.

Parsons, not sure what to say, gave a slight nod. "Can I expect you for the funeral services today?" he asked.

"Lola and I will be here," Jef said, opening the office door to leave.

Parsons blew out the candle on his desk and followed.

"You two look as if you had been sharing ghost stories," said Shirley, who was still in the midst of cleaning the chapel when the pair stepped from out of the office.

"Close," Jef said with a grin.

Prior to racing home to get ready for Means' funeral, Jef had one more stop to make.

When Jef exited the church, Ranger was there waiting for him with a tail wag. "I wish I knew what you knew," Jef told Ranger.

Chapter 33

Squeak look dumbfounded when Jef first told him a vampire, or vampires, were likely behind the killings.

Squeak scratched his head before uttering any sort of reply. "What?" he asked, as if he didn't hear Jef the first time.

"You heard me. Now help me," Jef pleaded in having captured Squeak's undivided attention.

The pair, leaning on Squeak's blood-stained work bench where victims had been laid out in preparation for examination and burial, brainstormed over how they could take their fight to such an attacker.

"If the killer is in fact a vampire, then he can only be killed by a stake through the heart," Jef said, sharing what vampire lore he knew with his simple friend.

"All right," Squeak said, waiting anxiously for more information.

"So, we need to find out if our killer is a vampire," Jef said.

"Don't look at me. I'm not asking him," Squeak quickly replied.

"Don't be ridiculous. We need to draw the attacker out," Jef said.

"Like a worm on a hook?" Squeak asked.

"Yes," Jef replied, proud of Squeak, who was doing his best to contribute.

"We need someone strong, able to handle themselves, yet, naïve and overconfident, to want to take the challenge," Jef said, thinking out loud as he paced back and forth in Squeak's cluttered work space.

"Well, I am certainly neither of those, as bad as I hate … ," Squeak said before being cut short by Jef.

"I don't mean you," Jef reassured his friend. "But we will have to provide our would-be bait with some backup protection, which is where you and I do come in. We follow our decoy, then when they encounter the vampire – eureka! – we pounce before it can pounce."

"Who?" Squeak asked. "Who would be so brave and yet so gullible?" he said, his voice trailing off.

"Gullible, good word," Jef said, complimenting Squeak's word choice before answering him. "It has to be someone who isn't aware of what they may be up against. Someone so full of themselves they believe any task requiring physical strength would be easy for them to perform," Jef said.

"Ajacks?" Squeak asked.

"It can't be the law. We'll be breaking the law by violating curfew," Jef reminded.

"Then who?" Squeak asked. "Dry Springs is only so big."

"What about Otis Thumper, the blacksmith? He is a bear of a man, doesn't seem to fear anything or anyone." Jef said.

"Otis Thumper? He is a big guy. He might do it," Squeak said, proud to be part of Jef's scheming.

"We'll approach him after Means' funeral," Jef said.

"Knowing Thumper," Squeak said, "he may want some sort of rate of exchange."

"I have no money, you know that," Jef said, reaching into his trouser pocket to provide Squeak with a visual reminder.

"Thumper loves to eat," Squeak said. "We offer him some of Lola's stew or a couple of jars of her raspberry preserves."

"I go walking out of the house with a couple of jars of preserves and my wife is certain to ask questions," Jef said.

"You want your vampire story or not?" Squeak said.

"Of course I do," Jef said, now growing impatient with Squeak's input. "You just make sure you don't turn chicken on me."

Squeak smiled. "Me, afraid? Huh! I'll be there. But just in case you're wrong about your vampire theory, I'm bringing a gun along," he said.

"That's all right with me," said Jef, who at this point would say anything to get anybody to buy into his plan.

Jef had never killed another human being before. His Mormon values put killing as a sin. Although, along the trek his family and he made from upstate New York to Wyoming, there were times he wanted to choke a few people.

Maybe the best way to rationalize all of this scheming with his conscience, Jef thought, is that his hope was that it would be Thumper who would drive the stake into the monster's heart.

"In situations like this, it's all right to kill, right?" Jef asked Squeak, looking for reassurance.

Squeak threw him a puzzled look. "When in battle with a vampire, I would likely think it is kill or be killed," he told Jef.

"Then that's the plan. After Means' service we talk to Thumper," Jef said.

Squeak nodded. "If I help kill a vampire, do I get my name in the newspaper?" he asked. "I've never been in the paper before."

"We rid this town of its attacker, especially if it's a vampire, we may well all get our names in all kinds of newspapers across this land," Jef said.

"That would be fun," said Squeak, wanting nothing more than to see his name in print.

"The hard part may be getting the jars of preserves out of my house without Lola noticing," Jef said.

"Tell her you've got a monster appetite," Squeak said, laughing hard at his own humor.

Chapter 34

Todd Means, despite every effort to be brave during the services, sobbed so hard his entire body shook.

For years he had worked with his father at the saloon, unboxing crates and wiping tables. Despite Russell's line of work, he never did let Todd serve drinks to the patrons.

And now, they were burying Todd's father.

Had he only stayed with his father that night and accompanied him to the courthouse, Todd thought, maybe his dad would still be alive. But other town members had dismissed such a notion, explaining to Todd that he was fortunate he wasn't with his father when the attack occurred or he too might have been a victim.

Seeing the boy in despair at the services, Jef walked over to Todd and laid his hand on his shoulder, giving it a slight squeeze. Jef figured that was what his father would have done had he seen someone in such distress.

"Russell was a good man, and you, Todd, well, you will be even a better man," Jef assured the teen before walking back over to where Lola and his two children were seated in the chapel.

Once again, the whole town had turned out for another funeral. Jef, being overly suspicious the killer might be among them, surveyed the faces of the crowd, taking note of who was there and who wasn't.

Sheriff Wily had yet to return from his venture into the wilderness. Stan Peterson was also not in attendance, which raised a flag. But Ike explained his brother was out of town tending to their parents' estate in the hope they could have everything wrapped up before winter.

"With the curfew and all, don't you think it best my brother and I move into town?" Jef overhead Ike Peterson asked Wolcutt prior to the service beginning.

Wolcutt, being the grizzled cowboy he was, told Ike both his brother and he would be safe as long as they kept doing most of their work on their ranch during the daylight hours.

"If that situation should change, you need to let me know," Ike Peterson told Wolcutt.

Peterson and Wolcutt were just two of the many passing back-and-forth idle chit-chat prior to Parsons taking his position behind the church pulpit.

Once Parsons stepped to the pulpit, the crowd out of respect went silent, with those still standing quickly finding a seat on the hard wood benches.

The toll on Parsons' square-shaped face was beginning to show in being called to see over the burial of another town member.

But Jef figured everyone in town was pretty much wearing these murders. No one in the chapel appeared comfortable. Even at his own home Lola had begun sleeping with her Boxed Colt 45 underneath her pillow.

And although Jef's newspapers were selling like flapjacks, some of his editions selling equally well in neighboring Twin Bridges, he too was hoping for a quick end to the madness. It was with that in mind Jef felt justified in moving forward with his plan of attack.

Jef had overheard many town members murmuring, many expressing their lack of confidence in Deputy Ajacks and Wolcutt. But in fairness to the men, Jef thought, based on what he suspected, they were all in over their heads. And like trying to stand in quicksand, town members' confidence was beginning to sink.

The words Parsons offered during the service gave Jef some peace. But it was the wink and nod Parsons gave him prior to him wrapping up his sermon that really gave Jef the comfort he was looking for. Jef received a similar gesture from Squeak and Otis Thumper before they left the chapel and made their way to the cemetery where Means would be buried next to the other victims.

The winks and nods meant they would be putting Jef's plan into action this night in the hope of being able to restore peace to their town.

CHAPTER 35

Wolcutt gazed hard at the faded black and white picture of the woman in the copper frame.

He then formed a comb with the fingers of his right hand, passing it through the thinning gray hair that stubbornly remained on his head. Before putting the framed picture of the woman back down on the mantel of his stone fireplace, he took one last long gaze into it as if he were trying to memorize it. He then licked his thick moustache hiding the bottom half of his face, much like Ranger would wrap his tongue around his snout after having tasted meat.

The night would be long for Wolcutt. It was his turn to provide Dry Springs's curfew control. He didn't mind. Sheriff Wily had still not made it back from his adventure, so Wolcutt felt obliged to help Deputy Ajacks.

Ajacks would be glad to see Wolcutt offering him his midnight relief. Besides, Wolcutt was well aware the young deputy longed every minute he wasn't on duty to be at the side of his true love, Prudy Richards.

On the other hand, Wolcutt was alone with only his memories of a 10-year marriage that near its end had gone horribly wrong under the grind of the long hours of daily law work.

Although she had left years ago, he still swore he could smell her scent now and again in his empty home.

But at 55, Wolcutt was no longer looking for love. He realized Ajacks appointing him as a deputy was his last opportunity to go out in a blaze of glory. It was a second chance at a lifestyle he had put aside a few years ago, thinking one day his ex-wife, the woman in the frame, would return and give him another chance. But it was not to be.

Sometimes with relationships you only get one chance, he figured, as he moved himself away from his thoughts by picking up the tin star Ajacks had given him and pinning it to his vest.

Even in the dark of his home, only lit by a single candle burning, Wolcutt could see the charred tin star shimmer.

Prior to pinning the star to his vest, Wolcutt, using his thumb, had tried for the umpteenth time to rub off the black smudges now decorating the emblem.

The star, the same star Gibby wore, still carried the burn marks from where the old cagey lawman tried to escape his attacker by jumping into the fire.

Despite the blackened mark, Wolcutt could see in the reflection of the five-pointed star all the long days he had put in as a former sheriff, bounty hunter and now deputy.

It was that same devotion that had garnered him the respect of many brave men – and chased his wife away.

And now, the town he swore to protect was under siege. The murders had him baffled because there was so little to gain in Dry Springs. Dry Springs, off the beaten path, provided a hiding place for many, Wolcutt figured. Others there were just too lazy or feared going anywhere else.

Wolcutt sensed he was one of the lazy ones, because he feared or hid from no one.

With that thought, Wolcutt picked up his Colt 45 he had left resting on the kitchen table. Leaving the gun out was another habit his former wife despised. Wolcutt meticulously checked to be certain a bullet had been placed in each chamber, before sliding the gun into his worn holster.

Next he took his fashionable brown Stetson hat off the coat rack next to the door of his modest home. There, near the coat rack, also lay his boots, mud and manure caked on the heel and toe.

Wolcutt threw on his duster, and his prep work was complete.

Before walking out the door, Wolcutt blew out the candle and rubbed his fingers one last time over the charred star pinned to his vest. For Wolcutt, that fine piece of jewelry meant he remained one of the good guys.

Now all he needed was his spit mix bag, and he'd be on his way.

Exiting his dark home, Wolcutt felt the surge of the law once again flowing through his veins. It had an intoxicating feel, more powerful than any adversary he could face.

It was enough to make him spit and so he did.

CHAPTER 36

Sneaking through the backstreets of Dry Springs, where no gas lamps or torches burned, was difficult for Jef and his rag-tag bunch.

Just to get to this point it had taken three jars of Lola's preserves to convince the 6-foot, 5-inch, 300-pound Otis Thumper that he was up to the task.

The gentle giant complaining less about having to chase down a would-be vampire with nothing but a wooden stake and his blacksmith hammer, than having to lose out on a good night's rest.

It was almost midnight. Some insects could still be heard, but the crisp fall air had knocked most of them out of the air.

"I don't think you know the magnitude of what we are trying to accomplish here," Jef told Thumper. Thumper's thick black curly hair and similar-like beard made it so Jef felt like he was speaking to two gray-colored eyes.

"Magni- what?" Thumper asked, as if Jef were speaking French.

"He means the importance of," Squeak intervened, casting Jef a stare he likely didn't see in the dark of the night. "Excuse him, Thumper, Jef just can't speak plain speak."

Squeak, given the task of carrying an old fish net once belonging to Jef's late father-in-law, Amor Sanchez, wondered why he was a participant in Jef's wild scheme. And then it donned on him, he was here to serve as an interpreter so Jef and Thumper could communicate.

But Squeak, who had hung garlic around his neck on the chance Jef's hunch may be right, was enjoying the excitement of the night. He had also darkened his face with mud, as if the group were on some sort of secret mission for the U.S. Cavalry.

Parsons, ironically, this night was playing the role of the unbeliever having only joined the group to make certain Jef would recognize the error of his ways with his vampire theory.

Despite his lack of faith in Jef's rationale, Parsons had taken the time to arm himself with a wooden cross he had blessed prior to joining the group this night.

It was Parsons's hope his presence would prevent the group from being thrown in jail should Ajacks or Wolcutt catch them violating curfew.

Parsons hated to admit it, but he was also curious as to what the town might be up against. So curious, he fought with his wife, Shirley, in order to come along this evening.

Shirley found Jef's idea to be harebrained.

And Jef, well, his motive kept shifting back and forth from wanting to do the right thing to being able to write that one big story that proved his worth as a newspaperman. The kind of article, he thought, that would bring him regional, if not national, attention.

"We're working in the dark because of, why, again?" Thumper asked.

"We're actually in violation of the law," Parsons explained. "So, not only might we go to jail for being out here on a chilly fall night when we all could be home in a warm bed, but in serving as vampire bait, we could accidentally be mistaken for an attacker and shot by a deputy sheriff."

"If we are to accomplish what we have come to do, we must keep our voices down and our eyes open," Jef warned, trying to get the group to refocus on the task at hand.

Noticeably missing from the group was Ranger. Jef feared the dog would give away the position of their group with the noise he would have made. Leaving him home, Jef was hoping, would also pacify Lola if she were to awake and find him gone. His wife and children had quickly become attached to Gibby's dog, and based on how the dog was reacting to the family it appeared the feeling was mutual.

The small group of men continued to shuffle their way behind the stores and shops making up the three-block radius of the town. Jef figured keeping to the backside of the buildings neatly lined up in a row would provide them adequate cover just off Main Street, where Ajacks or Wolcutt would likely spend most of their time making their rounds.

While most of the group looked to the ground to avoid tripping over, or stepping in, something with all the horse-pulled wagon deliveries made to the back side of the buildings, Jef kept his eyes peeled upward. He fully expected their attacker would drop in on them from the sky.

Before devising his plan, Jef searched the small town library for any books dealing with vampire lore. There being none, Jef resorted to rumors he heard while living back East with his family. One of those rumors included having to pound a wooden stake into the heart of the vampire in order to kill it.

But rather than let the group in on where he had obtained most of his information, Jef played the only card he had and bluffed, acting as if such information was common knowledge among those well-read.

Jef was confident they were looking for a vampire, so a gun would be of little value, but he, like Parsons, had packed his own vampire repellant: his wife's 1849 Colt 45 pocket model. He had also brought along his well-worn Book of Mormon. He had tucked both items neatly away in the poncho he normally wore to carry newspapers.

"Should we whistle for him?" Thumper said, growing impatient with having to creep along like a three-wheeled wagon.

"I don't think it wise to trifle with such a beast," Jef reminded his friend, whose biceps, from pounding horseshoes every day, were likely bigger than his brain.

"Tri- what?" Thumper asked.

"Tease," Squeak interjected, again playing the role of interpreter between Jef and Thumper.

The group was beginning to think nothing would be happening this night when they heard the groan of the boards bending on the Main Street board-walk. The noise stopped each of them dead in their tracks for a moment, before they all scrambled for cover behind the available crates, barrels or garbage discarded behind the shops.

Staying ever so silent, the group could hear Wolcutt and Ajacks share a short greeting, with Ajacks apparently heading home and Wolcutt settling in to play night watchman.

"Great," Jef said dejectedly. "We get Wolcutt."

In his encounters with both men, Jef had found Wolcutt to be much more diligent in following through on a task.

But the group did let out a collective sigh of relief once Wolcutt and Ajacks parted ways. They could hear Ajacks whistling as he worked his way toward the direction of Prudy's house. And while his whistling faded into the night, the noise from Wolcutt's boots pounding the boardwalk grew.

Thumper, growing increasingly anxious in wanting to hit something, had been hoping the noise made by Wolcutt was the vampire.

Over the years Thumper's muscles had developed, as the simple man, at his mother's urging, had carved out quite a business for himself, being the only farrier in the region. Even folks from the neighboring town of Twin Bridges would frequent his blacksmith shop.

But despite his success, Thumper had yet to find his one true love, remaining at home with mom, who had a reputation for being unpleasant. Thumper was a Dry Springs original, living in the same home he had been born in.

"Shush," Jef said, trying to keep his heavy-footed, heavy-breathing group quiet long enough for Wolcutt's silhouette to pass them as the deputy began to make his way to the other side of town.

"We'll wait until he doubles back and starts heading the other direction before moving," Jef said in a hushed tone, motioning for his friends to find a place in the dirt to sit for a few minutes.

Wolcutt's thumping boots along the Main Street boardwalk made him easy to track.

"Maybe this vampire doesn't attack groups," Parsons said, his doubts growing over Jef's theory that the town's attacker was a vampire.

"Splitting up is not wise," Jef warned. And then looking around at the impatient group, he relented some. "Alright, I guess it wouldn't hurt to have Thumper walk a few yards ahead of us. We'll stay close," he said, giving Thumper the nod.

Once Wolcutt had made his way to the end of Main Street and back, passing the group and heading in the other direction, Thumper got braver, moving off the side street where the group had been hiding and onto Main Street to make certain he could be seen by any would-be attacker.

Realizing the boardwalk would creak and groan under his mighty frame held together by hair, muscle and a pair of suspenders stretched to the point to where they were about to snap, Thumper walked down the middle of the dirt street, heading the same direction Wolcutt had just come from.

With Thumper's long strides, it was only a matter of minutes before he had put a distance between himself and the group. The chasm concerned Jef, who for the first time was beginning to question the sense of his own plan.

"I wish Thumper would slow down," Jef muttered, his request only making the others more nervous.

But Thumper continued down the road at a good gait, his body language sending off signals that he was ready for anyone or anything.

Reaching the end of the street, Thumper stopped, turned and looked around before raising his arms to his shoulders as if to say to the others, "Where is it?" before beginning to make his way back toward the group.

Thumper hadn't quite closed the gap between the group and him when the wind picked up, blowing the hanging signs posted outside each of the shops back and forth like swings, creating a symphony of squeaks.

The wind then began accelerating, raising dirt from up off the road, sending sagebrush rolling and papers flying.

"Odd," Jef said to the others of the sudden wind, squeezing its way through the spaces between the Main Street buildings, in creating an eerie tune.

The bluster was even annoying ol' Stu, Gibby's pull-horse, finishing out its last days of its 10-day hold in the sheriff's unclaimed property corral. The unnatural wind had Stu baying, as if it had blown angry life into the otherwise docile animal.

"Thumper, we'd better call it night," Jef yelled in a hushed tone. But his call was too late.

CHAPTER 37

Even in the dark and blowing dust, Jef could see a shadowy form make a bird-like landing just behind Thumper.

"It's him," Jef screamed into the wind, pointing wildly at the figure fast approaching their friend from behind.

But the wind killed Jef's warning. By the time Thumper realized Jef was trying to get his attention, and turned to face their adversary, he was caught off-guard.

The figure hit Thumper with an uppercut in raising the bear of the man 15 feet off the ground. The sweat-stained bucket hat Thumper always wore to cover his dirty hair went flying in the wind like a dandelion seed.

"Looking for me?" the figure said smartly to Thumper, who landed on his back with such a thud on the dirt road that the air escaping his lungs could be heard over what was now a dying wind.

Before Jef and his friends could run to Thumper's aid, who had regained his feet, the pasty-faced cloaked figure landed a second haymaker to Thumper's chin, this time sending the blacksmith reeling like he had been shot from a cannon, knocking free from Thumper's waistband the wooden stake he had been carrying to pound into the creature's heart.

"Ooof," Thumper exclaimed, the wind being knocked from him like a bloated cow upon him landing a second time hard on the dirt.

Jef realized then their group was overmatched. "There, Parsons, now do you see what we're up against," said a frustrated Jef, before realizing now may not be the best time to be telling the pastor "I told you so."

Lying flat in the dirt like a bear-skin rug on a cabin floor, a determined Thumper again rose to his feet to face his foe.

"Why, you dirty no good...," said Thumper, who, during the attack, had managed to hold onto his hammer, swinging it in a round-house motion in gaining some space between the vampire and himself.

Thumper was finally up on two shaky legs, his friends close by cheering as if Thumper were on an 8-second bull ride.

"Let him have it, Thumper," Jef coaxed. His yell distracting the attacker just enough to allow Thumper to land his first heavy blow with his hammer, smacking the creature in the side of his head.

The noise of the strike sounded like thunder clapping. But the strike caused little in the way of damage, merely causing the creature's head to turn.

With encouragement, Thumper began swinging his sledgehammer even faster, hoping his foe would run into one of the swings.

But the attacker, albeit smaller, appeared to have superior strength, moving about with the grace of a stage dancer and the power of a desert flash flood, fending off Thumper's hammer strikes with his forearms.

It was obvious to the on looking group that Thumper's swings were slowing down as a result of his arms quickly tiring.

"He won't last," Jef said of Thumper, pulling his wife's gun from the pocket of his poncho and taking aim at the monster, before firing.

But nothing happened, outside the flash, and a loud noise.

"Fire again," Squeak told his friend. And again Jef fired the gun, only to find it had no effect on the creature.

"You're missing him," Squeak claimed, before drawing his own gun, and firing at the creature, now within 20-feet of the group.

"What gives," Squeak stammered, before Jef screamed from the bottom of his lungs, "He's a vampire."

Chapter 38

The gun fire had done nothing but annoy the vampire, who remained persistent in his pursuit of Thumper, grabbing ahold of the big man by his bib overalls, and lifting him above his head with both arms stretched upward, as if Thumper were a bale of hay about to be pitched into a wagon.

But the creature, rather than tossing Thumper as before, slowly walked with him while holding the blacksmith aloft, moving toward the direction of the general store.

Before any of the onlookers could utter a word, Thumper and the hammer he was carrying were again airborne. This time Thumper was flying like a prehistoric bird into the large pane glass window of the store.

The explosion of glass shattering and wood splintering from Thumper crashing through the window created a sound that reverberated through the entire town.

Wolcutt, patrolling on the other side of town, heard the crash and immediately began making his way to the noise.

Throwing Thumper about 20 feet through the window wasn't enough for the vampire, who moved swiftly in making his way through the busted out window and into the store, in haste to finish the fight the barrel-chested blacksmith had picked with him.

Squeak hoped he could distract the vampire from going into the store after Thumper by firing a couple of more shots at him. But the bullets again passed through the creature like he was made of water. The vampire's only reaction to the gun fire being an icy glare he cast in Squeak's direction, as if to say with his dark eyes, "I'll remember you."

But other than that, the vampire ignored Squeak's frivolous attempt in pursuing Thumper, who had found refuge in the store by curling up behind a pile of neatly stacked 100-pound bags of flour.

"We've got to do something," said a panicked Parsons, pulling out his large wooden cross from beneath his coat. Based on his actions, Parsons was now a believer.

While Jef pulled a lit Main Street lantern from its hook and began to hurriedly search the street for the wooden stake Thumper had dropped in the fight, Parsons and Squeak quietly entered the general store through the broken window, keeping their distance from the vampire who had his back to them in his continued search for Thumper.

Being this close, Parsons and Squeak were hoping to be able to create some sort of diversion in freeing Thumper from his hiding place. The thought of Thumper having to hide from anyone, with the exception of his mother, was a new experience for all of them.

The vampire, gliding about with confidence of a new born bull, had come to a stop where the flour bags were piled, as if he could smell Thumper's fear, and knew exactly where his prey was hiding.

Being ever so careful, the vampire began systematically removing one flour bag at a time from off the top of the stack, forcing Thumper to crouch even more in trying to become even smaller behind the stack of flour bags.

It would not be long before the vampire would be revealing their frightened friend, Parsons thought.

"Come out," the vampire said in a voice that cut the silence. And with each flour bag the vampire removed from out of his path, he would send little wispy flour clouds into the air.

By this time an out-of-breath Wolcutt reached the scene, taking a position just outside the broken store window behind a wood column holding up the boardwalk awning.

Wolcutt had drawn his gun from its holster, but was having a difficult time finding a clear shot. Looking into the store, Wolcutt could see the backs of two figures, those being Parsons and Squeak. "You fellows best step back out of there," Wolcutt said, prior to spitting.

"We can't do that," said a whispered voice from the dark of the store Wolcutt recognized belonging to Parsons.

"And why not?" Wolcutt steamed back. But before another word could be exchanged, Wolcutt could see Jef fast approaching with a torch in hand and screaming some kind of warning.

"What is it?" Wolcutt asked, always out of patients with Jef.

"He's a vampire. The killer is a vampire," Jef screamed.

"Just more of your craziness" Wolcutt shouted back.

No sooner had Wolcutt finished scolding Jef, that Parsons could be heard screaming from inside the store, "Thumper, pick up a bag of flour and bust it over his head."

The call by Parsons caused the vampire to turn for only a moment to see where the call had come from, giving Thumper the time needed to react by rising to his feet out of his crouched position, and dropping what appeared to be a cloudburst of flour over the vampire's head, in giving him the chance to push his way past the creature, nearly knocking everyone else down in his haste to get out of the store through the broken store window.

The vampire, wiping white flour from his eyes, did not see the wooden cross Parsons was holding at arm's length out in front of him until he quickly spun and was upon it. Parsons standing his ground pushed his cross into the creature's face, while Squeak took cover behind the pastor.

Recognizing Parsons's faith, the vampire let out a shrill before burying his face into his cape and spinning like a top in transforming from a man into a large-winged bat.

The frightening metamorphosis sent a cold wind through the store, sending flour particles still hanging in the air swirling, creating the look of an indoor blizzard. The force of the wind generated by the vampire's furious spinning action also knocked store items off the shelves.

Parsons froze in place, transfixed by what he was seeing, as the flour-speckled bat with a 3-foot wingspan zipped over his head in an effort to exit the store.

CHAPTER 39

"**G**ot you!" Squeak exclaimed.

Before the vampire bat could exit from the store window, Squeak's hunting instincts kicked in, with him throwing the stinky fish net he had been packing all night over the creature, and then holding tightly to the net's edge.

The unexpected force of the bat's flight pulled the skinny Squeak across the store's wooden floor made slick with flour. Its pull causing Squeak's wobbly legs to buckle at the knees, sending him sprawling face-first out of the broken store window and into a belly-plant onto the Main Street boardwalk near Wolcutt's feet.

Wolcutt said nothing, his mind trying to process everything his eyes were seeing.

Despite Squeak's somewhat comical clumsiness, his large hands remained firmly gripped to the net, holding the flailing bat captive.

Wolcutt now had a clear shot at the bat and took aim, but before he could fire, the creature began dragging Squeak by his belly off the boardwalk and down the street.

Squeak, fearing what the vampire might do should it escape the net, took the punishment of being dragged through the dirt, mud and manure, with the taste of the road bouncing into his mouth, causing him to spit a lot like Wolcutt.

Despite the weight of the net over its body, the vampire bat continued to flap its powerful wings, pulling Squeak like a plow harnessed to runaway Clydesdales.

The group chased after, hoping for an opportunity to kill the vampire while in bat form.

Wolcutt ran after Squeak, his unbuttoned duster flying behind him, while Jef, armed with the wooden stake Thumper had once carried, followed the pack, hoping to save face with the group over what was beginning to appear as a failed plan.

"We have got to stick this stake into its heart," Jef told Wolcutt. But Jef was uncertain whether Wolcutt understood or even heard him.

Parsons was also in hot pursuit, gripping his wooden cross like it was a weapon, while pleading with Squeak, who had now been dragged some distance, to hold on for dear life.

Under the dark of the night and the chaos surrounding the event, none of them noticed the bat was quickly gnawing its way through the netting. It would only be a matter of distance and time before the bat would break free, enabling it to return to what appeared to be an invincible human form.

Squeak, having no other options, held tight, his trousers filling up with dirt once belonging to Main Street.

"Stab it! Somebody stab it!" Squeak cried in a herky-jerky voice, while the bat managed to chew its way through the net, freeing its head.

Then Squeak came to a sudden halt in a cloud of dust. The bat was free, flying only a short distance from the group before perching on top of a store roof ledge. There it made its transformation from bat back to man.

As before, the coming and going of the foul wind signaled the vampire's presence. Squeak remained laying in the street wearing a shocked expression, his shredded shirt and the road rash on his belly for the time being forgotten.

"You are annoying me," the vampire proclaimed from his new perch, before approaching the group, this time on foot.

Before Jef could make a run at the creature with the stake, or Parsons thrust his cross outward in an effort to once again repel the vampire, Wolcutt, being the dedicated lawman he was, stepped out away from the group and into the path of the vampire.

"No, Wolcutt. This dude is a vampire!" Jef screamed.

Wolcutt simply ignored Jef's chatter.

"I am the law and you're under arrest for the murders of Abe Vigil, Gibby Jones, Homer White and Russell Means," Wolcutt told the vampire as the two continued to advance toward one another.

"Let him go, Wolcutt. We'll get him another day," Jef said, running up and grabbing the sleeve of Wolcutt's duster. "Tell him, Parsons."

"Wolcutt, please, in the name of everything that is holy, back down!" Parsons yelled.

"Don't embarrass me. I got a job to do," Wolcutt said, turning and telling the group, before jerking his arm away from Jef's grasp.

"This creature is nothing but a common criminal who deserves to have his fate sealed at the end of a rope," Wolcutt said, pointing his gun at the vampire.

The vampire ignored Wolcutt's threats and continued to approach.

"I step aside for no man," Wolcutt told the vampire before spitting to the ground.

"I'm no man," the vampire calmly replied before flying at Wolcutt, who immediately began firing his pistol.

The group of men screamed one last time, trying to warn Wolcutt that his gun was no match for the vampire. But it was too late. The smoke coming off the end of the barrel of Wolcutt's pistol, and the smoke coming off the vampire's cape where the hot bullets had torn through it, had yet to dissipate when Wolcutt stumbled backwards and fell to the ground like a toppled wooden soldier.

Wolcutt's cowboy hat popped off his head like a cork, revealing even in the dark a look of astonishment on his face. Outside the trail of the fresh blood line that ran across his throat, Wolcutt looked as if he had lay down to take a nap.

The vampire, in mocking fashion, knowing he had killed the deputy, spit to the ground.

But before the vampire could come any closer to the group, Parsons jumped in his path, his wooden cross extended.

The vampire stopped in his tracks. "We'll all dance another day," he told the group, before throwing his dark cape over his face and raising a small dust storm in spinning away.

The wounds to Wolcutt's neck inflicted by the vampire's fingernail talons had been fatal. The lawman, in the throes of death, lying flat on his back in the dirt, didn't utter a sound or shed a single tear. Instead, he reached up with his right hand and firmly grasped the deputy sheriff star pinned over his heart.

Squeak, looking like he had taken a mud bath, appeared to be in shock, while Parsons huddled over Wolcutt's body muttering a prayer. Jef too began to pray for Wolcutt's soul, feeling the full weight of responsibility for what had happened tonight. It was a plan that failed. It was a calculated risk that ended up getting Wolcutt killed. The man died defending his first true love – the law.

Jef would have cried had he the energy. "You'd better go wake Ajacks," Jef told Parsons upon the pastor completing his prayer.

"Tell him Wolcutt's dead," Jef said matter-of-factly.

"And what are you going to do?" Squeak asked Jef.

"I'm going to go home and hug my wife and kids. After that, I am going to devise a better plan. This town will have its revenge," said Jef, who was mentally trying to place the face of their attacker.

While the group conversed near Wolcutt's limp body, a dazed Thumper, minus hammer and hat, having a few cuts and scrapes to his face and arms, staggered out from wherever he had been hiding, in walking slowly toward the men.

"Preserves are a puny payment for what I just went through," a dazed and complaining Thumper told Jef, not even noticing Wolcutt's body lying still in the dark street until nearly falling over it.

Chapter 40

Lola and Ranger were posted like sentry guards in the living quarters of the house. The small flickering candle cast dancing shadows across their faces. Most of the tall thin candle Lola placed on the fireplace mantel had already melted into the tin cup holding it upright. But there was still enough wax to throw off what light Lola and Ranger needed.

"Wear it out," had always been Lola's mantra when it came to making ends meet.

Jef had annoyed her by sneaking out while she lay sleeping, leaving her no word of where he was going. But she assumed his absence had something to do with his search for the vampire he claimed was behind the murderous attacks in their town.

After checking on her children, Lola brought out her butcher knife and put it within arm's reach of where Ranger and she had posted themselves in the hard wood furniture Squeak had crafted for them in trade for meals.

Lola would have brought out her pistol, but it was nowhere to be found. It was apparent Jef had taken it with him, even though he couldn't shoot straight.

And now he was taking on a vampire, no less for nothing more than a story, she thought.

Lola worried for Jef's safety. He was an intelligent man, but one who lacked the skills to shoot or ride. Two needed traits to thrive in the West. But what could she expect of Jef, whose father, James Furst II, a banker from upstate New York, having never owned a firearm.

But it was Jef's inner strength Lola admired. He was tenacious in seeking the truth and in pursuing justice for the underdog. Lola often suspected some days Jef envisioned her as the underdog, being the daughter of a Mexican farmer who had difficulty making ends meet due to the hurdles put before him by others.

That is why at a young age her brother Martino and she would find work to survive. Sometimes the work included the two of them leaving their father's farm in Dry Springs and heading north during the warmer months to feed those passing settlers making their way west.

Lola had been taught to cook at an early age by her mother, Maria. It was those skills that Martino and she put to use at Fort Laramie, where they offered plates full of fresh beans and rice, generally to hungry men, for an affordable price.

After working at the fort for a few years, Martino took off to find his fortune in California, leaving Lola with a new chuck wagon partner in Hyme Rodriguez. Rodriguez, an older man, after warming up to her, turned friendship into flirting, leaving Lola looking for a way out of the cantina.

It was about that same time an innocent hazel-eyed Mormon traveler agreed to accompany her back to Dry Springs to help care for what little property her father had left her mother following his untimely death.

Soon after arriving in Dry Springs, Jef and Lola married, caring for Lola's mother for about two years prior to her dying. With the family unable to locate Martino, Lola was left the estate, consisting of the small piece of land she and Jef now farmed, and the small one-level house that they lived in.

Being thrown against the elements of the West had made Jef and Lola each stronger in different ways. Jef was the only man Lola had ever loved, besides her father and brother, and it was moments like this that she felt compelled to protect him.

Ranger's barking made Lola aware someone was approaching the house. The dog, moving closer to the door, let out a short snuff after hearing the shuffling of footsteps outside. Lola reached for the butcher knife she had placed close by.

"Jef, is that you?" Lola asked through the locked door, anxious to unlatch it and swing it open.

CHAPTER 41

"It's me," Jef replied. "Open the door."

But the voice Lola heard through the door sounded nothing like Jef. And when Lola opened the door, the man standing in the doorway in no way resembled the man she had married.

The man at the door appeared broken, head down, and when he did look up, he revealed red-rimmed eyes swollen from earlier tears.

Not even Ranger, who had to sniff him prior to licking his hand, seemed to recognize Jef.

But no matter, for the time being Jef was safe and Lola was relieved to have him home. She threw her lightly freckled, thin, olive-skinned arms around his neck.

"Where have you been?" Lola asked, squeezing Jef so hard she could feel the impression of her pistol he was packing in his worn out newspaper poncho push up against her frame.

Jef made no effort to hug back, entering the home silently, ignoring Ranger, whom he always had a pat on the head for.

"Obviously you found your vampire," Lola said, her curiosity piqued by her husband's body language and deflated spirit.

"Wolcutt's dead," Jef uttered, as if it took all the energy he had to get the two words out of his mouth.

"He's dead?" Lola asked in a shocked tone. "What happened to him, James?"

"My plan went bad. Wolcutt stepped in. The vampire killed him," said a visibly frustrated Jef.

"What plan?" Lola asked, still trying to get her mind around the fact Dry Springs really had a vampire and, as a result, another town death.

"I helplessly looked on," Jef said, his tone growing louder from the guilt he was packing. "I watched the vampire throw Thumper around as if he were a toy; I saw Squeak being pulled through the dirt like he was a plowshare after the vampire transformed into a large bat; and I looked on while it killed Wolcutt with one fatal blow when the deputy stepped between the vampire and us," he said.

"And our gunfire was useless," Jef said, adding that part of the evening to his memory for the first time.

"You went out in the middle of the night in search of a vampire?" Lola asked. "Are you crazy?"

"Yes to your first question, maybe to your second," Jef said.

"And it appears we're helpless until this vampire decides the Dry Springs feeding ground has gone dry," Jef said. "I just can't figure out what he is doing here," he said, returning to the same question haunting him from the beginning.

"So, what's next, besides more funerals?" Lola asked frustrated by the killings taking place in what had been once a tranquil little town.

"We have got to find some sort of way to kill this thing," Jef said.

"What?" Lola quickly replied. "James, no more plans. This fight is someone else's responsibility. You have got too much at stake."

"This well may be my Goliath. As if my dad would say, that moment of your life when you have to push through no matter how difficult the task at hand," Jef replied.

"So we're going to hit this thing in the head with a rock?" Lola asked. "I don't know about you, but I don't have that much faith in your aim."

"The term Goliath, it's a metaphor. Don't be silly," Jef said.

And then for a few seconds there was complete silence between Lola and he, before Jef offered, "We need something that can fire a wooden stake from a distance, like a crossbow, only smaller, something easy to operate, easy to conceal."

"Where do we find such a weapon in Dry Springs?" Lola asked.

"We design it, make it ourselves," Jef said, his mind already moving on to his next new plan.

Lola looked at her husband in disbelief. "A primitive crossbow is going to kill this thing?" she asked, questioning the simplicity of her husband's idea.

"If he is a vampire, he plays by all the vampire rules. And rule No. 1 is a stake to the heart kills him," Jef said.

Lola looked at her husband as if he had two heads. "Where do you come up with this stuff? In trekking West, prior to you meeting me, did you Mormons encounter vampires? And where are we going to get the materials to build these mini-crossbows? I got news for you, you can't order such items out of the Sears and Roebuck catalog," she said smartly.

"I told you, I'll design something Squeak can rig up," Jef said, his life returning back into his eyes. "Then, once we get such a weapon, we'll need to practice with it. That's where you come in."

"No, Jef, I'm not serving as your moving target," Lola said forcefully.

"Not a target, but you can help me become a better shot. We don't want to get any closer to this thing than we have to," Jef said.

"Well, that's a comfort," Lola said, before blowing out what remained of the burning candle. "Let's get some sleep. Obviously tomorrow there is much work to do," she said, removing her pistol from Jef's poncho and taking it back into their bedroom and tucking it underneath her pillow.

"You didn't hear a word I said," Jef said, prior to removing his glasses and wiping his eyes in preparing for sleep. "That gun is nothing more than a noisemaker when it comes to repelling a vampire."

But it did please Jef to see his wife was still up for the fight. Her willingness and understanding, however, did nothing to ease his conscience when it came to Wolcutt's death.

Watching Wolcutt die hung over Jef's heart like a hangman's noose.

Prior to falling asleep, a frustrated Jef rolled back out of bed and got down on his knees by his bedside to pray, asking God specifically to make a place in heaven for ornery old Wolcutt.

The next morning's headline: "VAMPIRE ON THE LOOSE. HERO DEPUTY KILLED."

The headline captured the attention of the whole town, the frustration of Mayor Howard and the ire of young deputy Ajacks, now the only lawman in town.

CHAPTER 42

"These commoners have no respect for European dress," the vampire said to the other person in the room.

"Look, my inheritance, handed down from generation to generation, is taking a beating in this shanty town," the vampire said, sliding his pasty white fingers into the bullet holes now riddling his cape.

"We have been here longer than expected. But remember, friend, revenge is a dish best served cold," the second voice in the room said.

"Had he not run while I grieved, I would have never come to this backwater Western town. A place I certainly would have never otherwise visited," the vampire said with a growl. "And now we wait," he conceded. "But while we wait, we must continue to remind others of the pain of losing a loved one."

"We will make them all pay," the second voice in the room added, trying to calm the creature.

But all he did was agitate him.

"WE? Who is this WE you speak of? It has been I who has been wounded in the heart as these frontier plainsmen turn their gunfire on me, catch me in nets that smell of rotting fish and attempt to bully me with their size and numbers. For that reason, before I am done here, I will give that annoying newspaperman a story to write.

"In addition, I will leave this sleepy little town my family's 300-year-old curse that my father so willingly passed down onto me," the vampire said, again rubbing his fingers over the bullet holes in his cape in the hope his family's dark coat of arm and title alone would take them away.

"But first, revenge against the lawman who claims to protect this town," the vampire said. "The same lawman who shot and killed my beloved and ran to the river in an effort to float away from his past."

"We'll get revenge for you and your love. And then we'll get out of here," the second voice in the room said.

"You are not mocking me when you speak of the only woman I ever loved?" the vampire asked his company. "If that be the case, we can quickly trade places."

"So sensitive," the voice replied. "Remember, I'm one of the few friends you have."

"Why, what do you mean, you're my brother," the vampire said with a fiendish laugh, before returning to their original conversation, their purpose of being in Dry Springs.

"The lawman wears my mark," the vampire said proudly.

"I'm certain it's the first thing he sees in the morning and the last thing he feels at night when he rubs his eyes to sleep," the second voice said.

"Oh, how I hope he has had to explain his mark to others," the vampire said, smiling coolly.

The second voice remained silent, hoping this would all soon end.

CHAPTER 43

The raindrops pattering off the brim of the big black hat did so in a rhythmic fashion. Just as the rainwater would begin to pool, the hat would shift ever so slightly, sending a trickle of water cascading down the neck and across the broad shoulders of Sheriff Harry Wily.

Despite Wily's light buckskin coat being soaked to a dark brown, the sheriff continued to point his granite-chinned face into the storm, toward the direction of Dry Springs.

Wily glanced up at the sky for only a moment, letting the rain briefly patter off his tired, sunburned face before bowing his head again to the force of Mother Nature.

His quick look skyward revealed he had been out in the elements. For a week he had been in Piute country chasing down Crazy Max Dooley, a horse thief wanted out of Colorado.

Wily's sunburn pained him some. But he wore the look with honor, having captured his man. The only part of Wily's face not red from the sun was the noticeable pink scar stretching from his left eyebrow to his lower left cheek. Outside the old wound, appearing to have been caused by someone dragging a nail down Wily's face, the sheriff was ruggedly handsome.

His steel blue eyes and light red hair, protected from the rain by his signature Stetson hat, served as warning that Wily was a no-nonsense lawman who didn't need the star pinned to his chest to gain respect.

Following closely behind the sheriff atop a horse he was towing with a rope sat Crazy Max.

The horse thief's arms were securely tied behind his back, while his bright yellow bandana covering his head was now soaked to the point of forming to his round head. Max didn't look like much. But the infamous horse thief was a valuable commodity to Wily, who was about to cash-in on a $75 reward for bringing the wanted man in alive.

Had Wily had to kill Max, the reward would have only been $25. The Colorado ranchers who put up the money for Max were more interested in carrying out their own justice.

Wily expected his pursuit of Crazy Max into Piute nation would take two or three days. But the thief was elusive, delaying his capture for nearly a week. Spending the extra days out under the hot fall sun had worn Wily ragged. But the sheriff was in no position to quit, becoming dependent on bounty dollars where the Dry Springs sheriff job paid only $60 a month.

Having been out under the sun for such a period, the rain came as a relief to Crazy Max and the sheriff, who quietly plodded past the weather beaten wooden sign welcoming folks to the town of Dry Springs and offering all who read it an outdated population count.

But the all-too familiar sign had been mischievously altered due to someone's handiwork to now read: *"Blood Springs: Population, Dead."*

The word *"Blood,"* written in what appeared to be dry blood and gouged deep into the wood with a knife or nail, covered most of the word *"Dry,"* which could now hardly be seen.

"Vandals, Sheriff?" Max asked in observing the sign.

Rather than say anything to Max, Wily shifted in his saddle, taking in a deep breath, and blowing out a long exhale, before giving his horse the order to plod past the warning.

In reaching town, Wily was anticipating some sort of welcome from someone. But it appeared due to the heavy rain, the streets, and even most of the businesses, were deserted.

The only sign of life in town was Gibby's ol' horse, Stu, who for whatever reason was in the sheriff's unclaimed property corral. To keep the rain from bouncing off of his back, Stu had found partial refuge in the wooden lean-to Wily had built to keep any unclaimed livestock out of the sun.

Wily's horse hadn't clomped through the town's muddy red clay streets very far when the sheriff began to take notice of some other subtle changes around town.

Chapter 44

A new sign, obviously painted by a steady hand based on the lettering, caused Wily and his horse Chocolate to stop dead in their tracks.

The sudden stop even caused Crazy Max to raise his chin, catching with his young, whiskered face some of the rain that continued to fall under the dark sky.

Nailed high on a wooden porch pillar outside the general store, oddly its front window boarded-up with plywood, was a sign that read: *"Dawn to Dusk Curfew by Order of the Law."*

Looking down the empty street, Wily could see similar signs posted along the street. Likely all carrying the same warning, he assumed.

The curfew raised many questions in Wily's tired mind. The first of which, had Ajacks lost his mind, and all his power of being deputy sheriff gone to his head? Or was the little sleepy town he had left seven days ago under some sort of attack?

Wily hadn't ridden much farther when he began noticing wooden crosses, like those Parsons wore, dotting the storefronts. It was as if the pastor had run out of people to bless and was now giving his blessing to buildings.

"Normally this quiet, sheriff?" Crazy Max asked in a cocky tone, the rain continuing to pound down on the both of them.

The question caught Wily off guard, who nearly responded to Max, before thinking better of it. His first task was to get the two of them out of the rain. After that, he would go to search for life, answers and food. He was hungry. It had been a long ride.

Chapter 45

The small sheriff's office only made the vertical iron-barred cell Crazy Max was to temporarily occupy appear even more claustrophobic.

After getting a day or two of rest, Wily would be taking Max on to Denver for trial.

Until then, the 12-foot by 12-foot seldom-used brick-sided cell would provide little privacy for the horse thief, just like those petty criminals who had been held there before him. Not only was space limited in the cell, but so was air flow, with only a 1-foot-wide by 2-foot-long barred opening sitting about 10 feet high on the back wall.

The vent brought little air from the outside into the cell, preventing even the smell of the prisoner from escaping. With its 1-inch in diameter iron bars on the swinging cell door and its bar columns set 3 inches apart, no prisoner had yet to escape from the cell.

So when the iron cell door clanked shut behind Crazy Max, Wily knew his prisoner was there to stay.

Looking at his surroundings, Crazy Max resigned himself to the fact he had been captured, immediately retreating to the corner of the cell, plopping his backside to the ground and resting his back against the cell's wall.

"Got anything to eat or drink?" Crazy Max asked in his unnerving voice. The horse thief, infamous for his ability to run, was now too exhausted to stand.

In slamming the cell door shut so it clanked, Wily figured this would be a good time to find where the town members were hiding, including his deputies, Gibby and Ajacks.

"I'll be back," Wily told Max before stomping out of the sheriff's office.

Walking beneath the eaves of the covered boardwalk stretching along Main Street would keep him dry until he had to venture out in the rain to find his friends. But Wily didn't have to look far before spotting wagons and horses clustered outside Parsons's church.

It was a funeral, he suspected. And whoever's funeral it was, he likely knew them well, being the town was so small.

He walked across the muddy red clay street, exposing himself to more of the rain falling from the blackened skies, in approaching the church. Fears were now beginning to mount in his head that the funeral service may be for one of his own deputies. It was a notion that had popped into his head after seeing the curfew signs and Gibby's old horse in the unclaimed property corral.

Moving closer to the church, he spotted more posted signs bearing the same curfew warning as well as several more wooden crosses on the doors or over the entryways of the businesses.

Knowing the even-keeled Pastor Parsons, there had to be good reason for it, Wily figured.

Just outside the door of the church sat Ranger, he too trying to avoid the rain showing no sign of letting up. Upon seeing Wily approach, Ranger stood and began wagging his tail, the dog being the first to welcome Wily home.

Seeing Ranger gave Wily a sense of relief. Gibby must be inside the church, he thought.

Standing on the porch, Wily could already hear Parsons's thundering sermon coming from inside. He was curious as to whom Parsons was referring to in using the words "brave" and "loyal" in his message.

As quietly as a rough-and-tumble cowboy wearing spurs could be expected, Wily opened the door to the church just wide enough for him to slip in so as not to disrupt the service. The service appeared to be holding the entire town captive, as magic healing words of faith rolled off of Parsons's tongue.

So as not to offend anyone with his prairie smell, his sunburned and un-shaven face and his lack of formal dress, Wily stood at the back of the church behind the pews, trying to figure out who was in the coffin resting atop the altar at the front of the chapel.

Listening to Parsons, whom he had finally made eye contact with, ac-knowledging him with a nod, Wily was hoping the pastor would give him a clue.

The sheriff's concern once again turned to Gibby, who he could not find among those in attendance. Another clue that concerned Wily was Parsons mentioning on more than one occasion the responsibility that comes with being a deputized lawman and how no man has any greater gift to give than to give his life for his fellow man.

There was no doubt about it. All signs were pointing to this being Gibby's funeral.

But before the sheriff would let his heart sink from guilt, he would scan the chapel one more time. He had no emotion to waste.

The sheriff had already spotted Ajacks and Prudy Richards sitting next to one another holding hands. Both of their heads were bowed in reverence as Parsons continued with the service.

Others he spotted sitting in the pews were the Furst family; Parsons's wife, Shirley; Squeak, the man responsible for making sure everyone in town received a respectful burial; Thumper and his mother; and Ike Peterson, son of the late Darwin and Mabel Peterson.

But there was no sign of Gibby. So who was Ranger diligently waiting for outside on the church porch, Wily wondered.

And then Parsons, as if he could see the puzzled look on the face of Wily standing at the back of the room, mentioned Ray Wolcutt as the dead whom he was speaking of.

Wolcutt was a sheriff's deputy? He wasn't when Wily left town eight days ago, the sheriff thought, his mind now racing. It was obvious he had some catching up to do. But this was not the time or the place for it.

There was a prisoner he had to attend to, and a warm bath at the saloon calling his name. Thinking of his bath brought to mind he also hadn't seen

Russell Means, the saloon owner, among the congregation. But oftentimes Means would skip services in order to work. Means was always interested in making a buck.

Wily quietly snuck out of the church the same way he had snuck in, patting Ranger on the head prior to making his way back across the muddy street. The rain once again began pattering off his hat he had failed to remove upon entering the church.

The dark clouds hanging over Dry Springs had only gotten bigger.

CHAPTER 46

Wily ducked into Means' saloon, which was only a few doors down from the sheriff's office. His first task: Get Crazy Max and himself something to eat and drink. The bath could wait. It had already been a long day.

And it was about to get longer.

The saloon was unusually quiet. Its oak chairs and tables, normally filled with people, sat empty. The only soul in the place stood behind the counter. It was Ever Peppers, one of Means' card-playing buddies and sometimes workmate.

"It's good to see you, Sheriff," Peppers exclaimed, his round shape, short dirty apron and thick black mustache making him look the part of someone who would tend a saloon.

"I guess everyone is at Wolcutt's funeral," Wily said. "Although I didn't see Means there," he added.

Peppers generally upbeat face turned downward upon hearing Wily's words. It was apparent nobody had told the sheriff of the tragedy that had befallen Dry Springs while he was away. Before Peppers could muster up an explanation, Wily posed the question: "Curious, what did Wolcutt die of?"

"Sheriff," Peppers said, starting slowly, before eventually answering Wily's question in a hushed tone, "it was a vampire."

"A what?" Wily recoiled. "It sounded like you said vampire."

"I did," Peppers said, his voice cracking, before pulling from behind the bar the latest edition of the Dry Springs newspaper.

"The same vampire got Means, Sheriff," Peppers said with a gulp and a nod. "There is an eyewitness account of the vampire attacking Wolcutt," he said, pointing to a story in the newspaper written by James Edward Furst.

"Give me that. Furst will say anything to sell a paper," Wily said, angrily snatching the newspaper from Pepper's reach.

During his time spent in Dry Springs, Wily had already had his fair share of verbal encounters with the newspaperman.

"Jef wasn't the only witness, Sheriff," offered Peppers, who was beginning to hate being the bearer of bad news.

"Who else?" Wily demanded. "Not that fleabag friend of his he shares an office with?"

"Well, yes, Squeak was an eyewitness. But so was Otis Thumper and Parsons," Peppers stressed. "Parsons," he reiterated, the person who had gained the reputation for being the most trusted man in town.

Now it was Wily's face that shrunk.

"A vampire?" Wily questioned in a tone loud enough to shake Peppers to the core.

"Read it there for yourself, Sheriff," Peppers said, again pointing to the article bearing the headline: VAMPIRE ON THE LOOSE, HERO DEPUTY KILLED.

"It's all there in black and white," said Peppers, who didn't hold the same resentful feelings toward Jef that the sheriff did.

Wily was a poor reader, but was able to glean from the article enough to understand that many of his fellow town members had fallen victim to this so-called vampire while he was away.

The murders of Gibby, Wolcutt, Means and Vigil put the sheriff's red, sunburned face into full bluster.

"What would a vampire want in Dry Springs?" Peppers asked, sharing his thoughts out loud with Wily.

"I don't know," Wily snapped, who appeared already lost in thought.

"Got any soup or better yet, chili on the fire?" Wily asked quickly changing the subject. "I've got a prisoner to get back to."

"You get your man, Sheriff?" Peppers asked.

Wily rolled his eyes. "Don't I generally?" he said, silencing Peppers, in hoping it would rush the bartender with his order.

While Peppers went to the back of the bar to work the ladle to pour what looked to be some watered-down chili into two tin cups, Wily began to reread Furst's article so as not to miss a detail.

But the word "vampire," and the frequency in which it appeared in Furst's article, was making the news difficult for Wily to digest.

"Can you believe that, Sheriff?" Peppers asked Wily, who now had the newspaper clasped in both fists and his nose buried deep in it.

Wily remained uncomfortably silent.

"Here's your chili. I also threw some bread in there for you and your prisoner," Peppers said, placing the meal neatly in a crate.

But Peppers talk did little to bring the sheriff out of the trance-like state he had fallen into. The sheriff seemed fixated on the article.

"Put that on my tab," Wily said of the meals, while quickly folding up the newspaper, unwilling to wait around for any further explanation from Peppers as to what had taken place since he had been away.

Wily quickly exited the saloon, but not before tucking the newspaper under his arm for further reading.

"Hey, Sheriff, that paper cost me 4-cents," Peppers whined.

But the sheriff was already out the saloon door and down the street, making quick time to his office, packing two cups of chili, bread and a newspaper he expected he would be reading several times over.

Outside the sheriff's office, the welcome rain continued to fall, and the skies remained black, while inside his cell Crazy Max could be heard slurping up chili and gobbling down a piece of bread like it was already his last meal.

CHAPTER 47

The Peterson ranch house had always impressed Sheriff Wily since he first moved to Dry Springs six months ago. He coveted the three-story structure, the top of which could be seen from a distance. A nearby neatly planted corn field on the property screened the ground floor from sight. But the elevated wrap-around porch, signifying a hint of wealth and dignity, was visible to passersby from the main road. The wooden white bench swing on the porch added to the structure's hominess.

The number of windows in the house, all accented with open white-painted shutters making the western mansion seem quaint, served as notice that visitors were welcome.

Darwin and Mabel Peterson had obviously done well for themselves, Wily thought. How the couple had amassed their fortune was uncertain, but there was talk it centered on a gold discovery and their desire to live out the rest of their lives in a quiet place.

What had happened to the sweet old couple still remained a bit of a mystery. One day they went missing, before both of their nearly decomposed bodies were discovered a few months later out in the desert a few miles from their home.

It appeared the deaths were due to overexposure to the elements, those elements including the scorching temperatures Dry Springs was known for.

Wily suspected the pair went out for a walk, wandered too far from home without a water source and became disoriented, falling victim to nature.

Mayor Howard was quick to close the case as deaths related to natural causes, putting an abrupt halt to any investigation.

"They were eccentric," Howard said of the elderly Peterson couple he knew best.

Wily was fond of the Petersons, both of whom were supportive of the mayor's decision to hire him as the town's full-time sheriff.

The whole mystery surrounding the Petersons' death hadn't been spoken of much until the recent arrival of their two sons, Ike and Stan Peterson.

The two sons had arrived to settle the family's estate.

Wily had mentioned more than once he didn't know either of the men well, but being a deputy short Ajacks was certain one of the two men could lend them some temporary help while things were in chaos.

Ajacks was hoping by bringing one of the two Peterson brothers onboard with them that it would make amends with Wily, who was openly agitated with the deputy for sending Gibby out to retrieve the dead body reported by the river.

Had it been Ajacks who performed the duty as assigned, Wily had explained to his young deputy, he likely would have survived the attack, or better yet, been able to avoid it altogether.

Gibby, being old and of poor eyesight, stood no chance, Wily had scolded Ajacks.

Now the sheriff and deputy were on their way to the Peterson ranch because Ajacks had rattled on about how Stan and Ike Peterson willingly volunteered for posse duty in the recovery of Abe's and Gibby's bodies.

Ajacks was obviously sold on the two men. But Wily seemed reluctant to deputize either of the brothers. Despite that fact, the sheriff was packing in his vest pocket the charred tin star Wolcutt and Gibby had both worn prior to their deaths.

Wily, having to soon leave town again to transport Crazy Max to the courts in Denver, had talked to Ajacks about getting him some help. But for whatever reason, Wily was having a difficult time embracing Ajacks's selection, although the sheriff recognized the pickings were slim in Dry Springs.

Upon first moving to Dry Springs, Wily had an immediate dislike for Furst, who was always sticking his nose into other people's business. And the sheriff dismissed Squeak as being awkward and quiet.

Wily did like Parsons. But it seemed strange to ask the only pastor in town to tote a firearm. Besides, he was uncertain whether he could get the mayor's support in naming Parsons as a deputy where the pastor on numerous occasions had chided the mayor for his lack of support for the church.

By process of elimination, Ajacks figured that made Ike or Stan Peterson a logical choice for deputy.

After what seemed a long ride, the pair arrived at the Peterson ranch.

Ajacks, always eager, was the first off of his horse, bouncing up the porch steps and rapping hard on the front door of the house.

After standing there in silence for what seemed an eternity, Ajacks and Wily surmised that maybe no one was home.

"They've got to be around here somewhere," said Wily, scanning the area with his sunburned face that had already begun to turn into a tan.

"Give it another knock," Wily told Ajacks impatiently, motioning his head toward the door.

Chapter 48

Ajacks gave the front door of the house another hard knock, causing the door that apparently had not been latched properly to open a crack.

Using that as a welcome, Ajacks poked his head around the door and into the dark structure in hopes of being able to see something or someone.

Wily followed Ajacks's lead, which was unusual for the sheriff, who generally took charge. "Ike? Stan? It's Sheriff Wily. You folks home?" Wily announced in stepping through the door and into the dark of what he suspected was the formal greeting quarters of the house.

But the sheriff got no response.

"Ike? Stan?" Wily announced, this time louder, his voice echoing through the halls of what was nearly a mansion.

Ajacks stood next to Wily, carefully surveying their surroundings, before cautiously taking another small step in making certain they weren't going to be falling over anything.

"ANYONE HOME?" Wily screamed, his eyes finally adjusting to the dimness of the cavernous house.

Ajacks too was having difficulty seeing.

Despite the numerous exterior windows in the house, no sunlight was entering the main level of the home where each window had been tightly boarded up from the inside.

"Odd," Ajacks said, noticing the handiwork of the Peterson brothers.

"It keeps the house cool," Wily said, explaining the blocked windows.

"But it's fall," said Ajacks, continuing to move slowly through the dark, his boots making drawn-out clomping and scraping sounds on the home's hardwood floors.

Had it not been for the sunlight coming in from the crack in the front door, they wouldn't have been able to see the outline of the furniture in the room.

"I need a little light," Wily said, using his thumb to pop the top off of a wooden match he pulled from his vest pocket. The small flame briefly illuminated the massive room and the few furniture pieces in it before the match burned out.

At a glance, it appeared the furniture was a high quality Victorian-era style, maybe rosewood hand-crafted furnishings the likes of which only the Petersons would be able to afford.

It was also apparent the Peterson brothers were not very good housekeepers. A thick layer of dust had accumulated on the furniture.

Even a glass-topped oil lamp resting on a small walnut designer table situated in the corner of the room appeared as if it hadn't been lit in months.

"Pigs," Wily said, demonstrating such by blowing on the oil lamp and sending into the air what seemed enough dust to cover a standing cow in a meadow.

"Obviously," Ajacks said, feeling some of the dust Wily had stirred settling on him.

"Certainly a different way to live," Wily said, brushing the dust from his signature black vest that matched his black hat.

Ajacks figured Wily owned a whole closet full of the same vest based on how they were always so neatly pressed and clean.

"Let's hope their guns are cleaner than their living room," said Wily, his eyes having fully adjusted to the dark.

"Ike? Stan?" Wily yelled one more time before thinking it might be time for Ajacks and he to exit the home.

"They might be sleeping," Ajacks said.

"Deep sleepers," Wily said.

"Maybe they're both already out working in the yard," said Ajacks, who had taken a liking to the two brothers and was willing to defend them, even if it meant annoying Wily.

"Well, rather than trespass any more than we already have, we had better go have a look outside," Wily conceded.

The pair exited the house, once again finding it difficult to see as their eyes readjusted to the sunlight.

"Maybe they're in the barn out back," Ajacks said, leading the sheriff off the porch and toward a neighboring red barn that stood as high as the house.

Darwin and Mabel Peterson once had it all.

CHAPTER 49

The red barn, with its white framing, stood about 30 feet tall and had a second-story hayloft with swing doors. There was also a pulley on a hook used to lower the hay bales into a waiting wagon down below.

The barn, with its brown rounded roof, pitched against the backdrop of the wide-open blue sky and surrounding green pastures, appeared as if it were an oil painting.

Wily and Ajacks, who were paid sheriff and deputy wages respectively, couldn't help but be envious. Each of the men ached to find their own fortune and shake off the dust of Dry Springs forever.

Wily wanted to law in a larger town, while Ajacks wanted enough fortune to allow him to run away with Prudy Richards and take her for his wife.

"IKE? STAN?" an impatient Wily screamed toward the barn.

Wily had left Crazy Max at the jail under the watch of Mayor Howard. Leaving such a prisoner for someone else to watch always made the sheriff anxious, and he was growing tired of not being able to locate either of the brothers.

With their pointed, dirty boots crunching the gravel beneath their feet, Wily and Ajacks reached the barn. One of the two barn doors was swung wide open, almost inviting the pair to enter.

In the barn there were about a dozen sectioned-off horse stalls, with only two stalls having horses in them. The others sat empty. Apparently the two brothers had already sold off most of the Peterson livestock.

"Ike? Stan?" the sheriff called again, looking for any sign of life other than the two horses. The only sound was the horses grazing on fresh feed, indicating one of the brothers had to be nearby.

The sheriff was about to turn and leave when a voice from behind asked, "Can I help you?"

Ajacks was so startled he instinctively brushed the pearl handle of his six-shooter while at the same time spinning around.

"Ike," Ajacks said, relieved they had found someone home. "Ike, this is Sheriff Wily," Ajacks said, making the formal introduction between the two men.

Wily extended his hand for a handshake, but Ike brushed it aside, informing Ajacks he had briefly met with the sheriff when the Petersons first arrived in town.

"I know all about Sheriff Harry Wily," Ike said.

"Oh," Ajacks said in a surprised tone.

"Some through my folks," Ike said unconvincingly. "Now, what can I do for you two hardworking lawmen?"

Wily always believed the best way to talk to any man, or woman for that matter, was straightforward plain speak.

But before Wily could say a word, Ajacks interjected.

"We're looking for another deputy. These past few days the town has had a run of bad luck, and I know firsthand you and your brother are both good with a horse and gun," Ajacks said, confident Ike would respect his request.

"Is that what you call that, Deputy, a run of bad luck? It sounds like to me the entire town of Dry Springs is having a run of bad luck. My brother and I fear even going into town at night anymore. Some crazed newspaperman who deserves to be locked up says the town has a vampire," Ike said. "For that reason, I don't know that being a deputy is for me."

"Well, we're not certain it's a vampire. That newspaperman has a history of embellishing stories in order to sell papers," Ajacks said. "But we certainly have a problem on our hands," he added, looking at Wily for some sort of confirmation.

"We could use your help," Wily added. But it was obvious the sheriff wasn't going to plead.

"No vampires then, Sheriff?" Ike asked.

"We're not certain," Wily said, backing away from the whole vampire notion.

"Ike if you're not willing to be deputy, what about your brother, Stan?" Ajacks asked anxiously.

"My brother is not much of a night person. I fear he'd be found sleeping on the job," Ike said.

"Besides, Stan is often out of town wrapping up the affairs of our parents' estate," Ike said. "No, if it is going to be one of us, it would have to be me."

But just as Wily was beginning to think Ike was about to decline their request, Ike asked if he could see the tin badge that came with the job.

Wily reached into his vest and pulled from his pocket the charred tin star both Wolcutt and Gibby had worn, flipping it in the air to Ike, who caught it in his clasped hands.

"What would my duties be?" Ike asked, examining the star.

"I figure the three of us could work the streets around the clock, rotating shifts every third day, making sure no one has to pull the night shift on consecutive days. At least until we solve this mystery," Wily said. "Or the vampire moves on to another feeding ground."

"And the pay?" Ike asked.

"It's $32 a month," Ajacks added.

"There is not a lot you can do with $32 a month? Besides, I may not last a month. Like I said, my brother, Stan is wrapping up our work here, and then we'll both be on our way," Ike said.

"It comes with some special privileges," Ajacks said, trying to sell the job. "We get meals at Means' saloon for half price, and if we need to stay in town, 50 percent off our room at Annie's Place."

"Do I get the same privileges with Miss Prudy Richards?" Ike asked with a laugh.

Ajacks didn't find Ike's question funny or proper. "No, can't help you there," Ajacks said, staring at Ike and trying to determine whether the cowboy was serious.

"Maybe you should ask Prudy first before you go making those decisions for her," Ike said, not letting it go.

"You in or not, Ike?" Wily asked, trying to cut the tension between the two young bulls. Being nearly 40 years old, Wily figured he didn't have time for such idle chit-chat anyway. Ajacks and he had already spent more time than he wanted at the Peterson place.

"I'm in, Sheriff," Ike said, clutching the star, all while keeping his eyes glued on Ajacks.

"You start tonight just before sundown," Wily said. "You got the first shift. I'll relieve you at midnight," he said. "Bring something that shoots straight."

"It sounds like to me you've been vampire hunting before," Ike said, taking one last playful jab at the two lawmen before they departed.

But Wily, nor Ajacks, offered any sort of response.

CHAPTER 50

On the ride back to Dry Springs, Wily couldn't help but wonder if they had made a mistake bringing Ike on board. Causing him further annoyance was the fact Ajacks was no longer singing the praises of Ike and Stan Peterson as he had been on the three-quarter mile ride out to their ranch.

As a matter of fact, Ajacks had become as quiet as a stump.

Wily figured Ajacks's feelings had been hurt by Ike's teasing.

After all Ajacks was young and at times shallow. That's why the deputy always had to wear his hat just so and spent nearly three months' pay for his pearl-handled pistol. But still, Ajacks, who was just dying to leave Dry Springs, found Prudy Richards to be his most valuable commodity. Not only did the auburn-haired beauty look good hanging on his arm, but Prudy gave Ajacks the confidence he needed to be a lawman. He figured Prudy was equally in love with him, and that may have been why the deputy was visibly annoyed by Ike's disrespectful chatter.

"Let it go," Wily said, almost able to hear what Ajacks was thinking as the two rode back to town. "Don't let him get to you, Ajacks," Wily said, well aware his deputy had been silent since his verbal sparring with Ike. "Men will be men. Next time Ike sees you, he'll likely apologize all over himself for the remarks he made," Wily said, even though he didn't believe that.

Ajacks just looked at his riding partner, generally respecting his wisdom, but in this instance not believing a word of it.

Ike Peterson had an ego and was as brash as a Spanish bullfighter, Ajacks thought.

Wily shared similar thoughts about Ike. The sheriff figured he might need a bucket full of cold pump water handy whenever the two cowboys crossed paths.

"Prudy would never go for such a man," Ajacks said out of nowhere, as if one of his thoughts had accidentally escaped him.

Wily let out a snort before shifting in his saddle, causing the leather of his saddle to squeak some. Wily felt it best to keep his eyes forward and his mouth shut. He had enough to deal with.

"You ever been in love, Sheriff?" Ajacks asked from nowhere.

The question was like a bolt of lightning striking Wily on the head.

"Once," Wily stammered, "it was a long time ago. And I, unlike you, am not willing to share it," he said, his steely eyes remaining forward.

"Well, regardless, what Prudy and I have is special, and no fast-talking visitor from wherever Ike comes from is going to interfere with that," Ajacks said matter-of-factly.

"Oh, this is going to be fun," Wily said, his chiseled face cracking a smile, revealing a row of teeth that appeared as clean as a mountain stream.

Chapter 51

The sketch of the primitive looking device Jef slapped down on Squeak's work bench made the quiet craftsman blink twice before he spoke.

"And what is that?" Squeak asked.

"That is what I need you to build for us to kill the vampire," Jef replied.

"Really," Squeak added, further examining the pencil drawing Jef had put before him. The weapon design resembled a pistol-size handheld crossbow.

"Mmmm," Squeak said, eyeing the faint drawing. "And what will this weapon shoot?"

"Wooden stakes," Jef said, pulling a sample from the back pocket of his trousers.

The stake, an inch in diameter and 8 inches long, is large enough to fly and long enough to be able to pierce the heart of the vampire from a safe distance, he said.

Squeak again eyed the design. "The only difficulty in crafting such a weapon is finding the material to produce the tension, the firing mechanism, or force, needed to push the stake hard enough, fast enough, to penetrate the monster," Squeak said, sounding more like a weapons expert than a carpenter.

"You will think of something, my friend, and my hope is you will think of it fast," Jef said, brushing his moppish hair out of his eyes and pushing his glasses back onto the bridge of his nose. "Now the vampire knows who we are, it will be only a matter of time before he comes a calling," Jef said.

Squeak gulped. The vampire having seen him up close the night they attacked did cause Squeak some concern now Jef had mentioned it.

"You have to keep our weapon work out of the newspaper," Squeak cautioned Jef. "We're already under enough pressure."

Squeak lived in Dry Springs because life was simple there. Here, he fit. In Dry Springs he could build tables, chairs and water wheels without being rushed, and more importantly, without having to be told how to do so. But those projects of late had been put on hold due to the high demand for coffins. Work orders temporarily transforming his woodwork bench into a morgue slab.

"Do you think you can build three of them, one for you, me and Parsons? I don't want to experience what we experienced the other night ever again," Jef said, hoping the combination of specially designed weapons and his endless faith in God would keep his family safe.

"Mmmm," Squeak responded, beginning to visualize where Jef was going with the weapon. "Let me be, I have to work to do," Squeak said, trying to rush his demanding friend away.

"I like the way you think," Jef said, slapping Squeak on the back before exiting the shop with Ranger. Jef was hoping Squeak, who normally plodded, would step it up on this particular project before the entire population of Dry Springs called the city cemetery home.

As he was leaving, Jef could hear the pondering craftsman giving the weapon design he had been provided another reaffirming "Mmmm."

Squeak's odd expression made Jef grin with hope that the next time they encountered the vampire they would be ready for the creature, with the intent of killing him, despite how much killing anything panged Jef's soul with guilt where the act ran so contrary to his faith.

CHAPTER 52

The tin star glistened under the dim light of the lantern, all but the portion charred by fire.

"Where did you get that thing?" the other person in the room asked.

"The sheriff gave it to me, like it were a key to the city," the man wearing the star cackled.

"This makes things so much easier," the other voice said.

"Yes, but we can't stay long. I think the newspaperman and his friends are up to something," the other male voice warned.

"That is where Crazy Max comes in," the second voice said confidently. "I just know he would love to help out rather than sit in a jail cell waiting to be extradited to Denver. We will punish the sheriff, but first we are going to have some fun with that newspaper boy. Then we'll leave a curse on this town the likes which none of these plain-speaking folks living here have ever seen."

"You've thought this out, haven't you, brother?" the second voice asked.

"I have. But remember, friend, we only play brothers," the voice reminded. "But I will allow you to share in the spoils. After all, you now possess the key to the city."

The two men then laughed heartily.

"Now, give me my rest. I've got a night ahead of me," one voice said menacingly before the house went dark.

Chapter 53

After studying Jef's design for nearly an hour, Squeak decided a walk down Dry Springs's unusually quiet Main Street to clear his head was what he needed. The sun, peeking between the clouds, warmed him from head to toe as he strolled.

There was some foot traffic out, but the murders had robbed the simple little town of much of its friendly character.

Sheriff Wily's bold promise he would soon have the attacker behind bars provided little in the way of hope. It was Squeak's own personal run-in with the vampire that caused him to doubt the sheriff's ability to deliver on his word.

Squeak still carried from that encounter with the vampire a purplish-yellowish bruise on his forehead, mostly concealed by his long blond bangs. The scrapes on his chest and stomach from him being dragged through the street by the winged creature were also beginning to scab and heal.

Being a man with very little religious conviction, Squeak was now beginning to question in his own mind whether anything could be done to stop the vampire. He hated that feeling of helplessness.

Certainly, Parsons's wooden cross held the monster at bay. But Squeak conceded he didn't have Parsons's faith. Of course, outside of Jef, who did?

Squeak was the type of man who had to be able to put his hands on something to believe it existed. And he figured if there was a heaven and hell, like the one Parsons and Jef spoke of, than he had already cashed in on his gift from heaven – it being able to craft something out of nothing.

He figured God didn't owe him anything else.

Just the same, Squeak was hoping his morning walk would inspire him to create and build the killing tool that would gain him and the rest of the town members their freedom.

With his lope, the tall, skinny-framed man had no real destination in mind. But while on his stroll, Squeak couldn't help but subconsciously stop once to hand-turn a loose screw on a Main Street business sign, allowing the sign to once again swing with dignity without squeaking.

It was while adjusting the sign that Squeak had a brainstorm that the person he needed to go see was Miss Higginson.

Miss Higginson, another lonely heart living in town, was kind, smart and eccentric, possessing a wide array of imported furnishings in enjoying what many observers considered a world traveler lifestyle.

The hope was in visiting with Miss Higginson, Squeak might get some idea as to how he would develop Jef's anti-vampire gun. But Squeak had no intention of letting Miss Higginson know the purpose of his visit.

If word got out about their effort, it was likely the townspeople would chastise them and remind them ridding the town of the vampire was a job best left to Sheriff Wily.

And should those in the vampire's camp find out about their effort, it could mean Jef and he would likely be the targets of any future attacks.

No, Squeak wanted to keep this information to himself.

Besides, it appeared Sheriff Wily hadn't yet bought into the whole vampire story. The sheriff gave the impression that the attacker only thought himself to be a vampire. That, despite the eyewitness accounts provided to Wily by Jef and Parsons.

Thumper had been oddly quiet since the incident occurred, likely embarrassed by the fact that the vampire had handled him with such ease, ruining his reputation of once being the strongest man in Dry Springs.

The warnings given to the sheriff about hiring Ike Peterson as the new deputy also seemed to be ignored by Wily, Squeak thought.

No sooner had he run all these different scenarios through his mind than Squeak had arrived at Miss Higginson's side door where she regularly took in her guests. Squeak rapped only once on the door before it quickly swung open. Miss Higginson was apparently aware Squeak was approaching her home and, having been cooped up for some time due to the murders, was eager for his company.

She smiled wide upon seeing it was Squeak at her door.

"Hurry in," Miss Higginson beckoned, as if the vampire might be nipping at Squeak's heels.

CHAPTER 54

"**B**eing a frail, single woman, I must avoid all manner of evil," Squeak could recall Miss Higginson telling Jef in an earlier chat after the first two murders occurred.

But the overbearing, well-traveled woman in her late 20s seem to be anything but frail as she engulfed the rail-thin Squeak into her big-boned arms, giving him a welcoming hug while using her foot to quickly close the door behind him.

Squeak, in catching his breath from Miss Higginson's loving squeeze, couldn't help through his deep breathing catch a whiff of tea brewing.

"What brings you out on this fine day?" Miss Higginson said, dabbing with her handkerchief at a single drop of sweat having beaded up on her forehead.

"Just a social call," Squeak shyly replied, already surveying Miss Higginson's living room packed full of treasures.

It was like Miss Higginson lived in a museum.

There in her living quarters, a French imported sofa; an accordion standing upright on a mahogany-wood base table; an artist rendering of a schooner on a storm-tossed sea that hung on the wall; an M Singer & Co. sewing machine; and a large framed picture of what appeared to be a famous New York Broadway entertainer. The print was of great worth, Squeak figured, as a result of the autograph near the bottom right corner of the frame.

"Social call? Why, you flatter me, Mister Squeak," said Miss Higginson, whose constant banter provided the necessary balance for the usually quiet Squeak.

"Most recently a visit from Jef, and now you stop by unexpectedly," Miss Higginson said, loving the attention.

Oftentimes, the formally educated Miss Higginson would grow impatient with Squeak's quietness, mistaking it for ignorance. But the truth be known, Miss Higginson had a bit of a crush on Squeak, who was about four years her junior.

"Would you like some tea?" she offered as he continued to stand, his mouth gaping open, but nothing coming out except the slight wheezing noise created by him inhaling and exhaling.

"Yes, yes, I would like some tea," Squeak replied in an effort to catch up on their conversation.

"Then sit, please, dear boy, sit," Miss Higginson said motioning to the furniture before quickly darting to the kitchen where she already had tea boiling.

Squeak made his way over to the French sofa, sitting down as softly as possible so as not to make the furniture creak or raise any dust from the dirty trousers he had now worn for three days straight without a washing.

"Oh, I just can't get over you paying me a social call, Mister Squeak," Miss Higginson said upon returning from the kitchen.

"Just Squeak, ma'am," Squeak replied, removing his old brown bowler hat from his head with the hope it would make him more comfortable.

"No ma'am. Just miss," Miss Higginson corrected him.

But Squeak was lost in thought, scanning the room so full of interesting items, including a feathery boa hanging from a nail in the wall, apparently a remnant from Miss Higginson's earlier dancing days.

There were some fine glass goblets, likely from some sort of important toast she shared with a friend, and a wooden chest that, based on the thin layer of dust on top of it, had not been opened for some time.

Squeak's eyes then fixed on a six-string guitar standing upright in the corner.

"Oh, do you play?" Miss Higginson asked, noticing where Squeak's eyes had focused.

"No, I don't play," Squeak said, seemingly distracted by the question. "But I didn't know you played," he added.

"Oh, I don't play," Miss Higginson giggled before jumping up and running to her stove to pull the whistling teakettle off the burner. She shortly returned with two cups of tea she balanced in one hand, and a small wooden folding table about the size of a footstool she balanced in the other.

Miss Higginson then set the footstool before Squeak, before daintily placing a teacup on it. The woman then sat down on another sofa positioned directly across from him.

But rather than the tea, Squeak was fixated on the six-string Hohner acoustic guitar Miss Higginson had tucked away in the corner, realizing the musical instrument is what he needed to make Jef's weapon work. The guitar strings, Squeak was already envisioning, would provide the perfect triggering mechanism to send the wooden stakes flying.

"That is my prize. If I were to find the time to play an instrument, that would be the instrument I would play," Miss Higginson said, not being able to help notice Squeak's interest in the guitar.

Squeak flashed Miss Higginson an odd look, before turning his attention back to the guitar.

"My instruments are merely for show. Why, that particular brand of guitar is so new, most in these parts have never even seen such a fine instrument," Miss Higginson said with a slight crow in her voice.

"Oh, someday I intend on playing. But it is difficult to concentrate on music lessons when Dry Springs is encountering the possibility of having a vampire roaming loose," she said.

Miss Higginson was a master at changing subjects.

"It has gotten to the point that I don't enjoy even picking up the paper anymore," Miss Higginson said, referring to Jef's published reports on the vampire and its victims.

Squeak gulped his tea in one continuous slurp before setting it down and rising to walk over to the corner of the room where the guitar stood. Upon closer inspection, it was apparent Miss Higginson had not picked up the instrument for some time based on the dust collected on it.

"May I borrow your guitar?" Squeak asked, grabbing the instrument by its neck, before nestling it into his body in order to slightly strum his callous fingers over the tight nylon strings of the instrument. He was now certain the nylon strings would provide the right amount of tension to make Jef's weapon work. But he feared what her reaction might be if he mentioned to Miss Higginson his intent to take her guitar apart to piece together such a weapon. She had already mentioned how she was becoming annoyed with Jef's nonstop coverage of Dry Springs's vampire problem.

"I had no idea you had such culture," Miss Higginson said. "You are a surprise," she added, hoping her flattery would bring Squeak back for a return visit in the near future.

"But who will teach you how to play such an instrument?" Miss Higginson asked. "Maybe we could take lessons together."

Before Squeak could craft a story in his mind, the name Jef slipped from his lips. "Jef plays the guitar," he said.

"I did not know Mister Furst played the guitar," Miss Higginson said.

"He is shy about it," Squeak said, further growing his lie.

"Well, yes, of course you can borrow it, on the condition someday you teach me how to play," Miss Higginson said, batting her long dark eyelashes at a blushing Squeak.

"Should we all live long enough for that," Squeak said, rubbing his bruised forehead hid by his hair.

With the guitar strings, Squeak figured he could have a weapon fashioned for testing within the day for his friends.

Squeak than tucked the guitar under his arm, wanting to leave with the instrument before Miss Higginson had a chance to change her mind.

"Maybe one day you and I could do a church number for Pastor Parsons," Miss Higginson said, while Squeak tried to move his lanky body, with the guitar in tow, closer to the door.

"That would be my hope," said Squeak, whose mind was already floating with ideas as to how he was going to make the guitar strings work. His only fear was that he didn't break too many of the strings in the process, as he lacked the means to buy new ones for Miss Higginson.

But if he saved her life with the advent of Jef's new weapon, it would be likely Miss Higginson wouldn't mind how her new guitar was put to use.

"No sour chords now," Miss Higginson told Squeak jokingly as he exited her house.

Not funny, Squeak thought to himself as he walked down the street, placing his bowler hat back on his head and straightening his black bow tie, as if he had accomplished something.

Looking at the six-string guitar, Squeak figured he had six chances to get it right.

Chapter 55

Like a wounded greater sage grouse, the wooden stake fluttered before falling out of the air.

The stake had again fallen short of its intended target.

"It isn't that I'm a bad shot," Lola rationalized, taking aim at the vertically stacked hay bales and firing again.

The noise the weapon made with each firing was a distinct PING.

The lightweight stake again drifted a few feet off course, completely missing the circular target the Furst family had pinned to the hay bales.

"Step closer," Jef encouraged his wife, despite fearing her response.

Shooting practice was not going well.

"Yeah, step closer, Momma," James Jr. said, parroting his father. The child's response came somewhat as a surprise, considering both boys normally sided with their mother in her chiding their father.

The chiding was especially forthcoming when it came to comparing Lola and Jef and how they each participated in the customs of the West, such as roping, hunting or shooting any type of weapon. Although in this instance, at issue was the weapon, almost resembling a toy, crafted by their father's friend, Squeak.

The children were totally unaware their mother and father were taking turns practicing with the weapon in the event they had to defend themselves against a vampire.

Oh, the two young boys were totally aware the town was on guard for something, but they were purposely left out of every conversation as to what.

Jef and Lola felt that was best kept a secret so as not to frighten them.

While Lola and Jef took turns taking aim with the new weapon, the Furst boys used the extra ammunition, the wood stakes, to play a rollicking game of fetch with Ranger.

"Look how good he has gotten at this game," James Jr. bubbled after throwing the stick and having Ranger bring it back to him. Lola and Jef, concentrating on the target, had heard what the boys said but weren't fully registering it.

"That's nice," Lola replied, like a good mother trying to concentrate on one thing and do another.

Again the PING of the nylon guitar string sent flying the rounded stake Jef had shaped using the wood from the native Box Elder trees. But the 8-inch-long stake fell woefully short of the target.

"Unless you're rubbing elbows with the monster, this isn't going to work," said Lola, who had the reputation of being able to hit a running rabbit at 40 feet, even in her Sunday dress.

"Move up," Jef said, determined the crossbow contraption would work.

PING.

"See there," Lola said, pointing, her wooden stake barely hitting the bottom edge of the 2-foot circular target they had drawn using barn paint.

"Daddy, it needs weight," offered James Jr. between his play with Ranger.

"Son, please," Jef said, already beginning to lose confidence in what Squeak and he had built as their vampire killer.

Grabbing the weapon from Lola out of frustration, Jef stood close to the target.

PING. "There. At 5 feet it appears it would work," Jef told Lola.

"Willing to stake your life on it?" Lola said, not realizing what she had said until after the words had escaped her mouth. But the children did not hear what was said having been still actively involved in playing with Ranger.

PING. "From 10 feet back the stake appears to have enough velocity to fly straight with enough force to strike the vampire with a fatal wound," Jef said, before realizing what he had done.

"James Edward Furst III, might I remind you, your children are present," Lola scolded.

"Momma, I know what fatal means. It means dead, huh, Dad?" James Jr. added, the 5-year-old totally unaware he wasn't helping his father's cause.

"Please, son," Jef said, before taking another few steps backward and firing the weapon again.

PING. "Twelve feet away is about the weapon's range," Jef conceded.

"That is much too close," Lola said. "We need a weapon with a range of at least double that distance."

"Weight, Momma. Give the wood a little weight," said James Jr., proving to be intellectually advanced beyond his years.

"Weight?" Jef said, holding one of the stakes in the palm of his hand. "How do we add balanced weight to this?" he thought, almost hoping the stake would answer his question for him.

"A tail," James Jr. said, interrupting his father's thinking. "Like an arrow," he said.

"We need something heavier than that," said Jef, who couldn't believe he was now exchanging ideas with his young son.

The back-and-forth conversation had Lola doing double-takes.

"We need lead, the same thing that makes a bullet travel at such a high rate of speed," Jef said.

"But doesn't the stake have to be made of wood to be effective against a vampire?" Lola asked.

Jef gave her a look, holding a finger up to his lips as if to remind her of the use of the word "vampire" while the children were present.

Jef abruptly stopped talking and immediately began gathering up all the wooden stakes, some of which had Ranger's chew marks in them, before making his way to their small barn to saddle their horse.

"I need to go see Squeak," Jef said. "Son, a tip of my cap to you," he said, removing from the top of his head the dirty gray flat cap he always wore and waving it in the direction of his son as if he were curtsying before a king.

"I'll soon be back with much improved vampire ammunition," Jef said.

"Please, Jef," Lola asked, putting one last shush on her husband before he left the yard.

"Does that mean extra dessert for me?" James Jr. turned and asked his mother, seeing how pleased his father was with him.

"We'll see," Lola said, whose mind was more on Jef, hoping whatever fixes he was intending to make to the wooden stakes, he would do it in a timely manner in order to return home before dark.

CHAPTER 56

Crazy Max, frustrated at being held captive for two days, furiously shook the iron bars of the cell until he was red in the face.

"Wily," the prisoner screamed. But Sheriff Wily was gone, having some time ago blown out the oil lamp in the sheriff's office and gone home to get some rest.

It seemed everyone in Dry Springs turned out the lights early, as if the night moon might give them a burn, Max thought.

This whole curfew thing was new to Crazy Max. He had never seen such.

And while Max was holed up in his cell, newly appointed deputy sheriff Ike Peterson was out patrolling the city.

Crazy Max was already looking forward to Wily moving him to Denver for trial. Anything to be away from here, the thin, wispy-bearded man thought to himself.

Max had designs of escaping during the trip and being able to elude the sheriff. The same sheriff he was able to elude for nearly a week in Piute country before his capture.

This time would be different, he schemed.

But Crazy Max's scheming was soon interrupted by a fierce howling wind outside, that like a dust devil with a charted course, was beginning to squeeze its way through the small air vent at the top of his cell, allowing a blast of air to circulate throughout the musty sheriff's office, throwing papers about that had been left out on the sheriff's desk.

Although, this particular wind had an unnatural feel to it, chilling Max to the bone, as if it were a forewarning that there are worse things than being in jail.

The wind was now pushing its way through the cell vent at a hurricane-force rate, with small particles of dirt spraying into the cell, causing Max to shield his eyes by holding his forearm over his face.

And then as if he had stepped inside a twister, the wind began to swirl around him, ripping his signature yellow bandana from his head, revealing his receding hairline and stringy hair as dirty as the Mississippi River bottom.

The mini-windstorm within the cell swirled for what seemed an eternity before subsiding as abruptly as it had begun, allowing Max to take away from his face his shielding arm just in time to catch a glimpse of what appeared to be a large bat.

Based on instinct, Max initially cowered into a crouch position, trying to move as far away from the bat as possible. But in the tiny cell there was little room to maneuver.

The large bat, in a continued swirl, then began to take a new form, the shape of a human, a devilish looking character with pale white skin, cloaked in a black cape. Once the wind went still, Max was sharing his cell with another man, who now stood over him.

The normally confident horse thief was unable to utter a word, his eyes riveted on the imposing figure.

"Want out?" the caped stranger asked Max, nodding his head toward the direction of the jail bars.

At first, Max was reluctant to even nod, his tongue heavy like mud. But eventually he found the nerve to slightly bob his head, hoping that was the correct answer.

"I can arrange that," the stranger said. "But I'm a firm believer in a favor for a favor."

Max, a longtime criminal who generally had sharp words for others, remained silent, continuing to listen to whatever the intimidating stranger said.

"I'll get you out of here. But there is a task that needs to be performed before you leave town. There is a man by the name of James Edward Furst who lives just outside of town. He annoys me. I want you to rid me of my problem. Do you understand?" the stranger asked.

Max nodded as if to say, "I will obey."

"Where do I find this man?" Max asked fearfully.

"He is easy to spot. He wears a ridiculous grin, wire-rim eyeglasses and he walks like his words have power. But they do not. He is a coward, ignorant in the ways of the West," the stranger said.

"But Sheriff Wily...," Max said, before being immediately interrupted.

"I will deal with Sheriff Wily," the stranger said. "More importantly, do we have a deal?"

"What is my other choice?" Max asked, feeling a little braver by the minute.

"You have none," the stranger said, extending his right hand to seal the agreement. But Max was fearful, purposely placing his hand in his jacket as if to signal to the stranger that he feared touching him.

The stranger, although annoyed with Max's action, continued: "You can find shelter at a large home about a mile outside of town. You can stay until you have had ample opportunity to perform your task. But should you double-cross me, you common horse thief, I'll track you down and drain from you every ounce of pathetic life that lies within you. Are we clear?" the stranger asked forcefully.

Max nodded, realizing he had no bargaining power at this point.

"Now stand away," the stranger said before wrapping his bare white hands around the iron bars of the cell and slowly bending them outward as if they were wire, preparing a way for his new friend to escape from Wily's grasp.

After a few seconds of work by the stranger, who didn't break a sweat, the iron cell bars had been bent to a point where Max had more than enough room to slip between them.

"There is your exit," the stranger said. "Oh, one more thing before you go," he said, craning his head ever so slightly to apply a quick bite to the side of Max's neck.

"Oww, what was that for?" Max said of the bite inflicted by the stranger that had drawn blood.

"It is for strength. Within days you will begin to feel its effect," the stranger said proudly.

Max did all he could not to rub the wound.

"Now, remember, about a mile out of town there is a ranch. You can hole up there for a day or two until an opportunity presents itself. You can't miss the ranch, it's only the largest spread in the whole valley," the stranger said. "But remember, you owe me one newspaperman. Now, shoo, fly," the stranger said with a fiendish laugh before whirling out of the jail cell through the same small vent by reversing his transformation from man to bat.

A frightened, yet excitable, Crazy Max wasted no time squeezing through the jail bars and running out of the sheriff's office, occasionally rubbing his neck in hopes of alleviating some of the pain caused by the stranger's bite.

Making his way down the Dry Springs's Main Street with his yellow bandana in hand, Max out of excitement over being free failed to seize the opportunity to steal Ajacks's horse tied to the hitching post outside the sheriff's office.

He was free, or so he thought. The common horse thief did not yet realize he had just made a deal with the devil – or in this case, a vampire.

But Max figured this Furst fellow he promised the stranger he would kill would be less of a threat than having to make a getaway from Sheriff Wily during his transfer from Dry Springs to Denver.

CHAPTER 57

Rather than leave town after setting Crazy Max free – a mischievous deed still causing him to chuckle under his breath in envisioning Wily's reaction upon finding his prisoner was gone, and with him, the $75 reward he was to collect – the vampire was still thirsty for more.

It was the vampire's hope that his mounting evil acts would force Wily into a confrontation. The vampire was well aware Wily had come to Dry Springs to hide from his past, which had included an earlier bout with him.

In their first encounter, Wily had taken the life of the only woman the vampire ever loved. It was gunfire from Wily's pistol that killed her, just days prior to her having the chance to complete a full transformation into a member of his vampire family.

The deputy's escape, which left his face scarred, had allowed Wily for over two years to elude the justice of the stranger.

But now, the day of reckoning for Wily was near at hand. And to accelerate the process, the vampire was willing to make anyone his victim, so long as every victim buried in the town's dusty little cemetery reflected poorly on Wily's inept leadership.

Now out in the night air, the vampire realized he had not taken a victim since Wily's return to town. What better way to demonstrate to the sheriff who was in charge.

There must be someone not obeying curfew, the vampire thought, walking through the dark like he owned it.

In the shadows up ahead on Main Street, the vampire could see a lonely figure standing guard. Likely one of the sheriff's deputies making his rounds to ensure Dry Springs stayed safe after dark. Taking a second look he could see the cowboy guard was in no hurry to get in his way.

"Ike," the vampire said, formally greeting his acquaintance.

"Oh, it's you," Ike responded. "I saw Crazy Max making a run for it out of town in the direction of our place. I figured that was yer doing."

"It was," the vampire confirmed. "Anyone out?" he asked Ike, surveying the town.

"You may want to go get yourself a drink over at the saloon," Ike replied smartly.

"Thanks, friend," the vampire said, gliding past Ike as if the two were buddies. And they would remain that way as long as Ike remembered his place in their plans.

CHAPTER 58

Nᴇᴡ sᴀʟᴏᴏɴ ᴋᴇᴇᴘᴇʀ Ever Peppers knew he was running late and had let the hour slip past him. The sun had fallen. He was working on the saloon's weekly ledger, trying to determine what stock to reorder for the coming weeks. With the curfew taking people off the streets earlier in the evenings, business had been slow, and he was trying to keep cost down for the Means family, who were doing their best to keep the business going.

Peppers had stepped in to help Todd Means, the son of the late Russell Means, operate the business. While Peppers toiled in the back room over the books, Todd was out wiping down the bar counter and stools at a brisk pace in hopes the two men would be able to leave at the same time.

With a deputy on watch, Peppers figured any sign of trouble and the deputy would fire off some sort of warning round. So Peppers diligently continued with marking the order sheet.

It was during the quiet of their work, that Todd heard a shuffling noise from outside.

"Did you hear that?" Todd called out, from the front of the saloon to Peppers, who was in the back.

"Don't let your imagination run wild, kid. We'll be out of here in no time," Peppers said, calming his young co-worker. "Just need a few more minutes."

Again, Todd heard an unusual noise coming from outside, like a whistling, swirling wind was approaching the front door of the saloon. Todd could see from where he was standing the front door to the business was locked. To ensure his safety, Todd ran over to the two oil lamps that were burning to light the interior of the bar and blew them out. That left the candle Peppers was burning in the back room as their only source of light.

"What are you doing, son?" Peppers screamed out to Todd, noticing the lack of light in the saloon.

"Ever, somebody is outside our door," Todd said, poking his head into the little back room where Peppers was still working with his pencil in hand.

"Go get the shotgun from beneath the bar and make sure it's loaded," Peppers said, closing the books and dousing the single desk candle by squeezing the flame out with his fingers.

While Todd fumbled with putting shells into the gun and a few extra shells into his trouser pocket, Peppers grabbed matches and an old blasting cap that for weeks had been sitting in the saloon exchange drawer.

Months ago Russell Means had given a meal to one of his prospecting customers down on his luck and taken the dynamite stick in trade.

About 10 different times Means had said he had meant to take the dynamite home, but instead there it still sat in the same drawer with the other odds and ends Means had received in trade for a meal or a drink, including a pair of wooden dentures.

Todd and Peppers then met up to quickly formulate a plan of whether to try to hold their ground within the saloon or use their weapons and make a break for the church less than a quarter mile away.

Before Todd and Peppers were able to come to any sort of agreement, their decision was made for them when the front door to the saloon burst open, revealing an imposing figure in a black cape.

"Are you open?" the vampire mocked.

Before the attacker could complete his sentence, Todd and Peppers, were scurrying for the back delivery door to the saloon in making their getaway to the church.

Chapter 59

The attacker, seeking his prey, glided across the hardwood floor of the saloon like it were glass, his footsteps eerily not making a single sound.

What better way to get Sheriff Wily's full attention than to take out another member of the Means family, thought the vampire.

Todd and Peppers, frantic in getting the saloon back door unlatched and opened, had given the vampire the time needed in closing the distance between him and his prey.

Todd and Peppers ran out of the saloon like it was on fire, Peppers trailing the younger Todd, with the cold, lifeless breath of their pursuer blowing down his neck.

Realizing there was little chance for the both of them to make it safely to the church, the out-of-breath Peppers urged Todd to keep running, in turn hoping the step he had on the vampire would be all the time he needed to strike a match from off his boot top, and light the dynamite stick he held firmly in his hand.

"There," Peppers said, relieved at finally seeing the short fuse spark. All there was to do now was to turn and face his attacker, with the hope of the attacker reaching him at about the same time the dynamite exploded.

A rollicking BOOM sent dirt and pieces of Peppers into the night air with the force of a Texas twister.

It all happened so fast, Todd heard the blast and felt the percussion from it in his feet as he ran, fearing if he looked over his shoulder, the vampire would still be chasing him. Being young and in fairly good shape from handling constant chores assigned by his mother, Todd was able to cover a lot of ground as the last of the debris sent skyward by the explosion fell back to earth.

Nearly in shock, Todd realized his dad's best friend, Ever Peppers, had just joined his father in that big card game in the sky.

The church was now only 100 yards away. Todd made certain each of his long-legged strides counted. Within 50 yards of the church, Todd began yelling at the top of his lungs for Parsons to open the door. As thunderous as Peppers' blast sounded and felt, Todd still remained uncertain whether the dynamite had slowed their foe.

"Parsons open up," Todd screamed still carrying the shotgun. When he reached the door, it remained closed and locked, forcing him to begin beating on it like a child.

Looking over his shoulder, Todd could see a figure fast approaching, and it wasn't Peppers. The vampire had survived the blast, his cloak, now a little tattered and dusty, but the determined look on his face just as menacing.

There was a scuffling noise from the other side of the church door. Someone had heard his cries and was in the process of unlatching the door.

"Hurry, please hurry," Todd screamed through the door standing between him and safety.

At the same time the door cracked opened and someone reached from within the church to grab Todd's arm, the vampire reached Todd, firmly latching onto his shoulder.

The two forces, good and evil, were now pulling on him at the same time, as if he were a piece of saltwater taffy.

"God, help me," Todd cried, pleading for some divine intervention.

The shotgun he was carrying fell to the porch.

Chapter 60

Parsons pulled Todd through the narrow opening in the church door with enough force to rip the worn cotton shirt Todd was wearing right off his back.

The vampire held in his right hand what remained of the shirt, while Todd was able to safely slip inside the church.

To get the door shut behind Todd, Parsons momentarily flashed his wooden cross into the open door space, while using his other hand to stick a small wooden stake into the hand the vampire had been able to reach inside the door.

Sticking the stake into the vampire's hand drew a shrieking reaction, with the creature quickly withdrawing his hand from the door opening.

Once the door was shut, Parsons yelled out to his son John to help him latch it by sliding a plank back in place. Parsons and his son then moved Todd away from the door, fearing their fight with the vampire may not be over.

"Parsons, you are a dead man," the vampire painfully squealed on the other side of the closed church door.

Parsons let out a deep sigh and crossed himself in a silent prayer. His son John followed his father's example.

"Good thing your shirt gave," Parsons told a bare-chested Todd, while Todd returned thanks and praise on the pastor, who the whole town was beginning to appreciate a whole lot more.

In response to Todd's gratitude, Parsons merely pointed skyward to the heavens, saying nothing, while catching his breath.

"I'll be in church Sunday," Todd said, patting Parsons on the chest.

"It is the work of the Lord that saved you, not I," Parsons said, grateful to find Todd safe.

"Peppers is dead. I heard the explosion. It shook the ground," Todd said.

Parsons nodded as if he already knew. The pastor was sleeping in the connecting house portion of the church when he heard the explosion. It wasn't until he heard Todd screaming that he thought there might be a survivor from the blast.

"You can sleep here for the night. We'll go out come sunlight," Parsons said, rubbing his hand through Todd's already messed-up hair. "Bless you, my son," he added solemnly.

Upon that, Todd hung his head and began to cry.

"Your mother will be relieved you are still among us," Parsons said, trying to console the boy.

While Parsons was outwardly trying to console the teen, he worried inwardly who would be a comfort to himself. The town's rising body count had begun to even rattle Parson's faith.

CHAPTER 61

The headline read: PEPPERS BLASTS VAMPIRE, SAVES TEEN.

Sheriff Wily was in a snarly mood as he looked over the one-foot indentation in the dirt where Peppers made his last stand. Outside of a few tattered pieces of clothing here and there, there was not enough left of Peppers to fill a shoe box.

Wily heard the explosion but arrived late to the scene, armed with his pistol and a shotgun he had packed over his back using a sleeve.

The earth where Peppers once stood was scorched black. It was as if the explosion had vaporized most of him. Yet it apparently did little to the charging vampire who was able to recover and chase down Todd.

The whole scene was beginning to give Wily a heavy dose of guilt, where he suspected he was the individual responsible for bringing this curse on the town.

Wily never imagined the bizarre stranger he crossed paths with in St. Louis County, Missouri, would have tracked him this far west. In recalling the encounter, Wily was digging up memories he thought he had permanently buried.

The late Sheriff Pete Cochran and he had gone to the riverbanks of the Mississippi River to check on a man living in what resembled a circus wagon. Fur traders working that stretch of river had come into St. Louis city proper complaining of the man rumored to be dealing in black magic. The fur traders said the stranger, who kept to himself during the day, ran wild at night.

According to stories, there were even a few fur traders who had approached the stranger, never to be heard from again.

The odd man, dressed like a traveling salesman, was not alone. There was a younger woman living with him in the wagon he had brought to a rest in a heavy wooded clearing near the river's edge.

No one knew for certain how long the man had been camped there.

Wily could recall when Cochran and he entered the camp it was nightfall, the stranger having a low fire. Based on rumors of the man's odd behavior, Sheriff Cochran insisted Wily and he split up in entering the camp from different directions. Their intent was to have the stranger leave the area at first light.

But in drawing closer to the unnatural looking man and the beautiful young woman, who seemed mesmerized with her beau, things quickly went from calm to chaotic.

Sheriff Cochran, in getting within 20 feet of the couple, was immediately charged by the stranger. Reacting, Cochran drew his pistol and began firing without warning.

The blast of gunfire from point-blank range did nothing to slow down the man, who struck Cochran with the force of a mighty wind, sending him flying backwards through the air and nearly out of the campsite before landing.

Wily, out of instinct, also drew his pistol and began firing, hoping to catch the stranger off guard. It was then that the beautiful young woman running to the aid of the odd-looking man took a bullet in the back, suffering a vicious wound.

Seeing the woman fall to the ground in a shout of pain, the stranger became enraged, turning his anger on the person closest to him, who at the time was Cochran, who was back on his feet making his second charge at the creature.

The stranger latched onto Cochran's shoulders with his hand before placing the sheriff in a one-hand choke-hold in an effort to squeeze the life out of him. In trying to save Cochran, Wily fired his last two rounds into the back of the cloaked man. But like before, the shots had no effect. Wily then rushed to the campfire, grabbing from it a half-burned log, bouncing it off of the top of the head of the stranger, sending embers into the night air.

But the attacker was unfazed by Wily's effort, while Cochran continued to frantically thrash about in an effort to break the grasp of his killer.

As a last resort, Wily tried to pry the attacker's hand off the throat of the sheriff.

"You're killing him," Wily yelled. It was then the attacker turned and backhanded Wily across his face with his razor-sharp fingernails. The blow knocked Wily to the ground and opened a large wound down the left side of his face.

Wily instinctively put his hand up to the wound, it coming away blood red.

The stranger then turned his full attention back on Cochran, now barely holding onto life.

Using his shirt sleeve to wipe the blood from his face, Wily scrambled to his feet, deciding then to flee from what appeared to be a hopeless situation. His hope was while the stranger was preoccupied with Cochran, and his dying love, he would be able to reach the nearby river.

Wily recalled looking back over his shoulder one last time, seeing the odd man holding in his arms his dying love that Wily had unintentionally shot during the melee. Cochran's body lay motionless near the pair.

Wily ran, uncertain whether the suspect would follow, his running taking him to a 20-foot cliff, which he jumped from down into the cold river below.

It was Wily's hope the cold river water would slow the flow of blood coming from his wound until he could find someone nearby who could crudely stitch it up for him. It wasn't long after that he came upon a fur trapper who helped treat his wound in exchange for his deputy badge.

From there, Wily took the long road that eventually led him to Dry Springs.

It had been just over two years since that night. But the memory was once again as fresh in Wily's mind as a loaf of Shirley Parsons's baked bread.

CHAPTER 62

"**W**here were you?" Wily said, directing his question at his newest hire.

"I didn't see a thing," Ike Peterson said defensively. "How would I have known Todd and Peppers were in trouble?"

"And Crazy Max?" Wily asked, annoyed his prisoner had escaped.

"It was dark, Sheriff, and Crazy Max and that vampire creature likely did all their dealing when I was safeguarding the other side of town," Ike said, the rising sun shining on his face.

"You seen those iron bars. They are all twisted like rope in there," Ike said, pointing toward the jail office. "Personally, Sheriff, I think we're in over our heads here," he added.

Wily winced at hearing the words, scowling at Ike, the two men exchanging stares just a few feet from where Peppers had given his life to save the boy.

Even if Ike Peterson was right, Wily figured, he didn't want to hear that they were in over their heads, especially from someone like Ike.

"Sheriff, Ike did all he could do," Ajacks said, trying to break the tension between Ike and Wily that appeared to go well beyond them being just two bantering cowboys.

The conversation between the three lawmen abruptly stopped upon them hearing the mumblings of Parsons, who had walked out into the street to offer a semi-silent prayer over the site where Peppers had died.

Out of respect for Parsons and Peppers, the lawmen remained silent, with Wily and Ajacks removing their hats.

After the brief prayer, when only the gentle rustle of the fall breeze could be heard, Ike Peterson reignited his verbal sparring with Wily. "You're just annoyed Crazy Max took out of here and took with him $75 of your money."

"You watch your tone with me," Wily warned, emphasizing his message by pointing at Ike Peterson as if he were a child. Wily had reached the end of his rope, feeling both frustrated and helpless against a creature that had tracked him across the country for one of the oldest motives in the book, revenge.

"So, what's next, Sheriff?" Ajacks asked trying to get the attention of Wily and break off the stare down he had going with Ike Peterson.

"I don't know," Wily responded, not realizing he was rubbing the scar on his face.

Chapter 63

Finger-flipping the silver dollar and watching the coin spin on its edge on the oak desk until it came to a tumbling stop, only to repeat the process, was proving to serve as a bit of therapy for Wily.

There he sat behind his office desk, staring at the bent iron bars of the jail cell, a stark reminder of what he was up against.

The sheriff had so many secrets buried inside him that he was about to combust.

Wily had little holding him to Dry Springs. He had no children; he had no wife. The only thing keeping him in Dry Springs now was his unwillingness to run a second time from the monster.

Prior to becoming a sheriff's deputy in Missouri, Wily worked for a man who operated a ferry service across the Missouri River. There, those heading West, excited about a new beginning, would board the wooden ferry and traverse the river that always ran with a strong current. Wily was but a young man, and pulling on the rope to move the ferry back and forth across the river had made him strong and accustomed to hard, physical labor.

It was in working for the ferry service, Wily witnessed two bandits rob a family of their belongings. He remembered the family pleading for their lives as they were held at gunpoint, turning over all their treasures in the hope it would keep them safe.

Wily was unarmed and felt helpless looking on, questioning the justice of it all. The father eagerly complied with the bandits, but in spite of it, the bandits shot and killed the man. Prior to riding off, the bandits warned the surviving family members just how tough the West was, and not just anyone had better enter.

That was the last day Wily went without a gun belt.

Now, once again, he had taken a solemn oath to protect those under attack.

Wily's intention was that he was not going to be backing down a second time, as he gave the silver dollar on his desk another hard flick with his finger, sending it spinning.

There had to be a way out of this, he thought.

CHAPTER 64

Stan Peterson could still hear the ringing in his ears from the dynamite blast he had encountered. That was his first experience with someone trying to blow him up.

Over the years, people had tried to kill him with all manner of weapons, mostly guns.

One man doused him with water, thinking he was a witch. That only served to get him wet and annoyed. Another tried to push a boulder from a cliff over on top of him. It narrowly missed. Had it hit him, it likely would have done little harm to his powerful frame. The man they call Squeak netting him when he was in winged creature form was also a new experience. But the dynamite blast from the previous night had left him with a lingering headache, his ears ringing like the bells at the church, a place he religiously avoided.

Stan, whose real name was Roman Oscuro, came from a long line of vampires having been cursed by his father Mickel Oscuro. Mickel had been cursed by his father Nikoli Oscuro.

The Italian family curse, passed down from generation to generation, had become a staple for the Oscuro family, who was able to use the dark powers to their advantage in gaining independence and wealth.

Mickel Oscuro sent his son to America to take advantage of the growing wealth in the somewhat backwards nation.

It was his father's hope that someday he would be able to share his riches, and curse, in having children of his own. But Sheriff Wily had unknowingly interfered with his plan when he took the life of Beth, the only woman Roman had ever loved. Beth was merely days away from making her full transformation into a vampire. Had that been the case, Wily's reckless shooting would have proved to be useless against her, and Roman would have never heard of the dirty little town known as Dry Springs.

But now that he was here, his prideful thoughts had turned to capturing what wealth the town had to offer, including a new potential bride, all while taking out a priceless act of revenge on his nemesis.

Roman and his drifter friend, whose real name was Ike Fuller, had been put up at the Peterson place, which was sitting empty. In ransacking the home, the pair found Darwin and Mabel Peterson had acquired a great deal of wealth, some of which was stored away in a strong box tucked inside their bedroom wall.

In addition to the coins, the Petersons, who had gone missing months prior to Roman and Ike's arrival, possessed some gold.

Posing as Darwin and Mabel Peterson's children was proving to be the perfect cover for Roman and Ike.

It was a plan that had nearly been foiled before it began, when a relative of the Peterson family had come to town to settle the estate. However, Ike quickly made that individual disappear, preserving their secret.

Besides, the home provided the pair with the comforts they desired and the solitude needed in keeping Roman's nighttime habits secret. It also put them within striking distance of Wily.

It only added another layer of revenge to Roman's plan that Wily was town sheriff.

Over the few weeks the pair had been in Dry Springs, Roman and Ike had been successful in selling off most of the Peterson's assets to people in the small neighboring towns. That put a great deal of much-needed cash into their pockets, where Roman or Ike had not been regularly working before Ike landed his deputy job.

But what the pair hadn't counted on was local town members meddling in their affairs, particularly the newspaperman.

Jef seem to relish the role of sticking his nose in the business of others.

However, they would soon be rid of Jef at the hands of Crazy Max, who currently lay asleep in the spare bedroom awaiting Roman's next order.

"How much longer are we going to stay? I don't want to play deputy sheriff anymore," Ike whined after only a few days on the job.

"In a few more days we should be out of here," Roman replied. "I have a few things that need finishing up."

"Well, we had better hurry. Wily is going to start grousing as a result of losing out on his prisoner and the reward money that was to come with him," Ike said.

Roman laughed. "Can you image the look on Wily's face when he saw the bars bent into the shape of an hourglass?" he asked.

"But first, Mister Furst," Roman said. "When sleepy Max awakes, give him a weapon and directions as to where he can find Jef during the nighttime hours. While Max is visiting the Furst family, I have a girl in town I have to see," he said with a sneer.

"You are evil to the bone," Ike said.

"And because of it, you, a common drifter, have money in your pocket, food in your belly and a roof overhead. I expect you to remember that," Roman said, wagging his long, pale white finger with its long nail in Ike's face.

"I haven't forgotten. And If I did, I'm certain you would remind me," Ike said, always one for having a smart mouth. "But just a warning, the longer we stay here, the better chance of them discovering what we are up to," he added.

"You worry too much," Roman replied. "Besides, what are they going to do, sic Wily on us?" he laughed. "Now, go away Ike. I've got a headache I need to sleep off," Roman said, making his way to a brass rail four-poster bed the Petersons owned that he insisted Ike not yet liquidate for cash.

CHAPTER 65

Crazy Max was beginning to feel the first effects of his transformation from human to vampire. Since Roman had applied the bite to his neck in the jail cell, he had noticed an increase in his strength and energy. But his dull brown eyes had become sensitive to any natural light.

It would still be a few more days before his full transformation into a vampire would occur, Crazy Max had been told. But being an outlaw on the run, he was impatient. The sooner he took care of the newspaperman for the Peterson brothers, the sooner he was out of Dry Springs and away from Wily. Even though he had every bit of confidence in Roman to be able to handle Wily based on what he had seen.

But staying with the Peterson brothers was eerie. The two appeared to have loyalty to no one and did not include him in any of their conversations.

Everything that was shared amongst the two men was done in whispers, making Max's skin crawl.

The Peterson's plan was for him to strike tonight. Max figured a task he had to complete to avoid Roman and Ike's wrath. He was well aware he could not afford to disappoint his two new friends.

Chapter 66

The auburn hair on Prudy's shoulder barely twitched under the crisp fall breeze. The sun had cracked over the eastern mountains that lined Dry Springs.

Sitting on the bench behind the schoolhouse, Prudy and Ajacks seemed to hear the sound of every chirping bird that called the desert home. Despite the world falling down around them, the couple was doing everything they could to remain intact. This morning they were enjoying homemade cinnamon biscuits, a recipe Prudy had been experimenting with for some time before daring to have Ajacks sample it.

The undercooked biscuits were a little doughy, but Ajacks was smart enough not to mention it. He had learned over the last several weeks how the game of love was played.

The two sat side by side on the bench Squeak had handcrafted for the schoolyard, holding hands and chatting about their future.

"Prudy, these are some tasty biscuits," Ajacks said, swallowing hard to get the last piece of biscuit to slide down his throat and into his belly.

"Would you like another?" Prudy asked so sweetly Ajacks nearly said yes.

"If I eat any more, I'm not going to be able to run down bad guys," Ajacks said, out of habit rubbing the handle of his six-shooter.

Ajacks's mention of bad guys and his halfhearted effort at humor had brought the model-looking couple back to their present-day problems.

"What are we going to do, Ajacks?" Prudy asked, her eyes pleading for an answer.

Ajacks didn't know how to respond. He knew he didn't want to lie to her, and he didn't want to destroy the peaceful moment they were having.

Before he could respond, she was back at it.

"We need to leave town. Find us a new life, a better place. Somewhere where I can teach and you can be a lawman," Prudy said. "Maybe back east, Boston. I have an aunt living there."

"I can't leave Sheriff Wily at a time like this," Ajacks said, again instinctively rubbing his pistol handle.

"You hardly know Wily, Ajacks. He has only lived here for a short time," Prudy said. "It isn't like that we go about visiting with him."

"But Wily is the first person who didn't see me as some kid with a gun. He gave me responsibility, some pride. And if it weren't for this badge, Prudy Richards, you would have likely looked the other way when I came calling," he added.

Prudy's eyes bubbled with tears momentarily in hearing Ajacks's words, partly because she knew they had a ring of truth in them.

"Let's marry then," Prudy said looking into Ajacks's eyes. "Oh, I know I'm being forward when I ask, but why wait? Let's marry, and be happy like Jef and Lola," she added.

"Kids too?" Ajacks said with a panicked look on his face.

"Well, if you want we can wait for children. But we shouldn't have to wait for marriage," Prudy said, softly rubbing her hands through Ajacks's hair.

Ajacks gulped, and not because of the earlier biscuit.

"Prudy, I'd be honored to have you as my wife. I just want you to be certain I'm what you want," said Ajacks, who generally never lacked for confidence. But at this moment talk of marriage had made him weak in the knees and tongue.

"I love you, Ajacks," Prudy said, squeezing his hand tighter and planting a kiss on the side of his face. "We could have Parsons perform the ceremony," she said, pressing the matter. On other occasions Prudy had dropped hints of wanting to marry. But she had never applied such pressure as she was now.

Ajacks was fumbling for words, wishing he still had one of those cinnamon biscuits in his mouth. He feared his facial expression was giving him away, sending a signal to the girl he loved that he didn't know what to say next. So he said what most men say when they have no real answer to a woman's emotional questions.

"Can we talk about this later?" Ajacks asked his heart beating so hard inside his chest it seemed it was shaking the pine wood bench the pair was sitting on.

"We can talk later, but that isn't going to change my feelings about you," Prudy said, trying to prevent any delay in furthering their courtship.

"Let's go have another biscuit before I have to get off to work," Ajacks said, sounding more like a punch-drunk brawler than the tough deputy he portrayed.

"Biscuits it is, for now," Prudy said disappointedly.

Chapter 67

The wooden stake flew straight and fast, hitting the hand-drawn target dead center.

It seemed Squeak had given the ammo new life having added weight to the stakes by carving a niche into them and filling the opening with hot lead.

It wasn't like Lola's shooting needed much help.

"Man, you can shoot," Jef said. "Maybe you should be the one hunting the vampire."

Even facing the sun, Lola was able to fire the wooden stakes and hit the center of the target 20 feet away with regularity.

Jef, well, his shooting, albeit improved, left much to be desired. PING. There would be a hit. PING. And there would be a complete miss.

Jef's hands often shook when he shot, regardless of which hand he used.

Lola hated shooting with Jef because she generally had to round up his misses.

While the couple continued to practice behind their house, the children played nearby, giving Ranger a full workout as they had the dog fetch what stakes their parents weren't using.

James Jr. would throw the stake as far as he could, with Ranger pouncing on it within seconds of it finding ground. On occasion, to show off, Ranger would leap, plucking the stake from out of the air.

It seemed Ranger had also found new life in being reunited with Gibby's horse, Stu, after Jef had been the only town member to make a claim for the old horse.

Jef figured the only reason Sheriff Wily personally delivered the horse to their house was because he was tired of having to feed and water the animal himself. But James Jr. and Bobby loved the fact they now had a horse to ride.

The only thing standing in the way of the Furst family being totally content was the dark cloud in the form of a vampire hanging over the town.

Jef had ceased writing newspaper articles about the town's murders in trying to find some peace with Sheriff Wily and Ajacks. However, Deputy Ike remained ornery towards him.

Jef figured he best remain quiet for a few days about the murders while Parsons, Squeak and he worked on a better plan to rid Dry Springs of its vampire problem using the weapons Squeak had crafted.

Should word leak out about the weapons, which Parsons and Squeak were also practicing in secret with, Jef was fearful it might put the three men in peril.

Having Lola as his personal instructor, Jef realized, served as an advantage for him. But his progress was still slow. And each shot, an education.

PING, the guitar string would zing, flinging the stake at a high rate of speed at the target. Jef had wanted his children to also practice using the weapon, but Lola said absolutely not. Lola's thinking was if Jef, Ranger and she couldn't handle the vampire through their practice and prayers, then shame on them.

At night Jef continued with his study of his scriptures, particularly in Luke, Chapter One, verse 37, which reminded him that with God all things are made possible. In his Book of Mormon he also read that those who do their best to live a good life are encircled about in the robe of God's righteousness.

Jef figured that was what he needed, a robe of righteousness to hide behind while taking shots at the vampire. A fight, he knew now, he should have never had picked.

His arrogance for wanting to succeed as a newspaperman had put his family in harm's way. A selfish act, Jef realized, that his father would have scolded him about.

But despite all the sorrow the town had experienced—many good people having been lost—Lola stood firm in wanting to continue to live in Dry Springs and farm the land her parents had given her.

"These will work, Lola. We just have to get close enough," Jef said, taking aim and firing another wooden stake at the target pinned to the stacked hay bales.

PING. Jef's shot completely missed the target, but hit the hay bales.

Lola sighed.

"I know of no man who has more faith than you, James Edward Furst. Now exercise that faith and envision yourself being able to protect yourself and your family by hitting that target," Lola said, stoking her husband's confidence like one would stoke a coal-burning stove.

"You know the opportunity will present itself to take this monster down," Lola said, giving Jef a wink and a flirty nod.

"Now, don't go making me more flustered than I already am," Jef said, "or I am going to miss."

"You'll likely miss anyway," Lola teased, her dark brown hair flipping about with every turn of her head.

Jef said no more and fired the weapon.

PING.

"Closer," Jef crowed, pumping his fist as if he had just roped a steer.

The children, who were busily playing, stopped long enough to see what their father had done. "Hooray, Daddy," the pair screamed, young Bobby following the cries of his older brother.

"See what I mean," Lola said, her smile sending him a signal that someday Jef would have this ol' West thing whipped.

"Beans and rice," Jef said, who at moments like this was happy with his decision to leave his family's trek to Salt Lake City to join Lola at the bottom of the territory and start a family. Although Jef still missed his family.

"Give it to me," Lola said, holding out her hand for the weapon, with Jef turning it over to her.

PING.

"Bull's-eye," Lola said confidently.

"Hooray, Mom," the children yelled once again, but not nearly as loud or as quickly as they did for their father. They had become accustomed to their mother getting bull's-eyes. Yet, the children, being so young, had no idea why their parents were regularly playing with the toy Squeak had built for them.

Chapter 68

Ranger's non-stop barking in the direction of the field had become annoying.

Jef was already grumbling about having to clean the barn so late in the day. It was a chore Lola insists he perform. He was just grateful they had few livestock to care for.

Having practiced with Squeak's weapon most of the day, Jef had neglected some of the work needing to be done around the property. One of those unenviable tasks was cleaning the horse stalls.

Taking more time than he thought he might in tidying up, Jef had swung the barn door wide open to let the last light of the setting sun in.

Tidy is the way things were in the Furst household, particularly if the work was to meet with Lola's approval. She had a keen eye for wanting things just so. It was a trait that at times worked Jef's patience. That is why at his office he enjoyed letting things go. His desk so cluttered, that at any moment the pile of newspapers stacked on it could topple like some old barn under the weight of snow.

Squeak, whom Jef shared office space with, was even less tidy, having many unfinished projects scattered about.

"A slothful person is an offender of God," Lola would tell Jef. But finding that exact scripture in the Bible he possessed was something Jef had yet to accomplish.

"It's in the scriptures there somewhere," Lola would charge. And if it wasn't, the feisty woman would rationalize her claim: "If it isn't in there, it is likely due to someone's slothfulness."

Even the smell of the manure under his nose couldn't prevent Jef from smiling as he reflected on his wife's peculiarities.

And it was Mormons who were considered a peculiar people, Jef thought with a laugh.

While Jef was lost in thought, Ranger's barking had intensified, with the dog now taking a more defensive position just outside the open barn door.

"Please," Jef pleaded with his noisy friend as he lifted another shovelful of manure from the stall, then walked it out of the barn and sprinkled it over the ground where the family would be gardening come spring.

Ranger's temperament had taking an unusual twist. The dog's incessant barking had now turned into guttural growls. The kind of growls the dog first exhibited when Jef found him near Gibby's burned-out wagon.

"What's up with you?" Jef asked Ranger, the two looking out over the property, partially filled with chest-high corn and wheat.

It was dusk, but not yet dark, so Jef dismissed the thought that the town's vampire could be close by.

"What is it?" Jef asked Ranger, who pitched his ears up and then down again.

Jef pushed his wire-rimmed eyeglasses farther up onto the bridge of his nose to get even a closer inspection of his property, all while holding his empty shovel in hand.

Everything appeared quiet. Lola's horse, Windy, and Stu, were both lazily chomping on some grass in the nearby pasture.

The setting sun highlighted a silhouette of their little house. Fresh wisps of smoke were escaping from the chimney of the cabin where Lola was preparing one of his favorites: black bean and tortilla soup.

"I don't see anything," Jef said impatiently to Ranger, questioning the dog's mood.

No sooner had Jef shared his sentiment with his canine friend than he spotted in the field at a distance a flash of bright yellow, like someone was wearing a bright banana-yellow hat or possibly a yellow bandana.

Then the yellow flash was gone as fast as it had appeared, lost in the setting sun.

Jef gave Ranger a passing glance before taking a few steps farther away from the barn and out into the yard.

From there, Jef could pretty well see the layout of the land. There was no movement now. Yet he had still not convinced himself to take the shovel he was tightly holding onto back to the barn in getting another shovel of manure.

And then he spotted something that alarmed him. "Did you see that?" Jef asked Ranger. But before he could finish his question, Ranger gave him a resounding yes by going into full protection mode, snarling, snapping and growling toward the same direction Jef was now looking.

The degree of Ranger's viciousness even raised old Stu's head up from the pasture grass.

"There is definitely someone out there," Jef said, his armpits filling with nervous sweat.

The yellow flash Jef had seen was a bandana, with the man wearing it moving closer to where Ranger and he stood.

"Squeak?" Jef called out, hoping it were his friend. But he got no response.

"Ajacks?" Jef called, wanting to eliminate whoever he could from the list of their occasional visitors.

"Sheriff Wily?" Jef called, again getting no response.

The man wearing the yellow bandana was now running in a crouch, trying to flank Jef and Ranger on the right. Whoever it was didn't appear friendly, causing Jef to wonder if the man was preparing to attack once the sun set.

"We had better make our way back to the house," Jef told Ranger. But that plan was thwarted when the man in the yellow bandana cut off their route.

CHAPTER 69

"To the barn," Jef warned Ranger. His shovel in hand now being carried more like a weapon than a gardening tool.

"We'll have a better chance there," Jef said without breaking stride. His heart racing like it had the night Parsons, Thumper, Squeak and he went vampire hunting.

The figure chasing after them appeared to be no vampire. This attacker moved more like a desperate man than a monster. In spite of that, the man in the yellow bandana was gaining on them.

Running full speed toward the barn in hopes of getting the door shut behind him in time, a frightened Jef began to pray under his breath. In his short but fervent prayer Jef asked for strength and speed before closing his prayer with a solid amen.

Ranger was right by his side.

"James Edward Furst, you're dead," their pursuer called out.

By then Jef and Ranger were only a few feet from the open barn door. Had Jef not left the door swung wide open, he was certain their attacker would have caught them in the yard.

As soon as Ranger and he were in the barn, Jef quickly began to pull the big red wooden door shut behind them using its inside wooden handle. Lola had told Jef probably a hundred times to tighten the handle. Now the shaky, loose wooden handle with the weak wooden screws was all that stood between Ranger and him and an apparent killer.

Before Jef could get the barn door closed, the attacker managed to wedge his foot in the doorway, preventing it from closing and, more importantly, preventing Jef from being able to latch the door shut to secure their safety.

Ranger, in a rage, buried his teeth into the exposed boot of the attacker, causing the man to yell out in pain.

"Both of you are dead," Jef heard their attacker scream through the narrow opening in the doorway.

Ranger was relentless, releasing and then re-burying his teeth even deeper into the attacker's boot, wildly shaking his head back and forth to get the bite grip he was after.

While Ranger was mangling the man's boot, Jef was doing all he could to find the footing he needed to keep the barn door from being pried open.

Despite Jef and Ranger's best efforts, the attacker managed to squeeze his left arm inside the door, giving him additional leverage in trying to pry it open.

It then dawned on Jef who their attacker was. Based on wanted posters he had seen in the area, their attacker was none other than Crazy Max Dooley, who had slipped through the bars of Sheriff Wily's jail cell. But what did Max want with him?

Whatever it was now was not the time to be asking.

Jef began using his right hand to beat on Max's left arm with the pointed end of the long-handled shovel he was still packing.

The shovel raised large red welts on Max's bare arm but drew little blood.

"What is it you want?" Jef screamed through the door's narrow opening while continuing to keep pressure on the door in preventing it from flying open. Jef was already beginning to tire from the fight, sweat filling the palm of his left hand as he tried to maintain a grip on the wobbly door latch.

Max offered no words, continuing in his tug-of-war with Jef over the barn door, while Ranger continued to gnaw away on Max's boot, reshaping its pointed toe.

And then there was a loud SNAP.

The inside door latch handle gave way, sending the barn door flying open like a rodeo chute, allowing Max to stumble into the barn.

Chapter 70

"**I know who** you are," Jef said accusingly, dropping the door latch in his right hand to the ground and cocking his shovel back in preparation of taking a swing at Max. But before he could land the shovel head on his enemy, his swing was interrupted by Max tackling him, sending them both tumbling to the ground just inside the barn.

Jef was out of breath, his glasses hanging from one ear and his shovel out of reach, resting a few feet away.

In all the commotion, Jef could still hear Ranger's snarls and growls. The dog having sunk his teeth into the lower leg of Max, who lay on top of Jef.

Max grimaced but had the presence of mind to keep Jef pinned beneath him while reaching for a knife he had tucked in his boot.

Ranger, sensing Jef was in trouble, repositioned himself around the two-man pile, latching on to Max's right hand, forcing him to drop the knife to his side. But even then Max remained in control, as Jef and he continued to roll across the barn floor in their impromptu wrestling match.

While Jef and Max were grappling for position, Ranger remained tenacious, circling the pair, every chance he got jumping in and inflicting a new bite wound to Max's legs or back. Meanwhile, Jef continued to flail like a fish out of water, trying to get out from underneath Max.

Ranger then changed his approach, nipping at Max's face, causing the attacker to raise an arm to shield him from the impending bite.

The move by Ranger was just what Jef needed in breaking free from Max's grasp, giving him the time needed to roll away in getting back to his feet. But in making his move, Jef lost his glasses amongst the scattered hay in the barn.

Despite having difficulty seeing, Jef began to search for his shovel, while Max dropped to his knees in rummaging through the hay to find the knife Ranger forced him to drop.

Once Jef was reunited with his shovel, he began swinging it wildly at Max, catching him on the shoulder with his first swing, whacking him in the head with his second swing.

Connecting on a few swings with the shovel, Jef had made time to reach down and snatch back up the wooden door handle, which he wrapped his bare fingers around in filling his fist with something that would give him some punching power.

But by the time Jef turned back to the fight, even without his glasses he could see Max had found his knife and was now brandishing it at him.

"It's you or me, buddy," Max said, knowing there was no way he could return to Roman Oscuro having failed to rid Dry Springs of its newspaperman.

Meanwhile, Ranger was relentless, continuing his assault on Max from every direction. From the side, then from the back, darting at Max's feet, letting Jef know he was not in this fight alone.

Max then changed fight strategy, kicking hard at Ranger before bolting for Jef with his knife in hand.

Panicking, Jef ran at Max at a full sprint, hitting his attacker with a hard push and a low flying tackle, enabling him to duck under the outstretched knife, causing the two men to spill back out into the barnyard.

The sun had not yet set, leaving just enough light for both combatants to find the other.

Before Max could regain his footing from Jef's unexpected charge, Jef moved in, throwing a right punch to Max's head with the hand wrapped around the broken wooden latch, the force of the blow causing Max to stagger, but not lose his feet. But Jef's second punch landed square on Max's jaw, causing his attacker's knees to buckle.

All those years steadying the plow behind the horse was beginning to pay dividends, Jef thought.

Hitting Max hurt Jef's hand, but the first two blows made the third blow easier. This time Jef punched Max deep in his midsection, hoping it would be softer than Max's head.

The air escaped Max's lungs like a dust storm, as the punches continued to back his attacker up.

Jef was gaining confidence: His fourth and fifth punches landed with precision to Max's face, with Max's nose cracking under the crunch of the one-sided fistfight.

The sixth and final punch, an uppercut, sent Crazy Max Dooley to the dirt, his body thudding to the ground, raising a small cloud of dust in the barnyard.

Jef was out of breath, his knuckles scraped, bruised and bleeding from the force of the blows inflicted on Max.

Ranger looked on with approval.

Realizing Crazy Max Dooley was merely stunned, not knocked out, Jef rushed back into the barn grabbing the needed rope to tie up Dooley. Maybe Sheriff Wily and he could share the reward posted for the capture of Max Dooley, he thought.

Jef was just beginning to envision how he would spend the money when he was brought back to the moment by Ranger's barking.

By the time Jef returned from the barn with the rope, Max, whose face was battered from the punches he had absorbed, was back on his feet, preparing to make a wild bull-rush at Jef. In Max's right hand was his knife, the attacker displaying it like it was a pretty girl at a dance.

"Roman and Ike won't have it any other way," said Max, just before beginning his charge.

Then there was a distinctive familiar noise that pierced the commotion in the barnyard.

PING.

Max dropped to the ground like a downed buffalo, 15 feet short of where Jef was standing in preparing for impact. It was as if Max had been hit with a cannonball and stopped dead in his tracks.

The weapon designed by Jef, crafted by Squeak and now in the hands of Lola proved to be effective.

There in the shadows of the rapidly falling sun stood Lola in her cotton dress, her white apron attached, as if she were just completing another chore around the farm.

Her aim as good as she always said it was.

"I heard voices. I came running. I had to do something. I figured it was the vampire," Lola said, nearly in shock as a result of having to shoot Crazy Max with their wooden stake contraption.

"I've never killed a man before," Lola said, almost in a cry. "Nothing like shooting at lizards," she added, still in disbelief at what she had done.

"He would have certainly killed me," Jef said, slowly approaching his wife, taking her empty hand and gently kissing it.

"Thank you," Jef said, opening his right still-clenched fist and letting the latch handle fall from his already swelling right hand.

Seeing it, Lola cracked a grin, before letting a few tears roll down her face. It was the first time that Jef could remember Lola crying since the death of her mother.

"What a toughie," he thought to himself. His whole ordeal with Crazy Max had made it so that he wanted to cry.

"Who is that?" Lola asked, gesturing at the limp body in the yard. "And what did he want with you?"

"That's Crazy Max," Jef replied. "And I don't know what he wanted with me."

The pair then embraced, not far from where Max's body lay. Max's yellow bandana still tied to the top of his head, albeit slightly askew from the fight.

The small wooden stake that had pierced Max's left side near his heart was barely visible from where Jef and Lola stood.

"What a shot," Jef said. "How many of those wooden stakes did you bring with you?" Jef asked, the newspaperman coming out in him.

"One," she replied.

"One?" he exclaimed. "What if you had missed?"

"Ranger would have taken him down," Lola said, using her free hand to tousle her husband's hair.

"One shot?" Jef said, throwing his right arm around his wife. But with the setting sun, the newspaperman was well aware this was not the time to be hugging-it-out with his wife.

Before leaving the scene, Jef threw an old horse blanket he had retrieved from the barn over Max's body lying in the barnyard. Ranger, Lola and he needed to get back to the house where the children were. It was getting dark. And when it was dark in Dry Springs, nothing good happened.

Jef figured it would be easier to care for the dead body and find his eyeglasses in the morning.

As the three made their way to the house, Jef carried the small cross-bow weapon that killed Max, while Lola carried the guilt of having to have had kill a man – even if it was in defending her husband.

Jef's mind was already elsewhere, as he tried to figure out who the Roman and Ike were that Max had mentioned just prior to his charge. Jef figured he had a pretty good idea.

Later that night, while everyone slept, Jef lit a candle and went to the kitchen table to write a letter to his father. Something he hadn't done in months.

Dear Dad,

Tonight Lola and I wrestle with the guilt of having had to kill a man. Although done in self-defense, and law enforcement authorities will be notified, reflecting on the incident doesn't make taking the man's life any easier. Killing a man is nothing like wringing a chicken's neck for Sunday dinner or taking a steer to slaughter for a winter's worth of beef. I am hoping you will be able to give us words that may help in removing this burden from our souls. I have kept the faith, and through prayer have asked my Father in Heaven for the same counsel. My fear is more killings may yet come as our town is under attack from someone who is not of this earth. We have buried many friends here this past week, but Lola and I and the kids remain safe. I pray this letter finds you well and that we may one day be reunited in company.

Miss you both you and mom much, James Edward Furst III.

CHAPTER 71

The lock on the door to the cottage home snapped like a matchstick under the force of Roman Oscuro's hand.

The break-in was done so quietly Oscuro knew his beautiful victim would still be sleeping.

The home was dark. The victim was alone. Her beau, Ajacks, was working the night shift, keeping the town safe. The thought of Ajacks patrolling the streets made Oscuro smirk. What was that old American saying, "While the cat was away, the mice would play," Oscuro thought to himself, gliding across the floor of the cottage to the woman's bedside.

Prudy Richards lay in a deep sleep. Her porcelian-doll face slightly creased from the feather pillow she was laying on. Her small frame appeared almost that of a child.

But this was no child, Oscuro thought. This was his new love and treasure, and it was important he get to know her where she was the woman he would be spending the rest of eternity with.

A woman, who would soon forget any promise or memory of Ajacks she once loved, out of a craving for the vampire's love.

The only thing Oscuro couldn't decide was whether to wake the beauty or inflict his bite while she slept, meeting up with her at a later date when she would desire him more deeply.

In pondering his dilemma, Oscuro took a seat in the pink padded chair situated close to where Prudy lay. There he sat in the dark for a moment, getting lost in what their life together would be like.

Yes, he could envision it, what a beautiful bride she would be.

Then Oscuro pictured his former love, Beth, and how Sheriff Wily had taken her from him with his reckless gunfire. Oh, how quickly a memory can turn someone from love to hate.

The only thing that would have made revenge sweeter would have been had Prudy Richards been Wily's woman. Then the sheriff would have experienced the same agonizing pain Oscuro had felt for the past two years.

But Oscuro didn't care for either Wily or Ajacks, two men who were full of fire and confidence when packing their guns. But now the confidence of the two lawmen was eroding away with each victim buried in the Dry Springs cemetery.

Prudy's stirring brought Oscuro out of his thoughts. But soon the woman, dressed in a rose-colored nightgown, fell back into a slumber, totally unaware she was being studied by the town's most eligible bachelor.

So innocent, what a perfect victim Prudy was. What a perfect soul to steal to help carry his curse, Oscuro thought.

This evening he would leave his bite without waking her. He didn't want to cause her any pain. It would sting for only for a moment, and then after a few days it would change her disposition on life forever.

"My beauty, welcome to my exclusive club," Oscuro whispered, bending down over Prudy and gently sinking his teeth into the right side of her neck.

The sting caused Prudy to flinch and spring up in bed like a wind-up doll. But after seeing no one in the room, she thought it just to be a dream in rubbing the painful spot, not even noticing the splash of blood now on her hand.

Before falling back to sleep, she looked over to her bed stand to see the turquoise necklace Ajacks had given her just a few days earlier. The simplicity and brightness of the necklace reminded her of her love.

Meanwhile, Roman Oscuro quietly exited her home, shutting the door with the broken lock behind him. Even in the shadows Oscuro could be seen smiling, a spot of blood dripping from his unusually white teeth.

What a lucky fellow Ajacks is, Oscuro thought as he purposely wound his way through the streets of Dry Springs, taking the long way home in hopes of running into Deputy Ajacks.

Oscuro had a new girlfriend in Prudy Richards. She just didn't know it yet. He could hardly wait to tell Ike about his new love. It would be only a few days for his bite to take full effect, and then the prettiest girl in town would be his.

Chapter 72

Squeak was sitting on a bench outside his workshop chomping on a tomato fresh from his garden when Jef come riding up on Lola's horse, towing behind him ol' Stu, who was packing what appeared to be a body draped over the side wrapped in a worn bedroll.

Ranger followed after Jef, making it a parade.

At first glance, Squeak, who regularly rose early to catch the sunrise, feared Jef might be packing another victim of the vampire. But on second look, Squeak determined the body in the bedroll was that of Crazy Max Dooley, his yellow bandana poking out of the top of the roll.

For the last 48 hours, Sheriff Wily had been taking Dooley's name in vain. The reward dollars for his capture having slipped through his fingers when the common horse thief slipped out of his cell.

It wasn't until Jef reached the hitching post to tie his horses and unroll a portion of the bedroll Max was wrapped in that the wooden stake could be seen protruding from Max's side. Noticing his handiwork, Squeak began a barrage of questions.

"He's the vampire?" Squeak asked loudly, as if he were about to leap up from the bench where he was sitting and dance.

"This is just Dooley," Jef said, calming his friend.

"But he's got my vampire stake stuck in his side," Squeak said, pointing to the wound as if Jef wasn't aware of it.

"Dooley attacked me last night in my barnyard. Lola shot him with our contraption," Jef said.

"Why did she do that if Dooley's not the vampire?" Squeak asked.

"She didn't know it at the time," Jef said. "Lola heard a commotion in the barnyard and came running with our weapon. One shot, PING, and he was dead," Jef said, gesturing some with his hands in recounting the story.

"I brought the weapon in, because I know Wily is going to ask to see it," Jef said, reaching into his saddlebag and pulling from it the miniature crossbow.

Squeak remained preoccupied. "One shot?" he asked.

"One shot," Jef replied.

"Remind me to never poke fun at your wife's cooking," Squeak offered.

"You know what that means?" Squeak asked. Before Jef could respond, Squeak answered his own question. "It means our weapon works."

"It does at that," Jef said, while working to lift Dooley's body off Stu.

"How close was Lola when she shot Max? Like, 10 feet away or 30 feet away?" Squeak said, begging for details.

"I don't know, maybe 20-25 feet," Jef said. "I was a little busy. Did I tell you Dooley attacked me in my barnyard?" he said with a slight raise in his voice.

"Yeah, that's odd. Why would Dooley attack you? I found your article on him to be accurate, at least what I could read of it," Squeak said.

Jef shrugged, realizing Squeak's simplicity would allow him to live forever.

"Prior to charging me with a knife, Dooley mentioned the names Roman and Ike. He said they would be displeased with him if he didn't kill me," Jef said.

"I don't know a Roman. And the only Ike I know is Ike Peterson," Squeak said matter-of-factly.

Squeak's words struck Jef like lightning.

"I've got to go talk to Wily," Jef said. "Come give me a hand with this body. We'll take it inside to your makeshift morgue before the streets get busy."

"That's unbelievable," Squeak said.

"What's unbelievable?" Jef asked.

"That our weapon works. Wham," Squeak said slapping his right fist into the palm of his left hand. "You must be proud, Jef."

"Delighted - now give me a hand," Jef said impatiently.

As easy as it had been to share his story of Dooley's death with Squeak, Jef realized sharing the same story with Sheriff Wily wasn't going to go nearly as well.

CHAPTER 73

Sheriff Wily was annoyed with Jef and making no secret about it.

Jef had killed Dooley, costing the sheriff $75 in reward money. That was money Wily needed if he was ever going to be able to leave Dry Springs.

Wily was also bothered that Jef, or Lola, shot Crazy Max with a custom-made weapon.

Jef tried to temper some of Wily's frustration by agreeing to split with the sheriff the $25 reward he had coming to him for bringing in Max dead rather than alive.

"The Colorado ranchers will be glad to pay the sum in having rid themselves of the infamous horse thief," Jef pointed out.

The way Jef saw it, the right thing to do was to share the reward money. Crazy Max wouldn't have had been anywhere near Dry Springs had the sheriff not brought him in from Piute country.

But Wily was having a difficult time understanding why Max Dooley had a wooden stake sticking in his side.

The sheriff, along with Ajacks and Ike, had gathered at Squeak's woodworking office to examine the body. Mayor Howard was nowhere to be found.

Ajacks and Ike remained quiet, aside from Ike offering a few snide comments, while the sheriff asked Jef questions. "It appears the barbecue is done," Ike joked. But his attempt at humor did little to break the tension in the room.

"Let me see that weapon again," Wily said in re-examining what resembled a miniature crossbow. "You did this," Wily said, pointing to Dooley's wound, "with this?" he said, holding up the weapon for everyone to see.

Wily's first impression of the deadly weapon was that it resembled a toy. But under closer inspection, he was impressed with its design and craftsmanship.

However, Wily remained a bit suspicious of Jef's account regarding his run in with Crazy Max.

"You're telling me Lola shot him," Wily asked Jef for the third time, hoping his tough questioning was at least impressing his deputies.

"Crazy Max attacked me in my barnyard. Lola shot him just before he was about to stick a knife in me," said Jef, who had also brought Dooley's knife along as evidence to help show the killing was in self-defense.

"And whose knife might that be?" Wily asked Jef.

"I don't know. If you figure that out, you'll likely be able to determine who sent Max to kill me," Jef replied.

Squeak, who remained conspicuously silent during Wily's questioning, nodded in support of Jef's notion.

"Is there anything else I need to know?" Wily asked Jef.

"Well, Crazy Max did…," Jef said, before catching himself mid-sentence and abruptly stopping.

Jef was thinking about sharing with Wily how Crazy Max mentioned the names of a Roman and an Ike. But then the newspaperman thought better of it where Ike was present.

"I am going to have to take possession of your weapon," Wily said, planning to store the wooden stake shooter in the locking storage cabinet in the sheriff's office.

Jef was about to tell the sheriff taking the weapon away from him might be a mistake when Squeak gave Jef one of those passing looks as if to say just let it go.

"The weapon will remain under lock and key, and should any more of these weapons surface, they too will be seized," Wily said, staring down both Jef and Squeak.

"Understand?" Wily asked.

Squeak and Jef both offered a feeble nod and a mumbled "yes."

"I also expect a written statement from your wife to be forthcoming about this whole incident," Wily said, placing his black hat over his thick brown-red hair before stomping out of their office.

The cowbell on the office door clanged hard.

Ajacks and Ike stood silent, with Ike eventually breaking the silence by offering a low, shrill whistle as if to tell Jef he had done it now.

The two deputies then left the office, ringing the same cowbell, leaving Jef and Squeak standing alone.

"Tell Parsons to keep his weapon out of sight of the sheriff. You do the same. Wily finds out we're holding out on him, he is likely to throw us all in jail," Jef said in a whisper.

"What are you going to do next?" Squeak asked.

"What any newspaperman would do," Jef replied. "I've got a story to write, and I'm going to let the whole town know Lola took down Crazy Max, hoping it flushes out whoever put Crazy Max up to killing me," he said.

"Wouldn't it just be easier to poke Wily and his two deputies in the eye with a stick?" Squeak said fully aware Wily was only going to grow angrier with each published account of the vampire saga.

"No worries. Remember, the sheriff can't read," Jef said stubbornly.

"Look, to make sure you and your family remain safe, take my stake shooter," Squeak said, who moved to the center of the office, pulling his shooter from a cubbyhole he had created in the floor boards. "I can craft another. I have a few guitar strings left," Squeak said. "Besides, it's apparent no one knows how to use the weapon like Lola," he said with a smile.

"Amen to that," Jef said.

CHAPTER 74

Prudy's once sapphire eyes now had a muddy look to them. They had lost most of their sparkle. Nonetheless, she remained a beautiful woman.

"Sick?" Ajacks asked Prudy, making his routine visit to her home following his graveyard shift. The sun was just starting to crack over the mountains, beating through the lone window in Prudy's quaint cottage.

"I'm just feeling a little sickly, like a bug has my tongue," she muttered, still lying in bed, her covers nearly pulled up to her chin.

"We still thinking marriage?" Ajacks asked, almost timid with his words. The young cowboy sitting on the edge of Prudy's bed had not been able to push from his mind the romantic conversation the pair had the previous day. Their talk had given him courage and hope, as he envisioned one day they would be able to live normal lives here in Dry Springs.

"Now is not the time for such talk," Prudy responded impatiently, holding her hand up as if to halt the direction of Ajacks's words.

Prudy's scowl froze any more sweet talk the cowboy may have had in mind, her body language dimming Ajacks's bright smile.

"Is there anything I can do for you?" Ajacks asked. "Soup? Crackers? A drink from the saloon?" he giggled, aware Prudy abstained from liquor of any kind.

Even if Prudy had a cough, she would never take from the bottle.

But Prudy offered no reply to Ajacks, occasionally scratching and rubbing the side of her neck.

It was like she had a never-ending itch as if Prudy had attended a mosquito gathering, Ajacks thought.

There was a red mark on Prudy's neck where she rubbed. But because of the high covers, and her head being turned in such a way, Ajacks couldn't see the two small bite wounds his beauty was reacting to. And based on the woman's morning mood, he wasn't about to get any closer to her to discover them.

The air in the bedroom remained still, Prudy showing no interest in Ajacks's visit.

Not knowing how to break the silence, Ajacks in jest began passing his open hand in front of Prudy's face to see if he could get a reaction, bringing her back from wherever she was mentally.

"You in there?" Ajacks asked.

Prudy slapped his hand away. "What kind of question is that," she chided. "Ajacks, you are so immature. If it isn't about you, it just isn't important."

"Whatdayamean by that?" Ajacks replied, his patience with Prudy wearing thin. "I asked how you were feeling. Doesn't my question show my concern for you?" he asked.

Again Prudy gave no response other than a sigh and a cold shoulder as she rolled onto her side, away from where Ajacks was sitting on the edge of the bed.

"Let me be. I'm tired," Prudy said sourly.

Ajacks relented, feeling he had no other choice.

"If you need anything, you know where to find me," Ajacks said, in getting to his feet and working his way toward the door.

"Well, if you were any kind of friend of mine, you would make yourself useful and board up my window," Prudy asked. "I don't ever recall that much sunlight pouring through there before."

Prudy's request sent a shiver down Ajacks's spine as he recollected the Peterson home and how all the windows there had been boarded up.

Sheriff Wily said he suspected the boarded up windows were in response to the Peterson brothers readying the home for winter before they departed. But Ajacks never bought Wily's explanation.

"This itsy-bitsy thing?" Ajacks replied, walking over to the 2-foot-wide by 2-foot-tall cottage window.

"Can you do it or not?" Prudy snapped.

"I'll go down to the general store and see what I can find," Ajacks said, saying anything he needed to at the time to make peace with Prudy. But the cowboy found his girlfriend's request alarming.

"You sure you're alright?" Ajacks asked, turning his attention from the window back to Prudy who still lay in bed.

But Prudy offered no response, having already pulled the blue-flowered quilt over her head.

Had Ajacks not been distracted about having to board up Prudy's window, he may have noticed the broken lock on her front door as he left.

Chapter 75

News of Crazy Max's death at the hands of the newspaperman shocked Roman Oscuro. He wasn't close to Max, only using the horse thief to do his dirty work. But he assumed the man with a wanted reputation would have been able to handle Jef.

"Who killed Max? Surely it wasn't the newspaperman," Oscuro asked.

"Wily suspects it was his wife," Ike replied. "Everyone knows Jef has no spine."

Before Oscuro was to sleep, Ike had shared with him about how Max had been killed by what appeared to be a miniature crossbow that shot wooden stakes.

Its drawstring made of what appeared to be nylon, Ike reported.

"It appears these wooden stake shooters were designed with you in mind, my friend," Ike told a tired Oscuro, who had been out all night. "We need to finish what business we have here."

"I have planted my seed. It should take only a few days to bloom, and then we'll go," Oscuro said with a smile.

"Prudy, Ajacks's girl?" Ike asked.

"One and the same," Oscuro said proudly. "But she is no longer Ajacks's girl. Her love for the dusty cowboy will wane, and she will come to me. I hold the keys for her to live forever."

Oscuro was proud of himself. If he could have cast a reflection in the mirror, he would have been able to see himself gloating.

Oscuro was making everyone's life in Dry Springs miserable. And that is what he had initially come for. The riches and the girl were just added treasure.

"So, who is next?" Ike said, hoping to move their plan along quicker.

"The newspaperman irritates me. And the pastor, who feels like he has command over me, needs to be put in his place," Oscuro said. "But if we are to lop the head off this dragon, we need to prevent any more wooden stake shooters from being built. We must eliminate Squeak," he said.

"The awkward one?" a puzzled Ike asked.

"Without Squeak, they have no weapon I fear," Oscuro said. "The pastor's faith may deflect me, but it will not kill me. Nothing will anger me more than to think I hold the upper hand on these townies, only to find one is secretly packing a weapon that could end my existence," Oscuro said.

"My heart just can't take it," he added with a menacing laugh. "And who wants to be looking over their shoulder for the rest of their life?" Oscuro asked, in taking an additional jab at Wily.

"Well, Wily has already done you the favor of taking one of the weapons off the street by locking it up in his gun cabinet," Ike said.

"Good," Oscuro said, rubbing his hands together, sending dead flakes of skin flying. "Soon, we'll make the awkward one who walks like a bird, run like a race horse, or should I say chicken," Oscuro said with a smile.

"And Wily?" Ike asked.

"The sheriff will stay out of our way," Oscuro replied.

"I like it," Ike said, relieved to hear there was an end in sight to their stay in Dry Springs. After all, the only reason Ike continued to play a role in Oscuro's little melodrama was because he too feared him and the wrath he would face if he abandoned Oscuro. He knew firsthand Oscuro would travel the ends of the earth to find anyone who crossed him.

"And Prudy, does she come with us?" Ike asked excitedly.

"She will," Oscuro said with pride, as if he had just been crowned as royalty. "But it wouldn't hurt for you to keep an eye on my girl while you're out patrolling for vampires," Oscuro mocked.

Before Ike could respond, Oscuro issued his daily early morning command, "Now, be off," Oscuro said with a flick of his wrist, issuing the command to Ike as if he were some sort of private in Oscuro's dark army.

Ike's thoughts were already elsewhere. He too was dreaming of a happy ending for himself. He was dreaming before this was all over with of having Prudy to himself. Ike had never been in love before. But he would be willing to risk Oscuro's anger for Prudy's hand.

CHAPTER 76

Making his way around Dry Springs, Squeak couldn't help notice Ajacks all curled up like a bug in a blanket on Prudy's porch.

It was obvious from Ajacks's wrinkled clothes and the tired look on his face he had spent most of the night there.

Lovers' quarrel, Squeak figured. It was moments like these that made him happy to be tall, lanky and single. Besides, one subject Squeak hated giving advice to others on was when the talk involved women. That is why he appreciated Miss Higginson. She kindly carried most of their conversations.

Ajacks glared at his friend, whose off-tune whistling had awakened him. It was obvious to Squeak the idea of Ajacks sleeping underneath the stars on what had been a rather cool fall night had not been his idea.

"Something is wrong with my girl, if you must know," Ajacks blurted out, confused over the recent changes in Prudy's behavior. The woman had gone from sweet to ornery and had a look in her eyes, as if she were sleepwalking through the days.

"We were talking marriage one day, and then get out of my life the next," Ajacks said, unbending his knees and rising from his resting position.

"I know nothing about women," Squeak replied, fearing the conversation was headed the very direction he didn't want it to go. "My mother didn't even love me. Or at least, I don't think she loved me. I was raised by my aunt - and then only up to 10 years of age. She found me odd and sent me away to work for a livestock outfit. No, I'm not much good when it comes to women problems," Squeak said, not realizing he had just shared more with Ajacks about himself in one moment than in all of the years he had known the deputy.

"I don't think there is much to understand. Prudy is smitten with another beau, and I am no longer of any use to her," Ajacks said dejectedly.

"There are not that many beaus in these parts," Squeak said, trying to lift his friend's spirits. Dry Springs was a small town, offering little variety, Squeak thought.

"Oh, I don't know? But what I do know is she is not the same sweet Prudy Richards I use to know," Ajacks said, tossing his single blanket to the ground and rubbing his face in bringing it awake.

Squeak could see the deputy was extremely frustrated.

"I think you two make a fine couple. There isn't a soul in town who isn't envious of you, Ajacks, with the exception of maybe Jef," Squeak said.

Squeak's words brought a slight grin to Ajacks's face as he straightened his now wrinkled button-down shirt and brushed off his trousers.

"You want to go get something to eat?" Squeak asked. "Sometimes eatin makes me feel better."

"Why not," Ajacks said. "I'm outta here," he turned yelling in the direction of the house in hopes Prudy would hear that he was leaving angry. Inside the home Prudy heard nothing. She was in a deep sleep, dreaming of someone else, and that someone being Roman Oscuro.

Chapter 77

The pancakes dripping in molasses Squeak was squeezing onto his fork and sliding into his face mouthfuls at a time were giving him his fill at Marv's Kitchen.

The all-you-could-eat value, a tab paid by Ajacks, was going to make it difficult for Squeak to push himself away from the table when the two were finished.

While Squeak devoured the flapjacks, one after another, lovesick Ajacks barely touched his meal.

"You're not going to get full that way," Squeak offered between mouthfuls.

Ajacks merely mumbled, his concern for Prudy Richards resting in his belly. It was obvious the cowboy was in need of a friend, someone he could tell his sad love story to.

But Squeak because of his backward nature only had two women in his life: a brother/sister-like relationship with Lola, and an odd relationship with Miss Higginson, who was just as eccentric as Squeak was odd.

There was also the relationship Squeak had with his Aunt Beth, who cared for him until she shooed him away. It wasn't until he was an older teen that Squeak found his footing.

"It is almost as if Prudy is in a trance. Like she has been cast under a spell," Ajacks told Squeak.

"With the goings-on here of late, maybe she is under a spell," Squeak said before filling his mouth with more flapjacks.

"Like a vampire's spell?" Ajacks asked. After all, Prudy did request to have her lone cottage window boarded up.

And when Ajacks shared that tidbit of new information with Squeak, the awkward cowboy found new interest in their conversation.

"Bite marks to her neck, or her wanting to shy away from sunlight, is all part of the vampire lore Jef has shared with me the last two weeks," Squeak said excitedly.

"You're telling me she could be under the vampire's spell?" Ajacks asked, generally not the kind of man to give in to folklore or superstitions.

"I'm just sharing with you some of the stuff Jef has been sharing with me," Squeak said, putting the last bite of flapjack into his mouth.

"If we kill the monster, could it break the curse?" Ajacks asked, unaware he was now nervously rubbing his hand over his pearl-handled pistol.

"What do you mean?" Squeak asked, slowly getting up from the table, wearing the weight of the flapjacks.

"If we kill the vampire, does it break the spell he may have over Prudy?" Ajacks asked.

"It may," Squeak said, as the two made their way out of the breakfast kitchen and onto Main Street.

From there, the two men walked in silence for a while before they noticed other people beginning to fill the sidewalk, going about their daily activities. Squeak and Ajacks both gave each passer-by their customary courtesy nod.

"The first thing you have to do is get close enough to Prudy to find out if she has actually been bitten," Squeak said. "It would be somewhere on the neck."

"She'll think I'm crazy for certain and leave me based on my mental weakness," Ajacks replied.

"We need to know," Squeak said. "If you're afraid, have someone else take a look at her – Parsons or Jef."

"They are no vampire experts," Ajacks replied, having always been sour at the level of confidence Squeak placed in his newspaper friend.

"I know Jef being a Mormon makes him a little different, and his whole attitude regarding freedom of the press can get annoying, but at the present he is the closest thing Dry Springs has to a vampire expert," Squeak said, trying to convince Ajacks.

"I do love Prudy," Ajacks conceded, hoping to convince himself to put his pride in his pocket by bringing Jef into the matter.

"You would do anything for Prudy, right?" Squeak asked, walking slower than usual due to his flapjack intake. It wasn't very often Squeak got someone to buy him breakfast. And where his breakfast generally consisted of a piece of dry bread and fruit, Squeak took full advantage of the opportunity given to him.

"OK, send Jef by Prudy's place. Have him make up some kind of story to get a closer look at her. But don't let Sheriff Wily know I asked you to ask Jef to do me this favor. Understand?" Ajacks said. "I don't want to disappoint Wily."

"Your mind should be on Prudy," Squeak said. "She is a whole lot prettier than the sheriff."

Talking with Squeak was often a waste of time, Ajacks thought. But breakfast with the soft-spoken carpenter this day was proving to be most beneficial.

"Move quickly, Squeak. Prudy has already got a faraway look in her eyes," Ajacks said.

"If we're successful, maybe we can do pancakes again another day," Squeak said, as the men parted ways. Squeak went off to his woodworking shop to build a stake shooter for himself, and Ajacks went off to the sheriff's office where Wily would be waiting for him.

Chapter 78

Squeak was within arm's length of his woodshop door when he heard the familiar voice of Miss Higginson shrill his name at the top of her lungs. She sounded eerily similar to an operatic singer warming up prior to a stage show.

"Oh Squeak, dear," Miss Higginson cried out from half a street away. Those out walking early that morning turned to see where the voice was coming from, while Squeak blushed, raising his hand halfheartedly in her direction, hoping it would suffice as a "Hello" and prevent her from screaming.

"Dear boy," Miss Higginson said, picking up her pace considerably in moving toward Squeak. Upon arrival, Miss Higginson was nearly out of breath, small beads of sweat rising on her forehead and upper lip.

Despite the warm morning and the fact Squeak was packed full of flapjacks, the latter being something Miss Higginson was totally unaware of, she was determined to give him a hug.

"So good to see you," Miss Higginson said, wrapping her peach-colored arms around Squeak's skinny torso and squeezing him hard enough to make Squeak feel every flapjack he had just devoured.

"Ooof," he responded to the squeeze, unable to help himself.

"So?" she asked excitedly.

Squeak at first was out of sorts, trying to figure out what Miss Higginson was referring to. And then it came to him.

"The guitar playing?" Squeak said aloud.

"Yes, how goes the playing? I'm still waiting for my serenade," Miss Higginson said, fluttering her long black eyelashes hanging over her green eyes.

"Yes, the guitar," Squeak said, repeating her words in a delay to find a few of his own, where Miss Higginson was unaware her very expensive guitar now had only two strings attached to it and stood upright in the corner of Squeak's workshop, serving as spare parts for Jef's wooden stake shooters.

"Have you been able to do anything with it?" Miss Higginson asked of her guitar.

"Well, actually we have been able to do quite a bit with it," Squeak said, working to prevent from smirking. After all, he did realize it was an expensive acoustic guitar he had been pulling apart.

"Jef has been real busy in helping me learn how to play it. But, why…yes, I've gotten some use out of it as well," Squeak said, carefully choosing his words to avoid lying to his friend.

The last thing Squeak wanted to do was upset Miss Higginson. Someone he had been able to share his thoughts with and not be judged for it. Besides, he loved the culture and energy she brought to dusty Dry Springs.

"I've gotten a few pings out of it, but nothing that would really qualify as music," Squeak said, now thinking himself clever, hoping Miss Higginson wasn't going to ask him to play for her. He was certain it would break her heart to see the guitar she treasured dismantled.

Squeak was about to take the fourth string off the six-string guitar in making a second stake shooter for himself. He had given Jef his stake shooter as a result of Wily having confiscated and placed under lock and key Jef's original weapon.

"Well, I must have Jef and you over for a bite to eat and for some music," Miss Higginson said. "Knowing you gentlemen, I'll bet you two strum a mean guitar."

Squeak thought to himself, she's partially right.

"Yes, another day would be much better," Squeak said, taking a deep breath. "Maybe in a few days Jef and I will be able to offer you some sort of duet," he added, relieved she wouldn't be coming into his wood shop.

"That would be lovely. You tell Jef I look forward to hearing from him," Miss Higginson said.

"Now, I must be going. I'm on my way to the general store for fabric and lace. I've got sewing to do," Miss Higginson said, giving Squeak a goodbye hug before making her way to the store.

Squeak could still feel the flapjacks.

CHAPTER 79

Wily made several trips over to the cabinet mounted on his office wall, before unlocking it to re-examine the weapon he had taken from Jef.

The stake shooter was light and small. But it was obviously a deadly weapon, based on it being used to kill Crazy Max, Wily thought.

Lola had to be some kind of shot, Wily thought, as he inspected the crude weapon, running his thumb over the carved-out notch where the round 8-inch-long stake would be placed before being drawn back against the tension of the nylon string.

Wily would never admit it, but he marveled at the resourcefulness and craftsmanship that had gone into making the device.

Wily had no respect for Jef. The newspaperman annoyed him from their initial meeting, with Jef insisting on an interview Wily was reluctant to give, fearing putting his name out there publicly might reveal his hiding location, which it apparently had.

Wily's thoughts then went back to the weapon he was holding and whether the weapon would be enough to stop a vampire.

The stake Wily, with the help of Mayor Howard, pulled from Crazy Max's side, was about an inch in diameter. But it wasn't just any wooden stake one could buy at the general store. This stake had been weighted, causing it to fly straighter and faster, obviously with enough force to penetrate deep into the flesh.

The stain from Crazy Max's blood covering nearly three-quarters up the stake gave Wily a good indication of how deep the stake went into the notorious horse thief.

Wily had yet to figure out where Jef and Squeak had gotten the nylon string, but knowing everybody in town the way he did, he suspected it came from Miss Higginson, the queen of clutter.

And then again Wily thought, maybe he had undersold Jef and Squeak, and it was time for them to work together to solve the town's vampire problem.

Every time Wily thought about the vampire and the victims he was leaving in his wake, a twinge of guilt would stab his soul. He feared he was responsible for having brought the monster to Dry Springs.

Two years ago when he escaped the stranger with his life, all Wily wanted to do was lay low and grab hold of his elusive dream of raising a family and leaving his law days behind him forever. But when Wily arrived in the town of Dry Springs months ago, the little town was desperate for a sheriff, and so as a result the town folk recruited him, giving Wily all the confidence he needed to be their sheriff.

At the time he measured out in his mind how much crime could happen in sleepy little Dry Springs. And the sheriff's wage at $60 a month seemed fair enough, so he didn't have to farm like many of the others who call the town home.

Over the time he had been sheriff, he had also regained some confidence, being able to on occasion track down wanted men in the Utah territory for some extra cash.

But this vampire was a burr under his saddle, shattering his confidence and destroying his soul with each townie killed.

Maybe it was time to join forces with Jef and Squeak. But then there was Wily's pride. Being the sheriff, he hated to approach Jef for help.

Wily gave the stake one last look before placing it and the device back in the locking cabinet.

Wily had just gotten the weapon put away and settled back down into his hard wooden chair - it too crafted by Squeak - when Ajacks walked into the office looking like a whipped pup.

CHAPTER 80

"**What's wrong with** you?" Wily asked, growing increasingly impatient for the heartbroken deputy.

"I wouldn't expect you to understand," Ajacks replied, realizing anything he said to the sheriff he'd get grief for.

"Well, if it will make you a better deputy, I'll go have a talk with this young lady who appears to have tied your tail in a knot," Wily said, himself not ever having known true love. Oh, there had been women he had whistled at, or smooched with behind the barn, but the sheriff had done no real courting.

"No thank you," Ajacks said to Wily's offer. "I'll fix what's broke. And if I can't fix it…I'll walk away so it doesn't make me crazy."

"Well, be careful how you go about doing things," Wily said. "If you haven't noticed, women here are in short supply."

"So, what's the plan, Sheriff?" Ajacks asked, wanting to move away from his own problems and onto the town's problems.

But Wily, going over in his mind what he had to do next, gave Ajacks little in the way of a response.

"I wish I knew," Wily said, scratching the red-brown hairs on his chin, his eyes fixed on the cabinet where the wooden stake shooter he termed as evidence was stored.

Chapter 81

Jef's short visit to Prudy Richards's place frightened the newspaperman. He had never seen such a transformation, making him suspect Oscuro had to be behind it.

Jef, being of good heart, figured he owed it to Ajacks, his acquaintance, but not often his friend, to make the visit.

"There is definitely something wrong with her," Jef told Ajacks. "And I suspect it has something to do with our vampire on the loose."

Ajacks shook his head in bewilderment, while Squeak, who was in their company, absorbed Jef's words as if he were a sponge.

"Her eyes are distant, color is pasty, and Prudy does not resemble the same woman that had been serving as our town schoolteacher," Jef said based on his short pop-in visit with Prudy.

"How long has she been this way, now?" Jef asked.

"A few days," the visibly annoyed Ajacks mumbled, before asking Jef, "Did you notice a bite mark on her neck?"

"I didn't. She was wearing a high-necked gown, and her conversation with me was curt and cold, as if she wanted me to leave before I even arrived," Jef said, pushing his glasses back onto the bridge of his nose.

"I appreciate you looking in on her," Ajacks said, trying to avoid making eye contact with Jef.

"If you want to know for certain if she has been bitten by the vampire, offer her a nice walk in the evening air," Jef said. "But be careful, because if she has been bitten, she too will soon be making a full transformation into a monster."

"See there, Ajacks, I told you Jef knows what he is talking about." Squeak said, as the three men stood not far from where Prudy lived.

"Transfor-what?" Ajacks asked.

"There are those that vampires will save with their bite in order to spread their seed," Jef said.

"So Prudy may be a vampire?" Ajacks asked with tremble in his voice.

"Well, not yet," Jef said. "But I would be lying if I didn't tell you she is showing some signs of going there."

"It ain't even dark yet, and you're scaring me. Stop," Squeak told Jef.

Ajacks looked totally dejected.

"We just have to be careful," Jef said, putting his hand on Ajacks's shoulder and giving it a squeeze.

"What we need to do is figure out who this vampire is and put a bullet in him," Ajacks said, becomingly increasingly frustrated at his helplessness.

"Bullets ain't going to work," Squeak said. "That's why Jef and I invented a weapon that can kill this beast. Right, Jef?"

And there it was. Squeak had just expanded the circle of who knew their secret. But Ajacks looked desperate, hopefully desperate enough that he would be willing to keep their secret.

"Absolutely," Jef said in getting back to Squeak's original claim after having given it some thought.

"Well, then let's use it," Ajacks said.

"The timing has to be right, and the shot has to be perfect," Squeak said.

Jef nodded. But he was reluctant to say a lot out of fear of the vampire finding out, and result in him knocking on his door.

The one thing the town could ill afford to have happen is for the vampire to figure out who had such weapons. The element of surprise was important if they were to defeat the vampire, Jef thought.

"We need to talk to Wily. We need to convince him," Ajacks said. "Anything to save my gal."

"We'll talk to Wily," Jef said. "But he is the last person we let in on our secret, agreed?" he demanded, passing Squeak a glare.

Chapter 82

Ping.

The stake springing from the shooter sank deep into the empty crate.

"That was about 15 feet," Jef said, retrieving the stake.

Jef got his legs resituated, backing up a few more feet from where he had been standing, and fired the weapon again for the group gathered behind the general store.

PING.

This time the shot was not quite as direct, but nonetheless, the stake again found its mark, striking the crate.

"Wow. I didn't know the newspaperman was such a shot," Ike said, rubbing the shadow of whiskers forming on his rumpled face this early morning. Ike was an uninvited guest who had stumbled upon the group as they were gathering at the sheriff's office.

When Ike heard the word "demonstration," he figured it was in his best interest to stick around to see just what was being demonstrated.

Having Ike there concerned Jef, making him feel uneasy about showing their weapon. Jef did not trust Ike or his brother Stan. But he had failed miserably to get Wily to investigate the Peterson brothers and had even less luck getting Wily to send Ike off on another errand so as to excuse him from the group.

"And you're telling me this will kill a vampire?" Wily said, looking on.

"Absolutely," Squeak interjected before Jef could respond.

"So, what's it made of?" Wily asked of the weapon.

"Pine wood and guitar string," Squeak offered before Jef could shush his friend.

Jef thought now was not the time for them to be baring their souls to these men.

The weapon demonstration for the sheriff was being done at the request of Ajacks, who was growing increasingly frustrated at the town's ineptness in ridding itself of its vampire problem.

Despite Jef and Ajacks pleadings with Wily to allow them to show how effective the weapon was, the sheriff was reluctant to pull the weapon from his locked cabinet.

Prior to making their trip to the sheriff's office, Jef had pulled Squeak aside, making him promise he would not reveal to the men they had other wooden-stake shooters made.

"Isn't this that same weapon you killed Crazy Max with?" Ike asked Jef in an accusatory tone.

"My wife used this weapon to shoot Max while he was charging at me with a knife," Jef replied, saying it loud enough to make certain Wily, Ike and Ajacks heard every word.

"Well, it seems you have been practicing with this weapon," Wily said, nodding toward the two puncture holes in the crates.

"How good are you at shooting that thing on the run?" Ike said, pressing Jef. "Like, could you hit something from 30 feet out? Or do you have to be right on top of them in order for the stake to stick?" he asked.

"Ike," Wily said, tiring of Ike's teasing tone.

"What I need to know is whether you have any more of these weapons," Wily asked in eyeing Jef.

Jef thought for a second before answering, realizing Squeak had just crafted for him a new shooter yesterday, which didn't include the ones Parsons and Squeak had hidden at their places.

"We don't have any more just like this," Jef said, purposely measuring his words to keep from lying.

"Can more be made?" Wily asked.

"Well...," Squeak offered, avoiding the question.

Wily then grabbed the stake shooter Jef was holding. "Well, I have seen enough," the sheriff said. "This here remains evidence and, as a result, will remain locked up."

"Sheriff, didn't you just see how effective the weapon can be?" Ajacks asked. "I say we get Squeak to arm each one of us with one of these. Then when that vampire fella shows up to steal my girl, PING, we shoot him dead."

"Don't you men have somewhere to be?" Wily responded, breaking up the group and the conversation.

"Good call, Sheriff," Ike said, flashing Wily the OK sign with his hand.

Wily offered no response and remained standing in the dust behind the general store as everyone slowly walked away.

Wily suspected Jef was lying, which annoyed the sheriff considerably.

With everyone having left, Wily placed the stake in the shooter and drew back the nylon string serving as its firing mechanism. The sheriff drew a bead on the crate before pushing down the wood lever that released the string and sent the stake flying.

PING.

The stake punctured the wooden crate like it was paper.

Jef and Squeak were no dummies, Wily thought. But as effective as the weapon was, Wily remained uncertain whether it was enough to stop a charging vampire.

CHAPTER 83

Ike was giddy to return home and tell Oscuro what he had just seen. He figured his spy work would find him favor with his boss.

Squeak and Jef had created a killing device, and Oscuro could no longer take the meddling pair lightly.

It was midmorning, which meant Oscuro would still be sleeping in his chambers - what was once the Peterson's storage room in the basement of the ranch house.

The windowless room admitted no light, just the way Oscuro liked it.

The news Ike had for Oscuro would have to wait, giving him a little extra time to return to town to look in on Oscuro's would-be girl, Prudy Richards.

Ike had a mad crush on the woman Ajacks and Oscuro were both claiming as their own. Being a longtime drifter, floating from place to place, Ike never had experienced a love crush before. But he was definitely crushing for Prudy and hoping some way the two of them could work things out and be together, even if it meant fleeing from Dry Springs.

Ike was tired of drifting and only fell in with Oscuro based on the promises Oscuro had made him that he would have wealth untold.

But Oscuro so far had taken most of the spoils, leaving Ike no better off than he was prior to meeting up with Oscuro and his black magic powers.

No doubt, his message to Oscuro could wait. Ike was going courting. Maybe even steal a kiss from one Prudy Richards.

Chapter 84

After showing Jef where he hid his stake shooter – in a cutout in the floorboard of their workshop – Squeak was on his way to warn Parsons that Wily had expressed a desire to know where the other stake shooters were.

"I'm off," Squeak told Jef as he bolted from their office, the cowbell clanging as he opened and shut the door.

Jef hardly looked up from the work he was doing on his press. "Be careful," he told his gangly friend.

The newspaper Jef was preparing for tomorrow would offer little news on the vampire killings, serving more as a reminder of how the townsfolk needed to come together and watch over one another while law officials searched for the killer.

He figured Wily, Ajacks and Ike could use the buttering up in getting them off his tail.

In the meantime, Squeak, in his own bumbling-stumbling way, was moving down Main Street toward the church. The excitable cowboy totally unaware of the piercing eyes closely watching him.

Unless it was blowing, raining or nightfall, Parsons always had the large church doors swung wide open, inviting all to come to Christ.

Squeak didn't hold much favor for religion but believed Parsons had nothing but the best in mind for the town and he was eager to share his warning with him. But the chapel was empty when he arrived. He figured the Parsons family was likely out back doing some family gardening. Gardening was something the Parsons family did in helping feed those in the town who may have otherwise gone without.

Squeak himself on occasion had been a recipient of the Parsons family generosity.

Quickly darting around the side of the chapel to the adjoining home where the Parsons family resided, Squeak, just as he expected, spotted the family working their garden, picking the last of the ripe tomatoes.

Shirley Parsons, a master cook, would use the overly ripe tomatoes in her salsa. Some in town said Shirley's salsa was so hot it would melt ice in the Arctic.

But Squeak wouldn't know, he had never been to the Artic, he thought.

"What brings you out this fine day?" Parsons asked, looking up from his work, always greeting Squeak with a smile. Working alongside Parsons in the garden was his oldest son, John, who, although a little huskier, resembled his father in so many ways.

"Sheriff Wily is looking to confiscate our weapons as a result of Jef and Lola having to use it to kill Crazy Max," Squeak blurted out. The normally quiet Squeak had become much more talkative since the town killings.

"Jef just showed the law how the weapon works. You wouldn't believe it. Jef was two-for-two in hitting the empty crate they had set up," Squeak said, recounting the event.

"Wily asked Jef if there were any more weapons like it, and Jef lied, telling him there wasn't," Squeak said. "Can't hardly blame him for lying, can we?" he asked Parsons, realizing what he had just shared about his friend.

"No, we may have to let that lie slip," Parsons said, lost in thought, turning over in his hand a tomato he had just picked off a plant.

Parsons cast a passing glance at his son John, who stood only a few feet from him. "It concerns me Wily would want those weapons," Parsons said. "Those weapons might be the only thing standing between us and the vampire."

Squeak nodded in agreement.

"Thanks, Squeak, for the warning," Parsons said. "We'll watch ourselves closely. Now, can I interest you in a few tomatoes?" he asked his friend, moving onto another subject.

But in his gut, Parsons feared for the town and what would happen if those living there placed their faith in Sheriff Wily and his deputies.

"Sure, pack me up a few of those tomatoes," Squeak replied, being one to never turn away free food.

The man with the rail-thin frame had an appetite that rivaled Thumper's. But Squeak's reply to Parsons's offer had done nothing to bring the pastor from his deep thought.

"Let me get those for you," John Parsons told Squeak, realizing his father's mind was elsewhere. And the most trusted man in Dry Springs this day was keeping his thoughts to himself.

CHAPTER 85

Ajacks was already frustrated that he was losing his girl. Now, Sheriff Wily had decided against getting Jef and Squeak to build them weapons that would kill the vampire.

Some days Ajacks wondered just whose side Wily was on. If they didn't soon kill the vampire, Ajacks was certain he would lose Prudy Richards forever.

"Tell me one more time why not," Ajacks asked Wily as the two stood in the sheriff's office.

Wily was visibly annoyed with Ajacks, the long scar down the side of his face more noticeable than usual.

"I don't want some newspaperman and a failed furniture maker determining how we handle our problem," Wily said, as if he were spitting out buttermilk. "And I would ask that you respect my opinion."

Ajacks realized he was pushing his limits with the sheriff, but his one true love was at stake. Wily didn't love anybody or anything.

"I'm telling you, Sheriff, I think Jef and Squeak may be onto something," Ajacks said.

It was that claim that proved to be the sheriff's breaking point. "Get out of here. Go patrol. Go shovel manure for all I care, but do not mention the names of those two men to me again or that silly contraption they built," Wily responded, his face now as red as the tint in his beard.

Ajacks stormed out of the musty office with its crooked cell bars to find anyone who would listen to his sad lover's lament.

CHAPTER 86

"**T**wo direct hits," Jef said with a grin. But it was the only grin he would offer in recounting his day. The newspaperman was visibly frustrated with the day's demonstration and Wily's unwillingness to act.

"I guess God really does help those who help themselves," he added.

"Oh, you have never liked Wily," Lola said, rebuking her husband.

"You're right. I don't trust him. I get a sense he is not coming totally clean, and in the meantime, the town suffers," Jef said.

"Yes, but it is not our decision who is to live and die here. That responsibility rests with Wily," Lola said in a low tone so as not to disturb the children.

"Pshaw," Jef said, waving his hand at Lola as if it would wipe her words away.

"I say we batten down the hatches and ride this storm out. Soon, this vampire is going to tire of Dry Springs," Lola said.

"Not acceptable," Jef said. "Action must be taken."

"By who, you?" Lola inquired. "Have you ever killed a man, James Edward Furst?" Lola said, using Jef's full name to stress her point.

"No," Jef replied.

"Well, I have, and the guilt that comes with it is enough to sink one to the bottom of the sea," Lola said.

"Lola, God forgives such acts when they are in the course of defending yourself," Jef said.

"So is it that little rule that excuses vampire hunting?" Lola asked.

"I don't know," Jef replied in a loud tone, one he never took with Lola before. "All I know is I am not turning the second shooter Squeak just built for me over to Wily. Wily doesn't understand what this town is up against. He has never encountered the vampire. He has never been attacked, nor anybody he loves," Jef said, readjusting the glasses on his face.

"Knowing Wily, I'm quite certain he is not frightened by the intruder," Lola said, poking holes in Jef's rationale.

"Now here come the children. We'll talk of it later," she said, trying to put an end to their conversation.

But Jef had more to say.

"I'm tired of talking," Jef said in a tone making Lola uneasy and causing Ranger, sitting nearby, to raise his ears.

The vampire had to go if the Furst family was going to have any sort of life in Dry Springs, Jef thought. A place Lola was obviously unwilling to leave.

"Go talk to Wily. Share with him your concerns," Lola said in a whisper before turning her attention to James Jr. wanting to know when dinner would be served. That child was always hungry, she thought.

"Sure, just knock on the sheriff's office door and let him know I lack confidence in him," Jef said smartly, loud enough for Lola to hear but not loud enough for James Jr. and Bobby to hear what he said.

The two boys ran for the kitchen for a slice of fresh baked bread dripping with honey, giving Lola the time needed to turn to her husband and remind him of his lectures of putting one's trust in God.

"Faith without works is dead," Jef said, citing scripture in his reply, before turning to Ranger and asking him if he wanted to go for a walk.

With Jef storming from the little house, Lola's children couldn't help but feel the tension. "Where is Daddy going with Ranger?" James Jr. asked.

"I guess for a walk," Lola said, having no other answer for her bewildered children.

CHAPTER 87

"It went clear through the crate," Ike said, telling Oscuro what he witnessed earlier in the day. "It is like one of those old medieval crossbows, only smaller, pistol size."

It was obvious what Ike had seen alarmed him.

"These two characters – Squeak and Jef – may have come up with something that might pose a threat," Ike said, certain his report to Oscuro would elevate his status with his captain.

"You're telling me they have designed a weapon for the purpose of killing me? A crude instrument made of pine wood and guitar string?" Oscuro asked in making certain he understood Ike correctly.

"It's time to leave Dry Springs. We've gotten what we're going to be able to shake from this little town. Let's kill Wily and be done with it. These non-cowboys are making me nervous," Ike said of Jef and Squeak.

"I won't be chased away. The Oscuro name will be honored," Oscuro said, as if standing his ground here might impress his ancestry.

"What we need to do is to find the weapons they have built, along with the material they are creating them from. That would put a knot in their rope," Oscuro said. "And I would recommend we start this evening."

"I'll pay Squeak's workshop a visit, and together, you and I, with the help of a friend, will find these weapons. Do you understand?" Oscuro said.

"Yes," Ike said disappointedly, not even registering Oscuro mentioning receiving help from another. "After that, can we leave this town?" Ike asked.

"There are other treasures here I wish to take before leaving," Oscuro said with an eerie smile. "By the way, Ike, how is my favorite girl?" he asked.

Ike blushed some before informing Oscuro that Prudy was fine and should be obedient to his command within a day or two.

It would be during that time that Ike was hoping to be able to steal from Prudy a few more kisses.

Deep in his soul, what Ike really wanted was for Oscuro to slip up, allowing him to slip quietly out of town with Prudy. Oscuro did not deserve a woman as fine as Prudy Richards, Ike thought. But he didn't dare tell Oscuro that.

"I do appreciate you looking in on Prudy for me, Ike. Because I know, regardless of her beauty, you are aware that if you were to ever double-cross me in coming between that lovely woman and myself, I would hunt you down like the no-good drifter that you were when I found you," Oscuro warned.

Oscuro's comments set Ike back. With his black magic powers, could Oscuro sense what Ike had been thinking? Or was Oscuro's veiled threat just a coincidence?

Either way, Ike, who hated moments like these, figured it best he offer no reply so as not to give his hand away.

But to Oscuro, Ike's silence spoke volumes. And the vampire was beginning to question in his own mind Ike's loyalty to him.

It was for that reason Oscuro was about to set into motion another plan to ensure he left Dry Springs with all of its spoils.

Chapter 88

Oscuro nearly screamed out of frustration when he found the guitar in the corner of Squeak's woodshop with only two strings on it. Out of anger, he smashed the guitar into splinters, taking the two freed nylon chords and shoving them in the pocket of his pants. Two remaining strings meant Squeak had likely crafted four of the killing devices.

And Oscuro was determined to find every one of the devices beginning now, even if it meant turning over every piece of unfinished furniture in Squeak's shop.

But his search was proving to be futile, making him want to cuss. But cussing was beneath the Oscuro family's coat of arms. So, instead he continued to ransack the little office, taking full advantage of his break-in by toppling Jef's printing press that stood in the back room of Squeak's woodshop.

With four guitar strings missing and Sheriff Wily holding one of the weapons in his evidence locker, Oscuro was pretty confident he knew where the other three weapons were and who possessed them.

But just thinking there was someone out there who may have thought they held an edge over him angered Oscuro to the point he grabbed one of Squeak's unfinished chairs in the shop and smashed it hard against the office door, causing the cowbell hanging over it to let out a weak clang.

The noise he created had alerted someone. Oscuro could hear footsteps clomping down the street boardwalk just outside the office. He silently watched from the dark of the room as the door latch turned and a figure entered.

"Oh, it's you," said Oscuro, prepared to pounce, but then realized he didn't need to.

Chapter 89

"You owe me $75," said the figure, closing the door of the workshop behind him. But not slow enough to prevent the cowbell from throwing off another sick clang.

"You owe me a bride. I would say that still puts you in my debt," Oscuro responded coldly.

"I said I was sorry. It was an errant shot," Wily said smartly, rubbing the facial scar Oscuro had given him that night.

"Watch your tone with me," Oscuro warned. "I'm in a foul mood."

"Foul mood?" Wily questioned. "I've made it so you can live like a king here."

"No one can live like a king in Dry Springs," Oscuro replied. "Besides, everything you have given me since I arrived has been owed to me. I loved Beth, you imbecile," Oscuro said, raising his voice. "Just because you have never found love, cowboy, do not take my wishes from me."

"So, what is it you need now?" Wily asked, trying to calm his dangerous friend. "I put you up in the Peterson home where I knew treasures awaited you. I even took care of your foul-mouthed friend by providing him a job. Heck, I even laid out the table for you to be able to take your first victim in your thirst for blood.

"But no, you continue to feast on the town, and that was not part of our arrangement," Wily said, scolding Oscuro.

"I needed to send a message. And Gibby was your fault. You told me Ajacks would be picking up Abe Vigil's body. And now that clunky cowboy is still around competing for Prudy's hand," Oscuro said.

"And Homer White?" Wily asked.

"He was a barfly nobody would miss," Oscuro said.

"What about Russell Means? And then after you took Russell's life, you tried to take the life of his son, Todd," Wily said. "What were you thinking?"

"I'm thinking I'm in control," Oscuro sneered.

"Russell Means was the type that would have organized against me," Oscuro said. "And Wolcutt, well, he challenged me, while Peppers took his own life in an act of foolishness. My ears rang for hours after that little stunt.

"Oh, by the way, Sheriff, you forgot one," Oscuro added. "Sterling Peterson showed up at the Peterson homestead to lay claim to his family inheritance a few days after you took off after Crazy Max. I had Ike remove him from the equation. His body is buried somewhere in the Utah desert if anyone is interested."

As the pair stood in the dark of Squeak's workshop, Wily, at a loss for words, merely shook his head in disgust. "Why are you still here, Oscuro?"

"I want you to join me," Oscuro said, extending his pasty white hand for a handshake. But Wily declined.

"I don't want to be your partner. Anyway, you've already got a diabolical partner in Ike," Wily reminded him.

"Ike?" Oscuro said. "I fear Ike may be double-crossing me when it comes to securing my interest in Prudy Richards."

"Still not interested," Wily said.

"I can make you rich," Oscuro said.

"No, I'll be leaving town soon after you do, and most likely heading the other direction," Wily said firmly.

"You were always so tough," Oscuro said. "Come to think of it, I think I have only seen you run once," he said, getting in one more dig at the sheriff.

"Well, I'm not running now," Wily said defiantly.

"If you're not going to run, then I am going to need a favor or two from you. After that, I'll be moving on," Oscuro said.

"What it is you need?" Wily asked.

"I need those shooters Squeak made," Oscuro said. "As crude as they are, I do not want anyone coming after me when I do decide to leave. I don't want to be looking over my shoulder for the rest of forever."

"Is that what you're doing here tonight?" Wily asked in surveying the mess Oscuro had made of Squeak and Jef's workplace.

"I have turned this place upside down looking for those things," Oscuro said.

"Oscuro, you have to think like a furniture maker. Have you checked the floorboards?" Wily asked, demonstrating by stomping his feet on the floor.

"When you hear a hollow sound, you know you have found what you're looking for," Wily told Oscuro.

No sooner had Wily provided his vampire friend with the insight than Oscuro was tap-dancing throughout Squeak's workshop, closely listening for that hollow thud.

By the time Oscuro had done a few taps, a couple of spins and a move that looked similar to a European folkdance, he had located the floorboard piece that wasn't like the others.

"Why, Oscuro, I believe you have just danced your way to finding treasure," Wily said, taking in the scene.

Oscuro offered only an audible gasp before dropping to his knees and using his strength to pull up the floorboards. Under his grasp, the boards came up as if they were made of cookie dough.

There, beneath the boards, sat one of the stake shooters.

"My, Wily, how smart you are," Oscuro said, reaching down into the hole to grab the weapon, before snapping it into several pieces.

"There are two weapons left. I need your help finding them," Oscuro said.

"If I help you?" Wily asked.

"Then I spare your life," Oscuro said firmly.

"I love being your friend," Wily said smartly. "How does Ike do it?"

"I suspect the last two weapons are in the possession of Jef and Parsons," Oscuro said matter-of-factly.

"I'd say your suspicions may be right," Wily added. "But I already collected one of these weapons from Jef. It would be hard to believe that he would have two."

"You don't suppose Ajacks is carrying one of these weapons? Squeak and he have become good friends of late," Oscuro asked.

"It might be worth looking into," replied Wily, who trusted no one.

"But once we locate these other two weapons, Oscuro, I want you to get your bride and leave town. And take Ike with you," Wily said.

"I may need one more thing before I go, Sheriff," Oscuro said. "I may need me a newspaperman."

With that, Wily flashed an eerie smile, as did Oscuro.

Chapter 90

"**D**id you see what they did to our shop?" an angry Jef told Sheriff Wily.

"You need to pay a visit to Stan and Ike Peterson, find out where they were last night," Jef demanded, while Squeak silently looked on, shaking his head in disbelief.

When Squeak and Jef had arrived to work, the pair found their little office had been broken into and ransacked as if someone was looking for something.

Based on Squeak's reaction, they found it. The floorboards of his office were pried up where his stake shooter once was hidden.

Jef suspected the Petersons were behind it, particularly because Ike had been a witness at the weapon demonstration.

Squeak helped Jef stand up the press, then the two marched down to the sheriff's office, Ranger close behind. When they arrived, Wily was sitting behind his desk drinking his morning brew from what appeared to be a badly stained cup.

Before Wily could even greet them, Jef let the accusations fly.

"You can't make such claims without proof," Wily shouted back at Jef. "And just what is it that you think they were looking for?" he asked.

Jef pretended he didn't hear the question, while Ranger closely watched the verbal exchange.

"You haven't even been out to the Peterson place to question them," Jef said. "What kind of sheriff works like this?"

"You're pushing your luck with me, newspaperman. And unless you want to find yourself locked up, you had better walk lightly around me," Wily said, staring a hole through Jef.

But this morning Jef had no give in him. He had reached his limit when it came to showing patience.

"Are you going to put me behind those bars?" Jef asked Wily, pointing at the jail cell Crazy Max had escaped from. "If you haven't noticed, your cell bars are crooked, Sheriff, just like you are," Jef said pointedly.

His comment brought the sheriff out of his chair, causing Ranger to prick up his ears and Squeak to take a step back.

Before the red-faced Wily could respond, Ike entered the musty-smelling sheriff's office, setting off Ranger, who had gone from peaceful observer to a snarling guard dog.

"Bridle your dog," Ike demanded of Jef, reaching for his pistol.

"Ranger, no," Jef said, grabbing onto the leather collar Lola had made for the dog for just such instances.

"There is something about you, Ike, that my dog just doesn't like," Jef said, doing all he could to hold back a snapping Ranger.

"Get that dog out of here," Wily demanded.

"I'll do that, if you'll question Ike on his whereabouts last night," Jef bartered.

"If it will bring me a moment of peace," Wily said, before taking a long draw off his drink.

"Question me for what?" Ike asked.

"Oh, Jef here is convinced you and your brother Stan were responsible for breaking into his shop last night," Wily said, gesturing at Jef, who finally had Ranger under control.

"Anything of value taken?" Ike asked.

Jef remained silent.

"Well, was there?" Wily added, wanting Jef to respond.

But Jef remained quiet, thinking better of telling the sheriff anything. Squeak also remained silent.

The awkward silence in the room was broken when Ranger offered a few more guttural growls toward Ike's direction.

"You'll let me know if you find out anything, right, Sheriff?" Jef asked with a smirk before heading out the door with Squeak and Ranger in tow.

Wily gave Jef a weak two-fingered salute off his forehead before acknowledging Jef's question. "You bet. I'll talk to Stan," he said.

Wily's sarcastic remark crushed Jef's hope that the sheriff was actually going to solve the office break-in. Who to actually trust in the town of Dry Springs was becoming a problem for Jef.

It wasn't until Jef was away from the sheriff's office that Ranger stopped growling and reverted back to his peaceful nature.

CHAPTER 91

Wily and Ike's ride out to the Peterson place was quiet. The clomping of their horses' hoofs trying to beat down the dust of the road was all that was heard.

From town to the Peterson place was just under a mile. Ike, who generally liked to chat, remained quiet, as did Wily, who was lost in thought.

Wily was annoyed he had to keep from Ike the fact he knew Stan Peterson was Roman Oscuro.

Wily suspected it was because Oscuro was going to double-cross Ike. But the sheriff feared the pair might be setting him up. For that reason, Wily was doing what he could to read Ike's body language during their ride, but his riding partner wasn't giving much away.

"I figure Stan will be out working in the field somewhere, Sheriff," Ike said, breaking the silence.

"You figure that, do ya?" Wily responded, his horse maintaining stride.

"Sometimes during the daylight hours, Stan can be outright ornery, Sheriff. Regardless of just how much sleep he has had," Ike said, pressing their conversation.

But Wily wasn't biting. The ride to the Peterson place was the sheriff's way of trying to find out where Ike stood with Oscuro.

The two continued their ride through the fall morning until the framework of the Peterson ranch house came into view. Seeing the enormity of the ranch house, Wily couldn't help but think Roman and Ike had made hundreds, if not thousands of dollars, with the treasures they had found in the Peterson place.

It was while thinking about what he could do with all of that money, that Wily heard Ike slowly start to slide his pistol from its holster. Ike hadn't gotten the gun all the way out before Wily, who had been on guard, had his pistol pointed in Ike's face.

"Wow, Sheriff," Ike said, sliding his gun back into its holster.

"I know what is going on. You don't have to kill me," Wily said. "Don't worry. I'll let Oscuro know that you're faithful. I just wanted to get a read on things," said Wily, who had yet to take his gun off Ike.

Ike appeared as if he had just been punched.

"So, you know?" Ike asked.

"In Missouri, Oscuro and I ran into each other after we lawman in St. Louis County received reports that someone was fleecing fur traders along the Mississippi and Missouri Rivers. In trying to run Oscuro off, an errant shot from my pistol during a melee struck and killed Oscuro's Beth," Wily said.

Ike let out a fake slight gasp.

"I was frightened by the mistake I had made," Wily continued. "I had seen what Oscuro could do. So, I made an all-out run to the river thinking it might be my only refuge. I must have stand in that river for hours, fearing to swim toward either bank out of fear Roman might be waiting for me," Wily said, his voice trailing off.

"Then the pair of you show up, of all places, in Dry Springs," Wily said. "So, I roll out the welcome mat after Oscuro pays me a nightly visit. I figured it was the only way to save myself. So, yes, I sold out, allowed you boys to live in the best place I could offer."

"So, you've known all this time," Ike said, nearly speechless after hearing Wily's story.

"Yes, it was I that made arrangements for you two to stay at the Peterson place, figuring if I kept Oscuro content he wouldn't kill me. I just figured you two would be gone by now. There isn't a lot to take in Dry Springs," Wily said.

"I think Jef aggravating Oscuro has kept him here longer than he expected," Wily said. "That is just one more reason why I share the same hatred for the newspaperman," he added.

"Oscuro isn't going anywhere until Prudy Richards has made her full transformation into a vampire," Ike said. "He has every intention of taking her with him."

"I know," Wily said, feeling bad for Ajacks, his loyal deputy.

"In the meantime Oscuro wants to enact revenge on Parsons, Squeak and Jef, specifically," Ike said. "But because Jef killed Crazy Max with a wooden-stake shooter, Oscuro fears the newspaperman. And Parsons frightens him because of his faith in a Higher Power. That is probably where you and I come in," he said.

Wily was now beginning to recognize his role in this whole scheme. "And then are you and me of any use after that?" Wily asked Ike.

"Well … one of us is. Oscuro is always going to need a mortal partner. Somebody to protect him while he sleeps," Ike said.

"Well, that isn't going to be me," Wily replied

"The story we tell Jef is we visited the Peterson home and found Stan working in the field. We questioned him and he knew nothing of the break-in," Wily told Ike.

"You've done this before, haven't you, Sheriff?" Ike said in appreciating Wily's scheming.

Wily offered no reply. "But if you double-cross me, Ike, I'll let Oscuro know you have been paying personal visits to Prudy Richards," he added.

"Well, then I guess we're friends," Ike said, extending his hand.

"No," Wily said, declining the handshake. Riding back to town, Wily felt uneasy about his new relationship with Ike, fearing for the second time he had sold his soul to a devil.

Chapter 92

The headline read, "VANDALS BREAK INTO NEWSPAPER. VAMPIRE AT WORK?"

What was even more aggravating for Sheriff Wily was that while Jef sold his newspapers on one street corner, Parsons was passing out wooden stakes and small crucifixes he had blessed on the other.

The day of reckoning was drawing near.

When Wily addressed the two men with his disapproval, Parsons and Jef reminded the sheriff of all those traveling salesmen with their liquid potions he had allowed to peddle from the same street corner.

Jef was pleased his newspapers were now selling faster than the pancakes at Marv's Pancake House. He was equally excited for the success Parsons was having, despite the fact that he was not a member of that particular faith. Lola would be proud of him. His LDS pioneering father, James Edward Furst II, he wasn't as certain about.

"Extra, extra, read all about it," Jef yelled, waving his papers in the air to catch the attention of all who walked by. "It had to be the vampire, no prints were left," he added to his call to entice passersby into buying a paper.

"Will you stop?" Wily asked Jef. "You're just stirring everybody up."

"They need to be stirred. Their life might very well hang in the balance," Jef shot back.

Parsons crossed the street in joining Jef and Sheriff Wily in their conversation.

"You have to admit, Sheriff, our town track record is not very good," Parsons said, always trying to be respectful.

"But the town doesn't need this," Wily said, gesturing at the newspapers and crosses the two were holding. "You're doing no one a favor here."

"Did you ride out and see Stan Peterson? Did you ask him questions as to where he was the other night, or where he has been any of the other nights?" Jef said, using the moment to quiz the sheriff.

"Your suspicions are way off, Jef," Wily replied. "Ike and I rode out, only to find Stan Peterson working his field, all lathered up in sweat. We questioned him of his whereabouts in the evening, and he explained he had been busy working their land to prepare it for sale. Just like Ike told us. He also told me to tell you that you had best quit slandering his good name or he is going to ride into town and trounce you," Wily said.

"Well, I have plenty of time for that. Stan Peterson won't be riding in until dark. That's the way vampires work," Jef said, doubting every word Wily had just shared.

"I don't believe you. I won't believe Ike either. So save your story," Jef said. "I have looked on as the people of this town hide beneath their blankets at night. You lawmen do little to protect them."

"Now, Jef," Parsons interrupted, trying to prevent his friend from finding trouble with Wily.

But it was too late.

"I have a message you can take to Stan Peterson. You tell Mister Peterson I'll be waiting for him to come to town. And I won't be waiting alone. You let him know that, Sheriff," said Jef, whose frustration was getting the best of him.

The air around the three men was so still Parsons was having difficulty breathing. That was the first time Parsons had seen the mild-mannered newspaperman deliver such a scolding.

Even Ranger, sitting nearby, cocked his head from side to side to make certain it was Jef.

It seemed an eternity before the silence broke.

"Now, Sheriff," Jef said, recomposing himself, "if you're not interested in purchasing a newspaper, you'll have to step aside for those customers who wish to."

"You'll get yours," Wily said, jabbing his index finger in Jef's chest before stomping away.

"I don't know if that was faith or the early signs of a man going over the edge," Parsons told Jef, trying to collect his thoughts over what had just occurred.

"What I do know is after that display you had best watch your back," Parsons added.

Jef gave the pastor a nod, as if to say he understood his words with Wily might find him in trouble, before barking out to anyone who might hear him: "Extra, extra. Vampire breaks into newspaper office."

Jef was about to find out if the Founding Fathers were right when they proclaimed: "The pen is mightier than the sword."

CHAPTER 93

The fire had licked one side of the log for some time before licking the other.

The repetitive sound of Lola shucking corn at the kitchen table had put Jef into a trance as he gazed into the fire he had set in the fireplace. It was almost as if Jef were seeing for the first time how fire danced around things before consuming them.

The warmth from the fire heated the little cabin. All was quiet at the Furst home. James Jr. and Robert had both found their beds early, having had quite a play day with Ranger. Ranger also looked exhausted, lying sideways on the floor not far from where Jef was on bended knee, looking into the flames.

"Gibby's body was burned from the waist up," Jef said as if he were recalling out loud all the terrible things that had happened of late. "Gibby crawled, or was trying to crawl, into the fire to get away from his attacker."

"I don't know what you're talking about," said an impatient Lola, not missing a beat in shucking the corn.

"Gibby crawled into the fire for protection because his attacker wouldn't go there," Jef said, his eyes glued to the flames in the stone fireplace.

"The fire would have been hot, Jef, even for a so-called vampire," she said, trying to silence her husband.

"That means his flesh burns," said Jef, who had gotten up off his knees and situated himself at the kitchen table where his wife was preparing dinner for the next day.

"Please, Jef, just because the kids are in bed doesn't mean I want to talk vampire talk," Lola said.

"I know, I'm just trying to figure out a way to kill this thing," Jef said apologetically.

"Well, you are obsessing. Stop it," Lola said, briefly looking up from what she was doing.

"You do realize someone needs to kill this creature, right" Jef asked?

"After what happened the other day, I don't want to hear another word about killing," Lola said sternly. "Eventually, this man, thing, whatever it is will move on."

"But then we're just wishing our problem on someone else," Jef said. "And that just means more victims whose names we don't know."

"Killing it is not your call, James Edward Furst. You leave those matters to Sheriff Wily and his men," Lola demanded.

"Sheriff Wily, what a joke," Jef said.

"That is so disrespectful. What is it about you and the law?" Lola asked. "You felt the same way about Wolcutt, and he laid down his life for you fools."

"I was wrong about Wolcutt. I'm not wrong about Wily," Jef said, raising his voice, something he was doing more often with Lola.

"I'm beginning to believe you just hate authority. That is why your own father bothers you." Lola said.

"I got a bad feeling about Wily," Jef said. "And don't drag my father into this. Because I know that you don't want your mother dragged into this fight. Your mother and the property we inherited from her is the only reason we are still sticking it out in good ol' Dry Springs," he said.

Lola was now enraged.

"I'm done talking to you. I don't know who the creature is, the one who is out prowling for victims at night or the one I share a bed with," Lola said, her eyes aglow.

With that, Lola left the room, leaving Jef sitting at the kitchen table, with a few remnants of unhusked corn on top of the table and a dog now resting beneath it.

"Ranger, I know I'm right," he said. Ranger's head bobbed once before he lay it back down to sleep.

Chapter 94

The boards of the Main Street boardwalk creaked under Squeak's weight.

Ike had delivered a message to Squeak that Sheriff Wily wanted to see him. The sheriff's office was only a block from where Squeak and Jef kept shop. Squeak moved at a brisk pace so as not to keep the sheriff waiting, and to hurry with his meeting in order to make it home before dark. With it being late fall, the sun was setting earlier each night.

Like Jef, Squeak was beginning to trust no one. Sadly, it was a trait that had not been a part of his character before. For years Squeak had gotten through life by keeping his life uncomplicated.

When Squeak walked into Wily's office, the Sheriff, as usual, was sitting behind his big desk that filled most of the room. Mayor Howard had promised Wily the desk if he took the job as sheriff.

"I know you're in hurry, so I'll be quick," Wily said, gesturing with his arm for Squeak to take a seat in the chair positioned in front of him. But Squeak declined, tightly holding onto his bowler hat he had removed from his head. His hope was holding onto the hat would prevent his hands from shaking if the sheriff began to ask him questions.

"The weapons, Squeak. We believe the weapons Jef and you have created, those miniature crossbows, pose a risk to other town members, and we're hoping you will have sense enough to turn all of them over to us," Wily said slowly and deliberately.

"You do realize you already asked Jef about the weapons and he told you we didn't have any more," Squeak replied.

"That's true. But with the recent break-in of your office, I suspect one of those weapons you guys claimed you didn't have was uncovered," Wily said, now eyeballing Squeak.

"Yes, but Jef...," Squeak started to say before being interrupted.

"The Mormon is lying. There were four strings missing from the acoustic guitar found in your shop," Wily snapped.

Squeak was concentrating on his answers to prevent his knees from shaking.

"I was to fix that guitar for Miss Higginson. I never noticed how many of its strings were missing when she brought it to me. I know there were a few," Squeak said.

Wily out of frustration rubbed both his hands through his thick brown-reddish hair, the long scar on his face turning a new shade of pink.

"Squeak haven't we have always understood one another? And I have always admired your craft to be able to build something out of nothing. But now is not the time to be putting those skills to use in creating weapons that pose a threat to everyone in Dry Springs," Wily said.

"I can't help you, Sheriff," Squeak said, hoping that would end the conversation.

"Loyalty is overrated," Wily said with a scowl that puckered his face like it was made of fresh dough.

"Are we done, Sheriff? I have to go," Squeak said, seeing the time was escaping him and he would be walking home in the dark - alone.

"Oh, we're done," said Wily, waving him away as if he were saying good-bye to him for the last time.

CHAPTER 95

I t was about two blocks to his house from the sheriff's office. Squeak had never stepped so lively. Usually sauntering, Squeak was moving more like he had hoe down music playing in his ear. He was aggravated by the things Wily had said to him. But now his only concern was getting home safely.

Outside of his two big wood-working hands, Squeak had no other protection. He was thinking he should have worn the crucifix Parsons had taken the time to make for him.

Squeak wasn't halfway home when a wind gust blew his bowler hat from his head, sending it rolling down the street in the direction he had just come. Let it go, Squeak thought, as he kept moving toward home. The last time he had witnessed such a shift in the weather was the time the vampire had shown himself to Jef, Parsons, Thumper and he.

Over the sound of his own clomping he made walking down the board-walk, Squeak could now hear other footsteps. Someone was following him. But they sounded much lighter on their feet.

Squeak was about to call out to ask who was there, but he didn't want whoever was following him to know he knew he was being followed.

Squeak's home was still a block away. He was halfway home. But if he cut through Grimley's pigpens, he might be able to find safety a little faster at the church.

If he was going to change his path of direction, now was the time to do it.

Squeak bolted from the boardwalk, running as fast as his long, gangly legs would carry him toward the pigpens that offered a welcome stink.

Possibly the flapping of a cape, or wings, is all Squeak could hear outside of his own deep breathing.

His long, right leg easily cleared the short fence keeping the pigs at bay. But his left leg caught the top rail, sending him face-first into the pen.

Squeak was only down for a second before jumping back up and running straight for the church, the night air filling his lungs as he began to cry for help like a child.

"Parsons, help me!" Squeak yelled, nearly out of breath from running and screaming.

It was then a lantern turned bright in the church house windows. His hope was Parsons would either fling open the door to the church prior to him reaching the church porch, or he would come running out of the church with his wooden cross held high.

But just when Squeak thought he had made it, he lost his footing for a second time, stumbling to the ground face-first. This time into the dirt, a few feet short of the church entryway porch.

Squeak would have cursed had he not been so dependent on the holy edifice. But then like the miracle it was, the church door swung open, and out came Parsons, like a cavalry soldier to the rescue.

In one hand Parsons held his wooden cross, in the other the wooden stake shooter Squeak had provided the pastor with. By all appearances, even in the dark, Squeak could see Parsons had loaded the weapon.

"Back to the bowels of hell you go," Parsons screamed at the shadowy figure pursuing Squeak. While Parsons positioned himself between Squeak and his attacker, Squeak continued on into the safety of the chapel where Parsons's son John stood in the open doorway, admiring his father's bravery.

"A pastor toting a weapon?" the attacker asked, closing the distance on Parsons to about 20-feet, while the two fighters' only audience, John Parsons and Squeak, had found space just inside the church door, it left slightly ajar in order for them to see the scene play out.

"Parsons, you are out of your league. Evil works abound, whether you're armed with the light of God or a makeshift weapon designed to kill," the figure in the black cape said as he crept closer to Parsons.

"If you come any closer I will be forced to kill you, and I do believe God would forgive me for such a killing," Parsons warned without a tremble.

"Your faith is honorable. But coming to the rescue of others, I am afraid, has led to your demise," the figure said coldly.

By this time, Shirley Parsons, having heard the ruckus outside, had taken a position behind John, and Squeak, who reeked of pig smell.

"Whoever you are, you are unwelcome here," said Parsons, before taking aim with his stake shooter in the direction of the intruder.

"Sorry, Pastor, but there is a higher order here in Dry Springs that is making the rules," the figure said.

With that, the figure drew a pistol from his cape and shot Parsons several times in the chest.

"Why, you," Parsons uttered, unable to react fast enough to pull the trigger on his stake-shooter.

The flashes of gunfire stunned Squeak, John and Shirley. It was the first time they suspected the vampire had used a weapon to take his prey. By the time the smoke from the gunfire cleared, all that remained was Parsons lying on the ground motionless, his black tunic splotched with fresh red.

John Parsons instinctively attempted to run to his father's aid, but Squeak grabbed onto the young man to keep him safe, while using his foot to close the church door they had been using as a window.

Shirley Parsons also latched onto her son, oblivious to Squeak smelling like pig slop.

"I know you can hear me," a voice from outside the chapel called to the group huddled behind the chapel door.

It was the voice of the vampire.

"Squeak, I want all the shooters," Oscuro yelled, breaking Parsons's wooden stake shooter in half and tearing away its guitar string and placing it in his trouser pocket.

"All of them. Do you understand? And until I have them in my possession, I will remain in Dry Springs. So, it's your call, carpenter," Oscuro said, his words penetrating the chapel door.

Even though the vampire couldn't see him, Squeak hid his dirty face in his dirty hands, trying to conceal his anguish.

"I wish I would have never made those weapons," Squeak bemoaned to John and Shirley Parsons.

But while Squeak crawled into a shell, John Parsons's anger was boiling to the surface. The young Parsons did not possess the calm, quiet demeanor of his father.

"God knows who you are, and he will find you," John Parsons yelled loud enough so the vampire could hear him through the closed door.

Squeak, although not an overly religious person, added to that a quiet "Amen," while Shirley Parsons wept bitterly.

The three would give it some time, maybe even morning light, before venturing out of the church to retrieve Parsons's body that lay about 40 feet from the church porch.

During the wait, Squeak racked his soul as to why he ever listened to Jef in creating the weapons. Had he not created them, there was a great likelihood Parsons would still be alive. Squeak was beginning to believe the vampire had brought a curse to their town that was never going to leave, even when the vampire did.

CHAPTER 96

"Isn't it bad luck to kill a reverend?" Ike gleefully asked his gloomy master, who was looking over what was left of the weapon he had retrieved from Parsons.

But as pleased as Oscuro was at taking out of the hands of the townies their only true defense against him, he was in no playful mood, unexpectedly grabbing Ike around the neck and pushing him up against the wall of their home.

"You can be replaced," Oscuro said, digging one of his long fingernails into Ike's throat to stress his point. "Do you understand?"

Ike nodded. "I just killed you a reverend," he reminded Oscuro. "A matter of fact, your cape is a little heavier than I thought it would be. I had a difficult time keeping pace with that ostrich man," he said, referring to Squeak.

"Yes, but it was a plan that worked to perfection," Oscuro said, taking pleasure in recollecting what had just occurred. "Are any of those people going to be able to identify you?" Oscuro asked. "I would hate to have Sheriff Wily chasing us down," he added laughingly.

"I stayed in the shadows to shoot him, and by then you arrived," Ike said. "I'll never forget the surprised look on the reverend's face when I pulled that pistol. It was worth gold, I tell ya. He thought he was messing with you and got me," Ike said, boasting of his accomplishment.

"That leaves one weapon still out there," Oscuro said, purposely interrupting Ike's boasting.

"I would think Jef has the last shooter," Ike said.

"Even though we know Wily has already confiscated a weapon from Jef?" Oscuro asked.

"Jef having the weapon is the only reason why he walks and talks with such confidence," said Ike, reminding Oscuro which town member appeared to be the most defiant.

"I thought that may have been his Mormon thing," Oscuro said, speculating on where Jef was getting his courage. "Oddly, he claims God watches over him, but he wears no cross."

"He's just trying to show off for his pretty wife," Ike interjected. "Besides, outside of Jef, the only other person Squeak may have crafted a weapon for is Ajacks," Ike said.

"You would go a long way to find yourself in favor with me, Ike, if you were to locate the last of these little gems," Oscuro said, holding up what was left of Parsons's stake-shooter.

"I'll find it," Ike said. "If I can shoot a reverend, I can sure as shoot a sheriff's deputy or a newspaperman."

Ike was now more eager to serve Oscuro, now that he knew Oscuro had Sheriff Wily as a potential partner.

"Ike, you are almost as evil as I," Oscuro said, prior to retiring to his sleeping chambers.

Chapter 97

The headline read: VAMPIRE RIPS THE SPIRIT OUT OF DRY SPRINGS.
Parsons's murder sent a ripple through Dry Springs the likes of the 1849 gold rush, with several families packing up their belongings and leaving town – some permanently, others temporarily, until it was safe.

Sheriff Wily could offer no reassurances.

But a determined Jef, at the coaxing of his wife, would be digging in, taking an active role in Parsons's funeral services.

John Parsons had called on Jef to offer his father's eulogy. "I know you believe differently than we do, but my father respected you for your faith," John Parsons told Jef when asking the favor.

"I don't think we thought all that differently, but yes, I would be honored to do so," was Jef's reply.

But he would do it with a heavy heart. Someone working in partnership with the vampire had come forward to shoot and kill Parsons. Jef suspected it was Ike.

CHAPTER 98

The sunlight poured through the church's stained glass windows, splashing with color all the black, white and gray being worn by the somber congregation.

There was a slight fall breeze blowing through the chapel as a result of the church door being swung wide open. It was as if Parsons had already made friends with God on the other side and had made a request for Mother Nature to attend his service.

Jef, standing behind the pulpit, felt butterflies in his belly. But he rationalized his nerves away, recognizing those in the crowd were his friends, albeit some looked mighty different sitting out there with their best dress on instead of their everyday wear.

One in particular who looked out of place was Ike, who had found a seat on the back row of the chapel. His sandy blond hair, normally covered by a hat, slicked back like an ocean wave.

Stan Peterson was nowhere to be seen.

Sitting on the front row of the chapel benches were Sheriff Wily and Deputy Ajacks. Jef was disappointed to see Prudy Richards was not on Ajacks's arm. He was hoping the pair would mend their differences. Although, after recently visiting with Prudy, he wasn't sure she was the same girl who use to warmly welcome all the school-aged children to school.

On the bench directly behind Wily and Ajacks was the Furst family, Jef's anchor. Lola looked stunning. Jef always got a kick out of those who would remind him: "What is that," referring to Lola, "doing married to someone like you," meaning himself.

It was such talk that made Jef proud of being able to secure her hand.

Before Jef had taken a place behind the pulpit, Mayor Howard stepped up to it and offered for Parsons what may have well been the shortest eulogy on record.

Howard, in a mumble, spoke briefly, then sat back down, as if he feared he was going to get struck by lightning if he stood up there any longer.

Now it was Jef's turn, the crowd now staring back at him.

Jef cleared a small hitch in his throat and latched onto the podium with both hands, much like Parsons did when delivering his sermons. Not being a full-fledged member of the congregation, Jef was uncertain how a Mormon would be received. But after some prayerful study, Jef had opted to share with the group a lesson of faith and how Parsons possessed that quality to the end.

"It says in the New Testament those who have faith the size of a mustard seed can move mountains," Jef opened, carefully sliding his glasses up onto the bridge of his nose.

"Parsons had that kind of faith," he proclaimed. The room was eerily silent.

Jef then recounted to the crowd how Parsons became town pastor after going through a series of jobs, and how it must have been the Lord that brought him to where he finally landed.

"This town was lucky to have him," Jef said, choking back emotion. But this day, Jef refused to relent to tears. The town cried out for someone to lead and whether Jef liked it or not, he was it.

Jef shared with the congregation how Parsons always desired to do the right thing, and how he was innocently gunned down by a ruthless killer while responding to the cries of another.

It was with those words that Jef forced Ike off the back bench and out the already open church door.

The crowd was now completely still. There was no squirming, twitching or rustling on the wooden benches, with all the breathing being done in a collective chorus.

And then Lola noticed a transformation of sorts taking place with her be-speckled husband. A man, at one time considered to be an outcast cowboy and an annoyance, was fast becoming the trusted voice of the town.

And in looking around the chapel, Lola realized, others could see the same transformation in her once timid husband. It was as if Jef's words were his weapon, and his compassion for those around him, his rallying cry.

Lola couldn't help but be overwhelmed by a warmth she could not explain.

Then Jef reverted to the Old Testament: "If I were in the lions' den, in addition to Daniel, I'd want Parsons by my side. I am at times so sorry that I cannot be as brave," Jef added apologetically, his eyes fixed on his family.

Lola stared back at him, wondering who this man was.

"But sure enough, now is the time for bravery," Jef proclaimed to the crowd. "We must gather like an army of angels against this force of darkness that has us clutched in its hands, and if need be, break one at a time each finger on that hand until the stranglehold is lifted.

"It would not only be Parsons's wish for us to do such, but God's wish as well," Jef said, pounding his fist on the pulpit. "Might I remind you all within the sound of my voice, that faith without works is dead. In the name of Jesus Christ, amen," Jef said in closing.

The crowd, seeing Jef in a new light, responded to his message with a collective amen in nearly shaking the pews, while Lola's mouth, after witnessing Jef deliver such a fiery message, was gaping open like an old mine tunnel.

John Parsons gave Jef an approving nod. But Sheriff Wily sat like a stone, as if he were annoyed by the services.

Chapter 99

While the town mourned at Parsons's funeral, Ike plotted. His first stop—Prudy Richards's place.

Ike, better dressed than usual, timidly knocked on Prudy's door, uncertain what he would find when it opened.

When Prudy looking half-asleep finally popped open the door, Ike realized her full transformation from schoolteacher to mistress of the dark was nearly complete.

"What is it," Prudy asked, before motioning with one arm for Ike to enter while shielding her eyes from the sun with her other arm.

Once inside, Ike's eyes quickly adjusted to the dark of the house.

"Is our plan to still on?" Ike asked.

"You promise to honor, love and obey me for the rest of eternity?" Prudy replied flashing a wicked smile, the likes Ike had never seen before.

"I'm in," Ike said, excited over his newfound relationship with Prudy. Ike was so happy he had come to Dry Springs. Almost happy enough to sing Oscuro's praises for bringing him here - but not quite.

"Remember, this is our secret," Ike told Prudy knowing what was at stake.

"Of course, darling," Prudy said, before offering a fiendish laugh that seem to shake her little cottage, while at the same time shake Ike's soul.

Chapter 100

Following Parsons's funeral, Jef took his family home before secretly returning to town to the general store.

There he spent what few extra coins he had made selling newspapers over the last few weeks to buy some extra kerosene he had the store clerk pour into two small glass jars.

Jasper, the clerk, said nothing, outside of giving the newspaperman an odd look.

It was Jef's intentions to use the bottled kerosene to combat the vampire. It was an idea he had come up with after reflecting more on Gibby's death. Jef suspected Gibby used fire to try to fend off the vampire.

"There is no need to alarm Lola," Jef sternly told the clerk. It was his way of politely asking Jasper to keep his purchase between them.

"Going to be doing some strange barbecuing?" Jasper asked Jef, his curiosity getting the best of him.

"You could say that," Jef replied, not wanting to give too much away.

"Well, be careful with those," Jasper said pointing at the jars now filled with the flammable liquid.

"Oh, I will," Jef replied, tightly wrapping the jars in an old flannel shirt he had brought along before placing them deep into his shoulder bag for the ride home.

"Let's get going, Ranger. There is work to be done," Jef said, leaving the store.

"Happy hunting," Jasper said with a smile. It was almost as if the store clerk knew what Jef was up to.

Chapter 101

Mayor Howard and his wife Sue in their packed wagon had reached the outskirts of Dry Springs, near where the town's chillingly altered Welcome to Dry "Blood" Springs sign stood, when they heard a fast galloping horse and a yell.

It was Deputy Ike who was quickly approaching.

Howard, trembling some, turned to his wife sitting next to him on the wagon bench, advising her to let him do all the talking. By the time the Mayor had finished warning his wife, Ike had reached them.

"Leaving town Mayor?" Ike asked. "Yer gonna miss all the fireworks."

"Just off to see family in Twin Bridges," Howard said, trying to remain calm, his round-face already starting to sweat.

"Well, by order of the law," Ike said, tapping the deputy badge he was wearing, "I can't have anyone leaving town at this time, even the mayor,"

"Oh, I checked with Sheriff Wily before departing," Howard said, hoping his explanation would keep his wife and him safe.

"Well Mayor, the problem is, both you and I know, Wily really isn't in charge, don't we?" Ike asked.

Howard reluctantly nodded.

"What I need to have happen is for you to turn this wagon around. Because it would be awfully embarrassing if I were to have to arrest the town mayor," Ike said with a grin.

"We're going," Howard said, patting Sue's knee, frustrated his intentions of escaping Dry Springs had been thwarted.

The Mayor's wife Sue said not a word, but carried a look of worry in her face.

Chapter 102

"**One more weapon** left," Oscuro said, becoming increasingly annoyed with Dry Springs, a town that was starting to get under his dead skin.

"It's likely Jef, possibly Ajacks," Ike said to console his master.

"Ajacks?" Oscuro asked.

"Squeak and he have gotten to be good friends," Ike said. "So, either Jef had two of the weapons, or Ajacks has the last weapon and is playing Sheriff Wily as a cow hand."

Oscuro stroked his bare chin while taking in the information.

"There is a way to resolve all this," Ike said. "We have Wily approach the two of them in getting them to come out to our place. Likely, whoever has the weapon will bring it with them. Then, we have Wily take it from them, worries over."

"You are so devious. That may work. If I wasn't a vampire, Ike, you would frighten me," Oscuro mocked.

"But the sooner we act the better. I caught Mayor Howard and his wife today trying to skip town," Ike shared.

"Good catch," Oscuro said. "Let's keep all the chickens in one coop."

CHAPTER 103

The headline read: VAMPIRE HAS IT COMING TO HIM.
The intention behind Jef's headline and story was to goad into action whoever was hiding behind the vampire's cape.

Jef had tired of being meek and lowly.

"You have got some nerve," Lola told Jef after seeing the morning paper. "Why didn't you just pull the vampire's cape? That would have been safer," she added.

Lola had always demanded Jef be a true cowboy, and now all he was trying to do was oblige her.

"If you and I are going to stay here, we need to be able to live. And this isn't living," Jef said. "I'm tired of having to look into the faces of those who have lost family to this …this thing. And if right makes might, as scripture tells me it does, then we will be given an opportunity to take this creature down."

"Is your pride worth our safety?" Lola asked tersely.

"Are we safe? If so, then let's take a leisurely stroll through town this evening," Jef fired back.

"You know, you're just a newspaperman," Lola reminded. "You're just chasing a story. And the day the subject of your story decides to no longer run, you're in trouble, and not even God can save you."

There, finally, Lola had said what she had wanted to say for days, and Jef was smarting from it.

"I did initially chase after this for ulterior motives," Jef said. "I wanted the respect of others, something I figured I didn't have with many folks, including you at times. But that changed. Now I'm in this for us, and this creature must go, if you and I, or our children, are going to be able to stay," he said.

"Lola, you've always wanted me to be a cowboy, cowboy hat, six-shooter and all," Jef said. "But that is not who I am. I am half of our 'beans and rice' team, remember, even though I often forget which of the two I am, beans or rice."

The wordsmith had again reached Lola's heart.

"So, what's your plan?" Lola asked, almost afraid to hear Jef's answer. "And please, no embellishing, I know how you newspapermen can be."

Chapter 104

Prudy Richards's eyes had slightly cleared, but there was still something alarmingly different about the woman Ajacks loved.

"It's good to see you up and out of bed," Ajacks told her, paying her a nightly visit. He feared saying much of anything would result in Prudy chasing him away with hurtful words.

Prudy offered no hand or response.

Ajacks had stopped by in hope of mending his broken heart. But he had no preconceived notions on how his visit was going to go.

"You're wasting your time with me, Ajacks. My heart belongs to another," Prudy said in such a matter-of-fact tone it wounded the young, tough, confident cowboy to the core.

"Our relationship is dead and buried, alongside so many others who have fallen victim to this town's curse," Prudy said, her words sharp like a knife.

"I'll survive, but I'm only a portion of who I once was. I am now part of a darker plan," Prudy said. "And it is only my memory of you that now keeps you safe from me.

"But you, on the other hand, Ajacks, might not survive. For I know the master will have more than words for you if you do not leave here soon," Prudy said.

"What are you saying?" said a confused Ajacks.

"I'm saying, I am awake, but only because it is dark. And I have awoken this night to find I have a thirst for blood needing to be quenched," Prudy said, her eyes now searing through Ajacks.

"What can I do to bring you back?" Ajacks said. "You're the only woman I have ever loved."

"Do not speak of love with me," Prudy said with a snarl. "I am someone else's bride, and the bridegroom will be along soon to claim me."

Ajacks was stunned into silence.

"Now go, or you'll be my first victim. And I wouldn't want that," Prudy said.

"You talk of ...," but before Ajacks could finish his sentence, Prudy took a swipe at him with her long nails, ripping over the front of his button-down shirt, leaving thin red rake marks across his now slightly exposed chest.

"Do not trifle with me," Prudy said in a voice that was not her own.

"How do I break the curse?" Ajacks said, pleading with her.

Prudy laughed a deep, maniacal laugh. "This is so beyond you," she said. "Your shiny gun can't fix everything."

"No, there must be a way. There is always a way," Ajacks said. "You tell me who your master is, and I will be able to fix it," he said.

"You already know him," Prudy said.

"Who is it?" Ajacks screamed at her.

"It's Roman Oscuro," Prudy said. "Oscuro has my heart."

"Who is Roman Oscuro?" Ajacks said, wanting to know more.

"There are some who know him by other names, including Stan Peterson," Prudy said. "But I warn you, out of pity, not love, that Roman Oscuro is not to be trifled with. He is not from this land, nor from this time."

"Look at me," Ajacks said, grabbing Prudy by the shoulders, forcing her to look into his eyes despite the pain across his chest from where she had scratched him.

"My love for you is real. And if I eliminate your master, I may well eliminate the hold he has over you," he said.

"You, a vampire slayer," Prudy mocked, shaking out of Ajacks's grasp as if he were a child. "He'll eat you alive."

"The next time we meet, you'll have that light back in your eyes," Ajacks said. Ajacks then caught Prudy off guard by grabbing her arms and, before she could react, kissing her on the forehead.

"I'll make this right," Ajacks said, before turning and walking out of Prudy's home.

It was only getting later, and the Peterson place was still about a 20-minute ride away.

In Ajacks's hurry to leave Prudy's cottage, the determined deputy failed to hear her faint warning: "Oscuro has help."

Chapter 105

Ajacks stormed out of Prudy's place and up Main Street to the sheriff's office. His cheeks, blowing out air like he was some sort of steam locomotive, kept his tears away.

Here the vampire had been right under their nose and they hadn't figured it out, well, with the exception of Jef. But nobody had been listening to him except Squeak and Parsons.

"Wily?" Ajacks yelled, bursting through the door of the sheriff's office, having long run out of patience for Wily.

But the deputy's voice merely bounced off the walls of the empty office.

Ajacks figured he would give one more good call outside the office before he moved on without the sheriff. "WILY?" he screamed at the top of his lungs.

And then there was a familiar voice.

"What are you doing?" asked Squeak, who had earlier spotted Ajacks storming up the street.

"It's Stan Peterson. Roman somebody," Ajacks sputtered, trying to bring his friend current as quickly as possible as he made his way to his horse tied to the hitching post just outside the sheriff's office.

"What are you talking about?" Squeak asked.

"The vampire is Stan Peterson. His real name is Roman something. Prudy just told me," Ajacks said, gesturing down the street from where he had come.

"So where ya headed?" Squeak asked.

"I'm a deputy. I'm going to go make an arrest," Ajacks said, jumping on his horse.

"Alone?" Squeak asked.

"Well, I'm not waiting for Wily," Ajacks said. "I've got to get out to the Peterson place before it gets any later."

Squeak grabbed the bridle to Ajacks's horse, preventing the deputy from riding off in a huff. "Hold on. I'll go with you. Let me run and get my anti-vampire bag. I got a sneaking suspicion we are going to need it."

"You're what?" Ajacks asked. But before Squeak could reply, he was already awkwardly running back to his workshop he had just locked up for the night. It wasn't but a few minutes before Squeak returned on his horse, holding a flour sack that based on its misshaped form, appeared to hold a number of items.

"Now we're ready," Squeak told Ajacks, straightening his bowler hat, before giving his horse a giddy-up command and a heel kick to its flanks.

Chapter 106

The unnatural swirling wind popped Wily's hat off his head, messing up his full head of reddish-brown hair.

"Enough with the theatrics, I've seen them before," Wily told Oscuro who now appeared before him, the two standing in the shadows behind the sheriff's office.

"I love to make an entrance," Oscuro responded as the sheriff busied himself by picking up his hat and knocking the dust from it.

"Is our plan still in place? You still intend on bringing me our famed newspaperman this evening so I can make him eat his words?" Oscuro asked with such sharpness his tongue could have split a tree.

"That is the plan," Wily said. "And then after that, my debt is paid. We go our separate ways, never to see or hear from each other again."

"You certain this is the way you want it? I can make you rich," Oscuro said.

"Not interested," Wily responded.

"Don't be so quick. There will come a day when age will creep up on you, and you too will desire to live forever," Oscuro said.

"Is that what you call what you're doing – living?" Wily replied.

"Watch your tone with me," Oscuro said. "I'm cranky and hungry, having gone without human blood for nearly two days now in waiting for you to formulate your plan."

"You have Ike. You don't need another henchman," Wily said.

"Ike? I am not certain he is to be trusted. But I will use him for the time being," Oscuro conceded.

"And we're certain our newspaperman is carrying the last shooter?" Oscuro quizzed Wily.

"It was either Ajacks or Jef, and when I confronted Ajacks about it, he flatly denied it, and was even offended I had asked," Wily said. "We are safe from Ajacks. He is nothing but a lovesick pup."

"I'm stealing his girl, you know, despite your miscalculation that Ajacks would be out of the way by now," Oscuro said.

"How was I to know Ajacks was going to hand off his duty to Gibby?" Wily asked.

"Well, be careful around Ajacks tomorrow, he will be angry," Oscuro warned.

"Tomorrow, I'll be gone," Wily assured Oscuro.

"I'll miss you, Wily," Oscuro said. "Your escapades have allowed me to see a part of the country I never thought of visiting. If you don't mind, I too will be leaving tomorrow. These wide-open spaces make me a little claustrophobic. But if you don't mind, before I go, I think I'll stop by Mayor Howard's place and give him a fright."

"Just a fright?" Wily asked out of concern for the man who had hired him to be sheriff.

"Just a fright," Oscuro repeated. "I promise."

For the last time, Oscuro extended Wily his hand. But the sheriff once again declined to take it, and instead gave Oscuro a nod.

Then, like the black magic he rode in on, Oscuro began twirling at such a speed that a dust cloud formed to offer him cover as he made his transformation from human to vampire bat, taking flight in the direction of the mayor's house.

Wily was again annoyed by the whole spectacle created by Oscuro's transformation, but grateful to be able to be completing his final transaction with the creature.

Wily made his way back inside the sheriff's office. About 20 feet from where the sheriff had been conversing with Oscuro was a small figure, huddled behind empty box crates once filled with stock belonging to the Means Saloon.

Todd Means, who had gone behind the saloon to break down crates as part of his work, had overheard the entire conversation between Wily and the man he called Oscuro.

Now the only question that remained for Todd was who he was going to tell first about the meeting. The teen, still reeling from seeing Oscuro transform into a bat, was having a difficult time trusting anyone with his father now gone.

Means decided his first stop would be the saloon to tell Carl Rogers what he had seen and warn him to quickly close up. His second stop would be home to tell his mother, with his third stop to Jef's place to warn his friend about the devious plan being hatched to kill him.

CHAPTER 107

Jef was just about to sit down and read his children a story when there was a rap at the door. The single knock had power behind it, causing the door to quake.

The knock brought Lola out of her nightly routine of sewing, this time the article of clothing being one of the children's britches. The Furst family motto when it came to fashion was to wear it out.

The knock also put Ranger in sentry mode. The dog giving one initial bark in letting everyone in the house know he was on duty.

"Who is it?" Jef called out, approaching the door so he could hear the reply of the person on the other side.

"It's Sheriff Wily," was the response.

"Wily?" Lola questioned Jef in a quiet tone. "Now what have you done, James," she said with a voice only Jef could hear.

Jef just shook his head in response and refocused his attention on the front door.

"Hurry, I know you're in there," Wily's voice could be heard. Wily had a distinctive voice, sounding a lot like he was storing glass marbles in his cheeks.

Before popping the door open, Jef flashed Lola and Ranger an odd look, as if to tell them to prepare for anything. Ranger added his own quizzical look to the equation by raising his ears and staring at the door latch in anticipation of his master lifting it.

When the door creaked open, even in the poor light, the first thing Jef noticed was Wily's long scar.

Based on Wily's cold expression, Jef knew it was no social call. Lola stood behind Jef, Ranger right behind her.

"I'm going out to the Peterson place to finish things," Wily said. "Can't find any hint of Ajacks or Ike. Hoping you might ride with me?" he asked.

Hearing Wily's words, Lola was initially relieved, breathing a deep sigh of relief. She just knew Jef was wrong about Wily. But then it donned on her, Wily wanted Jef to accompany him to the Peterson place, possibly the vampire's lair.

Jef didn't know how to respond to Wily's request. Was Wily coming around? Jef doubted it. So before answering the Sheriff, Jef looked to his wife for input.

Jef figured if Wily needed help, he would be the last one in Dry Springs the sheriff would turn to. And it wasn't customary for Wily to request help. The lawman exuded confidence. It poured through his vest, chaps and gun belt. Wily reeked of the cowboy Lola dreamed of.

"What will it be?" Wily asked, trying to get some sort of response from Jef. "You've written enough about the vampire's stranglehold on this town. If your suspicions are right, we can do something about that this evening."

Wily seemed to be making sense.

But Jef was having a hard time buying the turnaround. A calm, collected voice whispered to his heart to not let his guard down.

"Let me grab a few things. It will take me a few minutes," Jef said.

While Wily stood near the door way and waited, Jef rushed to the barn to retrieve his two tightly wrapped glass jars of kerosene, his wooden stake shooter and seven stakes, all items he had placed in a potato sack and buried under a manure pile so they wouldn't be disturbed.

Jef also checked his trousers for the flint stone he had a habit of carrying.

Jef had been preparing for this day, but figured while alone he would offer up a short prayer. In it, the only thing he asked for was for God to protect his family from harm.

While a seemingly brave Jef kneeled in silence out in the barn, an uncomfortable Wily was waiting on the front porch of the Furst family's cabin home.

It was several minutes later when Jef had returned.

"Got everything?" Wily asked eyeing the burlap potato sack Jef was now packing. The sheriff hoping the bag contained the last of the stake shooters.

Before Jef could jump aboard Lola's horse, his wife wrapped her slender olive-skinned arms around his neck. Wily would have to wait a little longer.

"Be careful," Lola said. "Your children need a father, and I need a man." She smiled before planting a kiss on Jef's lips, causing him to blush.

"It is times like this that I wish you were going. You are a much better shot than I am," Jef told Lola under his breath.

"Cowboy, aim straight," she said choking back the emotion. Lola was holding Jef so tight it was difficult for him to be able to see if she had a tear or two in her big brown eyes. But he could sense through her embrace he had married the right girl.

"Take care of him, Sheriff, or you'll have me to deal with," Lola said, reverting back to her tougher side as Jef jumped on his horse.

In the last few weeks, Lola had seen Jef grow from Mormon pioneer to town leader. Of late, there was no doubt the man who had her heart was beginning to show his mettle. If only her mother, who anguished over her marrying Jef because of the difference in their cultures, could see him now, Lola thought.

Almost from habit since wearing a sheriff's star, Wily assured Lola no harm would befall her husband.

Before departing into the night with Wily, Jef had only one question remaining: "Ranger, you in?"

Ranger's ears immediately picked up, his head rotating toward Lola for one last look before joining his new best friend on what was likely to be their wildest adventure.

Wily was agitated by the whole syrupy scene playing out before him. He too wanted to go finish this thing. Just not in the same manner Jef wanted to finish it.

CHAPTER 108

The Peterson ranch house, about a third of a mile off the road, was neatly sandwiched between pasture land to the west and corn fields to the east.

The corn fields, which appeared neglected, had a wagon-width road dividing the series of tall stalks. It would be that narrow road Ajacks and Squeak would take into the property.

Ajacks, having been there previously, was aware all the windows in the house had been boarded up for the approaching winter. Or at least that was how Wily had explained it to him.

With each trot his horse took down the dark lane, Ajacks became increasingly anxious, uncertain what the pair would find.

Squeak was equally nervous – wearing a facial expression like he had an appointment with a tooth extractor.

During their ride, the pair shared few words, Ajacks still stewing over the thought he was about to lose Prudy Richards to a demon spell.

"We'll get off our horses here and walk in," Ajacks said, the pair now 100 yards from the front of the house. "You may want to take off that ridiculous looking hat to avoid giving our position away," Ajacks added, referring to Squeak's bowler hat, which he had nearly lost earlier.

Rather than debate the issue of whether his bowler hat had character or was just plain unsightly, Squeak removed it from his head and, not saying a word, rested the hat on the horn of his saddle.

Ajacks had already begun checking the rounds in his gun, reassuring himself his pearl-handled six-shooter was fully loaded.

Squeak hated to interrupt the cowboy's routine, but based on his experience with the vampire, Ajacks' firearm would be of no use. "You realize your gun is useless against this thing, if in fact Stan Peterson is the vampire," Squeak offered.

"What would you suggest? We walk in there with rocks in our hands?" Ajacks said defiantly, his head gesturing toward the house.

"Besides, you ever consider the vampire might not be the only one in there?" Ajacks said. "Where there is Stan, there is Ike, and we know Ike is no vampire."

Squeak nodded in agreement. But just the same, the carpenter would be relying on those items he was packing in his anti-vampire bag.

"What have you got in there?" Ajacks asked Squeak of the sack he had untied from his saddle, and slung over his shoulder.

To avoid having to dump the contents of the bag onto the ground, Squeak used one long arm to hold the bag and the other to reach down inside it, in sharing what he had brought along.

"A flour bomb," Squeak said, holding up the first item. "Another flour bomb, this one packed a little tighter," he said. "These can be effective. I've also got a wooden stake in here in case we get close enough to stick it into the vampire's heart," Squeak said, before continuing to reach into the sack and pull out another surprise like he was Saint Nick.

"One ripe tomato," he added, continuing with his process.

"What's that for?" Ajacks asked curiously.

"It's to eat in case I get hungry. I didn't have dinner," Squeak replied. "Oh, a clove of garlic, and one mended fishing net the vampire has seen before. I also brought this wooden cross along Parsons made for me some time ago. But I think I lack the faith to make it work."

"Like you, I'm not much of a religious man. But I reckon in fighting a vampire, you'd want God on your side," Ajacks conceded. "Give it to me if you're not going to wear it."

Squeak then placed the wooden cross attached to a leather strap around Ajacks's neck like he was knighting a king.

Ajacks took a moment to stare down at the cross hanging from his neck, hoping it would keep him safe, before the pair tied off their horses and left the road, ducking into the brush in hopes of being able to come up from the back side of the house.

"Keep your head down and eyes open," Ajacks advised.

Squeak grunted, firmly clutching his bag.

From where he was standing upstairs, Ike was able to get enough of a look from out of the boarded-up window to be able to make out Ajacks and Squeak approaching the house.

But rather than alert Roman, Ike figured he would take care of these two guys himself. He figured he owed Ajacks.

Chapter 109

Jef and Wily hadn't been gone for five minutes when Lola heard a young man's screams and an approaching clomping horse, coming from outside the cabin.

"Miss Furst," she could hear her name being yelled. It was the voice of young Todd Means.

The commotion had brought Lola's two boys, clad in their nightshirts, from their bedroom. The boys stared at their mother, wiping signs of sleep from their eyes.

"You children stay there," Lola said, insisting they come no farther while she opened the door for Todd. For whatever reason, Lola's kids looked up to Todd, who treated the children with nothing but respect.

"Miss Furst, Miss Furst," Todd stood at the door sputtering while catching his breath between words.

"Come in out of the night," Lola responded, grabbing Todd by the arm and leading him into her house so as to close the door behind him.

"What is it, Todd?" Lola asked, trying to be patient while waiting for the boy to get his bearings.

"I overheard a conversation between Sheriff Wily and a man named Roman. It's a trap. Your husband is in trouble," Todd said. "The sheriff is taking Jef to the Peterson place where this Roman, who is the vampire, is waiting for him."

It was with Todd's words that Lola's bronze skin lost all color.

"I know of no Roman," Lola said.

"Roman is the vampire," Todd said, before realizing what he had just blurted out before Lola's young children.

"You're saying Wily is in cahoots with this Roman, who is staying at the Peterson place?" Lola asked, still with so many questions in her mind.

"So, where are Stan and Ike?" Lola asked, before realizing now was not the time to be playing 20 questions with Todd. If she was to save Jef, she would have to hurry.

"Todd, I'll need your help getting my children someplace safe," Lola said.

While Todd stood at the door, Lola grabbed her two boys, blew out the candles she had burning, and raced to the barn to saddle up old Stu, where Jef had taken her horse.

"If you can pack James Jr., I can take Bobby," Lola told Todd.

"Where are we going, Momma?" James Jr. asked, frightened and confused at her urgency.

"I'm going to go help Daddy and Ranger," she said, not wanting to reveal much more to her already traumatized children.

"So where are Bobby and I going?" James Jr. asked, peppering his mother with questions, much like his father would if he were here.

"Todd and I are going to find you guys a safe place to stay for a little while," Lola said, and with that the four of them were off to town.

But in her rush, Lola had forgotten her gun until she was already halfway to town. She thought maybe she could swing back to her cabin and get it on her way out to the Peterson place.

Chapter 110

Hiding behind a tree and waiting for the pair to pass by was Ike's way. With Ajacks out of the way, that was one less person he would have to compete with for Prudy Richards's hand.

But it would be a few minutes before Ajacks and Squeak would be making their way past his concealed position, giving him time to think about how he was going spend his share of the money Oscuro and he had collected from selling off the Peterson's assets.

Ike figured he had over $600 stuffed into the pockets of his coat that hung in his room. Oscuro's share was a little more than that. Ike wanted to keep his vampire friend happy.

The sound of fallen tree twigs snapping under the feet of Squeak and Ajacks making their way through the dense forest immediately brought Ike out of his thoughts.

Cautiously moving closer to the ranch house, Ajacks drew his gun, while Squeak armed himself with one of his flour bombs. He figured if the vampire couldn't see them, he couldn't rip their throats out.

Up ahead was a cluster of larger pine trees that Ajacks could envision Darwin and Mabel Peterson at one time huddling under to find shade from the heat of the day. It was the same sort of peaceful scene he had pictured in his mind for Prudy and he someday.

CHAPTER 111

Wily said little and rode.

Jef found it odd the two were riding partners. He realized some time ago he annoyed the sheriff the rest of the town had come to love and respect.

"Why tonight?" Jef couldn't help but ask.

"Why tonight, what?" Wily grumbled his horse maintaining stride.

"What makes you think tonight is the best opportunity to visit the Peterson ranch?" Jef asked.

"Call it a lawman's hunch," Wily said, keeping his words to a minimum.

Ranger kept pace with the two men, seemingly determined not to let Jef out of his sight.

"Well, I hope you're prepared for most anything, Sheriff," Jef said, trying to cut through the tension between the men.

Wily was a hardened man hiding behind a mystery, while Jef was an open book, his boyish face making him appear even younger than his 26 years. The flat gray cap and wire-rimmed glasses he wore only adding to his youthful appearance.

And while Jef had a face with nary a facial hair, Wily often wore a shadow of whiskers, the scar down his face serving as notice he had been battle tested.

Jef was glad the two of them were on the same side this time.

Chapter 112

Dry Springs resembled a ghost town. There wasn't a soul on the streets when Todd, Lola and her two children hurriedly rode into town, going directly to the church.

"You kids will be safe here," Lola said, helping the children off their horses. Despite Lola's assurances that everything would be all right, both children wore a look of fright and confusion.

"Todd, take them inside, let Shirley know I'm riding out to the Peterson place to help Jef," she said.

"But Miss Furst...," was all Todd Means could mutter before the fiery Latina interrupted him.

"I can't have you go with me," Lola said. "I couldn't live with myself if something happened to you. You're a good man, Todd Means. Help Shirley look after my children."

"Bye, Momma. Bye, Momma," her children said before Lola kissed them each on the cheek and rode off toward the center of town to see if Squeak was still up. Squeak, a longtime family friend, could help Lola execute the plan she had formulated in her mind while riding into town.

But when she arrived at the door of Squeak's small sleeping quarters tucked behind one of the Main Street shops, she saw that Squeak's horse, normally tied to a neighboring fence, was gone.

Out of desperation Lola banged hard on his door, but as expected got no response. Frustrated, she wadded up her fist even tighter and hit the door a little harder, yelling Squeak's name as she did so.

Still, no response, the place buttoned up tighter than a church dress.

Oddly, Lola noticed, there was also no deputy on patrol. Where was Ike or Ajacks? Had they gone with the sheriff?

Her plan would now have to change as she looked for any late lantern burning in any of the nearby homes.

Quickly glancing over the dark town, Lola spotted a light burning in the window where Otis Thumper and his mother lived.

Lola took her discovery as a sign from God.

Thumper's house was neatly situated next to the blacksmith shop where he pounded horseshoes and wagon wheels most of his days. Thumper never liked to venture very far from his mother.

Lola's rapid knocking on Thumper's door caused a stir within the little home. "Help," Lola cried into the door, hoping it would speed their response.

Mrs. Ora Jean Thumper opened the door just slightly to see who it was.

"Where's Otis? I need his help," Lola asked the woman, who had a face like a sponge.

"Mrs. Furst, being a married woman, you have no cause to be calling on my son at such an hour. You come back in the morning, you hear, when you can catch up with Otis at the blacksmith shop," Mrs. Thumper said, before attempting to shut the door.

Lola held out her thin arm as if it would prevent the door from closing. "You don't understand. My husband is in danger. It's the vampire. I need Thumper's—Otis's—help," she pleaded.

Lola generally was not one to beg.

"I told ya, he'll be at the blacksmith shop tomorrow. Besides, the last time he did you Fursts a favor, your husband nearly got him killed with his harebrained scheme," Mrs. Thumper said before slamming the door shut on Lola, leaving her once again alone in the dark.

Remaining steadfast, Lola would do what she could to execute her plan on her own. Jef needed her help.

The ride over to the sheriff's office was a short one. There, as expected, she found the office locked, the structure built more like a strong box than an office building.

Already in a frightened state, Lola picked up the biggest rock she could lift and began furiously pounding on the sheriff's office door like a mad-woman in love.

She hit the door handle repeatedly with the mini-boulder, hoping it would give. But all the door did was shudder under her blows. She needed in. Her hope was the last of the wooden stake shooters was still in the sheriff's wall-mounted locker. Thinking about Jef, and the valuable time that was wasting, made her pound harder. Again, and again, and again she banged the door handle with the large rock, its jagged edges inflicting small cuts to the palm of her hand. Lola switched hands and began pounding away again, oblivious to the noise she was making.

"Please God, help," she muttered, not missing a beat with her blows. As if each blow would beat down all the barriers she and Jef had already overcome in trying to make a go of it in the wild West.

But her effort appeared fruitless, tears beginning to pool in her eyes, making it difficult for Lola to actually see the door handle she was pound-ing on. Knowing what was at stake, she refused to relent. Each blow to the hard wooden door echoing through the little town she desired to call home.

Lola found sad irony in the fact the jail Crazy Max was able to break free from, she could not break into even in her darkest hour.

"Give up!" she screamed at the handle, as if it had taken on a life of its own. Tears were now streaming down her face. It wasn't very often Lola cried. Even after losing her mother, few tears were shed.

And now a stranger was trying to interfere with what was becoming a perfect union with Jef.

"I will not go away!" Lola screamed at the door, as if it were now the only thing standing in the way of everything she ever wanted.

Just as Lola was repositioning the rock in her hand to begin another se-ries of pounding blows to the door, there came a noise from behind her. It was the sound of heavy breathing and heavy feet.

"Stand out of the way, Miss Lola," Thumper said his blacksmith hammer in hand. "I'm just hoping you got good reason for breaking into the sheriff's office."

"Thumper, please, take down the door," Lola asked.

"Don't have to ask twice ma'am," Thumper replied, before winding up in taking his first swing.

Chapter 113

Despite it being a cool night, Ajacks could feel the cold steel barrel of the pistol pushed against the side of his head. He had done the very thing he warned Squeak not to do—walk into a trap.

"Ever so slowly, hand your fancy pistol to me, partner," Ike said in a hushed tone.

Ajacks had walked into a cluster of trees on the backside of the Peterson home, unaware Ike would be waiting there for him.

"Where is your stork-like friend?" Ike asked, taking possession of Ajacks's gun and shoving it into the front waistband of his pants.

"I don't know," Ajacks responded dejectedly, angry at himself for making it so easy for Ike.

"Call to him. Tell him your little adventure is over," Ike said, applying more pressure to the gun barrel he had pressed up against Ajacks's temple.

"Squeak, you'd better come in," Ajacks yelled, doing everything he could to keep fear from his voice. The last time Ajacks had seen Squeak he was about 60 feet behind him. Because of his awkwardness, Squeak lagged in finding his footing through the thicket.

And now, in the dark, his partner was nowhere to be seen.

"I mean it, Squeak. You had better turn yourself in," Ike yelled impatiently, all while keeping his focus on Ajacks.

Ike figured of the two, Ajacks and Squeak, it was Squeak who posed the least threat to him.

"I want you to know I stole some kisses from your girl," Ike told Ajacks as the two stood in the dark, Ajacks staring straight ahead, with Ike standing just off to his right.

"That Prudy, she is a real pretty girl. You should have paid more attention to her," Ike teased, hoping to provoke Ajacks.

"Oh, that girl," Ajacks said, "that's not the same Prudy I had come to love."

"Don't get smart me with me, Deputy," Ike said, ripping Ajacks's tin star from his vest.

It was at about that same time Ike noticed the cross hanging around Ajacks's neck.

"Don't tell me, Ajacks, you have found God in this desolate wilderness? Or is that to ward off any stray vampires? Well, you needn't worry about the vampire. I don't need his help to take care of the likes of you two," Ike said.

"Now where is that Squeak?" Ike demanded.

Often clumsy, Squeak made barely a rustle jumping from out of the brush with his rifle gripped in both hands, using the butt of it to quickly strike Ike on the back of the head.

The impact immediately knocked Ike to his knees, the pistol he had trained on Ajacks falling from his hand as if it were hot.

Before Ike could react, Squeak followed up his surprise attack by casting his stinky fish net over Ike, who seemed down, but not out.

Squeak's interference was all the distraction Ajacks needed in evening the playing field with Ike, who was a little older and bigger than the young deputy.

"What the...," Ike said, trying to rise back to his feet with the heavy net draped over top of him.

Before Ike could rise, Ajacks landed a windmill-like punch to the side of Ike's face, dropping their nemesis under the net, out for the count.

"Retrieve your gun. Retrieve your gun," Squeak stammered, pointing at Ajacks's pearl-handled pistol now visible through the net.

Ajacks reached under the net and pulled his six-shooter out from Ike's waistband.

"Should we hit him again?" Squeak asked excitedly, raising his gun stock in the air, poised to strike.

"No," Ajacks said. "Ike isn't going anywhere."

"I seen he had ya, I had to do something," Squeak said, nervous over the fact he may have to kill a man.

"I appreciate you coming along when you did," Ajacks said. "I believe Ike would have shot me. He would have shot you, too."

Ajacks's words put Squeak at ease.

"I'll hit him again if needed," Squeak offered, this time not raising his gun quite as high in the air.

"I don't think that is going to be necessary," said Ajacks, whose heart was just beginning to beat normally again. "We'll come back for Ike later," Ajacks said, gathering up Ike's pistol that had fallen to the ground. "Again, thanks, partner," Ajacks said, for the first time expressing some appreciation for his knobby-kneed friend.

"You're welcome," Squeak said, now beaming with confidence. "Don't forget your badge, Ajacks," Squeak added, pointing to Ike, who remained unconscious under the net.

Ajacks smiled before reaching under the net a second time in pulling his deputy badge from the side pocket of Ike's jacket, and ripping away the deputy star pinned to Ike's shirt. "Now, let's go find Stan Peterson," Ajacks said, feeling tougher by the minute.

Squeak nodded, his arms clutching his anti-vampire bag, now minus one stinky old fish net.

CHAPTER 114

The sweat from Thumper's face ran like a river, his black beard not big enough to hold the droplets from running down his neck onto his shirt.

Thumper was putting his heart and soul into every swing, as the sound from his thwacks shook the night.

The blacksmith had already busted through the door of the sheriff's office and was now working on the wall-mounted locker where Lola had hoped to find their stake shooter.

"Oh, Miss Lola, how I hope you're right about this one. Or both the sheriff and my momma are going to be mad at us until the end of the world," Thumper said.

"If we're unable to get this stake shooter, Thumper, it may well be the end of the world tonight. Hit it again," Lola said.

Thumper's next blow knocked the locker off the wall and to the floor. Then, with two more strikes of his hammer, Thumper was able to crack open the sheriff's evidence locker like a walnut.

When the locker burst open, it was as if Lola had found gold when the stake shooter and stake still stained with Crazy Max's blood were revealed.

"That's it?" Thumper asked disappointed in what she had grabbed up.

"This is all we'll need if we get close enough," Lola replied.

"Oh, how I hate the way you used the word 'we' there," Thumper said, reluctant to play any more of a role in Lola's scheming than he already had. But the large man couldn't desert the fair maiden in distress. Thumper knew all about that from his mother telling him all those stories when he was a child.

"We've got to get moving. Go get your horse," Lola said. "My husband's life is at stake."

"Yes, Miss Lola," Thumper answered like an obedient child. "Might there be some home cooking in exchange for my helpful deed?"

"Yes. Please, Thumper, hurry," Lola said, not wanting to waste another second.

Chapter 115

Roman Oscuro stared eastward out of the top window of the Peterson ranch house. He was beginning to wonder where Wily was, and the gift he had promised to deliver – James Edward Furst III.

Ever so anxious, Oscuro strolled to the other side of the house to see if he could see where Ike had disappeared to.

As he stepped out into the fall night air and onto the third-story deck the Petersons had built to enjoy the sunsets, Oscuro relished in the fact that he would soon be leaving Dry Springs and going back East where the weather would offer him not such a heavy dose of dry air.

The wood deck provided the vampire with the perfect lookout point over the Peterson property and had served him well as a landing point when making his nightly transformations from bat back to man.

Scanning the property with his keen night vision, he could see Ajacks and Squeak slowly making their way toward the house from the back of the property, as if they thought they could sneak up on him.

But where was Ike, he wondered. Upon closer inspection of the property, he spotted his partner, lying unconscious, wrapped in the same fish net Squeak had once dropped over his head. It was a pungent smell Oscuro would never forget.

"What in the world?" Oscuro muttered. Surely the two dim-witted fools approaching the house had not overpowered Ike, he wondered.

Now the question was, did Oscuro fly to Ike's rescue, and possibly miss out on Wily's special delivery, or guard the house.

What was a vampire to do, Oscuro mockingly asked himself. Ike would have to wait. Besides, if Oscuro could convince Wily into coming with him, there would be no need for Ike.

Chapter 116

Thumper almost looked too big for his horse. But Lola was glad he was joining her. She was also pleased to see that in addition to his blacksmith hammer, Thumper had gone back home and retrieved his shotgun.

"Thanks again," Lola said, hoping her encouraging words would be enough to keep Thumper motivated throughout the rescue.

But the pair hadn't traveled on horse more than 100 yards from town when they heard the fast gallop of an approaching rider.

"Get behind me, ma'am," Thumper told Lola, instinctively reaching for his shotgun, while Lola took aim with the stake shooter, hoping she wouldn't have to use it, as she only had one stake.

As the figure on the horse got closer, Thumper and Lola brought their horses to a stop.

"Like a third?" the rider yelled, just about the same time Lola recognized him.

"John Parsons Jr., what are you doing out?" Lola asked.

"I figure I got a stake in this fight, too," the junior Parsons said, wearing a gun belt around his waist and a wooden cross around his neck. It was the same cross his father had regularly worn.

"Well, if he is in, can I be out, Miss Lola?" Thumper enquired.

"No, you may not," Lola told Thumper, before turning to John.

"John, I love that you want to help, but your best to stay here, being our last line of defense should the vampire make his way back to town. I need you and Todd Means to protect my children, John. You understand, right?" Lola said.

A somewhat dejected John Parsons Jr. hesitated, remaining silent, before nodding in agreement, as if his place were to safeguard his mother and Lola's children.

"Dagnubit," Thumper said, who was hoping for the company.

With that, John Parsons Jr quickly spun his horse around. But not before reassuring Lola that he was not afraid. "I may be studying to be a man of God, but I've never hungered more to kill a man than Ike," John Parsons Jr. said with a sneer.

And with that, he was off, heading directly for the church.

CHAPTER 117

Little had been said between Wily and Jef during their ride. So when the pair arrived at the narrow dirt road that would take them into the Peterson property, Jef was relieved.

Working their way down the wagon-width road the Petersons regularly used, Jef spotted two horses tied to a tree.

"That Squeak's horse," Jef said quietly.

Wily glanced over at Jef as the two were now side by side in their saddles. "That other horse belongs to Ajacks," Wily added. The sheriff was hoping having Squeak and Ajacks here wasn't going to complicate his plan.

"Let's ride on," Wily said, determined to get closer to the house before dismounting.

Wily's leather gun belt squawked with every little move he made in the saddle, while Jef remained quiet, anxiously waiting for Wily to share his plan of attack.

The closer they got to the house as their horses clomped along, the more nervous Jef became, regularly looking over his shoulder to make certain Ranger was still following him.

"We'll put our horses here," Wily said, putting them about 100 yards from the front porch of the home.

Getting off his horse and grabbing his burlap bag carrying his unique weapon, its ammunition and two jars of kerosene, Jef took in his surroundings. On his right was an obviously neglected cornfield, based on the amount of dried corn left on the stalks. On his left, heavy vegetation and rugged forest terrain providing the ranch the shade needed during the hot summer months the southern Utah territory experienced.

Before throwing his burlap bag over his shoulder like a student headed off to school, Jef made certain his kerosene jars remained tightly wrapped, preventing them from clinking together. To bring their enemy from out of his hiding place, Jef had every intention of using the kerosene to burn the Peterson place to the ground if he had to.

Wily brought his pistol; apparently not realizing vampires were bullet-proof. "Let's go," Wily said, as the trio began making their way toward the house.

"Shouldn't we be looking for another way in?" Jef said in questioning the front door approach they were taking.

"Don't you think I know what I'm doing?" Wily snapped.

Rather than debate the point, Jef instead prepared by pulling from his bag his wooden stake shooter and loading it with one of the seven stakes he had brought along.

Chapter 118

Wily, Jef and Ranger had nearly reached the front porch of the Peterson house when Wily turned, pointing his gun at Jef.

Where it was dark, Jef didn't initially see what Wily had done until the sheriff alerted him to it.

"Give me your weapon," Wily said in a menacing tone.

Jef let out a nervous chuckle before realizing Wily was serious. "What do you mean?" Jef asked, shocked by the request.

"For us to make our problem go away, I'm gonna need that," Wily said, motioning with his gun toward the stake shooter Jef was holding.

Jef was having a difficult time making any sense of it.

"Sheriff, without this," Jef said, tapping the little stake shooter with his free hand, "we're as good as dead."

"No. We turn the weapon over and most of us are going to be able to stay very much alive," Wily replied. "So, I need your weapon."

"You know the vampire is bulletproof, right?" Jef asked. "This little contraption is the best shot we've got," he said of the crude device Squeak had crafted.

"First off, Jef, this guy has a name. It's Roman Oscuro," Wily said. "And I have made a deal with Oscuro that if I bring him the last of the stake shooters, he'll leave town peacefully, on the condition he get to take Prudy with him."

At first Jef remained silent, before everything the Sheriff had just said, registered with him. "WHAT? You sold us out? You sold all of us out?" Jef said, the pitch in his voice grabbing the attention of Ranger, standing nearby.

"If you don't give me the weapon, Jef, I'm going to have to kill you," Wily said.

Even in the dark, Jef could tell Wily wasn't bluffing.

"I thought we came here to capture this Oscuro. I tell you, Wily, we don't have to do it this way, I've got a plan that will work," Jef said coaxingly.

"I've already made my deal," Wily said. "I'm tired of looking over my shoulder and seeing Oscuro staring at me with those eyes full of fire. We two, we go way back," he added, touching the crimson scar that ran down the left side of his face.

"Now give me that thing," Wily demanded.

"I can't," Jef said, nervously pushing his eyeglasses farther up on the bridge of his nose, now standing eye to eye with the sheriff.

Out of frustration Wily reached out to grab the shooter, which in trying to wrestle the stake shooter from Jef's hand had caused it to accidently fire.

The only sound heard in the dark was a distinctive "PING" which the weapon made, followed by Wily's screeching howl.

The stake Jef had earlier loaded into the shooter sliced through the Sheriff's right knee as if were skewing raw meat.

"JEF," Wily cursed though clenched teeth, finally ripping the weapon from Jef's hands and tearing away the guitar string serving as its firing mechanism, before finding the wherewithal to raise his pistol and fire off a shot at Jef.

The bullet fired at such close range pierced Jef's right shoulder, knocking him to the ground for an instant before he could jump to his feet and scamper away.

"Run, Ranger," Jef screamed, as the two found cover in the nearby cornfield. Just as the two made it into the tall stalks, they heard a second shot ring out and Wily curse one more time.

"You are a dead man!" Wily screamed loud enough for the world to hear.

But chasing after Jef would be difficult for the sheriff, who remained in pain, the wooden stake having gone in one side of his knee and partially out the other.

In diving into the cornfield, Ranger and Jef had become separated. Jef, too in pain, blood running from his wounded shoulder down his arm, turning one side of his white pressed printer's shirt bright red. But he had managed to hold onto the burlap bag containing the two small jars of kerosene and six more wooden stakes. The plan, if he got close enough, would still be to stick one of the stakes into the vampire's heart. But in the meantime, he had Wily to contend with.

"I'll wait you out," Wily screamed before blindly firing a third shot into the cornfield at what he thought was movement. But Wily's shot found nothing but dirt a few feet from where Ranger was bounding through the stalks.

If Jef didn't know better, he would think Ranger was thrashing about in an attempt to draw Wily's gunfire. But if Ranger and he were to have any chance against the sheriff, Jef was going to have to draw Wily into the corn field and the sooner the better, based on the amount of blood Jef was losing from his shoulder wound.

Chapter 119

Squeak and Ajacks were about to enter a storm cellar door on the backside of the Peterson house to see where it would lead, when they heard gunfire and the cries of Sheriff Wily.

"Wily is here!" Ajacks exclaimed, relieved to know Squeak and he were no longer alone.

Ajacks, with his pearl-handled pistol drawn, quickly began making his way to the front side of the ranch house toward the sounds, with Squeak following after him. It was upon rounding the corner of the house, that the pair of heroes was surprised to find all the commotion they had heard was Wily actually locked in a battle with Jef, not the vampire.

Roman Oscuro had also heard the Sheriff's cries, moving back to the east side of the house in hopes of finding Wily arriving with Jef and the last of the stake shooters.

But when Oscuro peeked out over the boarded-up window, he found from his third-story vantage point that Wily did not have the situation under control, causing him to fear he may have picked the wrong partner in his diabolical scheming.

Wily, whose leg continued to bleed, throb and now stiffen due to the 8-inch wooden stake piercing his knee, had slowly began wading out into the cornfield after Jef.

"I'm writing this story," Wily yelled out to Jef, as he crept farther into the cornstalks.

Wily's constant bellowing helped Jef track him, allowing him to roll on the ground away from the slow-footed sheriff in hopes of being able to circle back behind him.

But just as Jef was beginning to think he had Wily figured out, the sheriff would stop and fire off another round. Most of his shots aimed Ranger's direction, who had continued to rustle about in the stalks in moving closer to Jef.

Wily's breathing was now labored as he tried to ignore the pain in his knee. "I have given it some thought," Wily called out. "Jef, maybe it would be best if we did team up to take on Oscuro."

The sheriff's words caught Jef's attention. But could Wily be trusted?

"I mean it, Jef, we can do this," Wily coaxed.

Had Wily finally figured out Jef was his best chance to rid the town of the vampire?

Jef wanted to reply but feared doing so would give his position away.

"Well, I'm going back to face this Oscuro fellow, whether you come with me or not," Wily said, turning as if he were about to make his way back out of the cornfield.

"Wait," Jef said, nervously popping up, revealing himself to the sheriff who was about 30 feet away through the stalks.

This would be Wily's last chance to succeed with the task Oscuro had given him. He quickly took aim with his pistol and fired, the bullet skipping off the dirt less than a foot away from where Jef was standing.

Immediately, Jef dropped to the ground, and in an effort to put some distance between the sheriff and he, he began rolling through the stalks, biting his tongue so as not to scream out each time his wounded shoulder made contact with the ground.

Once again finding himself concealed from Wily, Jef reached into his burlap bag and pulled from it one of the small glass jars filled with kerosene he had hoped to use in burning down the ranch house. But if he didn't escape Wily, he would never get the opportunity to get that far with his plan.

Before dousing the surrounding corn stalk with kerosene, Jef pulled from his trouser pocket the flint stone he had brought along in the event of such emergencies.

In making his Mormon pioneer trek with his family from New York to Wyoming, Jef was often given the task of building and starting a campfire using next to nothing.

For Jef, starting the dry cornfield on fire would be easy. And the kerosene would give the fire the flash it needed to cut off all escape routes for Wily.

"God, please forgive me for what I am about to do," Jef muttered before striking the flint over the kerosene-soaked corn stalks.

Immediately, flames filled the space between Jef and his pursuer, as the 5-foot undernourished cornstalks burned liked prairie cheat grass.

It then donned on Wily he may not be able to move fast enough to avoid being trapped by the flames.

At the same time, Jef and Ranger were taking the shortest route to safety, which was a direct route back to the narrow dirt road separating the cornfield from the rough terrain surrounding the Peterson place.

Jef, with his burlap bag draped over his good shoulder, figured the road would serve as the perfect firebreak.

By the time Oscuro could see from the upstairs window what Jef was up to, the entire cornfield was engulfed in flames, with Wily somewhere in the center of it.

Out of desperation, Wily took the time to reload his gun before firing into the wall of flame in the hope one of his bullets would find Jef.

"Come out, newspaperman," Wily said before firing again.

Jef could barely hear the sheriff over the popping cornstalks that now lit up the night.

Jef was proving to be quite the adversary, Oscuro thought, wondering if he should flee the ranch house now with his money in hand or face his nemesis. Certainly, he thought, the first thing he must do is rescue Ike, who could prove to be a valuable asset in the battle.

But when Oscuro made his way to the back side of the house and out onto the deck, Ike was no longer where he had been, and all that remained in the spot was the empty fish net once covering him.

Ajacks and Squeak, upon arriving to the front of the ranch house, couldn't believe their eyes as the cornfield burned before them, sending their direction a wall of heat.

There was no sign of Wily, but the pair could hear the sheriff screaming from within the flames, which were now throwing off a thick, gray smoke and an irritating smell.

"Roman, curse you," Wily could be heard screaming over the roar of the fire, realizing his exit out of the cornfield was now where a wall of flames stood.

"I held up my end of the bargain," Wily cried. "I know you can hear me Oscuro. You owe me, and I'll be taking my payment when I see you on the other side."

Wily realized his death would be painful. But despite that, the sheriff refused to cry out anymore. He refused to give Jef, or Oscuro that satisfaction.

Jef, who had huddled with Ranger a safe distance from the flames, was feeling the weight of his actions, having never killed a man before.

Now he had a better understanding of how Lola felt after shooting Crazy Max.

"Do you think God will forgive me?" Jef asked Ranger before placing his head into his hands as if he were already begging his Father in Heaven for mercy, and his mission not yet complete.

Ranger, flecked in ash, resting between pants, momentarily looked over at his friend, dropping his head in such a way as if to say they had both been caught doing something bad.

"That's what I think, too," Jef said, responding to Ranger's actions.

While the pair huddled in catching their breath, the cornfield burned at a torrid pace.

Squeak and Ajacks stood silently staring at the same flames unaware Jef and Ranger were somewhere on the other side of the burning cornfield.

Ajacks, who for months had hailed Wily as a hero, was stunned to find the sheriff in some way had been tied to the town murders. But he refused to jump to any conclusions before talking with Jef.

While Ajacks wondered what Squeak and his next move would be, Oscuro, looking down on Wily being consumed by fire, was already formulating his next move, knowing Jef was now without his shooting device.

"So, I do write the final chapter after all," Oscuro muttered from the third story window of the ranch house. From his vantage point, Oscuro with his keen eyesight could still see the newspaperman and his dog through the smoke and flames pouring off the cornfield.

CHAPTER 120

"James Edward Furst will now pay," Oscuro cursed, tearing away like it were paper the cheap wood Ike had used to board up the upstairs ranch house window.

Rather than take the time to slide the window open, Oscuro, in his rage, crashed through it, sending shards of glass flying through the air as he took flight in man-form.

The noise created by Oscuro's exit from the ranch house startled Ajacks and Squeak, causing the pair to run for cover under the ranch house porch. The two men not realizing at the time the vampire's anger was directed elsewhere.

Oscuro figured it was too late to save Wily, but he still had time to finish what he had started with Jef. It was Oscuro's plan to turn the tables on Jef, using the same fire the newspaperman had started in the cornfield, in cutting off any escape route for the boy and his dog.

Surveying the situation from the air, Oscuro spotted Jef and Ranger now trying to make their way back to the ranch house by way of the narrow dirt road.

Rapidly spinning in mid-air, Oscuro generated the wind needed to fan the flames from the cornfield in the direction of Jef and Ranger, throwing in their path a solid curtain of flame.

The swirling pillars of wind-driven flame appeared almost biblical in nature, with Oscuro being able to spray streams of fire as if the flames were his own personal whip, scorching the earth in front of Jef and Ranger, leaving the pair no other choice than to take another route.

But regardless of which direction Jef and Ranger run, the wind-spun flames being fanned by Oscuro licked at their heels and roared over their heads, as if a medieval fire-breathing dragon had been turned loose on them.

To protect him from the flying dirt, smoke and flaming cornstalks being twisted throughout the air, Jef used his good arm to shield his face. But that didn't stop what appeared to be fireballs directed his way by Oscuro. Fireballs that danced unevenly around Ranger and he, burning everything from the dry fall leaves still hanging on the trees to the long cheat grass surrounding the base of the tree trunks.

Even in crossing the plains during the winter of 1847, Jef had never experienced such elements.

But the flames didn't stop there, as Oscuro's continued spinning grew the flames in height and width, causing the fire from the cornfield to now roll like a wave over the road which Jef and Ranger had hoped to traverse.

It was as if Oscuro had found a new partner in Mother Nature, and he was going to use that relationship to barbecue Ranger and Jef.

"Toward the rocks, boy," Jef yelled in a panic, the pair ducking behind a series of large boulders seconds before another wave of flames roared over the top of their cowering heads.

Oscuro had cornered them, and like a cat toying with mice, was going in for the kill by intensifying his mid-air spinning, pushing flames up against the pile of gray boulders Jef and Ranger hid behind.

The flames hit the boulders with such intensity that the once-gray stones were beginning to blacken under the heat, forcing Jef and Ranger to burrow deeper into the dirt, hoping the cool earth would provide them with the oxygen needed to avoid suffocating under the bellowing smoke and flames.

Hearing the roar of the flame, and the heat and the smoke from it filling his lungs, Jef was finding it harder to push the doubts from his mind, thoughts he might not see his wife or children again in this lifetime. Being a Mormon, Jef believed in a life after death reunion if kept his faith. But even that reassurance wasn't enough to calm his fears.

All of this initially to have bragging rights to a story, Jef thought, questioning his original motive for putting himself in such a life-threatening situation.

Even Ranger wore a concerned look on his face.

And then the strange winds stopped, and the fire no longer stirred.

Oscuro had stopped spinning and was now back on foot, methodically walking toward the blackened boulders that hid his prey. On his way, here and there, Oscuro would have to skip over the small campfire-sized fires still burning, treating them as if they were puddles that might soil his shoes.

As lightly as Oscuro walked, the smoking fresh burnt ground still crunched under his weight. And as the distance between Oscuro and his prey narrowed, the vampire's smile widened, knowing his fight in Dry Springs would soon be over and he would be on the road with his treasures.

Oscuro was further encouraged by being able to see Jef's gray flat cap peeking from over the top of the rocks. The newspaperman had apparently frozen from fright, he thought.

"You can come out now," Oscuro said, within a few feet of the rock pile. "At least stand and face me like the man you claim to be," he called to Jef.

But there was no movement from behind the boulders.

It wasn't until Oscuro reached the pile of blackened stones that he realized why.

The gray cap Jef always wore had been propped up with a stick, the stick blackened, still smoldering from the vampire's earlier fiery blast. But there was no sign of the newspaperman or his dog. "You are beginning to annoy me," Oscuro cursed at the top of his lungs before grabbing Jef's worn, now warm cap and wadding it up into his clenched fist.

Chapter 121

Jef was relieved when Ranger and he reached the ranch house, his wounded shoulder still throbbing with pain. But his bullet wound was small potatoes compared to what he and Ranger had just endured, the smell of smoke on Jef's clothes and Ranger's fur, reminding them they had survived what was to be their roast.

Now the newspaperman had one more plan, it involving destroying Oscuro's sleeping chambers even if it meant burning down the Peterson place, with Oscuro in it.

Quickly stepping up onto the three-step porch wrung to the ranch house, a hand reached out and had latched onto Jef's wrist, startlingly the newspaper man until he heard two familiar voices, an excitable Squeak and a dismayed Ajacks.

Jef and Ranger were glad for the company.

"What was with Sheriff Wily?" Ajacks immediately asked Jef, having a difficult time shaking from his mind the image of his former mentor being consumed by flames.

"Wily was double-crossing us. I'll explain later. We don't have much time," Jef told the pair, aware Oscuro would be in close pursuit.

"You'll explain now," Ajacks demanded, flashing his tin star by pulling back his coat.

"Look," Jef began, before being interrupted by Squeak.

"Ajacks, Jef has never lied to us before. We have to trust him," Squeak said.

Hoping he had squelched the conflict, Squeak then turned to Jef. "Have you got your stake shooter with you?" he asked, motioning to Jef's shoulder bag.

"No, Wily took it from me during our fray," Jef said dejectedly. "But I do have a jar of kerosene I intend to use in burning Oscuro's sleeping chambers to the ground," he said, gesturing his head toward the Peterson place. "But first, we have got to find them."

"You mean like a coffin?" Squeak stammered.

"I don't know, maybe," Jef replied. "But whether we like it or not, this is where we are going to have to make our last stand," Jef said. "After this, there will be no safe place to hide from Oscuro."

Squeak and Ajacks hardly recognized the new bold Jef.

"But be on the lookout for Ike," Jef warned.

"We took care of Ike. He shouldn't be bothering us," Squeak boasted.

Ajacks gave a firm nod before reminding Jef a final time that he was the law. "Let me lead the way," Ajacks said, still gnawing on the bitter pill that Oscuro and Ike had every intention of stealing right underneath his nose, his girl.

Jef, Squeak, Ajacks and Ranger then darted into the dark ranch house, uncertain which direction they were headed from there.

The foursome initially moved together through the main floor of what now appeared to be an empty house.

"Man, they sold everything," Ajacks said, astonished to find the home empty of all of its fine furnishings.

Finding nothing on the main floor, Jef determined it would be best if the group split up to cover more ground more quickly. Any minute Oscuro would be making his return to the house in chasing him down.

"I'll take the downstairs, you two take the upstairs. Scream out if you find anything," Jef said.

"And again, what is it that we're looking for?" Ajacks asked.

"The place where Oscuro lays his head, his sleeping chambers, and yes it might involve a coffin," Jef said.

"Creepy," Ajacks said, before Squeak and he began their slow descent up the steep grand staircase, while Jef and Ranger made their way down into the darkened basement.

To move more quickly down the dark stairs, Jef let Ranger lead, following his canine friend, feeling his way along the walls.

While Jef and Ranger unknowingly made their way toward Oscuro's chambers, Ajacks and Squeak moved from empty room to room upstairs, looking for anything, but hoping to find no one, with the duo's biggest discovery being what appeared to be Ike's sleeping cot in a corner of one of the rooms.

Upon returning to the ranch house, an agitated Oscuro could hear the sound of shuffling footsteps within the house, giving him cause to wonder if Ajacks and Squeak, whom he had spotted earlier, had joined Jef and his dog in the fight.

"Where is Ike when you need him?" Oscuro mumbled under his breath.

CHAPTER 122

The fire and smoke in the distance only hastened Lola's ride, the back of her green flower-patterned dress and her long dark hair blowing in the breeze from the hard ride.

Old Stu had found new life.

Thumper's horse, carrying the weight of the blacksmith, was now breathing heavily, snot spraying from its nostrils, saliva from its mouth. Despite the horse being 16 hands tall, in the night it looked like a burrow under the weight of the large man.

Because of the flames in the distance grabbing their attention, Thumper and Lola failed to notice the figure and horse off to the side of the road hidden in the brush.

The eyes of the figure watched the pair gallop by and waited until the dust cloud from the horses dissipated before jumping on his horse and riding in the direction the pair had come from – toward Dry Springs.

There was a slight jingle to his saddlebag as he rode off.

Ike was headed to town to collect his other treasure.

CHAPTER 123

"Eureka," Jef exclaimed under his breath, making out in the dark the outline of two leather-bound traveling trunks resting on what appeared to be Oscuro's bed.

Unlatching the buckles on the first trunk, Jef found an assortment of some of the finest European clothing.

"Do you think this guy might be a Duke?" he turned and asked Ranger, with the dog offering him a quizzical look in return.

Jef's eyes had begun to adjust to the dark of the house. But it wasn't until he had unbuckled and opened the second trunk on the bed that his eyes were wide open.

Not only had Jef found Oscuro's sleeping quarters, but he had discovered leverage he could use as a result of the second trunk being filled with neatly stacked piles of American currency.

Having found a great deal of Oscuro's money Jef was hoping would give him the edge he needed in getting out of this situation alive.

It was evident Oscuro was not only a vampire, but a thief, who had stuck around long enough to line his pockets with most of the town's wealth.

It was Jef's hope that it would be that greed that would lend itself to the creature's demise.

"We'd better hurry, boy. We wouldn't want to be caught down here," Jef told Ranger, hurriedly shifting to his wounded shoulder his worn burlap bag carrying his wooden stakes and remaining jar of kerosene in order to make room on his good left shoulder for the trunk filled with money.

The trunk with the clothing would remain behind. Jef figured the clothing belonged to Oscuro, the money didn't. But hauling even one trunk up the narrow stairway would be no simple feat for Jef, already exhausted from the events of the evening and now working only on pure adrenaline in being able to see what he hoped was the finish line.

"Boy is Oscuro going to be surprised when he finds his money missing," Jef told Ranger before wrestling with the trunk to move it up the steep, dark stairway.

CHAPTER 124

Oscuro, being light on his feet, was able to sneak up behind Ajacks and Squeak as they moved from room to room in searching the upstairs of the sprawling ranch house.

Now it was only a matter of which of the two cowboys Oscuro thought he would wrap his hands around first and choke: The young love struck deputy or awkward carpenter?

But just as Oscuro was about to pounce, he heard an all-too-familiar voice calling his name from the main floor of the house.

"Oscuro, where are you?" Jef called, after positioning himself in front of the open doorway of the house in the event his plan went awry.

The sound of Jef's voice caused both Squeak and Ajacks to turn, finding Oscuro lurking behind them.

Instinctively Ajacks began firing his pistol at Oscuro, while Squeak, realizing bullets were of no use, reached into his anti-vampire bag.

Deep in the bag Squeak found something to latch onto and all in one motion he removed the item from the bag and threw it into the face of their attacker.

"A tomato?" Oscuro declared upon being splattered with the overripe vegetable.

"Oops," Squeak uttered. "That was for eatin'."

Ajacks glared at Squeak, but before he could say a word, Squeak was already reaching into his bag for another item.

This time Squeak located one of his flour bombs, pulling it from the bag and throwing it in the face of Oscuro who stood only a few feet away. The direct hit sent a cloud of flour spraying into the air.

The flour had temporarily left Oscuro blind.

The distraction was enough to allow Ajacks and Squeak to use the wide hall of the lavishly designed home to squeeze by Oscuro and run down the staircase to the main floor where Jef and Ranger were waiting.

For the second time Oscuro had fallen victim to the flour trick. The first time when he had Thumper trapped in the general store.

Failing to grab onto Ajacks or Squeak as they ran by like frightened children, Oscuro turned his attention to Jef.

"No matter, it is you I want," Oscuro called to Jef, who along with Ajacks, Squeak, and Ranger had gathered at the bottom of the staircase Oscuro was about to descend.

"Not so fast, Oscuro" Jef warned, and then gulped, hoping his plan would prove to be effective. "Look what I found."

Having spotted what Jef was referring to caused Oscuro to freeze in place.

There, from the flickering light of the burning cornfield shining through the open ranch house door, Oscuro could see the trunk full of money he had collected by liquidating the mansion furnishings over the last few weeks. His prize possession now laid out open at the feet of his adversary.

Chapter 125

Oscuro had filled his trunk with money in preparation for a quick getaway. Now, most of the wealth he had accumulated while in Dry Springs had been discovered.

Not far from where the money was displayed like a cake on display at the bakery stood Jef, hovering over it, holding in his left hand a small jar filled with kerosene. The jar serving as notice that Jef would burn the money if Oscuro approached.

"Going somewhere?" Jef smartly asked Oscuro, who stood on a step about midway up the staircase, the fingernails on his right hand noticeably tapping the stairway's ornamental bannister.

This was the first time Jef's group had actually gotten a clean look at their nemesis.

Oscuro had coal black hair he parted down the middle, his nose appearing to have a point and his dark, deep set eyes pitched close together.

Catching the group staring at him, Oscuro, as if he were European royalty, couldn't help but make an introduction as if he were at a formal coming-out party. "I am 173 year-old Roman Oscuro, son of the great Mickel Oscuro and grandson of Nikoli Oscuro, all from old Italy where we rule the night."

In hearing the introduction, Jef's jaw slightly dropped, while Ajacks and Squeak both released audible gasps.

"And I can admit, well played, newspaperman," Oscuro said, pointing to the bounty resting at Jef's feet.

"I was hoping I would get your attention," Jef replied, trying desperately to keep the tremor from his voice.

And while Jef sweat, wondering what his next move would be, Oscuro remained calm, looking as fresh as if he had just stepped off a steamship, his cape, despite all they had been through this evening, with hardly a wrinkle in it.

Beneath the cape, Oscuro wore a bolo tie, a white shirt, a black vest with large knobbed old English buttons and dark trousers, pleated at the pocket, to match. His rounded-toe shoes, the same shoes he wore to kick Thumper up and down Main Street, were neatly polished to where they would have reflected Oscuro's image if it were not for the fact that he was a vampire and did not cast one.

Oscuro stood on the stairs looking over the group like he was their king. But the trio of men did not appear to be willing subjects.

In addition to the jar of kerosene Jef was holding out where Oscuro could see it, he had tucked a wooden stake into the backside waistband of his pants. His hope was the money would lure Oscuro close enough to give them the opportunity to stab Oscuro in the heart. If indeed he had one.

It was hard to believe the bespectacled newspaperman, ignored over the years for not fitting in, was now standing toe to toe with a creature the likes of Oscuro. If Jef, flanked by Squeak and Ajacks, lived through this, what a story he would have to write, he thought.

"Why Dry Springs?" Jef ask Oscuro while he had his attention.

"The oldest motive in the book: Revenge," Oscuro coldly replied. "I initially came here to kill Wily."

"Vengeance is mine, saith the Lord," Jef responded.

"Oh, you are one to talk," Oscuro said. "I may have come to town to kill Wily, but it was you who did my handiwork for me. I can still smell the sheriff burning from here," he said taking in a deep inhale.

Oscuro's words pricked Jef's conscience. Jef didn't want to kill Wily. The sheriff's angry cries while he burned in the cornfield, would haunt Jef forever, he suspected. But it was better he heard the screams of Wily than the screams of his own family, who had been put at risk.

"I had no choice," Jef said, rationalizing his setting the cornfield on fire. "Wily would have certainly killed me."

After some silence, Jef needed to know more. It was just his nature. "Why Wily?" he asked Oscuro.

"In Missouri, Wily took from me the only woman I ever loved with his reckless shooting," Oscuro said. "She died as a result, and Wily, a deputy at the time, ran like a rabbit. Much like the way you and your friends have run from me," Oscuro added, getting in one more dig at the trio who stood facing him.

"But when Ike and I arrived in Dry Springs after having searched two years for Wily, the cowardly sheriff rolled out the red carpet for me unbeknownst to Ike, extending an invitation for us to stay here," Oscuro said, his hands gesturing at the spaciousness of the Peterson place.

"So what did happen to Darwin and Mabel Peterson?" Jef asked.

"We had nothing to do with their deaths. That was likely one of your own town members who did them in, likely for their riches," Oscuro said, the words drawing murmurings from Ajacks and Squeak.

"Ike did kill a member of the Peterson family who came a-calling to check on the property," Oscuro said. "But knowing the unpredictability of Ike, the body could be anywhere," Oscuro said, stepping down a stair, hoping Jef wouldn't notice.

"Speaking of Ike, has anybody seen him?" Oscuro asked in wanting to gain all the information he could.

"We had a run-in with Ike in the woods awhile back, and left him there," Ajacks said. "We didn't kill him, did we, Squeak?"

"No, we didn't. But I sure wanted to beat him over the head another couple of times," Squeak said, regretting he hadn't done so.

"Well, Ike will be along any minute," Oscuro said, causing both Ajacks and Squeak to stir.

"And what about you, Mister Newspaperman, what keeps you in Dry Springs and so interested in vampire chasing?" Oscuro asked.

"Family," Jef replied. "This is where they want to be."

"Yes, but to chase me?" Oscuro asked.

"Initially, as selfish as it sounds, the fact you are a campfire story no one is going to be able to top," Jef said. "But then you made it personal."

"I knew this had something to do with your own glory," Oscuro said. "Most men run and hide and wait for my dark storm to blow over. But for you, I am the trophy on the wall that you need to gain the respect of those you love. Which means you're not that much different than me."

"Not true," Jef replied. "I've sought respect without robbing others of theirs."

"You are always quick to turn a sentence, huh, wordsmith?" Oscuro said. "We would have made an unbeatable team."

"And your wooden cross? Where is it, Jef? I see nothing around your neck," Oscuro continued.

"My faith burns from within," Jef replied.

"Oh right, you're a Mormon," Oscuro said. "I've not had the pleasure of meeting many of them. They all like you?" he added.

"Not certain," Jef said with a faraway look in his eyes. "I've not been around some for some time."

"Well, I would think they would be right proud of you, Mister Newspaperman," Oscuro said mockingly. "You have represented yourself well."

"And now that I have given you your due," Oscuro told Jef, "I'll need you and your friends to stand aside. Oddly, you are standing over my money."

"What about all the victims who paid for this blood money?" Jef asked. "Where is their justice?"

"What do you know of justice?" Oscuro replied, his voice rising.

"Some of those so-called victims had to be taken to keep Wily in check, while a few others out of necessity in feeding my thirst," Oscuro said, taking another step down the staircase, moving closer to Jef and his friends.

But this step Jef noticed. "I mean it, don't come any closer," he warned Oscuro, at about the same time Squeak pulled a clove of garlic from his anti-vampire bag, and Ajacks gave a nervous tug on the wooden cross hanging around his neck, making certain it was still there.

"You stick your nose where it doesn't belong, and then I am forced to leave a place I'm just growing accustomed to," Oscuro said.

Oscuro's words silenced the group for a moment before Ajacks got the nerve to ask Oscuro what his intentions were with Prudy Richards.

"What have you done to my girl?" Ajacks asked.

"Your girl? I don't think so," Oscuro said, coming down the staircase another step. "If she was your girl, she wouldn't have been so easy to take. No, cowboy, you drug your feet, and I stepped in," Oscuro said, now five stair-steps away from the group.

"You wouldn't know love," Ajacks fired back.

"Don't try my patience, Deputy. I still have a lot of fight left in me," Oscuro said, hoping his stall would give Ike the time needed to show up and help him salvage their wealth.

"You can't even keep your friends, how you going to be able to keep a pretty girl like Prudy?" Ajacks asked bitterly.

Oscuro offered no response but cast Ajacks an icy stare and wagged a pale finger at the deputy as if to say he had tired of their talk.

But apparently, Ajacks, too, had tired of their talk.

"Roman Oscuro, you're under arrest for the murders of Gibby Jones, Russell Means, Ray Wolcutt, Homer White, Ever Peppers and Ronald Parsons, and the attempted murder of Todd Means and Otis Thumper," said Ajacks, whose frustration was quickly overtaking what was once a calm demeanor.

"Well, Deputy, I can't take credit for Parsons. Ike shot him," Oscuro said smartly. "But if that's the case, I suggest you walk on up here and put those handcuffs on me that are noticeably hanging from your belt," he added, extending both his arms outward in a surrender position.

Ajacks stood, uncertain what to do next.

"C'mon Deputy," Oscuro said, before bursting into laughter. The type of forced laughter indicating there is nothing really funny about the situation.

Like the animal he was, Oscuro was preparing to pounce.

CHAPTER 126

"Let it go, Ajacks," Jef said, turning his head only for a moment to calm the deputy. "Oscuro is not going anywhere without his money."

No sooner had Jef uttered his counsel, than Ranger barked and Squeak and Ajacks cried out in warning.

But they were all too late. By the time Jef had turned his head back around to face Oscuro, all he could see coming at him was a flying mass of black cape.

The force from the full-flight body tackle sent Jef reeling out of the open door he was once standing in front of, the unexpected impact causing him to fumble his small jar of kerosene near the door entryway.

Oscuro's flying charge had sent both Jef and he airborne, with the pair clearing the Peterson porch before landing hard in the ranch house yard. Hitting the ground under the weight of Oscuro caused Jef to temporarily lose his breath, and his grasp on the bag hanging over his shoulder containing the remaining wooden stakes.

Getting his bearings, Jef quickly tried to roll out from under Oscuro, but to no avail.

Ranger was the first to respond to help Jef, the dog burying his teeth deep into Oscuro's right leg, furiously tugging on the vampire, whom the dog had tasted before.

While Ranger tugged, Jef's dropped jar of kerosene remained puddled on the porch near the ranch house door.

"Squeak, torch the porch," a breathless Jef cried while still under the weight of his enemy.

Hearing the plea, Squeak dashed to a nearby tree in snapping off a limb, before running past Oscuro and Jef still tangled on the ground, in stealing flame from the burning cornfield, and taking it with him to set the front porch of the ranch house on fire.

Seeing what Squeak was up to, Oscuro jumped off Jef, pursuing after Squeak in an effort to prevent the carpenter from burning the Peterson home to the ground with Oscuro's money in it.

But just as Oscuro was able to tackle Squeak around the ankles, the stork-like cowboy in falling forward still managed to throw his burning branch onto the kerosene-soaked porch in causing it to ignite in flame.

The burning porch lit up the nighttime sky, making it impossible for Oscuro to recover his trunk of money, which was quickly consumed. Squeak than surprised a distracted Oscuro a second time, by stepping out of the night and driving the wooden stake he had been carrying deep into Oscuro's right shoulder.

Although Squeak had missed the monster's heart, the pain was still searing for Oscuro, who reacted angrily, knocking the carpenter to the ground with a hard swipe of his arm. Oscuro then followed that up with a solid punch to Squeak's face, rendering the carpenter unconscious.

Out of frustration over what he had just seen, Ajacks out of habit drew his pistol, firing at point-blank range the remainder of his rounds at Oscuro. But the gunfire had no effect on the monster. During the chaos, however, Jef had gotten to his feet, grabbing hold of the wooden stake he had earlier placed in the waistband of his pants and charging Oscuro from behind, burying the stake deep between the vampire's shoulder blades.

Oscuro let out a haunting scream before turning and raking Jef across the face with his razor-sharp finger nails, sending the newspaperman and his wire-rimmed glasses flying, while opening a sizeable wound on Jef's forehead.

Ajacks, recognizing his opportunity, reached into the bottom of Squeak's anti-vampire bag, finding nestled there the last of the flour bombs Squeak had made.

"Hey, Oscuro," Ajacks yelled, getting Oscuro's attention just long enough to hit him in the face with it.

Like before, the bomb popped open on impact, sending a mini-white cloud into the air, causing Ajacks to pump his fist in victory.

But Ajacks's celebration was short lived.

Oscuro immediately wiped the flour from his eyes, and impulsively turned his attention on the closest combatant to him, who was Ajacks, whom he belted with a haymaker to the chin, lifting the deputy a few feet off of the ground.

Now it was time to finish this fight, and salvage from the burning ranch house the gold coins that still remained inside.

Oscuro was hoping coins that would give him the traveling money he needed to leave Dry Springs. But first, there was one last item of business to be taking care of.

"You are a dead man, now," Oscuro said, his attention focused on Jef, who was scrambling to find in the dirt the other wooden stakes that had earlier spilled from his bag.

But a determined Oscuro was quickly closing in on the newspaperman.

Seeing that, Ajacks shook off the punch he had taken, and intervened, by jumping on the back of the vampire in hopes of being able to ride him into the ground like a steer. But Oscuro was having none of it, throwing Ajacks off of him as if the deputy were a Fourth of July rodeo cowboy and Oscuro the mad bull.

To finish off the deputy, still trying to recover from his hard ride, Oscuro wrapped his powerful hands around the throat of Ajacks, lifting him off the ground, before throwing him toward the direction of the burning house.

Jef seeing how close an unconscious Ajacks was to the flames of the home, stopped searching for the stakes, and redirected his efforts to drag the deputy away from the fire.

But Jef in trying to be the hero, had given Oscuro the opportunity to back Jef up against the burning house, allowing the vampire to finally get one of his pasty white hands around Jef's throat, squeezing it with such force that Jef immediately began to sputter for air before falling to his knees.

"Rather than kill you, I will do worse, I will make you one of mine," Oscuro said, baring his long, white fangs, now only inches away from Jef's sweat-and-blood-stained neck.

"I don't want to be a part of anything you have to offer," Jef choked out, thrashing his head about to avoid the bite. But resistance seemed futile, as Jef could feel Oscuro's warm saliva dripping on his neck.

CHAPTER 127

Riding down the narrow road leading to the Peterson place now resembling a large campfire only exhilarated Lola and Thumper. Between the burning cornfield and house, it appeared as if Lola and Thumper might be riding into Hades.

Lola was anxiously nervous, while Thumper remained silent. Spotting horses tied off on the roadside belonging to Squeak and Ajacks further invigorated the pair.

Lola was just hoping her husband was still alive.

Maybe Sheriff Wily had needed Jef, Squeak and Ajacks to execute a plan, she hoped. Yet, the generally reliable Todd Means told a different story.

In approaching the scene, Lola could see two silhouettes moving about, as if they were dancing, the high flames from the burning Peterson mansion, and the low flames coming off the burning cornfield, illuminating the yard in front of the house like it were a stage.

One of those still standing was Jef, the other obviously the vampire. And while the two players fought, Ranger could be seen circling the pair, trying to inflict damage to Jef's challenger.

"For me to have a shot at the vampire, I need to be within about 20 feet of him," Lola advised Thumper, as they quickly advanced on the two men locked in a fray.

"Twenty feet?" Thumper moaned.

But before Lola could respond to Thumper's latest whine, she had positioned herself close enough to her husband to get a clean shot at the vampire. After all, she only had one shot.

Chapter 128

Jef's body was a mass of wounds and bruises, but his spirit not yet broken by Oscuro.

Thanks to a bite and run strategy applied by Ranger, Jef had been able to avoid Oscuro's fatal bite in getting back to his feet.

"It will be me storyteller who will write the final chapter," Oscuro said, slashing Jef across the chest, ripping open his shirt as if it were newsprint, sending the newspaperman tumbling back to the ground.

Jef could feel his own warm blood run from the new wound, making the pain from the earlier gunshot wound to his shoulder and the cut on his forehead barely noticeable.

Unable to stay on his feet, an exhausted Jef merely running on survival mode began crawling on his hands and knees away from Oscuro, while pleading under his breath for some divine intervention. But Jef's pray was temporarily interrupted when the pointed tips of the European shoes Oscuro was wearing caught him in the back of the head, pushing him from his crawl position face-first into the dirt.

Then Jef heard the voice of a familiar angel. It was the voice of Lola.

"James, get up, run towards me," Lola screamed, now off her horse and shielded by Thumper, in moving toward Oscuro in hopes of getting off the one clean shot she needed with the stake shooter she held firmly in her grasp.

The cavalry had arrived, Jef thought, hoping to find cover behind the pair. But Oscuro wasn't about to concede, taking a short flight and catching

Jef, knocking him once again to the ground – 30 feet from where Lola and Thumper stood.

"Fighting vampires is not like pushing a pen," Oscuro gloated.

Lola, fighting off the shock of actually seeing the vampire for the first time as a result of the light from the burning house, regained her composure, quickly crossing herself in prayer before letting her wooden stake fly.

PING.

The shot was slightly off the mark, lodging in Oscuro's left side, causing him to scream out in pain and shoot her a scowl.

Lola's heart sank. The monster's heart still beat.

Jef too was discouraged but aware there were six other wooden stakes about, they just had to be found.

While Oscuro attempted to pull the stake out that was now protruding from the left side of his torso, Jef frantically began combing through the dirt once again on his hands and knees in hope his fingers would brush up against one, if not all, the stakes he had lost earlier.

While Jef sifted through the dirt like a 49er panning for gold, a leering Oscuro turned his attention toward Lola.

"Come to me, newspaper gal," Oscuro said in a lecherous voice in moving toward the fiery brunette. "Maybe Prudy Richards isn't the prettiest girl in Dry Springs after all," he added.

Recognizing Oscuro's advance, Thumper stepped forward in becoming the aggressor, swinging his hammer in connecting it with Oscuro's jaw.

For a brief moment, Jef, Lola and Thumper, were hoping Thumper's wild swing had been effective.

But Oscuro soon rallied, throwing an uppercut to Thumper's jaw, lifting him off the ground, before Thumper fell back to earth with a sleepy look in his eyes.

Then, as if manna itself had fallen from the heavens, Jef's fingers brushed up against one of the wooden stakes, and then another, and then four more. This fight would end, he thought. It was just a matter of getting the stakes to Lola, whom he had been cut off from.

Oscuro, unaware Jef was now holding the stakes, continued pursuing Lola. Acting out of desperation, Jef attacked Oscuro from the back, sticking one of the six wooden stakes he now held deep into the vampire's lower back.

Oscuro reacted immediately by spinning around, and tightly wrapping his hands around the throat of the newspaperman, lifting him off of the ground like he did so many other victims before him.

Jef's air supply had been cut off, his eyes rolling and losing focus. His arms, once used to hold his children, set print and embrace his wife, hung like wet noodles at his side, causing the wooden stakes he had finally found, to fall unnoticed to the ground – almost.

Chapter 129

As the wooden stakes Jef had been holding onto silently dropped to the dirt, Ranger easily spotted them and darted into action as if he were home playing a game of fetch with the Furst boys.

Ranger's teeth locked onto the first stake, his initial instinct to take it to Jef. But Jef appeared preoccupied, so Ranger did the next best thing, running over and playfully dropping the stake at Lola's feet.

Recognizing the miracle, Lola wasted no time picking up the stake, slick with dog saliva, and loading it into her shooter.

PING.

The stake zipped through the air, tearing into Oscuro's left thigh, causing the vampire to let out an audible "UGH."

"I must get closer," Lola muttered. "Fetch," she commanded Ranger.

No sooner had she given the command than the faithful dog returned with another stake.

Lola picked it up, this one just as wet as the first, in loading it and firing.

PING.

This stake again punctured Oscuro's left side, causing the creature to wince in excoriating pain, causing him to loosen the death grip he had on Jef.

"Still closer, I need to be closer," Lola told herself, Thumper still lying unconscious behind her.

"Fetch," Lola commanded. Again the dog darted playfully past where Oscuro was standing, gathering up a third stake before the vampire could react.

Lola, with shaking hands, quickly loaded the shooter. Her prayer, that she would finish this fight with this shot.

PING.

The shot missed, flying past Oscuro's head like a shooting star. But the annoyance of the near-hit caused Oscuro to change his plan of attack, as he pushed Jef to the ground like a doll, in turning to face Lola one more time. It was just what Lola wanted.

"Fetch," Lola shrilled, Ranger darting in for a fourth stake, with Oscuro helplessly kicking at the animal in his effort to prevent Ranger from reaching his objective.

Little did Oscuro know that this was Ranger's game, with the dog regularly while playing out in the yard outmaneuvering the two Furst boys.

Ranger followed the same pattern now, zigzagging around Oscuro, in giving him the space needed to latch onto another stake with his teeth and take it back to Lola.

With this shot, Lola was taking no chances, moving within 15 feet of the vampire.

Oscuro, beginning to resemble a well-dressed pin cushion, now squarely faced Lola, unaware he was leaving himself open for the shot she had prayed for.

With her heart in her throat and a prayer in her mind, Lola fired the weapon Jef had designed and Squeak had crafted for this very purpose.

PING.

The stake struck the vampire, burying deep into the left side of his chest, forcing Oscuro to let out a horrifying yelp, one likely heard all the way to Dry Springs.

Oscuro had frozen. The stake had found its mark.

Or had it? It was difficult to tell in the dark, as Oscuro remained on his feet, both hands clutching the stake now protruding from his chest.

Oscuro said nothing, staring straight ahead at Lola, who refused to blink.

The eerie stare down gave Jef the time he needed to rise to his feet just a few feet from where the frozen Oscuro stood with his back to him.

The last wooden stake now resting at Lola's feet where Ranger had dropped it.

And then Oscuro began slowly moving again, toward Lola, slowly putting one foot in front of the other. It was obvious he wasn't finished.

Jef, realizing his brave wife now needed his help, turned off his brain, and followed his instincts.

Thumper's hammer, Jef figured, had to be nearby. The very thing he needed if he was going to be able to drive the final stake home.

Lola, to protect her husband, mouthed the words to Jef to stay put.

But Jef being without his eyeglasses, either couldn't make out what she was saying or didn't care, in dashing past Oscuro, and running past his wife, to retrieve Thumper's hammer that rested not far from where the giant had landed from the punch he had earlier taken.

"Don't leave me" Lola cried, questioning her husband's actions.

Oscuro, seeing Jef was running away, began to pick up his pace toward Lola, who was now frantically back-peddling all while trying to load the last stake into the shooter.

"Jef, what are you doing?" Lola cried. But her husband said nothing in running past her back toward Oscuro, holding Thumper's heavy hammer in his right hand.

Oscuro's eyes remained transfixed on Lola. That was the woman he needed to have, a snarling dog being the only thing standing in his way.

And then out of the night, moving like a steam locomotive was Jef.

Even without his glasses, the newspaperman was hoping he could hit his mark before Oscuro could react. But his wind-up in swinging the heavy hammer resulted in Jef stumbling forward, missing the end of the protruding stake altogether.

For a split second Jef's heart sank.

And then as Jef tumbled into Oscuro from the momentum of his running attack, he felt a slight poke to his mid-section as the two long rivals tumbled to the ground, this time Jef holding the upper-hand over his vampire nemesis.

The air then magically rushed out of Oscuro like a popped hot air balloon.

Although the hammer had missed, strangely enough, the impact of Jef falling into Oscuro was just enough to push the stake into the monster's beating heart.

Jef didn't realize what he had even done until Oscuro went silent and limp.

"He's dead?" Jef yelled in a questioning fashion, before realizing Lola might be listening. "He's dead. I took care of that vampire," he proclaimed in correcting himself, this time saying it loud enough to be certain Lola could hear his words.

Oscuro, lying on his back in the dirt with a look of dismay splattered across his face, stared skyward, his eyelids slowly fluttering shut.

What had begun as a battle had ended with a whimper, with Lola rushing over to Jef, with the two embracing and exchanging soft kisses, Lola still holding tightly to her weapon.

"What were you thinking?" a shaken Lola asked Jef.

Lola's question put Jef on the spot. It being dark, and amid all the confusion, Jef was uncertain whether Lola was aware he had actually missed hitting the stake lodged in Oscuro's chest with the hammer. But it was certainly a detail he could share with her another day, he figured.

"I was just thinking of us dear," Jef said, realizing that it isn't often one gets to gloat about slaying a vampire.

As Jef and Lola exchanged more hugs and kisses, affection James Edward Furst III generally did not demonstrate in public, Oscuro had closed his eyes for a permanent sleep.

To make certain Oscuro was done Ranger approached the still body and sniffed once, giving Jef and Lola further confirmation the fight was over.

For a moment all that could be heard in the night was the crackling of the fire from the cornfield and ranch house, both of which had almost been entirely consumed.

"I can envision the headline already," Jef said, gesturing toward the still vampire lying only a few feet from where Lola and he stood.

"Oh, there is the Jef I know," Lola said, having already dropped the stake shooter to the ground in attending to her husband's wounds. And while Lola nursed Jef, Ranger through a medical remedy of sniffs and licks, began making the rounds in bringing the others out of their semi-conscious or unconscious states.

As a result of most everyone missing the end of the fight with Oscuro, Jef would be given many opportunities to recount his own version of what had actually happened.

"What a story you are going to have to tell, cowboy," Lola told Jef, rubbing her hand through his moppish hair.

"Don't you mean write?" Jef ask.

"That is exactly what I meant," Lola said.

THE ROUNDUP

VAMPIRE DEAD, WILY **BURNS, IKE FLEES,** the headline read.

There was no kicker. But the byline clearly read: By James Edward Furst III.

Jef was reading the article for the fourth time through the cracked lens of his eyeglasses when the cowbell hanging over his office door let out a familiar clang.

"How is the eye?" Jef asked Ajacks upon him entering the Main Street office.

For two days Ajacks had worn a shiner where Oscuro had connected with one of his punches. But that was okay with Ajacks, who wore the swollen eye like a badge of honor.

Ajacks's head was also bandaged from a cut he sustained in the melee. But he had been able to hide most of the bandage beneath his hat. Once the wound healed, Doctor Howard expected it would likely leave a scar across Ajacks's forehead the likes of the scar Wily wore down the left side of his face.

"I'll be alright," Ajacks told Jef. Besides, the deputy's heart hurt more than his head. He was crushed when he returned to town to tell Prudy of Jef killing the vampire, only to find she was gone, leaving no note.

Ajacks suspected somehow Ike was involved.

"I'd give my pearl-handle pistol to get Prudy back," Ajacks told Jef, before dropping on Jef's desk a small dusty leather bag he had been carrying.

The bag made a jingle when it hit the pine wood desk Squeak had built Jef in gratitude for him saving the town.

While Jef was away in having his wounds tended to by Lola, Squeak had rearranged the office, putting Jef's newspaper business to the front of the building and moving his carpentry work to the back.

It had been a few days since their final encounter with Oscuro as Dry Springs dragged to get back to normal.

"What about your shoulder and forehead? Those were some nasty wounds," Ajacks asked Jef.

Jef's head wound was starting to heal, while his left arm rested in a sling. But the bruising around Jef's neck where Oscuro had grabbed him was still very noticeable.

"Where Wily's shot was fired at such close range, it tore right through my shoulder," Jef said. "Doctor Howard figured I lucked out, preventing him from having to go in and dig out the slug.

"But I got my story," Jef said, gesturing at the newspaper lying out on the top of his desk.

"You might well sell a million copies of that," Ajacks said.

"So, where's Squeak?" Ajacks asked.

"I sent him off to see Miss Higginson and tell her she wouldn't be hearing any sweet music from that guitar she lent him," Jef said.

The two friends shared a hard laugh. It was good to hear Ajacks laugh again.

"Remember, Ajacks, I'm not certain what you will find when you locate Prudy. Just because we killed Oscuro, I can't be certain the spell she was under has been lifted. You guys tread carefully, you hear," Jef advised his friend.

Ajacks nodded.

"By the way, what's in the bag?" Jef asked, his curiosity getting the best of him, particularly where Ajacks had yet to say anything about it.

"It's the $25 you, or should I say, Lola, is owed for the capture of Crazy Max," Ajacks said. "Of course I had to remind the mayor it was owed to her," he added.

Jef reached out and grabbed the top of the bag, barely lifting it off the desk before setting it back down. "So, that's what $25 feels like," he said.

The cowbell then interrupted their conversation with its usual clang.

It was Squeak, looking a little flushed and wearing a big, red lipstick mark on his right cheek.

"I were breaking the news to Miss Higginson that I used her guitar to build a weapon to kill the vampire, and she up and kissed me one," Squeak said sheepishly.

"Miss Higginson called me a hero," Squeak said, his story causing Ajacks and Jef to break out in laughter for a second time.

"Well, we'd better get going, Squeak. We've got some miles to make up," Ajacks said.

"Where you headed first?" Jef asked.

"I figure where they can only travel at night, we might be able to catch up to them at the old mining site on the territory's east border," Ajacks said.

"That's a safe bet," Jef said, as Squeak scrambled about, grabbing his bedroll and a few supplies, including a new stake shooter he had custom made using guitar string he was able to salvage from the Peterson ranch. It took Squeak hours of meticulously sifting through dirt to find the string that Wily had ripped from Jef's stake shooter.

"I want to thank you for seeing this through to the end. Prudy means a lot to me," Ajacks told Jef.

"No problem," Jef said brushing aside the compliment and comment as if it were a buzzing horsefly.

It wasn't until Ajacks and Squeak had said their final goodbyes and on their way to find Prudy, that Jef got the itch to reach inside the leather bag and touch the coins Ajacks had left him. Lola would be so surprised when he returned home with the money.

"What's this," Jef muttered, as he reached blindly into the bag, pulling from it, in addition to a few coins, a charred deputy star with a small note tucked inside the pin. The note reading: *"This belongs to you Jef. You have been so deputized, Sheriff Ajacks."*

Before Jef could get from behind his desk and out his office door where Ranger was dutifully stationed, Ajacks and Squcak were nothing more than two small specks against the desert.

Jef stood in the middle of Dry Springs Main Street looking in the direction of his two friends, Ranger having come over to stand by his side.

"I guess, Ranger, this means we're going to be doing some deputy work for a few days," Jef said, looking down at the tin star he was holding in his hand.

Ranger raised his ears and cocked his head from side-to-side, staring at Jef, as if he understood every word.

Made in the USA
San Bernardino, CA
04 November 2015